a Whisper *and a* Curse

DARCY BURKE

USA TODAY BESTSELLING AUTHOR

OLIVERHEBERBOOKS

For Toni,
a brilliant coworker, generous friend, and excellent travel pal

CHAPTER 1

London, April 1868

*H*adrian Becket, Earl of Ravenhurst, had been shocked when his mother had asked to invite his investigative partner, Miss Matilda Wren, to their biweekly Sunday tea. It wasn't actually the invitation that surprised him, but the purpose of it. The dowager countess wanted to *hire* Tilda to investigate … something, which she hadn't yet disclosed.

As Tilda poured the tea, Hadrian kept his curiosity in check. Barely.

The minutes stretched as they made small talk. Hadrian forced himself to sip his tea.

Then he could stand it no longer. He impaled his mother with his most direct stare. "I am on tenterhooks waiting to hear why you need Miss Wren's help."

His mother's blue eyes—so like his own—narrowed at him ever so slightly. "I don't want to hear any admonishment about any of this. Do you understand?"

Bloody hell. This did not bode well. Hadrian tried to temper his concern. "Of course, but such a warning does not herald a sense of comfort."

"I just don't want you to counsel me." His mother sniffed, as if she were already affronted.

"I will not, Mama." He tried not to sound beleaguered and likely failed.

His mother abruptly turned her attention to Tilda, and Hadrian took another drink of tea. "I have recently begun consulting with a medium," the dowager countess said.

Hadrian nearly choked.

Coughing, he set his cup down. His mother glowered at him briefly, then looked back to Tilda. "She says she can communicate with Gabriel. Miss Wren, I want you to determine if she is authentic."

Of all the ridiculous notions. Why would his mother want to speak with Gabriel anyway? Hadrian's younger brother had died five years ago of cholera in India. His death would always provoke sadness. Why would his mother want to stir that up?

Perhaps because she still missed her youngest child. And now some charlatan was going to exploit her grief.

A sudden flush crept up Hadrian's neck as anger at this unnamed medium swept through him. He clamped his lips together lest he speak out.

Tilda glanced at him, and he kept his features stoic. He could not tell what she was thinking, but she did not appear alarmed. She smiled at his mother. "I will be glad to help, Lady Ravenhurst. Allow me to take notes whilst you provide the necessary details."

Hadrian silently fumed. Had he really expected Tilda to deny his mother's request? She was a paying client, and Tilda needed those. Not that Tilda would take *any* case. But did she really think it was possible to prove a medium was authentic? Hell, Hadrian couldn't prove his visions were real.

The visions had started after he'd been stabbed a few months ago. As Hadrian had fallen to the pavement, he'd managed to remove a ring from his assailant's finger. Hadrian had struck his head and lost consciousness.

One terrible concussion and a few days later, Hadrian had touched the ring and seen visions in his mind. After much investigation and frustration, he'd realized the visions were the memories of the man who'd worn that ring. The visions had continued—memories from others—as he'd touched other objects and people, provided he touched his bare skin to the object or another's flesh.

There was no explanation for how he was able to see what he did or how he could often feel the person's emotions in addition to seeing their memories. The only other person who knew of his confounding affliction was Tilda. That was because these visions and sensations had been crucial in helping to solve multiple murders they'd worked together to investigate. Indeed, his visions were the reason they were an investigative team. She was the investigator, and his unique power often guided her inquiries.

He supposed the fact that his visions had never steered them wrong, nor were they ever proven to be false, was as good as proof that they were real. Nevertheless, he didn't plan to tell anyone else about them.

Hadrian gave his mother a patient stare. "I don't think Miss Wren's capabilities extend to determining whether a medium's power is real or not. Nor do I think you need her to do so. *I* can tell you that this medium cannot possibly talk to Gabriel."

His mother exhaled. "I knew you would say something like that. However, I have it on good authority that she *can* speak to the dead."

"Whose authority? And if you are so certain, why do you need to hire Miss Wren?"

Lips pursing, the dowager narrowed her eyes slightly. "I am *not* certain, but my friend, Mrs. Langdon, who has been to her séances, swears the medium can speak to the dead. The medium revealed things she could not know. I trust Evelyn—Mrs. Langdon. However, I want to hire Miss Wren to make sure the medium is authentic." She focused on Hadrian intently. "Wouldn't you like to speak with Gabriel again?"

Hadrian missed his brother. He was angry that his life had been cut short, particularly since he'd been in love and on the verge of marriage, according to the last letter Hadrian had received from him. But Hadrian did *not* expect to speak with him.

"Mother, Gabriel is dead," he said quietly.

"Yes, but that doesn't mean he is gone. He's in the spirit realm, and he can communicate with us. At least, that is what I hope." The dowager countess picked up her teacup and sipped before replacing it on the table.

"Is that what the medium told you, that he's in the spirit realm?" Tilda asked, snatching the question from Hadrian's mind but posing it in a much kinder tone. Indeed, Tilda gave his mother a gentle smile and appeared greatly interested.

His mother nodded at Tilda. "Yes. And my friend says they are happy and safe—and eager to speak with those here on earth."

Tilda glanced at Hadrian, but he couldn't at all tell what she was thinking. "I confess I am most curious," she said to his mother.

"I'm glad to hear it because the medium is conducting a séance tomorrow night, and I am to be the prime subject. I want you to come with me." She looked at Hadrian. "You don't need to accompany us."

Before Hadrian could respond, his mother cocked her head with a slight frown. "Actually, you *do* need to accompany us. The medium is very particular about the circle, and she's made it possible for me to bring precisely one male and one female."

Hadrian held up a hand. "One moment. How much are you paying this medium?"

"Nothing," his mother responded briskly. "They do not charge a fee for the initial séance." She turned her attention to Tilda.

"Which is why I agreed before I asked you to investigate. I hoped you would be able to come and provide an assessment."

"What if we are not able to attend?" Hadrian asked.

His mother's expression was skeptical. "Is that true?"

Tilda picked up her teacup. "I am available."

Hadrian realized there was no avoiding it, nor should he try. If someone was going to attempt to fleece his mother in some way, he ought to do his utmost to protect her. He exhaled, releasing most of his annoyance. They would attend this séance, prove the medium was fake, and that would be the end of it. "What time are we expected, and where are we going?"

"We are going to a house in Rathbone Place," his mother replied. "The séance begins promptly at eight. Dinner is served after."

There was a dinner? "We don't need to stay for dinner, do we?" Hadrian noted the lines around his mother's mouth. He was irritating her. He did not mean to. This was just highly unusual. And aggravating. "I don't mean to be lacking in enthusiasm, but your involvement with a medium is most surprising. You say Mrs. Langdon introduced you to this person?"

"Yes. Mrs. Frost is one of the mediums with the London Spiritualism Society. She is very sensitive and kind. You will like her immediately, as I did. You will also see that she possesses a marvelous temperament for communicating with the spirit world."

Hadrian could only imagine what that could mean. Fortunately, he did not have to ask.

Tilda returned her cup to the table as she regarded his mother. "What sort of temperament is that?"

"She's calm and approachable, very mild in her manner. Apparently, she puts the spirits at ease, and they are comfortable communicating with her."

"How pleasant," Tilda replied, as if conversing about spirits was completely normal. "You mentioned that you are allowed to bring precisely one male and one female. Why is that?"

Hadrian's mother grew animated. "Mrs. Frost explained that circles are assembled with an equal number of men and women due to the energy brought by the different sexes. When I said I wanted to bring my son, she said she would also need to add a female, which is when I thought to include you, Miss Wren. Mrs. Frost also explained that it sometimes takes a séance or two to achieve the correct mixture of people. She said that Hadrian's presence and that of a family friend would be most helpful for contacting Gabriel."

"Tilda is a 'family friend'?" Hadrian asked.

His mother looked at him as if he were daft. As if *he* were the one who wanted to speak with his dead brother. "What else was I to tell them?"

Certainly not that she was bringing an investigator to prove whether or not the medium was authentic.

"I am happy to be your family friend," Tilda said warmly. "I will do my best to ascertain if Mrs. Frost can truly speak to the dead, though it will be difficult to tell in just one meeting. I will need to do additional investigation. Can you tell me what she helped Mrs. Langdon with?"

"Evelyn—Mrs. Langdon—wanted to speak with her father. Her mother is ill and confused much of the time. Evelyn wanted to find something her mother has lost and hoped her father could help find it."

"And was she able to?" Tilda asked. "Find it, that is."

"Unfortunately, no, but her father was adamant that he was right about where it was located, and Evelyn determined that her mother had moved the item and didn't remember where she put it." Hadrian's mother shook her head gently, then fixed her gaze on Tilda. "Evelyn didn't doubt that her father was communicating with Mrs. Frost. She said there were too many things Mrs.

Frost knew that she could not have without speaking with Evelyn's father."

"Do you know what sorts of things those were? It will help me to make my assessment," Tilda added with a smile.

Hadrian could see that Tilda was doing her best to both put his mother at ease and conduct her investigation.

"I'm not sure." The dowager countess's expression brightened. "Would you like to speak with Evelyn? I'm sure she wouldn't mind. She enthusiastically encouraged me to see Mrs. Frost."

Tilda inclined her head. "That may be helpful, thank you. Let us attend the séance tomorrow first. Do you know Mrs. Frost's first name?"

"Deborah. I am so grateful you are eager to help." Hadrian's mother smiled broadly. "Now, I will finish my tea whilst you tell me about your father the police sergeant." She looked expectantly at Tilda.

Hadrian watched Tilda closely. She missed her father greatly, despite not speaking of him much. Hadrian believed it was too painful for her, though he'd been gone for at least a decade.

"He wasn't yet a sergeant," Tilda said. "At least, not officially. He'd received the promotion, but on his last night as a constable, he was killed." She spoke with barely any emotion, her posture stiff and straight.

The dowager countess sucked in a soft breath. "Gracious, how awful. I'm so sorry. When was that?"

"Just over ten years ago." Tilda lifted her cup for another sip of tea and moved her gaze to the table.

Hadrian understood that she didn't wish to continue that line of conversation. Before he could redirect the topic, his mother asked, "Is your mother still with you?"

"No." Tilda blinked, then gave her head a slight shake. "She is still living, if that is what you meant. She remarried several years ago and resides in Birmingham. I live with my grandmother and manage her household."

"I suppose that explains why you are not married," Hadrian's mother said. "That's a shame, for you are clearly intelligent and well-mannered—and you're pretty. That gown is far more attractive than what you were wearing when last we met. I suggest you dress more like this to increase your chances of gaining a husband." She spoke warmly and kindly, but Hadrian noted the tension in Tilda's jaw.

"Thank you for the advice," Tilda said, masking her impatience. But Hadrian knew it was there. She did not want a husband, and the idea of her choosing a wardrobe to snare one was ludicrous.

There was also the fact that Tilda's financial situation did not permit a constantly current wardrobe. She did not renew her clothing each Season as Hadrian's mother, sisters, and their entire class did.

Because Tilda was not from the same class.

Hadrian hadn't really thought of their economic differences in such a stark manner, and he probably should have. He had the sense that Tilda was aware of her outdated wardrobe but that she had no quarrel with it. She had taken her grandmother's advice, that Tilda would attract clients if she appeared well-dressed, and recently purchased a new gown. It wasn't that Tilda's old clothes were poor, just that they gave one the idea that she could not afford anything new. Which had been the truth. However, with the funds earned from her recent investigations, she'd been able to refresh her wardrobe, which reflected her success as a private investigator. She also looked beautiful.

But then, Hadrian was hopelessly attracted to her. Especially since they'd shared a kiss a few weeks ago. However, she'd informed him that he'd overstepped. Which he'd only done after thinking she wanted him to. They'd miscommunicated, and she'd apologized for her part in that whilst he'd apologized for not seeking her consent explicitly.

It had all been very awkward. He had spent much of the last three weeks wondering how things were between them. Then his mother had decided to engage Tilda's services, and now they would be working together again. At least, he hoped so. He very much wanted to continue as her investigate partner. He also hoped they were still friends.

Hadrian's mother finished her tea, then gave Tilda Mrs. Langdon's direction. "Thank you again, Miss Wren." She looked to Hadrian. "You'll pick me up tomorrow evening?"

"Of course."

"Try to keep your mind open to this, Hadrian. Wouldn't it be wonderful to speak with Gabriel?"

"I don't understand why you want to," Hadrian replied, worried that he sounded cold. He couldn't help it. This entire scheme was doomed to fail and disappoint his mother.

"He died alone so far away, Hadrian. We hadn't seen him in over a year. We will never see him again." Her features softened and paled faintly. "Why wouldn't I want to tell him how much he is loved, just one last time?"

Hadrian's throat tightened, and emotion gathered in his chest. "Gabriel knew he was loved." At least by his mother and siblings. "And he wasn't alone. He had Nisha." His fiancée.

"He wasn't with his family." His mother's gaze shuttered. "I should think you would understand my need for comfort. Perhaps not." She stood and turned to Tilda. "I'll see you tomorrow, Miss Wren."

Hadrian launched to his feet and started to follow his mother on her way to the door. Tilda put her hand up and shook her head at him.

When the dowager countess was gone, he exhaled. "Why didn't you want me to accompany her downstairs?"

"Because *she* didn't want you to," Tilda replied from her chair, where she'd remained seated.

Hadrian sat down heavily in his chair, his lips twisting briefly into a scowl. "She's going to be disappointed."

Tilda arched a brow at him. "Why?"

"You don't actually believe this medium is speaking to the dead?" He stared at her.

"I don't believe anything yet," she said with a shrug. "I am keeping an open mind, as your mother bade, and as my own experience with you and your visions urges me to do. Furthermore, I am an investigator, and I must seek evidence before I come to a conclusion—without bias." She pinned him with an expectant stare. "What I find perplexing is how you, after all you've seen and experienced these past few months, can be so adamant that this medium *can't* speak to the dead."

A full scowl stole over Hadrian's face, and he didn't bother masking it. "I am not a medium, nor do I communicate with the dead." Except he had, in a manner of speaking. He'd touched objects that had been handled by a deceased person, and he'd seen their memories. It was far more rare than seeing those of people still living, but it *had* happened. Still, it wasn't the same as talking *to* them.

"Aren't you splitting hairs?" she asked wryly. "You can't explain your ability. Isn't it reasonable to believe that other similar abilities exist, such as speaking to the dead?"

"None of this is reasonable," he said crossly. "Especially my ability."

She leaned slightly toward him across the table. "Has it occurred to you that this medium may, in fact, be able to help you understand and even manage your power?"

Hadrian blinked at her. "That would require me to believe that she is authentic."

"I am going to determine that—with your help. Your ability is going to be particularly useful in this investigation." She smiled at him. Indeed, she looked quite pleased.

"Why are you so giddy?" He knew he sounded grumpy and didn't care. He did not want his mother's heart broken again. His philandering father had already done enough damage to her, and the death of her son had driven her into an extended period of mourning.

"This will be fascinating, and I can't believe you don't think so. I hope you will change your mind. Unless ..." She hesitated a moment. "Would you rather not work with me on this case?"

There was no way he wasn't going to be at his mother's side when she inevitably learned this medium was a charlatan. He also could no sooner turn down a chance to work with Tilda again than he could believe this medium spoke with the dead. "I must. If only because it's apparently required that I attend this séance."

"It's more than that," Tilda said quietly, with a small smile. "I know you care deeply for your mother. I promise I will do everything I can to protect her. I will not allow this to drag on. I shall begin tomorrow morning by seeing what I can learn about Mrs. Deborah Frost. I think I must start with the London Spiritualism Society, which your mother mentioned."

Hadrian wanted to accompany her. "When you asked if I wanted to work with you on the case, the answer is I do. Not only because I feel as though I need to for my mother's sake. I enjoy our investigative work and have hoped it may continue whenever you might have need of me."

Her eyes flashed with something—surprise or happiness. Whatever the emotion, he was delighted to see it. "That's good to hear. I enjoy our work too. I'd be pleased if you would make these inquiries with me." Tilda stood but did not move toward the door. Faint swaths of pink appeared on her cheeks. "I am not entirely certain what to wear to the séance. Would the dress I wore to Northumberland House be acceptable?"

During their first investigation, they'd attended an event at Northumberland House, and Hadrian had sent her to a modiste for her outfit. She'd looked absolutely stunning. "That would be too formal for a séance. Do you have a gown that you might wear to a dinner party?"

"Er, no. I am not invited to dinner parties."

Hadrian had risen with her and now stepped around the table toward her. "Visit the same modiste who dressed you for Northumberland House," he said. "Include the cost when you bill my mother."

She shook her head. "I can't do that."

"Why not? I paid for your Northumberland House garments."

"That was different. You insisted I purchase a gown as an expense of investigating the case. Your mother does not know that I don't have an appropriate gown." The pink had faded from her cheeks but now bloomed anew.

"Nor will she," Hadrian said softly. "But you need the gown to complete the investigation."

"I should obtain something suitable—for this and future investigations. I will purchase it myself, but not at your modiste."

Hadrian knew she would not be able to afford that. "I'm sure you'll find something just right. You look splendid today. I believe that's a new gown, is it not?" The burgundy wool was most attractive on her.

She smoothed her hand along her skirt briefly. "It is. I felt it important to make a good impression on your mother."

"You definitely did that—and it wasn't at all to do with your clothing," he said earnestly. "Wherever you purchased that gown should have something appropriate for tomorrow evening."

Tilda nodded. "Thank you. I'll take care of that first thing tomorrow. We can make our inquiries into the spiritualism society after. Why don't you fetch me at one?"

He smiled. "I'll look forward to it. Now, may I walk *you* downstairs?"

She chuckled, her lips lifting in a charming smile. "You may. Just try to stop scowling. I'm not used to you doing that."

Smoothing his features, he moved toward the door with her. "My apologies. I promise I will be in a better mood tomorrow, once I've had time to … think this through."

He'd been about to say once he'd had time to make sense of things. However, he didn't think that would be possible. His visions and speaking to the dead made absolutely no sense at all.

CHAPTER 2

*T*ilda pivoted in front of the mirror, surveying—to the best of her ability—the gown she'd just purchased. As with the last two gowns she'd recently acquired, she'd bought this already made. She'd even gone to the same shop where she'd found the others. And, as with the others, this one had required a bit of alteration. Mrs. Acorn, her grandmother's housekeeper, had adjusted the first two gowns, but Tilda's new, *temporary* maid, Clara, would take up the hem a half inch and tighten the bodice.

"You're sure you can finish this by tonight?" Tilda asked the maid, who was just a year younger than Tilda's twenty-five.

Clara nodded. "I'll have it finished this afternoon, Miss Wren."

"You must call me Tilda."

The maid's brown eyes flicked downward briefly. "You've been too kind, miss. I don't know where I would be without you."

The maid had worked for a former client—a woman whom Tilda had been helping in the matter of seeking a divorce. The divorce had become moot when her husband had been murdered. The widow, Beryl Chambers, had been left nearly destitute, and she'd been forced to return to her parents' home outside London. That had left Clara Hicks without employment.

And since she'd no family and not enough savings to lodge anywhere that was safe or clean, Tilda had welcomed her into the household temporarily, until Clara could find a new position.

It could not be permanent, no matter how much her grandmother said Tilda ought to have a maid. They simply did not have the household budget to support another mouth to feed. Especially not after they'd so recently taken on a butler they didn't need.

Vaughn had worked for Tilda's grandfather's cousin, who'd been murdered several weeks ago. He was past seventy and hunched, and there was no pension for him. He'd been injured by the man responsible for Tilda's grandfather's cousin's death and had recuperated here with them. Then he'd simply taken up a post as their butler.

Two murders and two new members to their household. Tilda's grandmother had joked that if Tilda solved another murder, they may find themselves with a footman or even a groom. Since they didn't even own a vehicle, that would be ridiculous.

Taking on retainers on an already-thin household budget was also ridiculous. And yet here they were. Tilda was glad she had a new client.

Tilda changed from the gown for that evening into her gray dress, one of her two new day ensembles. After donning her hat, she grabbed her gloves and reticule and hurried downstairs. Hadrian would arrive shortly.

As she descended the stairs, she thought of her meeting with him and his mother the previous day. Indeed, it had occupied much of her thoughts, both because she was excited to begin her investigation and because she'd been concerned by Hadrian's reaction to his mother's request.

She understood his concern that his mother must not be disappointed by a fraudulent medium, but his assumption that Mrs. Frost would be a charlatan had surprised her. How could he not have even a shred of curiosity, given his own inexplicable abilities?

Spiritualism was quite popular, particularly amongst his class. Was he not aware of how many notable people attended séances?

There was a third thing on her mind since the day before—and for the past three weeks—and that was her relationship with Hadrian. Things between them following the kiss in his coach had been strained. They'd both apologized, but really Tilda was most at fault. She'd made him think she might be amenable to a kiss, though that hadn't been her intent. She was woefully unskilled in matters of romance, nor did she wish to alter that. Content to be a spinster, she had no plans to surrender her independence.

But she'd missed working with him and the friendship they'd developed. Hopefully, that would return, and things could go back to the way they were before the imprudent kiss.

"Is Clara working on your gown for this evening?" Grandmama asked as Tilda entered the parlor to await Hadrian's arrival. Her grandmother was seated at the small table drinking tea. Petite, with snow-white hair and twinkling blue eyes, she was as dear to Tilda as her beloved departed father, which made sense because she was his mother.

"Yes, she says she'll have it ready by this afternoon. Must I really wear the feather in my hair?" Tilda asked. Her grandmother had gone to the shop with her that morning and insisted Tilda needed a new pair of gloves and a feather headpiece that Clara would pin into her hair.

"You will look splendid," her grandmother assured her. "Trust me."

Tilda noted that Hadrian's coach had stopped in front of the house. His coachman, Leach, opened the door, and Hadrian stepped out. He cut a fine figure with his hat and exquisitely tailored ensemble, not that Tilda could see the specifics from this distance through the window. Still, in her experience, she'd never seen him look anything less than spectacular. And it wasn't simply his expensive, handsome clothing. With his thick, dark-brown hair and deep-blue eyes, he was exceptionally attractive. His features were those a sculptor might choose to copy—a square jaw, slightly fuller lips than one might expect on a man, and a strong, expressive brow. The only imperfection was the slight bump in his nose, but, in her opinion, that added to his allure.

"Lord Ravenhurst has arrived?" Tilda's grandmother asked, likely noting Tilda's focus.

"Yes." Tilda pulled on her gloves and moved toward the entrance hall.

"When are you going to ask him to tea again?"

After they'd finished their first case, she'd invited him for tea. Since the kiss, however, she wasn't sure doing so would be a good idea. And yet, she also wanted to return to the friendship they'd enjoyed, so perhaps tea would help ease any awkwardness the kiss had wrought. Still, Tilda didn't need a reason to see him, for they would be working together on his mother's case.

Clearly, she was thinking too much about this. "I will consider when it would be appropriate, Grandmama. For now, we must conduct our investigation."

"Of course," Grandmama said, though there was a flicker of disappointment in her expression. Tilda was fairly certain her grandmother was nursing a dream in which Tilda wed the earl. No, that wasn't a dream. It was an impossibility. Tilda could no more fill the role of countess than she'd be hired by Scotland Yard.

Vaughn shuffled to the door and opened it. "Good afternoon, my lord. It's a pleasure to see you."

"Likewise, Vaughn," Hadrian said with a broad, genuine smile. He was always kind to the members of Tilda's household. Indeed, he treated them as if they were friends too. She'd seen him interact with his own staff in small amounts but wondered if his overall relationship with them was more friendly than she would have anticipated in an earl's household. She supposed she expected everyone in his class to behave more formally.

Hadrian turned his attention to Tilda's grandmother. "Mrs. Wren, it's always a delight to see you. I hope you are well."

"Quite, my lord," Grandmama replied warmly. "Tilda told me about your new investigation. I confess I wish I could attend the séance with you this evening."

"Is that so?" Hadrian asked.

Tilda sensed a slight reticence in his query. He was firmly against spiritualism, it seemed.

"My friend, Harriet Richardson, attended a séance a couple of months ago and was most enthusiastic about the experience. She said the medium moved an object on the table, whilst it was tipping to and fro." Grandmama grinned. "I should like to see that."

"That does indeed sound extraordinary," Hadrian said without any of the zeal Tilda's grandmother displayed.

"We should be on our way," Tilda said, both because she was eager to begin her investigation and to spare Hadrian further discussion. Tilda bussed her grandmother's cheek and preceded Hadrian from the house whilst Vaughn held the door.

As they walked toward the coach, Hadrian asked, "Where are we going?"

"The London Spiritualism Society has a headquarters located in Cadogan Place."

"In Belgravia?" Hadrian asked, sounding incredulous.

"You think such an establishment should not be located in such an esteemed area?"

"I'm merely surprised," he said flatly.

She approached Leach where he stood holding the door to the coach for her. "Good afternoon, Miss Wren. I'm glad to see you."

"Good afternoon, Leach. I hope you've been well."

"Indeed, miss."

"We're going to number thirty Cadogan Place," Tilda said.

Leach nodded before helping her up the steps into the coach.

Tilda hesitated briefly. Hadrian had always encouraged her to sit in the forward-facing seat. And he'd sat opposite her. At some point, they'd begun sharing the forward-facing seat—right up until the blasted kiss which had happened on that very seat. Perhaps that was why Tilda was wavering as to where she should sit.

Aware that she was likely taking too long to situate herself and not wanting to discuss the matter, she sat on the forward-facing seat and pressed herself as far against the opposite side of the coach as possible to make room for him.

Her deliberation had been unnecessary, for Hadrian sat opposite her. She was at once relieved and disappointed. Whilst she'd hoped for a return to their warm friendship, during which they'd often shared the same seat, she understood why that may not be possible. Her disappointment made her realize she *wanted* it to be possible.

The coach moved, and Tilda resituated herself toward the center of the seat since she now had it to herself. She was torn between wanting to address the seating, and the new tension in their association, and simply ignoring that in order to focus on the investigation.

The latter won out.

"I learned more about the spiritualism society from my grandmother's friend, Mrs. Richardson. She only lives a short walk away, so I called on her earlier to ask about her séance experience."

"I don't suppose she started and concluded by saying Mrs. Frost is a fraud?" Hadrian asked with a quirk of a smile.

Tilda laughed softly. "She did not. In fact, the séance she attended was not conducted by Mrs. Frost. The medium was Victor Hawkins, who is also with the London Spiritualism Society. Mrs. Richardson was kind enough to tell me where I could find the society as well as where she attended Mr. Hawkins's séance. He lives in Clerkenwell."

Hadrian blinked. "I'm aghast that there is a society focused on spiritualism. Is that where one goes to find a medium?"

"Apparently so," Tilda said. "Mrs. Richardson has not been there. She was invited to the séance by a friend who'd gone to the society. I'm quite eager to learn more about it."

"It seems as though I must educate myself on spiritualism," Hadrian said. "I understand it's quite popular in America. It's not a topic that ever interested me."

"Does it interest you now that you have experienced things you cannot explain?"

"I suppose it should." He lifted a shoulder. "Honestly, I just considered this … ability to be a strange anomaly that would disappear over time. Instead, it seems to be growing stronger. I had so many successive visions together at the end of our last investigation."

Indeed, he'd had two or three in a row on more than one occasion whilst they'd been investigating. They were incredibly helpful, but they also caused him a great deal of pain. Each vision was accompanied by a headache. The longer or more intense a vision, the greater his discomfort. He'd needed time to recover from them when he'd had several in succession. Tilda had started telling him to try to avoid having visions—which meant not touching things or people with his bare hands—unless they agreed it was necessary.

Tilda met his gaze. "I am hopeful that Mrs. Frost, or perhaps another medium, might be able to help you with your visions."

He appeared very uncertain, almost alarmed even. "Do you propose we reveal my ability? What if Mrs. Frost, or some other medium, is, in fact, a charlatan? I would prefer not to expose myself to anyone. You are still the only person who is aware of my curse."

He hadn't called it a curse in a while. At first, that was almost the only way in which he'd referred to it. She knew it was confounding for him. If she were the one with visions, she wasn't at all sure how she would feel.

"I promise we won't speak to anyone unless we both feel absolutely comfortable doing so. I am merely hoping we can learn things that might help you."

He arched a brow. "Do you really think we'll encounter someone in this spiritualism realm who shares my abilities?"

"I retain a moderate optimism. You know I am insatiably curious. I will dig until I am satisfied." She grinned at him, and he laughed again.

"Insatiably curious is precisely how I would describe you. In fact, I am sure I have done so."

"Do you mind presenting your card when we arrive at the society?" His title often aided their investigation. People were annoyingly eager to speak with a peer. Besides, she didn't particularly wish to alert the society that she was a private investigator.

"Of course not. What about your cards?" he asked. "You did order them, didn't you? I've yet to see how they came out."

He'd suggested to her that she ought to have cards printed with her name and occupation, as well as her direction. She hadn't wanted to share her grandmother's address, so she'd asked her occasional employer, Mr. Forrest, a barrister who sometimes hired her to assist him with divorce cases, if potential clients could contact her via his office. He'd been eager to agree, since a client for her may also end up being a client for him.

Tilda removed a card from her reticule and handed it to Hadrian. She felt a rush of pleasure as his mouth curled into a brilliant smile.

"I love seeing this," he said, lifting his gaze to meet hers briefly before he returned to perusing the card. "This looks splendid. I hope you are pleased." He'd recommended the printer, and Tilda was certain she'd been given an excellent bargain thanks to Hadrian's status.

"Honestly, I still can't believe I have them."

"You should have given one to my mother. She would have been even more impressed with you." He held up the card between his middle and forefinger. "May I keep this?"

"Certainly." She felt another flash of pleasure but worked to ignore it as he tucked the card into his coat. "When we arrive, we should ask for the head of the society, though I don't know his name."

"I will do that when I present my card." Returning his attention to her, he asked, "Were you able to obtain a gown for this evening?"

Tilda nodded. "Clara is altering it now. My grandmother insisted I purchase a ridiculous feather for my hair." She rolled her eyes.

Hadrian laughed. "I look forward to seeing it."

The coach stopped, and a moment later, Leach opened the door. He helped Tilda to descend to the pavement, and Hadrian followed her.

They walked up the short set of stone steps to the front door. A brass plaque that read "London Spiritualism Society 1867" was affixed to the brick.

"This was just founded last year," Hadrian noted before knocking.

Tilda's pulse thrummed with anticipation.

A butler wearing spectacles opened the door. He looked to be in his early thirties and possessed the squarest shoulders Tilda had ever seen.

"Good afternoon." The butler's voice was smooth and low.

Hadrian presented his card. "Good afternoon. We'd like to speak with the head of the society."

The butler opened the door wider. "Do come in."

They stepped into a massive rectangular entrance hall. A stone staircase curled up the left side at the rear of the room.

"This way." The butler led them to the right, through a

doorway into a parlor that looked out onto Cadogan Place. A large circular table dominated the central area of the room, and a separate seating area was situated near the hearth. "I'll let Mr. Mallory know you have arrived."

"Will you tell Mallory that you're an investigator?" Hadrian asked softly.

"No, which is another reason I didn't wish to present my card. I think it's best if they don't know we're investigating one of the mediums in the society."

"That is probably best," Hadrian murmured as a gentleman strode into the parlor.

The man was tall and muscular with blond hair and a pleasing countenance. A smile lifted his mouth as he approached them. "I'm Lysander Mallory. Lord Ravenhurst, I presume." He glanced at Hadrian before turning his attention to Tilda. "And?"

"Miss Matilda Wren," Tilda replied smoothly. "Thank you for agreeing to see us. We've come to ask you about how séances work. Lord Ravenhurst's mother has invited us to attend one this evening. We aren't sure what to expect." Tilda clasped her hands and worried them slightly, hoping to convey a sense of anxiety. "We thought you or another medium might guide us. We want to ensure the most successful séance possible."

Mr. Mallory smiled again. "I'm more than happy to help." He gestured to the seating area near the hearth. "Shall we sit?"

Tilda turned and walked to a dark-purple settee with mahogany trim. She sat, and Hadrian lowered himself beside her.

The medium took an adjacent chair upholstered in dark gold. "What is it you'd like to know?"

"Lord Ravenhurst's mother is hoping to speak to her deceased son," Tilda said, glancing toward Hadrian. His profile revealed a blank expression. "We hope that is possible, for her sake. However, we are skeptical. Can you perhaps explain how this is accomplished?"

"I understand your doubt." Mr. Mallory's brow creased.

"Indeed, it is most healthy. I shared your skepticism until I first spoke with someone from beyond."

"The spirit realm?" Hadrian asked dubiously. To his credit, he did not sound disdainful, although Tilda assumed he must be.

A faint smile flashed across Mr. Mallory's features. "Precisely. The spirit realm is real, and your brother is there, probably just as eager to speak with your mother as she is to him. Don't you wish to talk to him?"

Hadrian hesitated. "If I could, I would, yes."

Mr. Mallory held up his finger and wagged it briefly. "You will see, my lord."

"I'll be able to see him?" Hadrian asked.

"You'll hear him—through the medium. May I ask who is conducting the séance?"

"Deborah Frost," Hadrian replied. "We understand she is a medium with the society."

"Indeed. We have the very best mediums in London." Mr. Mallory's brown eyes gleamed. "Mrs. Frost is wonderful. You will no doubt have success."

Tilda addressed Mallory. "You are a medium then?"

"I am," Mallory said proudly. "I founded this society with the hope of bringing mediums and spiritualists together with a common goal of breaking down the barriers between this world and the spirit realm."

"How fascinating," Tilda remarked. "You've managed to attract mediums, and did I hear the society offers patronages?"

"We do indeed." Mallory moved his gaze to Hadrian. "Are you interested in joining our society, my lord? We'd be honored to have you."

Tilda noted that the medium addressed Hadrian about membership—not her. Was that just because he was an earl, and his presence would lend credibility to the society? Or was it because Tilda couldn't hope to afford the cost?

Hadrian managed a tepid smile, and Tilda wondered how

difficult that had been. "For now, I'm just accompanying my mother to her séance this evening. I'm eager to see what happens."

"Can you tell us more about the society? Do you just hold séances?" Tilda asked. "I'm quite fascinated."

"We do much more than conduct séances, though we do that almost every evening, in addition to the séances our premier mediums conduct at their homes." Mallory's expression was bright, his enthusiasm evident as he spoke. "We host teas on Wednesdays and Fridays, and we have a library which we encourage people to visit if they wish to learn more about spiritualism. On any given day or evening, you will find people there."

"You have an entire library dedicated to that?" Hadrian asked with a touch of incredulity. Tilda tensed, but Mallory seemed flattered.

"Indeed we do," Mallory said with a nod. "I'd be happy to show you. We also train new mediums who have joined our flock."

"You mentioned 'premier' mediums," Tilda said. "Is Mrs. Frost one of them?"

"Yes. She is one of three, besides me, of course." His tone held a casual arrogance that Tilda believed many would find charming. "There is also Cyril Ward and Victor Hawkins. The three of them are our most experienced," Mallory explained. "They were with me when I founded the society in January of last year."

Before Tilda could ask more questions, the butler entered the parlor. His lips were parted and his cheeks flushed. He appeared distressed.

"I beg your pardon, Mr. Mallory, but I must speak with you."

Mr. Mallory inclined his head toward Tilda and Hadrian as he rose. "Please excuse me for a moment." He walked toward the doorway and moved out of the parlor with the butler.

"I wonder what that is about," Tilda said softly. "The butler seemed upset."

"How do you find Mallory?" Hadrian asked.

"A trifle arrogant and very enthusiastic about his society." Tilda cocked her head. "And you?"

"I can't imagine an entire library dedicated to spiritualism. I'd no idea there could be that much published information on the subject. Perhaps it is a very small room."

Tilda quashed a smile as Mr. Mallory returned. His forehead was deeply creased. "I'm sorry, but I must go. Tuttle has informed me that one of the mediums in the society has died in a most … indelicate manner."

Tilda stood and Hadrian joined her. "I'm sorry to hear that."

Hadrian pinned his gaze on the medium. "Pardon my curiosity, but what does indelicate mean?"

"He has hanged himself."

CHAPTER 3

"**I**'m sorry to hear that," Hadrian said as Tilda also murmured her condolences.

Mr. Mallory shook his head, his eyes unfocused. He seemed utterly bewildered. "It doesn't make any sense. Cyril was doing exceedingly well as a medium. He'd recently written a pamphlet for the society about spiritualism. He had a prominent benefactor. There was no reason for him to take his own life."

"He was not unhappy?" Tilda asked, and Hadrian could sense her curiosity and desire to investigate.

"Not at all. I just saw him the day before yesterday." Mr. Mallory blinked. "You must forgive me. I need to go to his house."

"Is that where it happened?" Tilda asked gently.

"Yes. He lives in Willow Street. I'm sorry I can't finish our interview. I'm confident Mrs. Frost's séance tonight will be most illuminating for you." He looked to Hadrian. "Just open your mind to hearing your brother speak. That is the best advice I can give you." He turned and departed the parlor.

Hadrian looked to Tilda. "I suppose we should go."

Tilda started toward the door. As she passed the circular table, she slowed. "I wonder if they hold the séances at that table."

"Must they always be at a table?" Hadrian asked.

"It seems they are," Tilda said with a shrug.

Hadrian moved closer to the table and removed his glove.

Tilda blinked at him. "What are you doing?"

"If they have séances at this table, I wonder what I will see. If anything." He grazed his fingertips along the surface of the mahogany table.

"I'm glad you're being careful," Tilda said.

He heard the worry in her tone. The last several visions he'd experienced in her presence had been intense. He'd had a few since—all ordinary, such as seeing the memory of someone who'd sat at a table at a tavern—but he was careful about what and who he touched. Thankfully, nothing in his own house provoked visions, including his valet who, by necessity, touched Hadrian regularly.

Nothing came to him from touching the table, so he pressed his palm to the surface. Sometimes greater contact was needed. And sometimes—more often than not—he didn't see anything.

The room dimmed. It was now lit by candlelight, with a branch of candles in the center of the table. People sat around the perimeter, including Mr. Mallory, and they clasped hands. The candles blew out for some reason, and the vision faded.

Hadrian lifted his hand and tugged his glove back on. "They definitely have séances here. I saw several people around the table, including Mallory."

"How is your head?" she asked.

"Fine, actually." He'd felt a twinge of discomfort, but it had passed immediately.

"That's odd, isn't it?"

He lifted a shoulder. "Not particularly. The pain seems to come with visions in which something notable happens."

"Such as someone being pushed over a railing." Tilda referred to a vision he'd seen during their last investigation. "Did you feel anything?"

Often, his visions were accompanied by strong sensations—emotions of whoever's memory he was seeing. "Nothing this time. And of course, I've no idea whose memory I was seeing. Shall we go?"

"I want to take a quick peek at the library," Tilda said.

Hadrian gave her a wry look. "I confess I am interested to see how much literature they have on the subject of spiritualism."

They walked back into the entrance hall and paused. Tilda meandered toward the staircase. "I hear voices this way."

Past the staircase, there was a doorway to the left, through which Hadrian glimpsed a few people. "In there, perhaps?"

Tilda preceded him into the room, in which a pair of bookcases stood against the left wall. "I think this must be it. But you were correct in that it isn't much of a library."

Hadrian chuckled. The butler was there, and he sent Hadrian a dark look. Sobering, Hadrian turned to Tilda. "Perhaps we should go. They've just received bad news about one of their own."

"Yes, we should." Tilda again walked before him, and he followed her from the library.

They departed the house and, on the way to the coach, Tilda looked over at him. "Would you mind if we passed along Willow Street on our way to my grandmother's house?"

"Once again proving your insatiable curiosity," he said with a faint smile.

She arched a brow. "Aren't you curious why this man who seemingly had no reason to end his life chose to hang himself?"

"I am." He glanced back at the headquarters. "The entire society has piqued my curiosity."

They continued to the coach, and Hadrian instructed Leach to drive them along Willow Street. Leach held the door for Tilda as she climbed inside. She took the forward-facing seat, and Hadrian sat opposite her. Since they'd shared a kiss whilst seated together on the seat she now occupied, and Tilda did not want to repeat that, he thought it best if he took the other seat.

He was glad she didn't ask why he was sitting there, nor was he surprised that she did not. She regretted the kiss, and he was doing his best to put it from his mind. Though he wished he knew whether her regret stemmed from a lack of attraction to him or her reluctance to act on their attraction due to her views on marriage. Perhaps someday he would ask her. After they'd reestablished their close working friendship.

He sincerely hoped he hadn't gone too far and behaved in a reprehensible manner. He was not his father, who'd treated women as objects that existed for his amusement—or disdain.

The coach turned onto Willow Street, and Tilda leaned closer to the window, nearly pressing her nose to the glass. "There's a police wagon. That's Teague."

She referred to Detective Inspector Samuel Teague, whom they had worked with on their past two investigations. The man was of average height—indeed, the minimum for the police—with dark-red hair and sharp brown eyes.

Hadrian rapped on the roof of the coach. Leach steered the vehicle over and stopped.

"We're stopping?" Tilda asked.

"Don't you want to?"

Her eyes sparked with anticipation. "Well, yes. Thank you."

Leach opened the door, and Tilda stepped down. She didn't wait for Hadrian as she strode along the pavement to where Teague stood speaking with a constable.

"Detective Inspector Teague," she said, drawing the man to turn. The constable returned to the house, moving quickly up the steps and into the open doorway.

Surprise flashed across the inspector's features. "Miss Wren. Lord Ravenhurst." His eyes narrowed slightly. "Don't tell me you are investigating this murder too?"

Murder? Hadrian wasn't standing particularly close to Tilda, but he could sense the change in her. Her spine straightened, and she notched her chin up. Eager anticipation for investigating a murder was written across her attractive features—from the top of her heart-shaped face to the edge of her gently clefted chin.

"We'd heard the medium had hanged himself," Tilda said. "But he's been murdered?"

Teague arched a brow at her. "You heard someone had killed themselves and thought that required investigation?"

"We were with Mr. Mallory—the head of the London Spiritualism Society—when he received the news about the victim. Mr. Mallory was surprised to hear the man had killed himself. He said it was most uncharacteristic. I confess my curiosity was stirred." Tilda revealed the last without a hint of irony. "However, the man did not hang himself after all but was instead murdered?"

Teague frowned. "I misspoke. The coroner must determine if this was a murder."

"Why do *you* think it was murder?" Tilda asked.

Teague glanced around and answered in a low voice, "Ward was found hanging from the staircase. The rope had been painted to match the stone of the baluster. At first glance, it looked as though the man was ... floating in the air." Teague shook his head. "There's something off about it."

"As though he were levitating, as some mediums do?" Tilda asked.

"Yes, that's exactly it," Teague said, his eyes glinting. "It seems more likely that a murderer would create such a scene. Unless Ward was trying to make some sort of statement with his death, though I can't imagine what that would be."

"I'm sure you'll ask members of the society about that," Tilda said. Hadrian imagined she already had a list of tasks in mind—if she were investigating Ward's death.

"I will indeed," Teague said. "I've many questions about Ward's demise, and I imagine the coroner will too. Graythorpe will be here soon."

Tilda looked toward the house. "The coroner is coming here?"

Teague nodded. "I want him to see the body before we take it down."

Tilda cast another glance at the house.

"Don't ask me if you can go inside," Teague said darkly. "I've already revealed far too much to the both of you."

In fact, in the first case Hadrian had worked on with Tilda, Teague had assisted them greatly. But he'd done so on his own time, and that had been before he'd been promoted to detective inspector. Even on the last case, they'd helped each other somewhat, despite Hadrian being an early suspect in the murder.

"I wasn't going to ask," Tilda replied. "I look forward to attending the inquest." She turned to Hadrian. "We should continue on our way."

Hadrian inclined his head toward the inspector. "Afternoon, Teague."

"I imagine I'll see you soon." The inspector nodded at Tilda with a faint smile.

"Do let us know if we can help in any way," she said earnestly.

"You are an excellent investigator, Miss Wren. If it would not endanger my job, I would consult with you without hesitation." His gaze moved past her and fixed on a coach moving toward them. "I believe this is the coroner arriving."

"Good luck," Tilda said before turning and making her way back to the coach.

Hadrian walked alongside her. "I'm a little surprised you're leaving so easily."

She cast him a sideways glance. "What was I to do? Force myself inside? Loiter about like a nuisance? I can be patient for the inquest."

Leach opened the door to the coach, and they took their positions inside facing one another.

Tilda's gaze was focused out the window as they passed the house where Mr. Ward had died.

"You wish you were investigating the murder," Hadrian observed.

"I am intrigued. Not that it signifies," she said, sounding disappointed. "I have not been hired to conduct an investigation into the murder. I'm not even sure who would hire me. Perhaps Ward has family who would do so, although I'm sure they'd rather employ a man." Her mouth pressed into a brief but disdainful moue.

"The society—rather Mallory—might hire you," Hadrian suggested. "If he was aware that you are an investigator."

"I suppose that is possible," Tilda mused. "For now, I must focus on your mother's case." She clasped her hands in her lap and sat ramrod straight against the squab. "We learned some interesting things about the society today. I am looking forward to the séance tonight, particularly since it is with one of their 'premier' mediums. I wonder if that means anything beyond their seniority in the society."

"Such as they are highly skilled in contacting the spirit realm?" Hadrian was unable to keep the sarcasm from his tone.

"Or perhaps they do more than that, such as levitate or move objects."

Hadrian snorted. "I should like to see how those tricks are accomplished."

Tilda slid him a dubious look. "You don't think it's possible these mediums can do anything supernatural? I find that short-sighted of you, given your own inexplicable ability."

"Speaking of that, I should have shaken Mallory's hand."

"Do you think you may have had a vision that instantly proved him to be a fraud?"

He heard the humor in her voice and dipped his head. "Touché. I have no idea, but it is my best contribution."

"It is not your best," she said firmly. "You possess a keen intellect, and you've been essential to our investigations—not just because of your visions."

He couldn't help feeling flattered. And pleased. "I appreciate you saying that, but you must admit they are deuced helpful."

"They are indeed, which is why I hope one of these mediums may be able to help you understand them better. Without realizing they are helping you," she added hastily.

Hadrian did not share her optimism. He couldn't imagine how he might learn how to tame his power without disclosing that he had it. Not unless a medium revealed the same ability and offered up their knowledge and experience. Perhaps Hadrian needed to adopt Tilda's abject curiosity in the hope of learning whatever he could. Which meant believing that these mediums possessed supernatural power in the first place.

Hadrian exhaled. "It isn't that I don't believe in the supernatural. I can't help but do so, I'm afraid. However, that doesn't mean I believe these mediums and this society aren't taking advantage of people."

"They may have a gift, just as you do," Tilda said. "Perhaps they are trying to help people."

"I fail to see how levitating or moving objects would help anyone."

Tilda grimaced faintly. "I hope we will learn more this evening."

"I plan to touch Mrs. Frost and see what I may learn." He could only hope his "gift" would work, for he had absolutely no control over it.

"Just be careful that you don't overdo it," Tilda cautioned.

"I will." Hadrian would never tire of her concern. "I will pick my mother up before we fetch you just before seven."

"I'll be ready." Her green eyes glinted in the afternoon light, and he could see that she was quite eager. "Try to keep your mind open," she added.

"As open as my eyes will be. I'll be looking for every bit of evidence we can find." He would be receptive to all they could learn, as a good investigator should be. And as Tilda had consistently demonstrated when they worked together.

But what would he do if the medium contacted his brother in the spirit realm?

CHAPTER 4

*E*xcited for the séance, or more accurately the investigation into the séance, Tilda followed Lady Ravenhurst and Hadrian into Mrs. Frost's terrace in Rathbone Place that evening. The countess held her son's arm as the butler admitted them into the entrance hall. He took the countess's wrap and directed them upstairs to the drawing room where the séance was to take place.

When Hadrian had arrived at Tilda's grandmother's house, he'd come inside to escort her to the coach. He'd also explained that he'd informed his mother of the death of one of the society's other mediums. She'd wondered if the séance would go on as planned, but since she hadn't received notice that it was canceled, she had decided it must be.

As Tilda ascended the stairs behind Hadrian and his mother, another party arrived. Tilda turned her head to see a couple who appeared to be in their fifties or sixties. As she moved her attention back upward, she noted Hadrian tucking his gloves into his pocket.

Upon reaching the drawing room, Lady Ravenhurst took her hand from Hadrian's arm. Hadrian held back slightly and addressed Tilda. "I wanted to be sure and tell you that you look lovely. Dark green is a stunning color on you."

Tilda worked to ignore the flush of pleasure that heated her. He often complimented her appearance, and she was glad that he was still moved to do so, given the awkwardness between them following the kiss. She hoped this was a sign that things between them had returned to as they once were. "Thank you. I made sure the dye was not made with arsenic."

Hadrian laughed. "Of course you did."

She was glad to see him laugh and in good spirits. They entered the drawing room together. His mother was speaking with a woman who looked to be around thirty. Her oval face was pale, and long, dark lashes framed her gray eyes. She wore a dark blue flower in her sable hair, which was pulled back from her face and swept into a simple style.

Smiling warmly, she fixed on Tilda and Hadrian. "Welcome, Lord Ravenhurst and Miss Wren. I'm pleased you could attend this evening."

Hadrian stepped forward and clasped the medium's hand as he executed a bow. "I'm glad to make your acquaintance, Mrs. Frost."

Mrs. Frost's expression turned solemn. "As I am honored to make yours, my lord."

Tilda eyed Hadrian until he released the medium's hand. There was no indication that he'd seen anything, but then he would strive not to react.

Returning her attention to Mrs. Frost, Tilda said, "I confess I'm a trifle apprehensive. I hope you won't mind if I ask endless questions." She laughed nervously to give credence to her words.

On the way there, Tilda had explained to Lady Ravenhurst her plan to behave as though she were anxious so that her questions would not seem suspicious. The countess had thought that was a brilliant scheme.

"I don't mind at all," Mrs. Frost said, her red lips—they

appeared to be rouged—curving into another smile. "I whole-heartedly encourage curiosity."

A round table sat in the center of the room. There were twelve chairs, and small cards printed with a number between one and twelve sat on the table at each place. Tilda inclined her head toward it. "Is that where you will conduct the séance?"

Mrs. Frost pivoted so that she could see the table, which had been behind her. "Yes. Please feel free to peruse it. However, do not sit until I instruct you to do so. Everyone must be seated where I direct them."

"Of course," Tilda murmured. "Why is it important that we sit in certain places?"

"Aside from the order being male, female, male, female around the table, I must place people where I think they are best suited for their energy. It is why I talk with everyone before we take our seats. And I may ask people to exchange seats after we begin, depending on what the spirits tell me."

"Will you be levitating?" Hadrian asked, surprising Tilda. She hadn't thought to caution him against saying anything argumentative or that might impact his involvement. If the medium thought he didn't believe any of this was real, she might not want him to participate.

Mrs. Frost's lips parted, and her brow furrowed. "Is that what you were hoping to see? I'm afraid that is not something I have ever tried to do. I don't even like looking over a staircase rail. Levitating sounds terrible. However, I know other mediums who are able to perform that task."

"Who are they?" Tilda asked.

"Unfortunately, the one I would most recommend just passed away today," Mrs. Frost said with a pained expression.

"My condolences," Tilda replied softly. "We visited the society earlier today and happened to be there when Mr. Mallory learned about Mr. Ward's … demise."

"May I also offer my deepest sympathies?" Hadrian said. "I'm surprised you are still conducting the séance."

"I did consider postponing, however I know how keen Lady Ravenhurst is to converse with her son." The medium smiled at Hadrian's mother. "Since I'd already assembled what I think will be an excellent sitting, I decided we should forge ahead. Cyril would have wanted that. He had a true gift for communing with the dead, and now that he is among their number, I imagine he is anxious for us to try and speak with him." Mrs. Frost blinked and lifted her chin, as if she were trying to keep a tight rein on her emotions.

"Will you be trying to contact him this evening?" the countess asked.

"No, no, tonight is primarily for you, my lady," Mrs. Frost said earnestly. "Reaching Captain Becket is our priority. However, if other spirits wish to speak to someone at the table, I never turn them away."

Lady Ravenhurst opened her reticule and removed a folded piece of parchment. "I brought the item you requested, Mrs. Frost." She handed what looked to be a letter to the medium.

"Thank you. This will be most helpful." Mrs. Frost turned toward the door. "Please excuse me. I must welcome more guests."

Hadrian's mother turned her gaze toward him, her brows pitching into a V. "Why would you ask if she planned to levitate?"

Hadrian shrugged. "I was merely curious what to expect. What did you give Mrs. Frost?"

"She asked me to bring something that had been in Gabriel's possession. I brought her the last letter I received from him."

"Why would you relinquish that?" Hadrian looked and sounded quite cross.

"I am not *giving* it to her. She asked to have it for the séance. She said it helps to have something that belonged to the spirit she is trying to contact."

Tilda's senses pricked. What if this medium had the same ability as Hadrian? Perhaps she planned to use the letter to see Gabriel's memories. She slid her gaze toward Hadrian and saw that he was also looking in her direction. His eyes were dark, and his features tense.

Lady Ravenhurst pursed her lips at her son. "I do hope you will be helpful tonight. I will be most disappointed if your … *energy* causes problems."

"I'm sure all will be well," Tilda said soothingly. She sent Hadrian a quelling glance. "Won't it?"

"Mama, I want nothing more than for you to be happy," Hadrian said, sounding slightly beleaguered. "I shall do my utmost to ensure the séance is a success."

The countess seemed to relax. "Thank you."

The sound of a bell drew everyone to turn their attention toward the table where Mrs. Frost stood. "Good evening," she said, using a tone that was both loud and somehow soft and gentle at the same time.

"I am glad you are all here for the séance." Mrs. Frost looked to Lady Ravenhurst. "Our primary goal this evening is to make contact with Captain Gabriel Becket. However, we are at the mercy of our spirit guides, and they may have other messages to send us. I'm going to make my way around the room and instruct you where to be seated."

As Mrs. Frost spoke, the butler, who seemed young for such a position, moved about the room and extinguished every source of light until only the large branch of candles in the center of the table remained lit. The room was now quite dim.

"Please do not be concerned if you are not sitting with someone you know. I've spoken to each of you this evening and have decided upon the best arrangement for the séance to be successful. I do appreciate your trust in me." She smiled placidly, then moved toward the nearest person.

The gentleman with whom she spoke moved to the place

marked with the number eleven. Next, she approached the countess.

"Lady Ravenhurst, you will sit at number ten," Mrs. Frost said.

The medium pivoted to Hadrian and Tilda. "Miss Wren, you will be at number two, and Lord Ravenhurst, you will be next to me at number one." That meant the medium was at number twelve. Tilda realized the table was like a clock and wondered if there was any significance to that.

They moved toward their places and waited behind their chairs.

Tilda leaned toward Hadrian and whispered, "Did you see anything when you touched the medium?"

"A flash of a séance," he replied softly. "She felt ... focused, almost tense. It wasn't long enough for me to see much, unfortunately. I do wonder if she shares my ability since she asked for something of Gabriel's."

"I thought the same thing," Tilda murmured.

"But is she trying to see one of Gabriel's memories? My ability to see the memories of the dead is extremely limited."

Tilda looked toward him with encouragement. "Wouldn't it be wonderful if you could learn more about that?"

When everyone had been directed to their locations, Mrs. Frost bade them all to sit. When she was seated, she said, "If you are still wearing gloves, please remove them."

Tilda took her gloves off and tucked them into her reticule, which she'd set in her lap.

"Please place your hands on the table, palms down against the wood," Mrs. Frost instructed. "If the number card is in the way, you may move it toward the center."

Everyone complied. Tilda looked over at Hadrian's bare hands. His fingers were long, his nails neatly trimmed.

Mrs. Frost continued, "Our circle relies on the energy between us. I need everyone to adjust their hand placement so their smallest fingers can touch those of the persons next to you.

This will allow the energy to flow between us all. I may ask you to join hands. That depends on the level of magnetism I feel."

Hadrian arched a brow at Tilda as he slid his hand toward her until their little fingers touched. Tilda wondered if he would ever see one of her memories. They'd touched on a few occasions, and so far, he had not.

She looked over at the man on her other side. He was the gentleman who'd entered after them, and the woman he'd arrived with sat on his other side. He offered Tilda an excited smile.

"This is our first séance," he said.

"It is mine as well," Tilda replied in a whisper.

The medium surveyed the table, appearing to make sure everyone's hands were placed appropriately. She closed her eyes, which seemed to indicate her satisfaction.

After a moment, she spoke again, her voice loud and sure but with that soothing quality that Tilda had noticed earlier. "Before we begin, I must pay tribute to a man who has just recently entered the spirit realm. Our number in the London Spiritualism Society is diminished with the loss of my dear friend, Cyril Ward. He was our most gifted medium, aside from our leader, Lysander Mallory, and a light to all who knew him—in this world and the next."

After a moment's silence, Mrs. Frost addressed them once more. "We are gathered here tonight to speak to Captain Gabriel Becket."

Tilda felt Hadrian's finger twitch. She looked over at him and saw he was watching Mrs. Frost intently.

"Captain Becket, your mother is here to speak with you," Mrs. Frost said, her eyes still closed. "As is your brother and your friend, Miss Wren."

Tilda winced inwardly. She hadn't ever met Gabriel, and they certainly hadn't been friends. She hoped that falsehood wouldn't ruin the séance.

"Are any spirits here?" Mrs. Frost asked.

The branch of candles in the center of the table flickered, as if there were a breeze. However, Tilda did not feel one. Her pulse quickened. She again glanced at Hadrian. His eyes were narrowed at the candles.

"John Tabor, are you with us?" Mrs. Frost asked.

Who was John Tabor?

Mrs. Frost's eyes opened briefly but only to slits. "Mr. Tabor is my frequent guide." Her lids dropped once more. "John Tabor?"

Silence reigned, and Mrs. Frost frowned slightly. "Please feel free to converse among yourselves. Sometimes that encourages the spirits to visit."

Tilda looked across the table at Hadrian's mother. She'd also closed her eyes. Her lips were moving. Tilda leaned toward Hadrian. "What do you think your mother is saying?"

Hadrian gave his head a slight shake. "I've no idea."

The table moved suddenly, the top tipping away from Tilda. A guest on the opposite side, but not Lady Ravenhurst, gasped. The air around them cooled, as if someone had opened the window.

"John Tabor?" Mrs. Frost asked again.

Three raps sounded from beneath the table, as if someone had knocked on the underside. Hadrian pushed back from the table and looked under it.

"Everyone join hands please," Mrs. Frost instructed, her eyes still closed.

Hadrian's head was still bent to peer beneath the table.

Tilda reached for his hand, and he straightened. The moment their palms met, she felt a power greater than whatever might be happening around them at the séance. His touch warmed her in the chill of the room.

"Three raps means yes," Mrs. Frost explained. "John Tabor is with us. John, can you lead Captain Gabriel Becket to us?"

The answer came with two raps.

"Is that no?" Hadrian asked.

Mrs. Frost's eyes remained closed. "That means he doesn't know. Will you try, John?"

Three more raps to answer in the affirmative.

"John, tell him that his mother is here," Mrs. Frost said. "And his brother."

Mrs. Frost finally opened her eyes and turned her head toward Lady Ravenhurst. "What will you say to your son when his spirit is here with us?"

Tilda felt Hadrian tense, his hand clasping hers more tightly. She watched his mother, who took a moment to respond. "I would tell him that I love him, that we miss him. I hope he is at peace. I pray he's not—" She stopped abruptly and looked down at the table.

The candles flickered again. Tilda wondered if Hadrian had seen anything beneath the table but assumed he had not. He would have likely halted the séance if he'd seen anything suspicious.

The table tilted again, this time toward Tilda. She pulled back from the table but didn't release Hadrian's hand or the hand of the man on her left.

"Why is the table tilting like that?" someone, a woman, asked.

"The spirits are here," Mrs. Frost said. "John Tabor and others."

The man next to the medium spoke to her in a low tone. The table tilted again, back and forth, twice.

Mrs. Frost looked to Hadrian's mother. "Lady Ravenhurst, perhaps you should talk to Gabriel about his horse, the one with the long forelock."

Hadrian jerked. His attention snapped to the medium.

Lady Ravenhurst smiled. "That was Angus. He loved that horse. You want me to talk to Gabriel? Now?"

"It would likely encourage him to come," Mrs. Frost said.

Nodding, the countess looked around the room, her gaze drifting upward toward the ceiling. "My dearest, Gabriel. Are you with Angus now?" She laughed, perhaps nervously. "What a silly thing to ask. I remember when you fell off during your second ride." She looked over at Hadrian. "Do you remember that, dear?"

"I wasn't there," Hadrian said, his voice flat. Tilda noted the stiff set of his jaw.

"Well, I remember," Lady Ravenhurst said. "Cook made Gabriel his favorite pudding to cheer him." She went on explaining about the pudding and named several of Gabriel's other favorite dishes. But Tilda was focused on Hadrian.

"Are you all right?" Tilda whispered.

"This is ridiculous," he hissed.

"Your mother seems to be enjoying talking about Gabriel. Surely that's something."

"Until nothing happens."

The table moved again, tipping in all directions as if it were being tossed upon a stormy sea. Hadrian pulled his hand from Tilda's. She saw he also released the medium's hand.

The medium put her palm flat on the table, and the rocking stopped. As the table stilled, Mrs. Frost took a deep breath. "John Tabor has gone. He says tonight is not the time to speak with Gabriel or anyone else." Her lids lowered as her mouth dipped into a sad frown. "I do apologize. I think Cyril Ward's demise today has interrupted the connection to the spirit realm. At least, for me. You may release each other's hands. The séance is concluded."

Tilda noted that Hadrian had clasped his hands together and set them in his lap beneath the table. His gaze was focused on his mother. She looked, as he'd feared, disappointed.

Mrs. Frost stood and walked around the table to Lady Ravenhurst's chair. The countess turned her head as the medium bent down to speak softly to her. As Lady Ravenhurst nodded, Hadrian abruptly rose and moved to join them. Tilda followed.

"I'd be happy to try again next week," the countess was saying as Tilda arrived at her chair.

"I'm so glad," Mrs. Frost replied with a smile. "Again, I am sorry tonight wasn't successful. Sometimes that happens."

Lady Ravenhurst's disappointment from just a few moments ago seemed to have disappeared. Now, her features were eager, her eyes bright. "I am sorry to hear of the loss of your colleague."

"Would you like to go home, Mother?" Hadrian asked. His tone was cool, but his eyes were angry. And they kept drifting toward Mrs. Frost. Tilda wondered if he'd seen something more when holding her hand.

"We still have dinner, my lord," Mrs. Frost said. "I do hope you will stay. Here comes Henry with wine." She drifted away before Tilda could ask any questions, such as who John Tabor was.

Hadrian held his mother's chair whilst she stood. The countess turned to her son. "I'd like some wine. And dinner too, of course."

Tilda noted Hadrian clenching his jaw. She sidled closer to him as his mother turned toward the young butler, who approached them with a tray of glasses filled with wine. "Did you see something when you touched Mrs. Frost during the séance?"

"Yes. The man on her other side spoke to her during a séance —not this one, the man was dressed differently. I couldn't hear what he said, of course, which is damnably frustrating." He could never hear anything when he saw others' memories. "But his lips were moving. I'm glad my mother wants to stay because I plan to touch him next."

CHAPTER 5

*H*adrian wasn't happy that his mother was disappointed—he'd seen her downcast expression as the medium had ended the séance. But he'd expected nothing different. Apparently, they'd have to go through this again in a week. Unless he could talk his mother out of it. Or prove that this was a fraud.

"I saw the man speaking to Mrs. Frost tonight too," Tilda said. "Perhaps he has a particular energy that supports Mrs. Frost's connection to the spirit realm," Tilda suggested.

Hadrian gave her a look of exasperation. "Don't tell me you've bought into this nonsense."

She pursed her lips. "I am keeping an open mind because I am conducting an investigation."

The man who'd been seated next to Mrs. Frost was at least five years older than Hadrian, with gold-rimmed spectacles and a thick, dark beard and mustache. "Pardon me for a moment," he murmured to Tilda before walking to the windows where the man had moved following the séance.

"Good evening," Hadrian said. "I'm Ravenhurst." Before he

could extend his hand to the man, the butler arrived with a tray of wine.

"Balthasar Montrose," the spectacled man replied. "Wine?"

"Yes, thank you."

Montrose picked up a glass and handed it to Hadrian, as if Hadrian couldn't have helped himself. But he was immensely glad he hadn't had the chance.

The moment Hadrian took the glass, he saw a vision. He immediately recognized the parlor at the London Spiritualism Society. There were several people present, all seated. Mrs. Frost was there, perched on a chair. A gentleman stood near the hearth, his body angled away from them. He rose from the floor, appearing to levitate. Everyone applauded. Then he turned toward them and did it again, this time showing them how he'd achieved the illusion.

The medium angled one foot forward with the other slightly behind. He rose on the front of his foot, elevating himself whilst lifting his back foot from the floor. The trick was achieved by the medium's stance, which gave the audience a perspective that made it look as though the man was levitating.

The vision faded, and a sharp pain stabbed through Hadrian's temple. He'd known they were frauds. However, he couldn't prove it using his godforsaken gift. He needed to find a way to expose them. Perhaps he could do that at next week's séance.

"You broke the circle of magnetism when you stopped holding hands with those next to you." Montrose spoke with a Welsh accent. He eyed Hadrian with curiosity. "Why did you do that?"

"I found the table movement distracting. It … surprised me." He returned the man's intense perusal. "Did I ruin the séance?"

Montrose shrugged. "Impossible to say. But now you know what to expect, and you can retain your composure next time." He offered Hadrian a bland smile.

The man's superiority prompted Hadrian's irritation, which

only made his head throb more. He hadn't lost his composure. Taking a deep breath, he reminded himself they were investigating the medium. He sipped his wine. "How do you know Mrs. Frost?"

"I have long been a supporter," Montrose replied. "She invites me to many of her séances due to my sensitive energy."

"Your magnetism?" Hadrian asked, careful to keep his tone free of sarcasm. At Montrose's nod, he continued, "Are you a member of the London Spiritualism Society?"

"Proudly. Are you considering joining?" Montrose asked. "I highly recommend the society for those interested in the spirit realm and in harnessing the natural energy around us."

For what? Summoning the dead? "I have many questions about the society," Hadrian said vaguely. "How did you come to support Mrs. Frost? Did you hear about her through the society?"

"Yes. I was looking for a medium so I could speak with my grandfather after he passed away. I found the society and attended a séance there. Mrs. Frost was the medium."

"I confess I wasn't even aware of the society until very recently. I am surprised I hadn't heard of it." He took another drink of wine as Montrose did the same.

"I suppose it would be easy to miss if you weren't seeking a medium or don't possess an interest in spiritualism," Montrose remarked. "Furthermore, the society was only founded in January of last year."

"Was Mrs. Frost able to communicate with your grandfather?"

"Indeed!" Montrose said excitedly. "John Tabor is my grandfather. He continues to help her from the spirit realm." Chuckling, the man glanced toward Mrs. Frost. "I'm grateful to her for helping me to communicate with him. I know he's thrilled to be of use."

Hadrian stared at the man. Did he really think he was talking to his deceased grandfather? Hadrian couldn't help feeling sorry for Montrose. He'd been utterly duped.

"I am curious. Do you pay a fee to attend?" Hadrian asked. "Since you are able to speak with your grandfather regularly."

"I do not." Montrose sniffed. "I am an invited guest."

"Who is able to regularly speak with his grandfather," Hadrian said with a smile. "How does that work? Are you only able to ask questions that have a yes or no answer?"

"Not at all. On occasion, my grandfather inhabits Mrs. Frost's body. That makes it quite easy to converse." Montrose's brown eyes glittered. "I hope that your brother will find his way into Mrs. Frost next week. Then you will see." He held Hadrian's gaze for a moment longer than was necessary, or perhaps even polite.

It was unnerving. Something about Montrose bothered him, but Hadrian attributed it to the man's absolute belief and faith in Mrs. Frost and spiritualism.

Hadrian couldn't think of anything more horrid than imagining his brother invading the body of a living woman in order to speak to them. Gabriel wouldn't do that even if he could.

Montrose's gaze moved past Hadrian, prompting Hadrian to pivot. His mother and Tilda were walking toward them. Montrose smiled. "Lady Ravenhurst, I was just telling the earl that I hope next week's séance will bring your son to you. It's possible Captain Becket may even decide to occupy Mrs. Frost's body in order to communicate with you."

"I had heard that could happen," Hadrian's mother said, her eyes round. "I am not sure how I would feel about that."

Hadrian looked at his mother and worked to keep his features smooth. "Mr. Montrose says he's seen Mrs. Frost do it. Her spirit guide, John Tabor, is none other than Mr. Montrose's grandfather. Apparently, he has inhabited Mrs. Frost during some of his visits." Hadrian glanced at Tilda, who was watching him. She pressed her lips together as if she were trying not to speak.

Turning her attention to Montrose, Hadrian's mother asked, "And how did you find that?"

Montrose smiled. "It was wonderful to hear him, even if he

didn't look like himself. It's a much easier—and faster—way to communicate. Far superior to the tapping. However, sometimes, it is not possible."

The butler announced it was time to move downstairs to the dining room. Montrose offered his arm to Hadrian's mother. "May I have the honor of escorting you, my lady?"

Hadrian's mother smiled. "You may." She took Montrose's arm, and they made their way from the drawing room.

Hadrian turned to Tilda. "They are all frauds." He kept his voice low, but the anger he'd hidden whilst talking with Montrose spiked his words.

"Did you see something?" Tilda asked, taking his arm. "I wondered if the table gave you a vision."

"Oddly, the table didn't present a vision at all. I find that strange since so many people were touching it and have touched it in the past. But when I held Mrs. Frost's hand, I saw another séance. Or perhaps more than one." Hadrian guided Tilda from the drawing room, depositing his wine glass, even though it wasn't yet empty, on the table as they passed it. "The visions flickered quickly through my mind. It was disconcerting."

"How badly did that make your head hurt?" she asked as they walked toward the staircase.

"Not badly at all. The real ache came with a vision I received whilst touching the glass that Montrose handed me. He was at the London Spiritualism Society headquarters." Hadrian went on to detail what he'd seen with the fake levitation.

Tilda's eyes rounded. "That means the society is aware of the fraud."

"I wager they originate it. They bloody well practice their deceptive tricks." He glanced at Tilda as they started down the stairs. "We *must* find proof of their trickery. I don't know how they tilted the table, but there must be a cheat involved, as with the fake levitation I saw in my vision."

"I'm trying to envision what you described," Tilda said. "I think we must try this later."

"I shall be happy to demonstrate." Hadrian's mind worked. "Perhaps at next week's séance, I can pretend a spirit has overtaken me and caused me to levitate. Then I can expose the trick to everyone."

"I'm not sure that will prove that *they* are frauds," Tilda said gently.

Hadrian paused at the bottom of the stairs and turned toward her. "You believe me, don't you?"

"Of course. I have never doubted your visions." Her eyes met his, and the trust within them settled him. "Are you sure your head is all right? You could plead a headache and we could depart —it wouldn't be untrue."

"My mother would be disappointed to leave."

Tilda arched a brow at him. "Then you see that this pleases her, even if it is false? Would it harm her if she thought she was talking to Gabriel, even though she wasn't?"

Hadrian scowled. "I hate the idea of someone pretending to be my brother. Especially for the purpose of fooling my mother."

"Even if it makes her feel good?"

"I can't believe you would think it acceptable for people to be swindled. And there is something shady going on with regard to the fees for these séances. My mother said there was no fee for the first one she attended and did not say what it would cost to attend another. I didn't think to ask, for I'd hoped tonight would be her only séance. However, now she must return next week in order to speak with Gabriel. Will they charge her for that? Have they lured her in with a free séance only to ensure she must come back for a fee? Will Mrs. Frost also fail to speak with Gabriel next week, which will require my mother to return a third time?"

Tilda frowned. "I understand you are concerned, but let us not move ahead of the facts we have."

Hadrian took a deep breath. "My apologies. Since I have seen evidence of their levitation fraud, I am inclined to distrust the mediums and this society entirely."

"Let us continue to collect evidence. In particular, we need to be able to prove they are deceiving people with regard to communicating with the spirit realm."

"So I'm to accompany my mother to another séance next week and permit them to perchance fleece her of whatever it may cost?"

Her gaze was warm with understanding. "I'm afraid you must, as it is vital to my investigation. Though you must also realize we will not wait until then to gather more evidence. I would like to visit the other premier medium, Mr. Hawkins, and see what we may learn. Please just wait to deter your mother until we have proof. I would hate for you to cause her upset—you have such a nice relationship."

Hadrian thought he heard a wistful edge to Tilda's observation. Perhaps that was due to the estranged relationship between Tilda and her own mother. "I don't want to upset her either. We should go into dinner. I imagine we are holding it up."

They started toward the dining room, and Hadrian turned his mind to what Tilda had said—collecting more evidence. "I want to investigate the table in the drawing room, but I don't suppose I'll be able to do that tonight."

"Why don't we arrange to return another day?" Tilda suggested. "We'll ask for a consultation with Mrs. Frost. I can distract her, and you can look at the table. I would like to try to ascertain whether she shares your gift. I'm curious how she knew about your brother's horse."

"As am I. I don't know what the letter that my mother gave the medium said. Perhaps he mentioned the horse in it."

"Along with a description of the forelock?" Tilda's eyes narrowed. "That is something that someone could have seen."

"As I am able to do. You think Mrs. Frost touched the letter and perhaps saw a memory of my mother's that included Angus?"

Hadrian shook his head, which still ached. "How many people have this ability?"

"Perhaps three," Tilda said. "The premier mediums. Or four, since Mallory is also a medium."

"They train other mediums too. Are they somehow able to recruit people with this ability? I find that exceedingly hard to imagine. I am afraid of anyone finding out about what I can do. Why aren't they?"

Tilda smiled at him. "You are thinking like an investigator."

He chuckled and then escorted her into the dining room, where they went to the two remaining seats, which were, fortunately, together. His mother was already seated next to Mrs. Frost at the head of the table, and Mr. Montrose sat on the medium's other side.

"I'll speak with Mrs. Frost after dinner to set an appointment for us to return," Tilda whispered as Hadrian held her chair.

Dinner would have been a tedious affair if not for Tilda's company. It seemed their friendship was intact following the kiss they should not have shared. Hadrian was glad. He wanted her as a friend, in addition to working with her on investigations.

At one point, he realized he'd missed a detail about the vision he'd seen after accepting the glass from Montrose. He leaned toward Tilda to tell her. "I saw Montrose in that vision I had when I took the glass from him."

She turned her head to meet his gaze. "Does that mean it wasn't his memory?"

"I have to assume so." When Hadrian experienced a memory, he did so from the perspective of the person to whom the memory belonged. If it had been Montrose's memory, he would not have seen him sitting next to Mrs. Frost, which was what he'd recalled during dinner.

"Whose memory was it, do you suppose?" Tilda asked.

"I can't be sure, but it had to be someone who was present at the society headquarters whilst someone else demonstrated how to pretend to levitate."

"That could be anyone who touched the glass, including the butler or any other retainer," Tilda mused.

"Why would one of Mrs. Frost's retainers be at the society headquarters?" Hadrian asked.

Tilda shrugged. "They would likely not. Montrose makes the most sense."

When dinner concluded, Tilda made her way to their hostess and thanked her for the evening. "I wonder if I might schedule a consultation with you."

The medium brightened. "Would you like to speak with your father?"

Hadrian noted Tilda's nostrils flaring slightly. He sensed her tension, perhaps because he knew how much she loved and missed her father.

"How did you know my father died?" Tilda asked pointedly.

Mrs. Frost glanced toward Hadrian's mother. "Her ladyship told me. When would you like to come for a consultation?" Her expression dimmed. "Not tomorrow. I've been summoned to attend the inquest into Cyril Ward's death."

"Of course," Tilda murmured.

"Perhaps the day after?" Mrs. Frost suggested. "Come at one, if that suits you."

Tilda smiled warmly. "It does, thank you."

"We will take our leave," Hadrian said. "Thank you again, Mrs. Frost." He guided Tilda from the dining room.

On the way to the entrance hall, where his mother was waiting, he looked over at Tilda. "I suppose we'll be attending the inquest tomorrow."

She met his gaze with the bright curiosity that fired her from within. "I wouldn't miss it, though I'll have to explain my presence to Mrs. Frost, lest she discover I'm a private investigator."

"Or you could disguise yourself," Hadrian said.

"I could, but then I wouldn't be able to speak with Teague without explaining myself," she said with a faint smirk. "Perhaps I'll just hide behind you."

He gave her a quick bow. "I'm happy to be of service."

When they were ensconced in the coach on their way to Tilda's, Hadrian decided to broach the topic of next week's séance with his mother. "Mama, you mentioned there was no fee for tonight's séance. Will there be one next week?"

"Yes, but I don't mind paying it, so do not give me any grief about it, Hadrian," his mother replied. Her tone was tense, and her mouth tight.

"I will not," Hadrian said. "I hope the fee is not terribly high."

"It is ten pounds." She lifted her chin and gave him a stern look that dared him to question the amount. When he said nothing, she added, "I realize Miss Wren has not yet determined if Mrs. Frost can actually speak to the dead, but I was most convinced this evening when she asked about Angus. Wasn't that remarkable?"

"It was indeed," Hadrian said evenly. "I do hope you will allow Miss Wren to continue with her investigation."

"I will, yes." His mother cast a small smile toward Tilda. "Did you learn anything this evening?"

"Only that I have doubts about the veracity of what they do during a séance. I would like to study the table to determine how it moves."

"If you find nothing, we must conclude the spirits are responsible," Hadrian's mother said. "How will you determine how Mrs. Frost knew about Gabriel's horse?"

"I am not yet certain, but I'm glad you brought it up," Tilda replied gently. "Did the letter you gave to Mrs. Frost include anything about Angus?"

His mother's face fell. "He did mention that he'd recently acquired a new horse with a long forelock like his first one. I'd forgotten that." She put her hand to her brow briefly.

Hadrian touched his mother's arm. "It's all right, Mama."

"Does that mean Mrs. Frost is a fraud? I will be so disappointed." She turned her head toward Hadrian. "I really thought Gabriel may have been close to us tonight. Didn't you sense him as I did?"

"I did not," Hadrian said apologetically. "However, that doesn't mean anything."

"Mrs. Frost said I must return next week, that spirits don't linger for long after they try to make contact. I fear if I don't, I will lose the chance to speak with him."

Hadrian met Tilda's gaze across the coach. It suddenly seemed as though it didn't matter whether the medium was authentic or not. He wasn't sure his mother cared.

And yet, she'd hired Tilda and asked her to continue her investigation. They would forge onward. He inclined his head toward Tilda, more determined than ever to discover the truth behind the London Spiritualism Society.

CHAPTER 6

"Lord Ravenhurst's coach just arrived," Tilda's grandmother said as she moved from the parlor into the entrance hall, where Tilda was drawing on her gloves. "Where is the inquest?"

"A tavern near Willow Street called the Boasting Goat," Tilda replied.

Vaughn opened the door and welcomed Hadrian inside. "Always a pleasure to see you, my lord," the butler said. "I understand today's business is another inquest. That medium who was found hanging from his staircase?"

The news had spread quickly, first appearing in last night's papers. Tilda's grandmother had read about it and asked if it was at all connected to the séance she and Hadrian had attended.

Her grandmother pierced Hadrian with a frank stare. "My granddaughter assures me you are not investigating this medium's death, but if that is true, why are the two of you attending the inquest?"

"We may learn information that pertains to the investigation Tilda is currently conducting," Hadrian replied with an affable smile.

Tilda had already explained that, but apparently her grandmother wanted to hear it from Hadrian as well. "There is no reason to worry, Grandmama. We are not investigating another murder. It is just that the deceased medium is a member of the same spiritualism society as the medium I am investigating for Lady Ravenhurst."

"I am not worried. Not when you are accompanied by his lordship," Grandmama said, returning Hadrian's smile. "Still, I am glad to see you investigate something other than death."

Tilda wasn't sure why it mattered, other than that her grandmother was always concerned about Tilda's safety. Unless she was with Hadrian. "I have conducted several investigations for women seeking divorce. That is, in fact, how my last investigation began."

Indeed, the investigation before that had also started with something other than a murder. Now that Tilda thought about it, perhaps murder investigations did have a way of finding her.

"What do you hope to learn today?" Grandmama asked.

Tilda exchanged a look with Hadrian. "We aren't sure. The person we are investigating will be at the inquest."

"I look forward to hearing about it," Grandmama said. "Except for any grisly details." She turned to Hadrian. "How did you find the séance last night? Tilda said it was somewhat anticlimactic."

"It wasn't much of an entertainment," Hadrian replied. "There wasn't any levitating to speak of." He smiled, and Tilda's grandmother laughed.

"Do they really levitate?" her grandmother asked.

"Anyone can," Hadrian declared. "Observe." He moved away from them, going to the farthest corner of the entrance hall. Putting his back to them, he angled his body so that his right side was more toward them. Very slowly, he seemed to rise from the floor and float a few inches above it.

Tilda's grandmother gasped. "How are you doing that?"

"He's only lifting his back foot," Vaughn said, who was standing closer to the side of the hall where Hadrian was conducting his trick.

"Show us how it's done." Tilda was glad he'd remembered to demonstrate what he'd seen in his vision the night before.

Returning to the floor, Hadrian turned and faced them. "It's all about putting distance between the trick and the audience so they can't see what is happening. And the performer must angle themselves in a specific manner so that the observers will only see the foot that is lifted. Meanwhile, I am rising on the front of my other foot, which remains solidly on the ground." He demonstrated for them as he spoke. Then he turned again to repeat the trick.

"Marvelous," Tilda breathed. She was most impressed with his mastery of the performance after having only seen it in a vision.

Hadrian lowered his foot to the floor and turned with a grin. "One must also not allow anyone to stand where they can see the front foot, as Vaughn was able to do."

Vaughn clapped, and Tilda and her grandmother joined in the applause.

"Well done, my lord," Vaughn said. "If your earldom is ever in need of funds, I'd say you could perform that trick all over England and call the act The Floating Earl."

Hadrian chuckled. "I would never want to bamboozle anyone."

Vaughn nodded. "Of course not. I didn't mean to imply you would. Perhaps I am too familiar."

"Not at all," Hadrian assured him with a smile.

They said goodbye to Tilda's grandmother, and Vaughn held the door for them as they departed. When they were settled in the coach, Hadrian asked, "Do you tell your grandmother everything about your investigations? Leaving out anything grisly, of course," he added with a smile.

"Not everything. I don't tell her about your visions, which are a vital part of our investigations. Is your head all right today?" His headaches didn't typically last into the following day, but Tilda wanted to ask anyway.

"Yes. Thank you for your concern. I've been thinking of the vision I had when I touched the glass that Montrose handed me. I'd like to know who else was in the memory, particularly who was doing the levitating."

Tilda nodded. "Thank you for your demonstration. You certainly delighted Grandmama and Vaughn."

"And you?" he asked in a teasing tone.

"Quite. Had you practiced?"

"I did, in fact. I confess I was eager to see if I could do it, so when I arrived home last night, I made Sharp, my valet, watch me try. He helped me perfect my technique. Then he had to try it too. By this morning, he'd taught two footmen and one of the maids. However, the trick doesn't work as well for women because the hem of the gown rather disrupts the effect of levitating."

"I'm going to have to attempt this for myself," Tilda said. "You've done a great investigative service."

Hadrian chuckled. "Happy to do my part."

"Do you plan to show your mother the trick?" Tilda asked.

"I'm considering it, although I'm not sure it will deter her from attending another séance. She isn't interested in levitation and likely won't care that it's a cheat. Furthermore, I believe she accepts that some mediums are frauds, which is why she hired you in the first place. She wants to be assured that Mrs. Frost is not among that number."

Tilda inclined her head. "We must prove that Mrs. Frost doesn't actually speak to the dead. Hopefully, we can do that tomorrow when we call on her. Or at least move closer to that goal."

"I wanted to ask you something about last night," Hadrian

said, his gaze cautious. "Did it bother you when Mrs. Frost asked about your father?"

"It surprised me," Tilda replied.

"I noticed you didn't answer," he said softly. "Would you speak to him if you could?"

"No, I don't think I would, if it was even possible." She eyed Hadrian a moment. He actually possessed a power that would allow her to recall something precious—one of her father's memories. "I have wondered, however, if you might see one of his memories some time. There are things in my grandmother's house that he touched in the past."

Hadrian leaned slightly forward, his blue eyes gleaming in the afternoon light filtering into the coach. "I would do that for you, if you wanted me to." He held her gaze. "Would you?"

Tilda exhaled. "I don't know. It only occurred to me that it might be possible."

"I can't quite determine if you believe the mediums can speak to the dead or not," Hadrian said, eyeing her intently.

"Because I haven't yet made a determination."

Hadrian leaned slightly forward. "Perhaps it's that I can't tell if you want to believe it or not. I am not sure of your overall impression of the spiritualism movement."

"I don't know that I have one yet. I tend to reserve judgment until I can gather as much information as possible. Like you, I'm inclined to disbelieve that these mediums speak to the dead, and I do not doubt that levitating and other tricks they execute are likely fabricated, though I would still like to find proof," she added pointedly. "However, I also know that I cannot explain your ability, nor can I discount the possibility that someone else is similarly gifted."

"I can't imagine how we'll find proof of that." He pressed back against the squab, squaring his shoulders. "And if we did, how would I explain it to my mother?"

"You could tell her the truth about yourself," Tilda said quietly, almost holding her breath as she waited for his reply.

She was not surprised when Hadrian shook his head.

"Why not?" she asked.

"For the same reason I didn't tell you—I am afraid she won't believe me. Or that she'll think I'm mad. Sometimes, *I* think I'm mad."

"I believed you. And you are *not* mad," she said vehemently. He'd been very concerned about that when the visions had started, and she understood why he would be.

"It isn't normal, Tilda."

Tilda heard an edge of revulsion in his tone, and it pulled at her heart. "Is that what you dislike? That you see yourself as abnormal?"

He shifted uncomfortably. "Because I am."

"I don't see you that way." She gave him a look that dared him to argue before directing her attention out the window. "The Boasting Goat is up ahead."

"What are you hoping to learn today?" Hadrian asked, probably glad that Tilda had abandoned talk of his ability and how he felt about it.

"I would like to know who else was in the vision you saw when you touched that glass last night. I hope you might recognize someone—or several someones—at the inquest."

Hadrian inclined his head. "I will certainly inform you if that is the case."

"Remember to block me from the mediums' sight, if at all possible," she said.

Hadrian chuckled. "They will no doubt recognize me. Why shall I say I am there?"

"You're a member of the House of Lords and you take an interest in public safety."

"You are so adept at coming up with believable lies to cover our investigations." His gaze was warm with admiration. "I am absolutely concerned about public safety, and you've accompanied me because you were moved by Mrs. Frost's grief over her friend's death." He grimaced. "That is not nearly as good as what you came up with."

"I'll come up with something," she said with a laugh.

The coach stopped in front of the Boasting Goat. Leach opened the door and as Tilda stepped out, she noticed a few journalists loitering near the entrance of the pub. "Some of the press has already arrived. I recognize them from the last inquest we attended."

"As do I," Hadrian said.

Tilda narrowed her eyes at one of them in particular. "The gentleman in the plaid trousers was most assertive in his quest for information."

"Shall we try to find another way in?" Hadrian suggested.

"I don't think so. I can't imagine they'll be troubling us as they did last time."

Because last time Hadrian had been a suspect in the murder. The press had been ravenous for details about an earl's involvement in the death of a man who'd stolen that earl's fiancée.

"I appreciated your efforts in blocking them from pursuing me," Hadrian said softly. She'd urged him into his coach after the last inquest and faced the press on her own to keep them from bothering him.

Leach said he would move the coach to the corner and await them there. Tilda took Hadrian's arm, and they made their way to the entrance.

The plaid-trousered gentleman approached them, his shrewd brown eyes assessing. "If it isn't the intrepid Miss Wren and her surprising companion, Lord Ravenhurst. Are you courting now?" he asked with a smirk.

"We are business associates," Tilda replied coolly.

The reporter turned his attention to Hadrian. "Ravenhurst,

surely you have more important things to do than squire this … private investigator about to inquests?"

"I beg your pardon, who are you?" Hadrian asked the question with a condescending boredom only an earl could affect. Tilda quashed a smile.

"Ezra Clement, reporter for the *Daily News*."

Hadrian offered his own smirk. "You report on romantic matters, such as courtships and marriages?"

The reporter pursed his thin lips. "I report on whatever may interest our readers."

"I daresay the most interesting thing here will be the inquest," Hadrian said. "Or perhaps your trousers." His gaze dipped to the man's brightly colored, blue-and-yellow, plaid garment.

"Why are you here for the inquest?" the reporter asked, lifting his notebook and pencil.

"I don't believe your readers would care," Tilda said blithely as she tugged on Hadrian's arm.

Hadrian looked over at her. "Agreed." He escorted her into the pub.

"What an annoying man," Tilda said. "But I suppose that is a requirement for his occupation. Some would likely find me annoying in the same way—because we both ask questions and persist with our curiosity."

"You are far more polite," Hadrian noted.

Tilda scanned the interior and saw Mallory as well as Mrs. Frost and several other people standing together. Tilda positioned herself so that Hadrian stood between her and them. Though perhaps it didn't really matter. Her presence here didn't reveal that she was a private investigator. Perhaps Hadrian was the investigator.

"There's Teague," Hadrian said.

The inspector stood near the head of a long table, upon which lay a body draped with a cloth. It would be the deceased, Cyril Ward.

Teague was not alone. He stood with the coroner who'd overseen the last inquest they'd attended, Julius Graythorpe.

"Let us speak with them a moment," Tilda murmured.

They moved toward the inspector and coroner, who both made eye contact. "I am not surprised to see you here," Teague said with a faint smile directed at Tilda.

"Why is that?" Graythorpe asked. He narrowed his blue eyes at Hadrian. "Are you involved with this murder too?"

"Not at all," Hadrian said. "I wasn't involved with Chambers' murder either." He referred to the last inquest, which was to determine whether Louis Chambers had been murdered.

"You knew the deceased and were a suspect," Graythorpe said. "That seems fairly involved." He turned his attention to Tilda. "Are you investigating this matter, Miss Wren?"

"Not specifically, no," she replied, glancing in the direction of the mediums, who were thankfully blocked from view by Hadrian. "I am making inquiries about another medium. She was acquainted with Mr. Ward, so I wanted to attend today."

The coroner inclined his head. "You will want to sit as we will be starting soon. I've decided to allow the press inside as this case will likely be of great interest to the public. It's rather terrible, I must say." His expression had darkened.

There were several chairs set into two rows near them. A few constables were seated in the front row, but the back was empty.

"If we sit there, the constables in the front may prevent the mediums from seeing you," Hadrian said.

"Splendid idea." Tilda moved quickly to sit behind one of the constables.

The jurors were seated in chairs set into two rows along the opposite side, whilst those who'd been called to testify, spectators, and the press were either seated or standing at the foot of the table. Lysander Mallory sat in the first row, and Mrs. Frost was next to him. Mallory cocked his head toward the man on his other side and spoke to him.

"Do you recognize anyone?" Tilda whispered to Hadrian.

"The man seated, with whom Mallory is speaking, was in my vision."

"Was he the one who levitated?"

"No, he was watching, as were two of the women in the back row. They are seated behind Mallory and the other man." Hadrian turned his head toward Tilda. "Hopefully, we'll learn who they are through the course of the inquest."

"Provided they are called to testify by Mr. Graythorpe." Tilda frowned. "If not, perhaps we should speak with Mr. Mallory and Mrs. Frost afterward and obtain introductions to the others."

"You would expose yourself after all the trouble I've gone to hide you?"

She heard the sarcasm in his tone and rolled her eyes with a smile. "You've convinced me that I can come up with a believable ruse for my presence."

The door opened, and Clement entered, along with a few other apparent reporters. They stood at the back of the room, their pencils poised above their notebooks. Graythorpe called the inquest to order and stated the matter plainly. The jury was to determine Cyril Ward's cause of death.

Graythorpe began by stating when and how Ward had been found. He paused and looked over everyone assembled. "We will expose the body now. Please avert your attention if that will distress you."

The coroner and a constable removed the covering to expose Ward's nude body. A cloth was draped over his groin. The man's neck was damaged and discolored.

"You may think the man died of hanging, however, he was dead before he was strung up from the staircase, which was done in such a manner as to suggest he was levitating. His death was caused by poisoning from prussic acid."

Tilda sucked in a breath. Her curiosity leapt.

Leaning close to Tilda, Hadrian said, "That's the man in my

vision. The one who levitated." Though he whispered, his tone was rife with excitement.

The coroner said it appeared as if someone had poisoned Ward, then positioned him on the stairs as if he'd hung himself. "I would say that whomever moved the body and strung it up had to have been very strong. Or multiple people worked together." He glanced toward the jurors. "I shall leave it up to these gentlemen to decide what happened. First, however, we shall hear from several witnesses, starting with Detective Inspector Teague."

Teague answered the coroner's questions regarding what he'd seen when he'd arrived at Ward's house, including how the rope had been painted and that the arrangement of the victim made it look as though he was levitating. The journalists' pencils moved quickly across their notebooks.

Next, the coroner spoke to Ward's manservant, who acted as a butler, and to the housekeeper, who was also his cook. Interestingly, neither of them lived at Ward's home. They left his house after dinner each night, and Ward had been alive when they'd departed the night before his death. When the manservant—a man in his late twenties called Nicholls—had returned in the morning, he'd found Ward hanging from the staircase.

The housekeeper had arrived shortly thereafter and fainted. Mrs. Radley was probably in her early thirties and appeared pale. She kept her back to Ward's body as she answered the coroner's questions—haltingly. As soon as he finished with her, she left the pub.

Next, Graythorpe addressed Lysander Mallory, who stood to respond. "Mr. Mallory, you are the head of the London Spiritualism Society of which Mr. Ward was a member?"

Mallory removed his hat and held it in his hand. He appeared earnest, his expression smooth and open. "I am. Cyril was one of our founding members and a skilled medium." He pressed his rather full lips into a tight line.

The coroner fixed him with an expectant stare. "Have you any idea who might benefit from his death?"

"I do not. Cyril was well liked." Mallory frowned sadly. "This is a great loss."

"Are you aware that Her Grace, the Duchess of Chester, had recently bestowed an allowance upon Mr. Ward and that she had added him to her will?"

Tilda leaned forward, her curiosity once again strenuously piqued.

Murmurs and whispers erupted about the room, prompting the coroner to lift his hand. "Silence, please. I must hear Mr. Mallory's response."

Mallory nodded. "Yes. Her Grace is a great patron of the society and considered Cyril her personal medium and confidante. She is devastated by his death," he added softly.

Graythorpe's bushy brows rose briefly. "You've spoken with Her Grace since Mr. Ward died?"

"I have. I'd hoped to be the one to break the news to her, however, Detective Inspector Teague arrived first." Mallory sent a cool look toward Teague, whose expression remained nonresponsive. The medium's eyes, however, seemed to glitter with … something.

The coroner concluded his questioning of Mallory, then turned his attention to the jury. It was a surprisingly short inquest, with the coroner now advising the jurors to render a decision regarding the cause of death. After a brief conversation in hushed tones, the gentlemen of the jury determined that Ward had been murdered.

Graythorpe thanked them, then addressed Teague. "Detective Inspector, I hope you will find the perpetrator and ensure justice is served."

Teague promised he would, and the inquest concluded.

Turning to Hadrian, Tilda inclined her head toward the detective inspector. "Let us speak with Teague."

Hadrian gestured for her to precede him. "After you."

Teague watched them approach and moved toward the corner, perhaps so they could converse more privately. "Do you have information to share?" He looked at both of them, but his gaze settled on Tilda.

"No, but I am offering my assistance, though I know you can't accept it. At least not officially."

"I will always welcome your unofficial input." He gave her an apologetic look, his chin dipping.

Unofficial meant unpaid, and Tilda could not afford to work without compensation, particularly not when she had an active case on which she ought to be focusing. Except this murder was loosely associated with her existing investigation, which made it doubly hard to ignore.

"I can see it pains you to not be involved," Teague said with humor.

Tilda smiled. "Quite. How did you determine the Duchess of Chester's involvement?"

"We found papers in Ward's desk," Teague replied. He looked at Hadrian. "Do you know Her Grace?"

Hadrian's brow arched. "You assume every member of the nobility is acquainted?"

Teague shrugged. "I thought I'd ask."

"I met her when her granddaughter was on the Marriage Mart, back when I was considering matrimony."

"Was that when you become betrothed to Beryl Chambers?" Teague referred to Tilda's former client.

"Yes. I do know that the duchess is somewhat eccentric," Hadrian said. "Her son died perhaps twenty years ago, and she was in deep mourning for nigh on a decade, if memory serves. It doesn't surprise me that she would seek to contact him through a medium."

Teague nodded. "Precisely. Her Grace told me about her son when I went to inform her of Ward's death and to ask about their connection. She said Ward had helped her speak to her late son, and she was most grateful—to the point of treating him like a family member."

"As a replacement for her son perhaps?" Tilda asked.

"I did have that impression," Teague confirmed. His auburn brows pitched low as he regarded them with a dubious glint in his eye. "Do you believe these mediums actually communicate with the dead?"

Hadrian did not hesitate in responding. "No."

Swinging his head toward Tilda, Teague asked, "You?"

"I am not convinced, but neither have I entirely discounted the notion that there is something happening when these mediums conduct their séances. In fact, I am currently investigating the authenticity of those in the London Spiritualism Society."

Teague's gaze flashed with interest. "Are you? I'd be interested in what you learn. If you don't mind sharing." They'd shared information with one another on past investigations, and Tilda saw no reason to keep anything from him. He'd been particularly helpful in her first investigation with Hadrian. In fact, Teague had aided them in catching the killer.

"I don't," Tilda said. "And if you find yourself in need of someone you *can* compensate, I hope you'll consider me."

"You know I would. You've a sharp mind, Miss Wren. Pity I can't hire you. The Metropolitan Police could use your talent." He gave her a wry smile, then turned and departed the pub.

"I know you're disappointed that you can't help," Hadrian said.

"I am not surprised, however. It's moot anyway. I need to focus on the investigation before me, since I do have a paying client." Tilda saw that Mallory and the gentleman he'd been sitting with had moved toward the door. "I would like to speak with Mr. Mallory. I shall tell him we felt compelled to come today since we were at the society when the news of Ward's death arrived."

"Brilliant," Hadrian said.

Tilda led the way, arriving at the door at the same time Mallory and his companion did. "Good afternoon, Mr. Mallory."

The medium had just set his hat atop his blond waves. "Good afternoon, Miss Wren. What a surprise to see you here." His gaze moved to Hadrian. "And you as well, your lordship."

Tilda gave him a sheepish look. "We were interested in learning what happened since we were with you when you learned of Mr. Ward's death. Please allow us to convey our most sincere condolences."

"If there is anything we can do to help, please let us know," Hadrian added, his gaze flicking to the other man, which prompted Mallory to introduce him.

"This is Victor Hawkins," Mallory said. "He's another medium in the society and was a friend to Cyril." He glanced at Hawkins. "This is Lord Ravenhurst and Miss Wren. They visited the society yesterday and were there when I learned of Cyril's death."

"I'm pleased to make your acquaintance," Tilda said. "I'm only sorry it's under these circumstances. A friend of my grandmother's recently attended one of your séances—Mrs. Richardson."

Hawkins was somewhat short of stature. His dark hair was slicked back from his high forehead and his light blue eyes were perfect for a medium. They were at once inquisitive and mesmerizing. "Mrs. Richardson was lovely," he said with a smile. "Are you hoping to attend a séance?"

"We were guests at Mrs. Frost's last night," Tilda replied.

"I'm sure you had a wonderful evening," Hawkins said.

"We did," Tilda assured him. "I can see why people keep returning. Is that what happened with the Duchess of Chester?" Tilda knew she was taking a chance by mentioning the duchess but decided it was worth the risk to learn more. "She enjoyed Mr. Ward's séances so much that he became her personal medium?"

"That is precisely what happened," Hawkins said sadly. "They were quite close. I plan to call on her shortly to offer my condolences."

"How ghastly that poor Mr. Ward was arranged to look as though he were levitating. Why would someone do that?" Tilda hoped Mallory or Hawkins would offer an opinion.

"I can't imagine," Mallory said almost angrily. "Only someone quite depraved would even think to do that."

"Perhaps someone didn't like levitation?" Hadrian asked. "Was Ward known for that?"

"He was, actually," Hawkins replied. He blinked twice. "Why would someone take issue with that and kill him? It doesn't make sense to me. I hope the police will discover the truth."

Mallory's brows dipped down. He appeared tense. "You must excuse us. We're having a small gathering at the society, and we need to be on our way." He turned toward the door, and Hawkins followed him after inclining his head toward Tilda and Hadrian.

Tilda glanced at Hadrian before quickly trailing them from the pub. Outside, the sun had emerged from the clouds. Tilda watched as Mallory and Hawkins caught up to the two women who'd been seated behind them. The quartet climbed into a coach and departed.

"They're all leaving together," Hadrian noted. "I presume the women are also mediums, since they were in my vision."

"I think it's safe to assume they are at least members of the society, since you saw them there and they are now returning to the headquarters for a gathering." Tilda reminded herself that the murder investigation was not what she needed to focus on. Except that investigating the society meant looking into the murder of one of their premier mediums.

Hadrian walked beside her as they approached the corner where Leach was waiting with the coach. "You have a determined look on your face."

"I was just thinking about my investigation into Mrs. Frost

and how the murder of Cyril Ward, another medium in the same society as Mrs. Frost, may be connected. Hawkins wondered who would take issue with Ward's levitation. Who indeed? Perhaps someone discovered their fraud—with levitation at least—and killed Ward." Tilda grimaced. "Though that kind of murder took planning and execution. It would not have been done in a burst of anger."

"Perhaps the killer is not entirely rational," Hadrian said. "If they felt they'd been cheated and that Ward was cheating others, perhaps they wanted to put a stop to it in a sensational way, so as to draw attention to the society as a whole."

"That is certainly possible." Tilda slowed as they were nearly to the coach, and she didn't want Leach to overhear what she said next. "You saw in your vision that the society is aware of and supports the levitation fraud. The killer could know that too."

"How do we go about finding former clients who may be angry about being cheated?" Hadrian asked.

Tilda flashed him a smile as she continued toward the coach. "We ask a great deal of questions."

Leach opened the door for her, and Tilda settled herself on the seat as Hadrian sat across from her. Perhaps this would be their seating arrangement going forward. That would be all right, so long as their friendship was intact. Tilda believed it was. Things certainly felt as they had during their prior investigations.

"So we are, in a way, investigating the murder," Hadrian said.

"As it pertains to the investigation into Mrs. Frost, yes."

Hadrian crossed his arms over his chest. "Good, for I am already rather invested in finding the killer."

"You want to investigate a murder," Tilda noted wryly. "I think I'm rubbing off on you."

"Most certainly," he replied with a fast grin. "And I have no quarrel with that."

There was a heat in his gaze that made Tilda turn her focus to the window. Her belly had done a little flip, indicating it was going to take time for her to develop an immunity to his charm.

If she could.

Except his charm was so much a part of him and why she liked working with him. She had to be careful she didn't succumb to the parts of his charm that encouraged kissing.

Navigating a relationship with a gentleman was proving difficult. Because it was more than that. He was a gentleman she liked and admired. A gentleman who could have perhaps been more than a friend if they were not from completely different classes and if she was at all interested in marriage.

But they *were* from different classes, and Tilda did *not* wish to wed. Tilda would make certain she did nothing to make him think otherwise.

CHAPTER 7

The following day, Hadrian fetched Tilda for their appointment with Mrs. Frost. He once again exchanged pleasantries with Mrs. Wren, as well as the housekeeper and butler. As he escorted Tilda to the coach, he noted how lovely she looked. She wore one of her new gowns—the gray one—and her hair was more intricately styled since she now had a lady's maid. At least temporarily. He decided not to say anything, however. They had settled into their familiar routine of investigating as a team, and he didn't wish to introduce any awkwardness.

"How are things with Clara?" Hadrian asked once they were in the coach and began moving.

"Very well," Tilda replied. "It is still a temporary situation. My need for a maid remains nonexistent."

"And yet she has kept busy, has she not?" he asked mildly.

Tilda gave him a light scowl. "You sound like my grandmother."

Hadrian hid a smile. "She wants Clara to stay on permanently?"

"Yes, but Grandmama does not understand our financial situation. Clara is hoping to find employment as a lady's maid, but her experience is rather limited. It may be that she must take a position as a maid."

"I'm still happy to provide a reference for her," Hadrian offered.

"Whilst that is helpful, not even the recommendation of an earl can overcome a lack of extensive experience, particularly when her only experience was working for the wife of a murdered gentleman."

Hadrian grimaced. "I can't imagine that helps her plight."

"I hope she will find something soon." Tilda set her reticule on her lap. "Let us discuss our visit with Mrs. Frost. Do you have a plan for investigating her séance table?"

"Not entirely. I hope to find a moment to slip away."

"And if we meet in the drawing room where the table is located?" Tilda asked.

"I'll walk near the table and drop something that I must search for." Hadrian was pleased to come up with a solution so quickly. "I'm confident we'll find a way—you taught me that."

Tilda felt a surge of pride. She hadn't intended to train him as an investigator nor expected that he'd take to it so eagerly and successfully.

When they arrived in Rathbone Place, Hadrian helped Tilda from the coach and escorted her to the door. It was ajar.

"How peculiar," Hadrian said, glancing at Tilda. He pushed the door open. "Good afternoon?" The entrance hall was empty.

"Is someone sobbing?" Tilda asked.

Hadrian listened, and he too heard someone crying. "I think so."

Tilda moved past him into the house. Hadrian followed, his senses on edge.

"I think the crying is coming from the back of the house." Tilda walked into the staircase hall and froze. "Hadrian!"

He rushed forward, moving to her side. Dread pooled in his belly as a chill swept through him.

Hanging from the staircase above them was Mrs. Frost.

"Oh no," Tilda breathed beside him. She put her hand to her mouth as she stared up at the body.

Hadrian swallowed, his heart pounding. "Let's find who's crying."

"Yes." Tilda shook herself and moved quickly toward the stairs.

They ascended to the first floor, where a maid was sitting against the wall, her knees drawn to her chest. She lifted her head and looked toward Hadrian and Tilda. Her eyes rounded with fear.

"Don't be afraid," Hadrian said kindly. "I'm Lord Ravenhurst. We had an appointment with Mrs. Frost. I'm so sorry for what's happened."

"We only arrived about an hour ago," the maid said with a sniff. "It was our morning off."

Tilda moved closer to her, but Hadrian remained where he was. "Who is 'we'?" Tilda asked.

"My brother and me." The maid took a stuttering breath. "He went to fetch the police, but he's been gone an awfully long time. I didn't want to stay here by myself, but he said I should—to guard Mrs. Frost." She flicked a glance toward the hanging body and shivered.

"You say you just arrived, and it was your morning off," Tilda said. "Where did you go?"

"We don't reside here," the maid said, sniffing. "We come to work in the morning and go home at night."

Hadrian looked toward Tilda, and she gave him a subtle nod. This was the same arrangement as Cyril Ward's servants.

"Where do you lodge?" Tilda asked the maid.

Before she could respond, the sound of masculine voices carried up the stairs. The maid's gaze darted in that direction, and she rose. Tilda offered her assistance, gently clasping the maid's arm.

Hadrian moved toward the railing and looked down. There were two men accompanied by several constables. Hadrian recognized one of them as Mrs. Frost's butler from the night of the séance. His name was Henry, if Hadrian recalled correctly. Presumably, he was the maid's brother. The men stopped and tilted their heads upward.

"Who's there?" asked the other man who wasn't in uniform.

"Lord Ravenhurst," Hadrian called down. "I had an appointment with Mrs. Frost. Her maid is most distressed."

"Ellen." Henry's expression was lined with great agitation as he hurried up the stairs.

Hadrian quickly removed his glove and touched the railing. The vision didn't immediately come, but when it did, a sharp pain exploded behind his eyes. The memory he saw was distinct and terrifying—the person whose memory he was experiencing carefully lifted Mrs. Frost's body over the railing and lowered her. Her neck was already encircled with rope and her face was deathly pale, her eyes closed.

"You must be Ellen's brother." Tilda's voice interrupted Hadrian's vision, and the memory slipped away.

Hadrian touched his forehead briefly before drawing his glove back on. He turned away from the railing.

The butler walked to his sister and embraced her. Tilda watched with a sad expression, then stepped around them to join Hadrian. Her gaze met his, then flicked to his brow. The small lines around her mouth told him she was concerned. She'd likely noted he'd touched his head and assumed he'd had a vision. She was particularly attuned to his reactions.

The police came up the stairs, led by the man who was not in uniform. Hadrian presumed he was an inspector.

The man, who wore a most impressive mustache, stopped in

front of Hadrian. His amber eyes surveyed his surroundings before he settled his gaze on Hadrian. "Ravenhurst?"

"Yes, and my associate, Miss Wren." He gestured to Tilda.

"I am Inspector Farrar from E Division. You had an appointment with the woman hanging from the staircase?"

"We did," Hadrian replied. "She is—was—a medium and had conducted a séance we attended here this past Monday evening."

Inspector Farrar's light brown brows rose. "Indeed? I imagine the detective inspector will want to speak with you when he arrives. I sent someone to Scotland Yard to fetch him."

"Can't you take her down?" Henry asked. "Mrs. Frost, I mean."

"I'm sorry, Mr. Henry, but we cannot do that until the detective inspector arrives," Inspector Farrar replied.

Tilda looked at the man and his sister with sympathy. "Perhaps we should go to the kitchen and have some tea."

Ellen wiped a handkerchief across her nose. "There's a pot steeping already. I did that as soon as I arrived. Before I came upstairs to see Mrs. Frost. I think I would prefer to go to the kitchen." She looked at her brother. "Jacob, will you come with me?"

Jacob Henry sent an uncertain glance toward the inspector. "May we go to the kitchen?"

"Of course," Farrar said with a nod. "I'll have one of the constables escort you if that would be a comfort."

Ellen's features lost a small bit of tension. "Thank you."

Farrar motioned for one of the uniformed men to accompany the siblings downstairs. They moved toward the back of the house, presumably to the servants' stairs.

Tilda walked to the railing and looked down at Mrs. Frost. Hadrian joined Tilda, his attention on Tilda, not the dead medium. Tilda's focus was now on the railing.

"See how the rope has been painted to match the wood of the staircase?" she noted. "And it's been twisted around the baluster. This matches what Teague described about Ward's death. It's clear to me that this was made to look as though she was levitating."

"Bloody chilling to think someone went to that much effort," Farrar said with a twitch of his shoulder as he moved toward the railing.

A figure appeared in the hall below. The man removed his hat and tilted his head up. It was Teague, and he was accompanied by two constables.

"Ravenhurst and Miss Wren?" Teague called up.

"We had an appointment with the victim," Tilda said. "I'd say she was likely killed by the same person who murdered Mr. Ward. Unless someone is trying to copy his murder."

"If so, they've done a damn good job." Teague's mouth pressed into a grim line. "Coming up." He turned and said something to the constables, which Hadrian couldn't hear. A moment later, one of them left the hall to return the way they'd come, and Teague strode toward the staircase.

The detective inspector eyed Tilda as he approached them. "For someone who is not investigating the murder of Cyril Ward, you are quite involved in this investigation."

Tilda's mouth quirked, but the expression was not quite a smile. "As I was investigating Mrs. Frost and she has been murdered, I must consider whether my investigation now includes her death."

"The press is going to make a meal of this," Teague said darkly. "In fact, one of their number has been loitering about Scotland Yard since the inquest. I think he may have followed me here. I've sent one of my constables outside to ensure he doesn't get in."

"I don't suppose he's wearing rather garish pants?" Tilda asked.

Teague's brows arched. "How did you know?"

Tilda exhaled. "He seems the most persistent of the lot. His name is Ezra Clement. He works for the *Daily News*."

"I can send one of my constables out," Farrar offered. "You likely need yours to conduct your investigation."

Teague turned toward the inspector. "That would be most helpful. You're Farrar?"

The inspector inclined his head. "I am." He looked toward one of the constables and directed him to relieve Teague's constable outside. Returning his attention to Teague, Farrar said, "There's a manservant and a housekeeper—Jacob and Ellen Henry, they are siblings—in the kitchen with another of my constables. You will want to speak with them."

"I will, thank you." Teague pivoted toward his remaining constable, who'd followed him up the stairs. "Go down to the kitchen and start their interviews. I want to know everything that happened today. And last night."

Nodding, the constable turned on his heel and went back down the main staircase. Hadrian assumed the man would find where he needed to go.

Teague moved closer to the railing, and Tilda edged out of his way so he could look directly down at Mrs. Frost.

"Looks damn near the same as Ward," Teague said as he bent over the railing. "I'd say it's the same person who committed both murders." He straightened. "I'll need Graythorpe to see if prussic acid has been used again."

"Shouldn't you be able to tell, given how that poison affects people?" Farrar asked.

"The killer cleaned the last victim up well enough that Graythorpe didn't know about the prussic acid until he looked inside." Teague turned toward Tilda. "We haven't yet determined a motive for Ward's death. Now we must consider why the killer also wanted Mrs. Frost dead."

Hadrian thought of what he and Tilda had discussed following the inquest, that someone was angry about being cheated by Ward. Now that two mediums from the society were dead, perhaps the killer blamed the society rather than the individuals. He wondered if Tilda would mention that to Teague and if the detective inspector would follow her lead.

"I'm sure you've looked into Ward's finances," Tilda said. "Does anyone benefit from his death?"

"Not that we can find so far. His house is leased by Her Grace, the Duchess of Chester. He'd just moved in at the beginning of March. And the duchess started giving him a quarterly allowance at the beginning of the year. From what we can discern, Ward directed nearly all of it to the spiritualism society."

"Does he have any family?" Tilda asked.

"A sister who lives in Margate, but they weren't close. We haven't found anyone else. His closest relationships were with the other members of the society." Teague looked at Tilda expectantly. "What do you know of Mrs. Frost?"

"Not much," Tilda said.

Teague appeared befuddled. "I thought you were investigating her."

"Only for a few days and only as it pertains to her work as a medium," Tilda explained. She flicked a glance at Hadrian. "To determine if she was authentic in her ability to speak with the dead."

"Didn't you attend a séance she conducted the other night?" Teague asked.

"We did." Hadrian glanced at Tilda. He didn't want to say too much. For whatever reason, he didn't want to share that his mother had wanted to speak with his dead brother. "I found it all very suspect. The table pitched about, and there were raps in response to questions the medium posed." He wished he could tell Teague about the fake levitating.

Teague's brows drew together. "Raps?"

"The medium asked questions that could be answered with yes, no, or I don't know," Tilda explained. "One rap for no, two for I don't know, and three for yes."

"And who does this rapping?" Teague asked. "Supposedly."

"The spirits." Hadrian kept from rolling his eyes. "I wanted to take a closer look at the table in the drawing room where the séance was held the other night. I suspect it contains some sort of mechanism that is controlled by the medium or someone else." He thought of the butler, Henry, who'd been present at the séance and wondered if he might play a role beyond greeting guests and serving wine.

Teague glanced toward his constable before lowering his voice. "I don't have a problem with you looking at the table now, but I shouldn't let you poke around too much. Go investigate the table and be on your way."

Tilda's expression tightened. "I was hoping to speak with the Henry siblings. Do you mind if we go downstairs for a few minutes to conduct a brief interview?"

"I suppose not, since you've been hired to investigate Mrs. Frost. But don't loiter. My constables won't mention your presence, but I don't know Farrar or his men." He gave her an apologetic look.

"Thank you, Detective Inspector." Tilda's gaze dipped to the floor. She removed her glove and bent to pick something up. Rising, she placed a pearl earring on the gloved palm of her other hand. Her gaze darted to Teague. "It probably belongs to Mrs. Frost, but you'll want to make certain."

The detective inspector took the piece of jewelry. "I will."

Tilda moved to where Mrs. Frost was hanging and crouched down for a brief moment. "She is not wearing earrings, so if she lost this one, it wasn't today. Unless she lost the other one too, which seems unlikely. I should note that I don't recall her wearing earrings the night of the séance either."

"We'll determine who it belonged to," Teague said. "If you'll excuse me now."

"Of course." Tilda pulled her glove back on and moved away from the railing.

Hadrian joined her. "To the drawing room?"

She nodded, and they moved into the room where the séance had been held the other evening. It looked quite different in the daylight. The curtains were open, and light spilled across the round table in the center of the room.

Tilda paused and touched his elbow, prompting him to turn. "What did you see when you touched the railing? And are you well?"

The pain in his head had diminished, but a dull ache persisted. "I'm fine. I saw the killer's memory. He—or she, I suppose—was lowering Mrs. Frost over the railing. The rope was already around her neck."

"What did you see of the killer's hands?"

Hadrian had learned to gather as many details as he could when he had a vision, but sometimes they didn't last long enough for him to be as thorough as he would like. "I think he—or she—was wearing gloves, but I can't be certain. The vision didn't linger." He concentrated, trying to recall what he'd seen, but he couldn't say more.

Removing his glove again, Hadrian started toward the table.

"Careful," Tilda said. "You don't want to overdo it."

Hadrian appreciated her concern. "I will make this my last attempt whilst we're here."

Going to the table, he dragged his fingertips across the top. Nothing came to him, so he put more of his hand on the wood. A vision flitted through his mind, like the wings of a bird taking flight. He pressed his hand more firmly, and a room came into view. Not a room but a workspace—a cabinetry shop. The memory was of a man building this table.

He took in the space. High ceilings, a few dusty windows. The scent of cut wood.

Hadrian froze. He'd never *smelled* anything in a vision before.

Inhaling, he let the aroma settle into him. He closed his eyes, and the vision disappeared. He'd always had to keep his eyes open to "see" the memories.

"Hadrian?"

He blinked his eyes open and turned toward Tilda. "I saw the memory of the man who crafted this table. I was in his workshop." He edged closer to her. "Tilda, I could *smell* it."

"What do you mean?"

"I smelled the cut wood as if I were there. I have never smelled anything in a vision before." He'd always wanted to hear what was being said but had yet to experience that.

"How astonishing." Her lips parted briefly.

For the barest moment, Hadrian was enchanted by her mouth. The memory of their kiss blazed through him. He could not think of that event or of Tilda in such a manner. Annoyed with himself, he pushed the recollection away.

"I want to look under the table." Hadrian knelt and crawled under the table, the fingers of his bare hand pressing into the carpet.

"What do you see?"

"There's a large pedestal in the center, which I suppose is necessary, given the size of the table." Hadrian ran his fingers along the wood of the underside of the tabletop. It was smooth with nothing notable or out of the ordinary. He tried not to expect anything, recalling what Tilda had once told him about investigating—it was better not to anticipate. That way your mind was open to whatever it may encounter. Even if that was nothing at all.

He didn't see another vision, which he supposed he appreciated. His head still ached from before, and he preferred it didn't worsen. "A light would be helpful."

"Let me see if I can find something," Tilda called.

He reached the pedestal, which had four large clawed feet. They were beautifully carved. The carpenter who'd made this table had done a fine job, even on parts that wouldn't be seen. Except by people crawling around.

Light shone under the table, and Hadrian glanced to his right to see Tilda on her knees holding a lantern. "How's this?" she asked.

"Good, thank you." Hadrian turned his head back to the pedestal. There was a word carved into the wood at the top. He ran his fingertip over it, feeling the letters as he read them. "Clifton. That's carved into the pedestal. Must be the carpenter."

"What are you doing?" A man voiced the question that carried to Hadrian beneath the table.

The light disappeared, and Hadrian looked to see that Tilda had risen. He heard her set the lantern on the table.

"I thought I lost a bracelet here the other night. Detective Inspector Teague said I could look for it."

Hadrian smiled. Tilda was so good at providing fabrications without almost no thought.

"Time to go," the man said. "We're conducting a murder investigation."

"Yes, we know," she replied drily.

Hadrian didn't want to cause trouble. And he had learned the name of the carpenter. He'd also seen that there wasn't any obvious method of moving the tabletop. To be sure, he crawled around the pedestal before making his way out from under the table.

Tilda was waiting for him near the doorway where the constable, whose uniform was labeled with E Division, meaning he was one of Farrar's men, stood with a perturbed expression. Hadrian brushed at his knees as he stood and made his way to Tilda's side. He offered the constable a smile. "Thank you for your patience."

They left the drawing room and went back to the staircase. Several constables were working to take Mrs. Frost down. Hadrian felt sorry for the poor woman.

When they reached the first floor, Tilda started toward the back of the house. Hadrian followed, and they quickly located the servants' stairs. They found the kitchen empty but heard voices from a room next to it.

They moved to the adjoining room, which had a small table and four chairs. The constable sat in one, whilst the maid and her brother occupied the others. They all looked at the door as Tilda and Hadrian entered.

"I'm sorry to disturb," Tilda said. "I wonder if we might speak with Ellen and Jacob about Mrs. Frost. We had an appointment with her today."

"Mrs. Frost was looking forward to meeting with you, my lord," Jacob said, his gaze fixing on Hadrian. "She was thrilled to have her ladyship, your mother, as a client."

Hadrian inclined his head. "My mother will be sad to hear of her demise."

Jacob grimaced as he nodded faintly.

Tilda gave the retainers a gentle smile. "Do you mind if I ask you a few questions about Mrs. Frost?"

The siblings exchanged looks, but it was Jacob who responded in the form of a nod.

"How long had you worked for Mrs. Frost?"

"Well, we don't—" Ellen began.

"About six months," Jacob said, interrupting his sister without so much as glancing in her direction.

"That is when Mrs. Frost moved into this house," the constable supplied. "They explained that the property is owned by the London Spiritualism Society. Mrs. Frost lived and conducted séances here. She also hosted teas for ladies who are members of the society."

Tilda inclined her head toward the constable. "Thank you." She looked back to the siblings. "Ellen, you mentioned that you had the morning off today. Was that typical?"

Once again, the constable answered. "They are off every Wednesday morning, and they don't reside here."

"Where do you live?" Tilda asked the retainers. She did not

sound as though she were bothered by the constable's interruptions, but Hadrian found it annoying.

"I was just getting to that," the constable said rather unnecessarily. He looked expectantly at Jacob and Ellen.

"We lodge elsewhere." Jacob glanced toward his sister. "We prefer that."

"What of the other members of the household?" Hadrian asked. He thought of the footmen who'd helped serve dinner the other night. And Ellen presumably had help preparing the meal.

"There aren't any," Jacob replied.

But Ellen had also answered. Her words came at the same time as Jacob's but in a softer tone so that Hadrian didn't catch them entirely.

Tilda turned her focus to Ellen. "What was that?"

"There are footmen and a maid who come to help with the séances." Ellen slid a nervous look toward her brother.

"We'll need to speak with them," the constable said, lifting his pencil to write in his notebook. "What are their names?"

The siblings hesitated, but Jacob finally answered, and the constable wrote them down.

The constable fixed his gaze on Jacob. "Where can I find them?"

"I'm not certain," he said quickly.

"Come now, Mr. Henry." The constable narrowed one eye at the retainer. "You work with these people. Surely you know where they can be found. It isn't wise to lie to the police."

"You'll have to ask the society," Ellen said, her voice squeaking. Taking a deep breath, she added, "The man in charge there."

Jacob frowned at his sister, and it seemed to Hadrian that the butler was troubled by something. And the maid was very upset. Perhaps it was that they'd just found their employer murdered in a ghastly fashion.

"Did Mrs. Frost ever speak to you about the séances or her work as a medium?" Tilda asked.

Jacob looked down as he shook his head. "No." The man seemed agitated, and again Hadrian wondered if it was simply due to the murder.

Ellen met Tilda's gaze, her soft brown eyes losing a bit of their timidity. "She told me yesterday that she was considering leaving the society. She was upset about her friend, Mr. Ward, who'd died."

"Was she afraid?" Hadrian asked.

"I think so." Ellen shifted her eyes away from them. "She said she wasn't entirely happy, that London was perhaps too fast for her."

Tilda's eyes narrowed slightly. "She wasn't from here?"

"She was from somewhere west," Ellen replied. "She said she came to London after her husband died."

"Was there anyone with whom Mrs. Frost was particularly close?" Tilda asked. "Perhaps a friend or even a gentleman?"

Jacob's brow furrowed as he regarded Tilda. "Why are you asking us questions about Mrs. Frost after she has died?"

"These are questions I am going to ask," the constable said. "So you may as well answer them."

"There was no one in particular," Jacob replied. "All the mediums in the society are close. And Mrs. Frost had regular clients who attended her séances and teas."

The constable scrutinized them. "I need their names. I'll repeat what I told you at the start of this interview—whatever you say will help us find the villain who did this to Mrs. Frost."

"There were a few ladies who came to tea nearly every week the past couple of months," Ellen said. "Mrs. Hemmings, Mrs. York, and Lady Gillivray."

The constable wrote the names down. Hadrian wondered why Tilda wasn't doing the same, but he suspected she was committing them to memory and would record them later.

"If you think of anyone else, I expect you'll let us know," the constable said with a tap of his pen against the paper of his notebook.

Ellen nodded, but Jacob didn't react. His features were locked in consternation.

Hadrian sensed the siblings' worry and perhaps fear. "What will you do now that your employer has died?"

Jacob blinked. "We'll manage." He took his sister's hand.

"If you require assistance, please call at Ravenhurst House," Hadrian said.

Jacob sent Hadrian a look of surprise. "That is most kind of you, my lord."

"I have one more question," Tilda said. "Ellen, did Mrs. Frost wear pearl earrings? I found one upstairs near … where she was."

Ellen's brows drew together. "No, she did not wear earrings."

"Thank you," Tilda said warmly. "Please accept my condolences." She pivoted to leave.

Without thinking, Hadrian brushed his hand against her lower back to escort her from the room. He immediately froze. After the kiss disaster, he'd resolved not to do things like this, but he'd forgotten. Recovering himself, he pulled his hand away.

Tilda snapped her gaze to his for a brief moment before inclining her head at the constable. Then she swept from the room, and Hadrian followed. They didn't speak until they started up the stairs to the ground floor. Thankfully, she said nothing about his lapse of judgment.

"It is interesting that Mrs. Frost spoke of leaving the society," Tilda said. "And of her discontent in London."

"It seems we should visit the society and make inquiries there amongst its members," Hadrian suggested. "I imagine you will also want to speak with the ladies who regularly came to tea with Mrs. Frost."

"We must speak to as many people as possible to determine who, if anyone, may have held a grudge against the society." Tilda paused at the top of the stairs and looked over at him. "We must also inquire with Mr. Mallory about the other retainers who help with the séances. However, first, I think I should like to call on Mr. Hawkins, since he is the sole remaining premier medium."

"Would you care to do so now?" Hadrian asked.

"I would indeed, if you are amenable," Tilda replied eagerly as they left the servants' stairs and made their way toward the entrance hall. "You don't have pressing matters in the Lords?"

"Not today." Though even if he had, Hadrian would almost always choose investigating with Tilda over his other duties—when he could.

As they passed through the staircase hall, they glanced up. Hadrian thought he glimpsed the coroner, Graythorpe.

"I'd like to attend the inquest," Tilda said, indicating she'd perhaps seen him too.

"It seems you are investigating these murders," Hadrian observed as they stepped outside. He swung his head toward her.

She sent him a smile bright with anticipation. "*We* are investigating them."

CHAPTER 8

Once they were on their way to Victor Hawkins's house in Clerkenwell, Tilda pulled her notebook from her reticule and made notes about what they'd just learned, including the names of the ladies who regularly had tea with Mrs. Frost.

"I wondered why you weren't taking notes during the interview," Hadrian said.

She glanced toward him and paused in writing. "Since the constable was recording their answers, I didn't want to do the same. I suppose I hoped I would appear more sympathetic, and that they might be more open to sharing with me."

"Clever. And probably helpful."

Tilda finished making notes as she thought back over their conversation with the Henry siblings. She tucked her notebook and pencil back into her reticule. "Did you find Jacob's demeanor nervous?"

"At times."

"It could just be that he is sensitive to his sister's obvious distress, and the fact that their employer was murdered," Tilda noted. "However, I do wonder if there is more that they could have told us and chose not to. They—Jacob in particular—

seemed hesitant to disclose the names of the ladies who attended tea. And they did not offer the location of their lodging."

"Does that matter?" Hadrian asked.

"It is if we want to find them to ask more questions." Tilda would trust that Teague would be able to locate them. "I found it odd that Ellen and Jacob did not live in her house, just as Mr. Ward's retainers did not."

"I did as well," Hadrian said.

"I wonder if Mr. Hawkins will also have retainers who do not live with him," Tilda mused.

Hadrian scooted to the side of his seat and stretched his legs out. The tips of his boots almost met her seat. "Hawkins will likely not have heard about Mrs. Frost's death."

Though Hadrian hadn't moved closer to her, the proximity of even his feet made her temperature rise. It had already spiked earlier when he'd touched her back. It had been the barest graze of his fingertips, but she'd still reacted. Thankfully, she'd hidden that reaction. He didn't need to know how he affected her, not when she was working to ensure nothing romantic happened between them.

"You're right. I hate to be the bearer of bad news, but we'll need to inform him. Let me consider how to do that."

Hadrian gave her a brief smile. "I trust you will handle it adeptly."

They arrived on Woodbridge Street a short while later. The neighborhood wasn't at all grand, but it was friendly enough, and it didn't take them long to find Hawkins's house, a double-fronted terrace of brick.

They went to the door where Hadrian rapped on the wood. A few moments later, an older woman answered. Short with deep-set blue eyes and wearing a white cap that seemed a bit large for her head, she surveyed Hadrian in particular. Nostrils flaring, she looked at them expectantly.

"I am Lord Ravenhurst," Hadrian said pleasantly. "This is Miss Wren. We'd like to speak with Mr. Hawkins if he is available."

"Come in, I suppose." The woman opened the door wider and admitted them into the entrance hall. "You can wait in the parlor there." She gestured to the left.

The woman started to turn, but Tilda stopped her. "Are you the housekeeper?"

"Yes. I'm Mrs. Wilson."

Tilda summoned an enthusiastic smile. "It must be exciting to work for a medium, particularly during the séances."

The housekeeper's eyes narrowed slightly. "I wouldn't call it exciting. It's a household, just like any other. I only work during the mornings and afternoons. I leave after I prepare dinner for Mr. Hawkins, which suits me fine as I only live down Sekforde Street with my son and his family."

"You aren't interested in spiritualism?" Tilda asked, pleased the woman had been so forthcoming.

Mrs. Wilson pursed her lips. "It's not my place to say." Her tone was crisp and, to Tilda, indicated her disdain. The housekeeper turned and disappeared into the bowels of the house.

"That was informative," Hadrian said.

"Quite. I was hoping to learn something, and she exceeded my expectations. As with the other mediums' households, she does not live here."

"However, unlike with the others, she does not work at the séances," Hadrian noted. "We know the Henry siblings were working during the séance we attended."

Tilda moved into the parlor, where an arched window faced the street. A large round table that looked almost exactly like the one at Mrs. Frost's dominated the room.

"Is this table identical to Mrs. Frost's?" Hadrian asked, echoing Tilda's thoughts.

"It appears to be. Should you investigate underneath to see if it looks the same there too?"

Hadrian crouched down. "The pedestal appears the same. I see the clawed feet." He removed his glove.

"Careful," Tilda warned. "Perhaps you shouldn't touch anything else today."

"I need to. We're here. Besides, my headache is almost gone."

"But you'll get another," Tilda said. "I hate that this useful skill causes you pain."

"I can manage." He touched the table.

Tilda watched anxiously as he fell silent, his gaze fixed somewhere beneath the table. A moment later, he blinked.

"I saw a séance. Whoever's memory I saw was seated at the table."

"Do you have any clue whose memory it was?" Tilda asked.

"I looked down to see the hands, and they definitely belonged to a man. There was an onyx ring on the left hand, which held a woman's hand. But his right hand clasped another man— Montrose."

The man who'd sat on Mrs. Frost's right the other night. "I thought the séances worked best when they sat everyone by sex —man, woman, man woman, and so on. You're sure the memory was that of a man?"

Hadrian nodded. "Completely."

Hawkins appeared in the doorway to the entrance hall. Tilda gestured for Hadrian to stand up.

"Lord Ravenhurst and Miss Wren, what a surprise." Hawkins's purple-and-brown striped trousers looked as though they'd been procured from the same shop as Ezra Clement's garments. The medium's dark hair was slicked back from his forehead, and his shockingly light-blue eyes fixed them with an eerie curiosity. Looking at the unearthly glimmer in his gaze, Tilda believed he could commune with the dead.

She noted he wore an onyx ring on the little finger of his left hand.

"Did you drop something?" Hawkins asked.

Hadrian had risen. "My handkerchief. I was also admiring your table. It's a beautiful piece. Might I inquire where you obtained it?"

"I don't recall," Hawkins said blithely. "How can I help you?"

Tilda took a step toward the medium. "We've come to speak with you about Mrs. Frost and the London Spiritualism Society. I'm afraid we have distressing news"

Hawkins's eyes shuttered, and his expression took on a guarded state. "What is that?"

"We had an appointment to speak with Mrs. Frost today, but she was, most unfortunately, murdered."

Eyes rounding, Hawkins gasped. He clapped his hand to his mouth. "How can that be?" He shook his head. "Please don't tell me she was killed in the same manner as Ward."

"She was, in fact," Hadrian replied. "Why would you assume so?"

Hawkins looked to Tilda. "You said she was murdered. I instantly thought of Ward. That was only two days ago."

"Of course it makes sense you would think of that." Tilda appreciated that Hadrian had asked for clarification. She sent him a quick glance of gratitude before returning her gaze to Hawkins. "Would you like to sit?"

Nodding, Hawkins walked stiffly to a small seating area near the hearth. He fell into a chair there without waiting for Tilda and Hadrian to take their seats.

Tilda perched on a settee, and Hadrian sat beside her. "I'm so sorry to deliver this terrible news."

Hawkins stared past them, his eyes glazed. "She was a friend of mine, of course."

"You were both members of the London Spiritualism Society," Tilda said.

"Yes. Founding members." He blinked, then focused on them. "My apologies, this is a great shock. Ward's death was awful enough, but to think it happened again—and to a fine woman such as Deborah." His brow formed deep creases. "The police must catch this dastardly killer."

"They are working on doing so," Tilda assured him. "Can you think of anyone who would want to kill Mrs. Frost and Mr. Ward?"

Hawkins opened his mouth, then snapped it closed. He was quiet a moment as his jaw quivered. Looking down at his lap, he brushed at his knee. "Forgive me," he whispered. "This is most terrible." When he lifted his gaze once more, there was moisture in his eyes. "It seems someone is killing mediums. *I* am a medium. This is incredibly distressing."

"Of course it is," Tilda said softly. "Since both Mrs. Frost and Mr. Ward were members of the society, I wondered if someone might have a quarrel with the group."

"Then why wouldn't they kill Lysander?" Hawkins snapped. He seemed almost angry, but Tilda understood his emotions were high. "I don't know anyone who would seek to harm the society or anyone in it."

"Do you know of anyone who was unhappy with how a séance went?" Hadrian asked. "Perhaps they weren't able to speak with their deceased loved one and were upset about that."

"That has never happened in my experience," Hawkins replied fiercely. "It may take a few séances to reach the desired person, but I always find them in the spirit realm."

If the man didn't actually speak to the dead, everything he'd just said was a lie. And if he lied about that, would he lie about someone being upset? Tilda could understand that the medium would not want to share that someone had believed him to be a fraud.

"Forgive me, Mr. Hawkins, but I must ask a question that may annoy you," Tilda said cautiously. "Did you or any of the other mediums ever have a client who accused you or anyone in the society of trickery or fraud?"

Hawkins pressed his lips together and looked away. At length, he said, "I suppose that has happened once or twice, but those people came to the society looking to create a scandal."

Tilda exchanged a look with Hadrian. "If you could recall who those people were, it would be helpful to the investigation of these murders."

"I do not," Hawkins said. "You could ask Lysander. He may remember." He narrowed his eyes at Tilda. "Why are you asking me questions? You sound as if you are investigating these murders? And you were at the inquest yesterday. You don't work for the police."

Tilda decided it was time to reveal herself. Since she was no longer just investigating the society's authenticity in contacting the spirit realm, there was no reason to hide her occupation. "I am a private investigator, and I *am* investigating the murders."

"I have never heard of a woman private investigator." Hawkins sounded dubious.

"Miss Wren is highly skilled," Hadrian said. "She has solved several cases, including murders."

Hawkins looked surprised as he gave Tilda his attention. "I am most eager to help catch whoever killed Deborah and Cyril."

Tilda gave him an appreciative nod. "Perhaps you could tell us about Mrs. Frost. It sounds as though you knew her well. I understand she was relatively new to London."

Hawkins's features relaxed slightly. "Yes. She moved here from Wroughton."

"How did you become acquainted?" Tilda asked.

"Through Lysander. I attended a séance at his house—what became the headquarters of the society—and met him and Deborah that evening. Cyril was also there."

Tilda would record everything in her notebook later. "Was Mrs. Frost already a medium?"

"Yes," Hawkins replied. "After the séance that night, Lysander told me he sensed that I would be able to communicate with the spirit realm. He'd already recruited Cyril to train as a medium, and the three of them convinced me to do the same. We formed the society soon thereafter."

"What did Mallory sense within you?" Hadrian asked.

Hawkins shrugged. "I'm not sure. He has a gift for identifying sensitive people. That is how he found Deborah. And Cyril too. We all trained together, and after working with Lysander a short while, we were able to speak with those on the other side." The medium smiled, but there was a sadness in it. "It has been most illuminating and gratifying. I am grateful that I met Lysander and the others."

"You hold séances here, is that correct?" Tilda asked.

"I do."

"A friend of my grandmother's—Mrs. Richardson—attended one recently," Tilda said. "You communicated with her deceased dog, if you recall."

"I do indeed," Hawkins said with enthusiasm. "Mrs. Richardson is a delightful woman."

"When is your next séance?" Tilda clasped her hands in her lap. "I ask because we attended Mrs. Frost's the other night and had planned to return next Monday. However, that will not be possible."

"I am conducting one Friday. The Duchess of Chester has asked me to try to contact Cyril in the spirit realm."

"If you are in need of another female guest, I should like to attend," Tilda offered.

"I would need another male guest to balance you. We require a certain and equal number of men and women."

"We learned that the other night," Hadrian said. "I would be happy to come as well. We also learned that guests are arranged by gender around the table. Do you ever stray from that rule and seat men and women next to the same sex?"

"On occasion, yes." Hawkins gestured with his hand. "It all depends on the energy that will be assembled. Sometimes modifications must be made."

Tilda was glad Hadrian had asked that question. She pressed on regarding Mrs. Frost. "How would you describe Mrs. Frost as a medium? What was her specialty?"

"Specialty?" Hawkins blinked. "What do you mean?"

"I understand some mediums are skilled at moving objects or levitating," Tilda said. "Did Mrs. Frost have a particular ability?"

"She was exceptionally gifted at communing with the spirit realm." Hawkins frowned sadly. "Her talent will be missed."

Tilda met the medium's gaze. "If you can think of anything that will help the police find the killer, that would be most helpful."

Hawkins's eye twitched. He looked away for a moment and seemed to be thinking.

"Has something occurred to you?" Tilda prodded.

The medium slid his gaze toward them. "There was a medium who used to work with Lysander Mallory, but they fell out. Lysander said it was because the man was jealous of his burgeoning popularity. After Lysander started the society, the man—Roger Grenville was his name—said he would warn people against it."

"Did you meet Grenville?" Hadrian asked, his expression intensely focused on the medium.

Hawkins nodded. "Several times, though I didn't come to know him well. He was older than Lysander, perhaps fifteen years, and supposedly a gifted medium. I never saw him practice. I can only say that he was most disagreeable. He insulted Lysander quite soundly. He left London not long after we founded the society. I suppose he was a founding member who abdicated his place."

"Do you know where he went?" Tilda hoped it wasn't far. She wanted to speak with him.

"Lysander believed he returned to his former home in Swindon." Hawkins cocked his head. "That's near Wroughton where Deborah was from. I hadn't realized that. What a coincidence."

"Indeed." Tilda's mind worked. This disgruntled medium was from near where Mrs. Frost came from. Had he known her?

"We met a gentleman called Montrose at Mrs. Frost's séance," Hadrian said. "Would you happen to know where we could find him?"

Hawkins glanced away, which piqued Tilda's interest. "No."

"Do you know him?" Tilda was curious how he'd answer that, since Hadrian had seen that Hawkins had sat beside the man. They had to know one another.

"He has attended a few séances, but I don't know him well. I'm sorry I can't help you."

Hawkins's demeanor was suspicious, and Tilda wasn't sure she entirely believed him. She summoned a smile to end the interview. "Thank you for speaking with us. Again, if you think of anything else that might help the investigation into your colleagues' murders, I hope you'll notify Scotland Yard. Ask for Detective Inspector Teague."

"I'll do that," Hawkins murmured. "I do appreciate you coming today so that I could hear the news about Deborah. So awful." He shook his head. "I pray the killer is caught soon."

Tilda pulled one of her cards from her reticule and handed it to the medium. "You can also contact me."

Hawkins looked at the card in his hand, then at Tilda. "Your father or someone in your family worked for the police, did they not?"

Tilda's shoulder twitched. "My father." This was the second time a medium had mentioned him. "How did you know that?"

"Mediums tend to be sensitive, and sometimes we just know things." Hawkins smiled benignly. "He'd be proud of you. I will let you know if we need additional people at the séance on Friday."

Tilda stood. "Thank you, Mr. Hawkins."

Hadrian removed his glove as he rose and presented his bare hand to shake that of Hawkins, who also stood. As they clasped hands, Tilda hoped Hadrian was seeing something, even as she also worried that he would suffer for it. That would be several visions in one day, and she did not want them to take a toll on him.

They made their way outside. As they walked to the coach, Tilda said, "I wonder if we ought to call on your mother next to tell her about Mrs. Frost before she can hear about it elsewhere and become distressed."

Hadrian frowned. "I should have thought of that. Thank you. Yes, let us call on her." He informed Leach of their destination before they settled into the coach.

"Did you see anything when you shook Hawkins's hand?" Tilda asked as they started moving.

"He was speaking to Montrose," Hadrian said darkly. "I do not believe for a moment that he didn't know the man well."

"Nor do I." Tilda turned her mind to the dowager countess. "Do you think your mother will want to see another medium from the society?"

"I wondered if that was what you were going to suggest when you asked to attend Hawkins's séance, but then I realized you probably wanted to go to meet the duchess and perhaps find out about her relationship with Ward."

"You know me too well."

Hadrian flashed a brief smile. "As for my mother, I would rather she did not see another medium. However, she believes she has a limited opportunity to speak with Gabriel and will likely want to make sure she doesn't miss her chance."

"Are you going to tell her you have reason to believe the mediums are fake?"

"I think we must. That is the purpose of your investigation, after all. I realize we don't have proof that we can show her, but we know they are cheating."

"About the levitating and probably the table movement," Tilda said. "We cannot prove they don't speak to the dead. I'm still wondering if these mediums share your ability. I gave Hawkins my card, and he asked about my father."

Hadrian stared at her. "You think he saw a memory of yours with your father in a police uniform when he touched the card?"

Tilda shrugged. "I don't know, but I found his comment eerie. And it was, of course, accurate."

"He could just as easily have made an educated guess," Hadrian said. "Which, in his line of work, would be a skill he'd honed, I should think. He surmised you are interested in investigation because of something or someone, and he vaguely suggested your father or someone else. He could have been fishing for the correct answer."

"That is a cynical view." Tilda smiled. "But you may be right. I imagine the mediums do whatever they can to obtain information from people. The more they know about someone, the better they can do their jobs. Perhaps one of the reasons they carefully select their séance guests is so that they can investigate them and have 'surprising' information to share."

Hadrian's brows arched. "That is an interesting theory. Do you think the society employs an investigator? You could offer your services," he suggested with a chuckle.

Tilda pursed her lips at him. "That is not amusing. I would not engage in that sort of investigation. Not for any price."

Hadrian sobered. "I was jesting. Of course you wouldn't."

"Thank you." Tilda grimaced faintly. She should have realized he was joking. "I do hope Hawkins will invite us to attend his séance, though he may not if he's hiding something."

"Which he seemed to be regarding Montrose," Hadrian noted.

"And perhaps the table," Tilda said. "He did not seem inclined to discuss it with you. We should find the carpenter—Clifton—and pay him a visit."

They fell silent for a few minutes, and Tilda noticed that Hadrian massaged his temple briefly.

"Does your head still hurt?" she asked.

"A bit. Rest assured, I am done for the day with touching people and things that are not in my house."

"What about your mother?" Tilda didn't think it likely that he saw visions when he touched her, since he didn't seem to see them with people he knew well, such as those who lived and worked in his household. "Do you ever see anything when you touch her?"

"I do not." He cocked his head and studied her a moment. "I haven't ever seen anything when I've touched you either. Not that we've done a great deal of that."

Tilda found it curious that he'd never seen anything. Perhaps they just hadn't touched enough. "No, we haven't," she agreed. Immediately, she hoped he didn't interpret that as an invitation. Nor did she want him to think that she found touching him distasteful.

"I wonder if it's because I've come to know you fairly well," he said, seeming to have moved past the touching, thankfully. "It does seem that the people and things most familiar to me do not provoke any sensations or visions."

A few minutes later, Hadrian said they were nearing his mother's house. He was looking out the window when his expression changed. His brows drew together sharply, and he frowned.

Now Tilda worried that their talk of touching had reinstated the awkwardness she'd thought they'd left behind. She sincerely hoped that was not the case.

They barely stopped before Hadrian bounded from the coach. He did not stop to help Tilda, and her wariness increased.

Leach hastened to offer her assistance. "My apologies, Miss Wren. I'm sure his lordship had good reason to abandon you like that."

Tilda looked toward the house and immediately saw why Hadrian had leapt out of the coach. It wasn't at all to do with her.

Ezra Clement stood in front of his mother's door.

CHAPTER 9

*H*adrian kept himself from lunging at Clement, but he raised his voice to stop the reporter from knocking on his mother's door. "Clement, a word."

Clement turned, his brown eyes glinting with surprise beneath the brim of his hat. "Lord Ravenhurst."

"Are you shocked to see me here?" Hadrian didn't bother disguising his irritation. "You must know this is my mother's house. Why are you here?"

"That's quite easily explained, my lord." Clement shifted his weight. It was the only sign of nervousness he displayed. *If* it was nervousness.

"I'm waiting." Hadrian saw Tilda approach. She stopped a few feet behind him, but she stepped to the side so she could watch the encounter.

"Another medium was murdered," Clement announced rather importantly.

"Deborah Frost," Hadrian clipped.

Clement's eyes rounded briefly. "You already heard? Then you must know why I am here to speak with your mother."

Hadrian glowered at him. "I do not."

"That seems unlikely," Clement said with a sardonic edge. "I spoke with Mrs. Frost's housekeeper, and she told me that Lady Ravenhurst attended a séance at Mrs. Frost's house the other evening. As did you," he added as he returned Hadrian's stare.

"I did as well," Tilda said, moving to stand beside Hadrian.

"My mother is not part of any news story you are writing," Hadrian growled. "Take yourself off."

Clement pursed his lips at Hadrian. "Of course Lady Ravenhurst is part of the story. Our readers will want to know of the association between her and the latest deceased medium."

The 'latest,' as if there were a succession and not just two. Although, two was bad enough. "You're sensationalizing tragedy." Hadrian stepped between Clement and the door. "Your readers won't know of the association if you don't tell them."

Tilda also moved so that she stood before the reporter. "Mr. Clement, I do appreciate that your job is to inform the public, however, there is no reason to share details of Lady Ravenhurst's attendance at a séance. Just say she was there, as was his lordship and I."

Hadrian frowned at Tilda. Why was she telling the man this?

Clement's brows rose. "Will you confirm that all three of you were there?"

"Yes," Tilda replied succinctly.

"Why did you attend a séance?" He glanced toward Hadrian but clearly expected Tilda to answer. And why not, since she was being helpful?

Tilda lifted a shoulder. "Why does anyone? That is all you need to know to interest your readers."

"You're an investigator, Miss Wren. Surely there is more you can share regarding these murders." Clement regarded her eagerly.

"I have not been hired to investigate a murder," Tilda said, which was technically true. "However, if I do learn of something that I think your *readers* should know, I will be sure to tell you."

She gave him a smile that didn't reach her eyes. "Good day, Mr. Clement."

The reporter appeared uncertain and perhaps peeved. But he ultimately turned and stalked away.

Hadrian exhaled. "Did you need to confirm anything to that hack writer?"

"He is actually a decent writer," Tilda said. "And yes, I confirmed something unimportant so he would leave."

"I don't think the dowager Countess of Ravenhurst attending a séance for the purposes of speaking to her dead son is 'unimportant,'" Hadrian grumbled.

"I didn't say a thing about Gabriel. However, you must prepare yourself that others at the séance may speak to Clement or other reporters. It's not the worst thing. There are plenty of other women of her status who are involved with the society," she added gently.

"I suppose that is true." He pivoted. "Let us speak to my mother about Mrs. Frost. I am glad we arrived when we did so that she didn't hear the news from the odious Mr. Clement."

Hadrian opened the door and held it for Tilda. His mother's butler, Peverell, strode toward the door.

"Come in, my lord. We weren't expecting you." The butler hastened to take the door from Hadrian. His mostly bald pate gleamed in the daylight before he closed the door. White hair clung to the sides and back of his head, and his bright-blue eyes surveyed Hadrian and Tilda.

"Allow me to present my associate, Miss Matilda Wren," Hadrian said, gesturing to Tilda.

"Miss Wren?" Peverell smiled at Tilda. "You are the investigator her ladyship engaged."

"I am." Tilda returned his smile. "I'm pleased to make your acquaintance."

Peverell looked to Hadrian. "Your mother is working on

correspondence. If you go up to the drawing room, I'll let her know you've arrived."

"Thank you, Peverell." Hadrian turned to Tilda. "Allow me to escort you." He offered his arm.

As they ascended the stairs, Tilda glanced at Hadrian. "You are so concerned about people knowing of your mother consulting with a medium and wishing to speak with Gabriel. Why is it that her retainers are aware?"

"My mother's household is very close—they are like family," he explained. "Peverell was our butler when I was growing up. When my mother moved out of Ravenhurst House, he accompanied her. She also took the cook, the housekeeper, two footmen, and, of course, her maid."

Tilda laughed softly. "She left you with a skeleton household."

"I didn't begrudge her," Hadrian said. "Peverell and Mrs. Denimore—the housekeeper—were kind enough to train everyone up."

Tilda paused as they reached the top of the stairs, her attention focused on a portrait of Hadrian's father, Hadrian, and Gabriel hanging there. "Is that you?"

"And my father and brother." Hadrian stood to his father's right, with Gabriel in front. "I was fifteen when that was painted. Gabriel was ten. It's one of my mother's favorites. She likes it here so she can see it every time she uses the stairs."

"You look very serious," Tilda said.

"My father wanted us to appear 'sedate.' If you only knew how hard it was for Gabriel to do that. He had boundless energy, which my father often found annoying." Hadrian frowned. He hadn't thought of that in a very long time. Their father had been difficult, and Hadrian often clashed with him. However, Hadrian was most disgruntled about the way he'd treated Gabriel, as if he truly were a spare and not worth their father's attention.

"It sounds as though your father may have been cold," Tilda said softly.

"As ice," Hadrian replied. "Particularly with my sisters and Gabriel. As the heir, I received the bulk of his attention. I did not, however, mistake it for concern or care. I don't believe my father was capable of demonstrating that sort of emotion."

"Not even for his family?"

"Not for anyone." Hadrian turned his head from the painting, hoping that could be the end of their conversation.

Tilda seemed to understand the hint, and they continued to the drawing room.

Hadrian urged Tilda to sit—but not in his mother's preferred chair—then waited for the dowager to arrive. She appeared just a moment later.

"What a lovely surprise," his mother said warmly, stopping beside him so he could buss her cheek. She continued to her chair, eyeing Tilda. "And Miss Wren. I trust this means you've come with a report on your investigation?"

"Somewhat, yes," Tilda said. She looked toward Hadrian, seeming to silently ask if she ought to tell his mother about Mrs. Frost.

Deciding it might be better if he told her, Hadrian took the chair nearest his mother. "We've some terribly unfortunate news, I'm afraid. Mrs. Frost is dead."

His mother gasped, her hand fluttering to her chest. "How can that be? She was just fine two days ago."

"I'm sorry to say she was, ah, murdered." Hadrian reached over and clasped his mother's hand briefly.

"Oh no." She looked to Hadrian, her eyes dark with concern. "Like that other medium I read about?" At Hadrian's nod, she added, "How dastardly." She diverted her attention to Tilda. "Are you investigating these murders?"

"Since Mrs. Frost is one of the victims, I am," Tilda replied. "More accurately, the investigation of Mrs. Frost has required investigation of the London Spiritualism Society, and since two of their mediums have died, their murders have become part of my inquiry."

"Good," his mother said firmly. "Poor Mrs. Frost deserves justice. Though I suppose the police are conducting an investigation."

"They are," Tilda said.

Hadrian's mother fell silent a moment, her brow pleated. He could tell she was thinking. Finally, she said, "I wonder if I ought to find a new medium in the London Spiritualism Society."

Tilda exchanged a look with Hadrian before speaking. "This may not be the best time since two of their number have died."

"Oh yes, of course." His mother waved a hand before settling it in her lap. "They are likely upset. Perhaps they won't be holding séances for a while."

Hadrian wasn't going to tell her that they were. "Perhaps this is a sign that you should not continue with your endeavor."

His mother arched a brow as she leveled a wry stare at him. "And here I thought you didn't believe in signs or messages from beyond?"

From the corner of his eye, Hadrian saw Tilda quashing a smile. "I think it's common sense to keep a distance from an organization whose members are dying."

"I'm sure they didn't deserve that," his mother said. "Perhaps now is the precise time the society needs support. Mrs. Frost mentioned membership to me and said she hosts weekly teas for some of the members. I admit I was intrigued and have been considering becoming a patron of the society."

"Mother, I must also tell you that news of your attendance at Mrs. Frost's séance will circulate. In the papers."

Her brows shot up. "Indeed?" She waved her hand again. "No matter. It's *de rigueur* to attend a séance."

Hadrian looked to Tilda. "We must inform my mother of what we've learned regarding their tricks."

They'd discussed whether he might demonstrate the levitation cheat for her, but telling her was enough. She needed to know the truth. Perhaps he could put an end to this nonsense once and for all. Regardless of the mediums' authenticity, he didn't particularly want his mother involved with people who were being murdered at an alarming rate.

Tilda gave him a slight nod before addressing his mother. "We've learned that some of the mediums in the society perform trickery to dupe those who come to their séances. They cheat at levitation, and we suspect there is something about the tables they use that allows the medium to make them move. Meaning, spirits are not responding with raps or moving the table."

Shockingly, the dowager countess laughed. "I've no interest in their flashy parlor tricks. I don't doubt those are fake. I understand some people are amused and enthralled. I've no quarrel with that. I only care that they can help me speak to my dear Gabriel."

"But if the raps aren't truly from the spirits, that is proof that they are not speaking to Gabriel." Hadrian kept a rein on his patience.

"You've proof that is happening?" his mother asked. "What about the information these mediums share about things they shouldn't know about? I realize Gabriel's letter may have helped Mrs. Frost with the truth, but from what I have heard from others, she revealed things she could *not* have known."

It was suddenly clear to Hadrian that his mother was warring with herself. She wanted to speak to Gabriel whilst also worrying about whether it was really possible. He wondered, as Tilda had suggested, if it wasn't just easiest—and best—to allow her to think it was, so she could accomplish whatever it was she wished to do in contacting her son.

"Mama, why is it so imperative that you speak to Gabriel?" he asked softly.

Surprise flashed in his mother's eyes. "I … I want to know all is well. To lose a child is terrible, but to lose him when he was so far away, when I hadn't seen him in more than a year, is truly awful. Things feel … unfinished."

Hadrian heard the ache in her voice and wanted his mother to find what she sought. But even if it was fake? "I hope you can find peace with Gabriel's death, Mama. We will do all we can to facilitate that." He looked toward Tilda, who gave him a subtle nod.

Tilda addressed his mother. "We can certainly find a new medium for you in the society. We met Mr. Hawkins today, and he seems most competent."

"I think I would prefer a woman, if possible. I have heard they are more sensitive."

"There are other women mediums," Tilda said. "We will inquire about upcoming séances and ask if you can attend one."

"Please tell them that I was to sit with Mrs. Frost again and it is imperative I find a replacement quickly, whilst Gabriel is ready and eager to speak with me." Her tone was urgent, her expression almost dire.

"We will, Mama," Hadrian assured her. Above all, he didn't want to see her upset, and she clearly was.

"I should like to call on Mrs. Langdon tomorrow," Tilda said. "Do I need an introduction first?"

"I will send a note of introduction," Hadrian's mother replied. "I would offer to accompany you, but I am otherwise engaged."

"Thank you," Tilda said. "We'll let you know what we learn about a new medium, and we will make that a priority since you are concerned about losing touch with your son."

His mother brightened. "I appreciate that very much."

Hadrian stood. "Pardon us for disturbing your day, Mama."

"You are never a disturbance, dear. I am sorry the reason for your visit was so tragic." She frowned sadly, then clucked her tongue. "Mrs. Frost was a kind soul. May she rest in peace."

They said goodbye, and Hadrian escorted Tilda back to the coach. "I hope you won't mind if I accompany you to Mrs. Langdon's tomorrow."

"Of course not," Tilda said. "I expected you would."

"I'll have to meet you there. I've a busy day at Westminster."

Leach opened the door to the coach, and Tilda climbed inside. Hadrian sat opposite her. They were shortly on their way to her grandmother's house in Marylebone.

Tilda met his gaze. "You seemed as though you may have been moved by your mother's desperation to speak with Gabriel."

He exhaled. "I was. And I thought about what you said. Perhaps it doesn't matter if anyone is really speaking to him. If my mother is happy to think she can communicate with him, isn't that enough?"

"It's good of you to try to understand that perspective." She hesitated briefly, her expression earnest as she continued. "But I want you to know that I recognize your struggle with it, and that it's bound up with your own feelings about loss and grief. And about your brother."

Hadrian was again moved, this time by her declaration. "Thank you." They rode in silence a few minutes before Hadrian said, "Should we also plan to visit Clifton if we can find him?"

Tilda nodded. "I am not sure when, however. I want to attend the inquest, and it will likely be tomorrow."

"Damn." Hadrian grimaced. He hadn't meant to curse in front of her, not that he hadn't done so before. It spoke of their familiarity, he supposed. "I don't think I can shirk my duties the entire day." He'd already ignored several meetings in Westminster this week. His secretary had obtained the necessary information, and Hadrian spent his evenings reading or at his club meeting with colleagues.

"I shall give you a full report," Tilda said with a smile. "Perhaps Friday we can find Clifton. And hopefully attend Hawkins's séance. We should also visit the spiritualism society since I just promised your mother that we would find a new medium for her."

There was a pause before he said, "Thank you for doing that. I know it gave her comfort. It should have come from me."

"Do not abuse yourself," Tilda scolded gently. "The important thing is that you are supporting her wishes to find some peace with her son's death."

Hadrian was sorry he hadn't realized his mother needed that. He'd thought their grief about Gabriel was long resolved. But the ache in his chest—though it had diminished in time—when he thought of his brother told him otherwise.

Perhaps there was peace to be had for everyone.

～

Tilda had received a note from Hadrian that morning saying they were expected at Mrs. Langdon's that afternoon, and he was able to pick her up in his coach instead of meeting her there. That had worked out well since the inquest had started at eleven o'clock, and Tilda had wanted to attend. She'd barely returned home when Hadrian's coach arrived to fetch her.

Seated in the coach on the way to Mrs. Langdon's house in Mayfair, Tilda began telling Hadrian about the inquest.

"Graythorpe again?" he asked after Tilda said the coroner had presided once more. "Someone is keeping him busy," he added grimly.

"It doesn't seem that Teague is any closer to finding out whom," Tilda reported. "I did tell him about our meeting with Hawkins and about Roger Grenville."

"Does he plan to track Grenville down?" Hadrian asked.

Tilda lifted a shoulder. "He was interested but wasn't sure when he'd be able to do that. He had constables interview Mrs. Hemmings and Mrs. York, whilst he interviewed Lady Gillivray. He said the only helpful information they obtained came from Mrs. Hemmings, who attended a séance at the society headquarters somewhat recently. She reported that someone charged angrily into the middle of the sitting and threatened the medium."

"How so?"

"Teague did not elaborate on that point," Tilda said. "He did tell me the medium conducting the séance was Cyril Ward."

"That is an excellent lead." Hadrian's eyes gleamed. "Did Teague tell you who interrupted the séance?"

"No. He apologized for not doing so, particularly after I'd shared the information about Grenville, but he didn't want to chance this person—the one who was upset with Ward—fleeing before he'd had a chance to interview him." Tilda gave him a determined look. "I'm confident I can discover the person's identity."

Hadrian chuckled as he settled back in the seat. "Of course you will."

Tilda smiled. "I haven't told you the best part. Hawkins was at the inquest, and he's invited us both to attend the séance tomorrow night. I accepted. I hope you don't mind."

"Not at all. I do hope there is fake levitating."

"You could always demonstrate your skills in that area," Tilda suggested sardonically.

"I am considering it." Hadrian gave her an arch look as he crossed his arms. "There was some discussion at Westminster today about these murders. They are capturing great public attention. Indeed, someone referred to the murderer as the 'Levitation Killer.'"

"I heard someone use that term today as well," Tilda said. "I can't say I'm surprised that public interest is so high. These murders were particularly spectacular and occurred in quick succession. Teague is concerned there will be another and advised the mediums in the society to be cautious. In fact, he's stationed a pair of constables at the society headquarters." Tilda recalled the conversation they'd shared prior to the inquest.

"Teague indicated that Lysander Mallory hadn't seemed overly enthused about having constables there but begrudgingly agreed it was necessary."

"That is interesting," Hadrian said, his eyes narrowing slightly. "Why wouldn't the man be thrilled to have police protection in this circumstance?"

"I wondered the same thing. I'd hoped to ask him if they would still be holding séances at the society headquarters, but I didn't have time after the inquest."

The coach stopped, and a moment later, Leach opened the door. Hadrian climbed down and helped Tilda to the pavement before escorting her to Mrs. Langdon's door. A butler shortly answered Hadrian's knock.

Hadrian handed the man his card. Tilda was content to let his title lead the way since it usually ensured they were well received.

The retainer welcomed them inside. "Mrs. Langdon is expecting you. She is in the drawing room, if you'll just follow me." He led them upstairs to the formal room at the front of the house.

Mrs. Langdon was a petite, angular woman with gray hair and half-moon spectacles, which she removed as they entered. Her dark-brown eyes focused on them as she smiled. "Lord Raven-hurst and Miss Wren, I presume."

"Yes," Hadrian said. "Thank you for receiving us today."

"It is my pleasure to speak with you about my experience with Mrs. Frost." Her features pitched into a deep frown. "I was so saddened to hear of her death. Absolutely dreadful business."

"Indeed," Tilda agreed as she sat on a settee across from their hostess.

Hadrian sat beside Tilda. "She seemed a very kind woman."

"That's right. Your mother's note said you'd attended the séance with her the other night." Mrs. Langdon's dark eyes gleamed with interest. "How did you find the experience?"

Tilda answered to save Hadrian from having to fib. "It was

most enlightening. We were looking forward to attending again, but alas, that won't be possible. How many séances were you able to attend?"

"Four with Mrs. Frost. I am a patron of the society, so I am able to attend one séance each month." Mrs. Langdon pouted briefly. "I must find a new medium, I suppose."

"I was not aware of that benefit," Tilda said. "What else does your patronage include?"

"Weekly tea with Mrs. Frost, though I have only been able to attend one since becoming a patron." Mrs. Langdon gestured with her slender hand. "Patrons also have access to the society headquarters, including the library, as well as teas and other events that they host there."

"It sounds as though the society headquarters is almost like a club," Hadrian observed.

"That could be," Mrs. Langdon replied. "But you would likely know more about that, my lord. Ladies do not have as many opportunities to belong to a club as gentlemen such as yourself."

Tilda wondered if most of the patrons were women and if the society was providing a much-needed place for them to gather. When they visited the society next, she would further her inquiries into their operations. She addressed Mrs. Langdon. "May I ask about your experience with Mrs. Frost? I am investigating her murder."

Mrs. Langdon nodded. "Lady Ravenhurst's note said you were conducting an investigation. I am happy to be of assistance. I visited the society to inquire about attending a séance and spoke with Mrs. Frost. I explained that I wished to speak with my father. He died a few years ago, and my mother thinks he sold a painting that she loved." Mrs. Langdon lowered her voice. "He didn't like it much." She laughed softly. "My mother said he wouldn't let her hang it in the house."

"Did you want to ask him if he sold the painting?" Hadrian asked.

"Yes, and Mrs. Frost was eager to help. Whilst she wasn't successful at the first séance, Mrs. Frost was able to contact him straightaway at the second." Mrs. Langdon smiled widely. "It was astonishing."

Tilda noted that, once again, the medium was not successful at the first séance. It seemed the clients were then encouraged to return and even become patrons. "How were you convinced it was him?"

Mrs. Langdon's expression grew animated. "Let me explain from the beginning. I'm sure you know how séances start since you've attended one. Mrs. Frost asked to speak with the spirit realm. We very quickly felt a cool breeze. It was most disquieting. She then asked if John Tabor—he is her spirit guide—was present. He rapped three times to say he was. Was he also present at your séance?" Mrs. Langdon looked from Tilda to Hadrian and back to Tilda again. "Mrs. Frost said he is usually her guide."

"He was there, yes," Tilda replied. "However, he wasn't able to help us much. It sounds as though you had the opposite experience."

"At the second séance, yes. Right away, he tapped out my father's name—Adam."

Hadrian kept his features notably blank. "How did he do that?"

"There was one tap for the first letter of the alphabet, then a pause, then four taps, and so on. Mrs. Frost said John Tabor was saying that he was with someone called Adam."

"That was all?" A bit of doubt crept into Hadrian's voice, and Tilda shot him a quelling look. She didn't want Mrs. Langdon to be put off by him.

"No, no. The table began to move quite violently then. Mrs. Frost closed her eyes tightly and bade us all to focus on the energy moving between us." Mrs. Langdon's eyes closed as she recounted the tale. "My father was glad to see me and pleased that I was wearing the yellow topaz necklace he'd given me. I knew right then that my father was there. I could feel his presence. The air grew warm, and I swear I could smell the scent he always wore."

Hadrian looked over at Tilda in disbelief. Tilda narrowed her eyes at him before returning her attention to Mrs. Langdon. The woman was smiling as she opened her eyes.

"Had Mrs. Frost asked you to bring something that your father had given you?" Tilda asked, thinking of how she'd done that with Lady Ravenhurst, who'd brought her son's letter. That could very well explain how the medium knew about the necklace.

"Yes, but I didn't tell her what it was," Mrs. Langdon said, which surprised Tilda, since Lady Ravenhurst had given the letter from Gabriel to Mrs. Frost. "She could not have known the necklace I was wearing was a gift from my father. But that wasn't the only thing that confirmed my father's presence. He asked if I was still attending the Henley Royal Regatta without him." Mrs. Langdon sniffed. "He took me to the very first one almost thirty years ago. It was the year before I wed. We went together every year since, except when I had a newborn babe and couldn't attend."

That was still something others might have known.

Mrs. Langdon smiled again. "My father recounted how, since I wasn't able to attend the regatta, he took me to Temple Island a few months later, after my confinement, and we sailed a small boat together." She giggled. "It is one of my fondest memories."

Memories … Tilda snapped her gaze to Hadrian. Again, she suspected that Mrs. Frost possessed the same ability as he did. "I don't suppose you were holding Mrs. Frost's hand?" Tilda asked Mrs. Langdon.

"No, those seated around the séance table must be in male-female order. Did you not notice that at your séance? I was seated near her—there was a gentleman between us. Mr. Montrose was his name."

Tilda found it interesting that Montrose was always seated next to the medium conducting the séance. At least with both Mrs. Frost and Mr. Hawkins. And, in the cases of Mrs. Langdon and Lady Ravenhurst, they'd sat on his other side. Perhaps Montrose also had the ability to see others' memories. Her curiosity about Montrose grew. "Was he at all of the séances you attended?"

Mrs. Langdon thought for a moment. "He was."

"What happened with your search for the painting?" Hadrian asked.

"Papa didn't sell the painting," Mrs. Langdon said with a light laugh. "He insisted my mother moved it somewhere in the house and simply can't find it."

Tilda wondered how Mrs. Frost had learned the painting hadn't been sold. Unless she really had spoken to Mrs. Langdon's father. "Did he not know where you might find it?"

Mrs. Langdon shook her head. "He could only confirm that he hadn't sold it. I'm afraid it remains lost for now."

It was notable to Tilda that no one could prove or disprove that since the painting was still missing. "I'm sorry you weren't able to find the painting," she said. "If you learned all that in the second séance, why did you attend two more?"

"Because it was such fun! Each week, Mrs. Frost spoke to my father and relayed what he said. It was like being with him again." Mrs. Langdon's shoulders jumped up as she smiled warmly.

Hadrian leaned forward slightly. "Your father said a great deal. How long did it take for all that information to be rapped out?"

"Oh, I forgot the most stunning detail!" Mrs. Langdon laughed somewhat sheepishly. "Once we established contact, Mrs. Frost closed her eyes and he spoke through her."

"I see." Hadrian sat back with a faint nod. He didn't appear at all convinced—at least to Tilda, who knew him well.

Mrs. Langdon eyed Hadrian as she clasped her hands in her

lap. Her gaze turned expectant. "You don't believe Mrs. Frost channeled my father, do you?"

"It is a great deal to accept," Hadrian said hesitantly.

"Your mother's note indicated that you are not entirely supportive of her desire to speak with your brother." Mrs. Langdon gave him a rather tolerant moue. "I understand your reticence, but let me tell you how extraordinary it is when the connection is made. I haven't the slightest doubt that my father was speaking to me through Mrs. Frost. She spoke details no one else could know—that my father wore a bright green cravat to the first regatta, which he'd bought especially for the event."

"You seem quite convinced," Hadrian said amiably.

Tilda noted he did not say *he* was convinced. "I am thrilled you were able to have that experience, Mrs. Langdon. Perhaps our next séance will be more fruitful."

"Will Lady Ravenhurst find a new medium?" Mrs. Langdon asked hopefully. "If she does, please tell her I would like to know whom she sees. I do think I want to attend another séance. It would be wonderful to speak with my favorite aunt. She died last year." She fixed her gaze on Hadrian. "If you would like further proof that Mrs. Frost spoke with the spirit realm, might I suggest you speak with Mr. Douglas Joslin? He saw Mrs. Frost a few months ago and raved about the experience. I'm sure he won't mind if you call on him." She provided the man's address in Montpelier Square.

Hadrian smiled at her. "We'll do that, thank you."

"We appreciate your time, Mrs. Langdon." Tilda stood, and Hadrian joined her.

They took their leave a few minutes later. Outside, Hadrian said, "I know Joslin. He's a member at one of my clubs— Brooks's."

"You belong to more than one?"

"Yes, but Brooks's is my primary. Come to think of it, I

haven't seen Joslin there in a while. But then again, I don't frequent the club as often as I used to."

"Why is that?" Tilda asked as they arrived at the coach.

He smiled broadly. "I've been too busy investigating with you."

Tilda couldn't help the shiver of delight that danced up her spine. "I hope I'm not keeping you from that."

"Not at all. I much prefer our work together."

She felt the same. Her life had somehow brightened since they'd met. Was it because of their investigations or was it him?

A clear answer was not forthcoming, and Tilda did not contemplate it further.

They climbed into the coach and started on their way back to Marylebone.

Tilda studied Hadrian a moment as she tried to determine the best way to broach what she wanted to say. Finally, she said, "Did you notice that everything Mrs. Langdon shared about Mrs. Frost's conversations with Mrs. Langdon's father appeared to be a memory?"

"I did. You think Mrs. Frost had the same ability as I do. Unfortunately, we can't find out for certain."

"Unless someone else knew," Tilda said. "As I've mentioned, I wonder if all the mediums have it. It would be extraordinary to discover that many people possess the ability to see others' memories. I must wonder how Mallory did that, assuming it was him, since he seems to have recruited the mediums. Though, after speaking with Mrs. Langdon, I am wondering if Montrose also possesses the ability to see memories. He was seated between Mrs. Frost and the person for whom the séance was being conducted."

Hadrian's eyes narrowed shrewdly. "We need to find Montrose. The society seems a good place to start. Should we go there now?"

Tilda shook her head. "No, I need to go home. My grandmother has invited a pair of friends to dine with us this evening, and I must ensure all is prepared."

"Perhaps tomorrow then. And we still need to find Clifton, the carpenter who built the séance tables."

"Don't forget Roger Grenville. Alas, he is a train ride away in Swindon."

"I'd be happy to escort you there." Hadrian met her gaze. "You're going to say you don't have the funds to do so, but it is part of your investigation, and you will include it in the invoice you provide to my mother."

"I suppose that is reasonable. I hope your mother doesn't dispute the cost."

"She won't," Hadrian assured her. "Especially since you have become her champion by promising to find a new medium for her."

"Yes, we must do that when we visit the society. Let's go tomorrow." Tilda frowned. "That will be the second day since Mrs. Frost was killed. If the pattern holds, there could very well be another murder."

"Not at the society," Hadrian said. "There are constables present. They will keep those who live there safe."

But none of the murders had happened at the headquarters. She worried about the third premier medium. "Perhaps Teague ought to put a constable at Hawkins's house."

Hadrian nodded. "That is a good idea. I'll stop at Scotland Yard after I drop you off and ask him to do so."

"Thank you, Hadrian. I am not sure how I would conduct investigations without you. I would certainly need to hire a great many hacks," she added wryly.

Hadrian smiled. "It is my privilege to assist you."

Tilda was glad to have settled back into their easy rhythm of working together. She supposed she should be grateful that the investigation had broadened beyond Mrs. Frost. It meant they could spend more time with one another.

And she had absolutely no quarrel with that.

CHAPTER 10

The following afternoon, Hadrian and Tilda arrived at the London Spiritualism Society. The butler greeted them by name, clearly remembering them from their last visit.

Hadrian smiled at the butler, who looked to be around Hadrian's age or slightly older. He was young for such a position, but it seemed as though all the mediums' retainers were youthful. The man in front of him was tall and muscular with sharp green eyes and a brilliant smile. "Good afternoon. Tuttle, is it?" Hadrian asked.

"That's correct, my lord." The man seemed flattered.

"We've come to speak with Mr. Mallory, if possible," Tilda said as they stepped into the entrance hall.

"Certainly. I believe he is meeting with someone in his office, but if you'd care to wait in the library, there is a group congregated there. I believe tea will be served in a short while."

"That would be lovely, thank you." Tilda followed Tuttle as he guided them to the library, and Hadrian trailed them.

At the door to the library, Tuttle stepped aside and gestured for them to go in. "I'll let Mr. Mallory know you are here." He pivoted on his heel and departed.

The library contained about a half dozen people. A few were seated and engaged in conversation, whilst others stood near the hearth.

Hadrian leaned toward Tilda and whispered, "I'd no idea we were coming on a day when others would be here."

"It's most fortuitous since we are looking for a new medium," she replied softly. "And to hopefully question members about the society."

A woman from the group at the hearth came toward them, her rouged lips spreading in a wide smile. Hadrian recognized her immediately from Ward's inquest. She was one of the women who'd been seated behind Mallory that day.

"Welcome, I am Mrs. Mercy Griswold, medium. I think I've seen you before." Her brow knitted. "Lord Ravenhurst?"

"And Miss Wren," Hadrian said, indicating Tilda.

Mrs. Griswold's blond brows arched over her aquamarine eyes. "Ah, yes, Lysander pointed you out to me at Cyril's inquest."

"I imagine it's been most disturbing to lose not just one, but two of your members," Tilda said with a sad frown.

The woman's gaze dipped to the floor. "We are devastated."

"I confess I am surprised the society is still welcoming visitors, though glad," Hadrian said.

Tilda nodded in agreement. "I am also surprised that the mediums have continued to hold séances."

"We did discuss pausing séances, and Lysander considered draping everything in black, but I convinced him that was silly."

"Silly?" Hadrian asked, surprised at her choice of words. Most people did not think of death and grieving as "silly." He noted that none of the people in the library were dressed in mourning clothes. Instead, they all sported black armbands.

Mrs. Griswold waved her pale hand. "I only meant that it's absurd to think that a society founded on communing with the spirit world would be put off by death. We commune with the dead every day." She smiled prettily, her gaze settling on Hadrian.

Sobering, she added, "We have many important patrons who rely on us, and we cannot let them down."

"Where do you conduct your séances, Mrs. Griswold?" Tilda asked.

"Here," Mrs. Griswold replied. "I love the energy that comes from this space, probably because many mediums have passed through these rooms and several live here at any time."

"Do they?" Tilda asked in a casual manner, though Hadrian could tell her curiosity was piqued. "I didn't realize anyone lived here, beyond Mr. Mallory."

Mrs. Griswold pursed her lips in thought. "There are three mediums in residence currently, aside from Mr. Mallory, including me."

"Why do you live here?" Hadrian asked. He found the arrangement odd, as if Mallory were running a boarding house, particularly if their stays were temporary, as Mrs. Griswold seemed to indicate.

Shrugging, Mrs. Griswold glanced toward the hearth where a man and woman were still speaking. The woman had pivoted so that Hadrian could see her face, and Hadrian realized she'd been seated with Mrs. Griswold at Ward's inquest.

"Lysander generously offers us lodging whilst we train to become mediums," Mrs. Griswold explained. Her expression grew serious. "It's important that we learn to harness our unique energies and learn to speak with the spirit realm."

Tilda cocked her head. "What if someone decides they don't wish to practice as a medium and chooses not to remain in the society?"

"I don't know that I'm aware of anyone who's done that," Mrs. Griswold said without a moment's thought.

Hadrian thought of Roger Grenville. Perhaps Mrs. Griswold hadn't known him.

"I understand Mrs. Frost was considering leaving the society after Mr. Ward was murdered," Tilda said.

Mrs. Griswold pressed her lips together before responding. "I had not heard that. And unfortunately, that rumor cannot be confirmed. Poor dear. I still can't believe she and Cyril are gone. I expect them to walk in at any moment." She glanced toward the doorway and blinked a few times.

"Can you tell us about the séances that are held here?" Tilda cast a look in the direction of the parlor where they'd seen the large séance table. Hadrian hoped he would have a chance to look at it and see if it was also made by Clifton. "They're conducted by the mediums who live here?"

"That's right," Mrs. Griswold said.

"It sounds as though the society is a kind of school for mediums," Tilda mused.

"More like a place to hone our skills," Mrs. Griswold said. "All of the society's mediums have a natural gift for communicating with the spirit realm. The society allows us to grow our energy and truly embody our talents."

"We heard about the person who interrupted one of Mr. Ward's séances here recently," Tilda said, her brows gathering with concern. She was very adept at playing a role when interviewing people. "I imagine that is upsetting, since he was murdered."

"Indeed." Mrs. Griswold nodded vigorously. "I do hope the police are being thorough in their investigation."

"I'm sure they are," Tilda said.

Mrs. Griswold looked to Hadrian. "Your mother attended a séance with Deborah—Mrs. Frost—earlier this week. Was she hoping to attend another?"

"She was, in fact," Hadrian replied. "We came here today to see if another medium would suit."

A dazzling smile lit up Mrs. Griswold's face. "I would be happy to conduct a séance for Lady Ravenhurst."

"Splendid!" Hadrian infused as much enthusiasm into his reaction as he could and only hoped he was convincing. He was not skilled at acting like Tilda—yet. "When will that be? My mother is anxious that it should be soon. Mrs. Frost mentioned there was a window of opportunity to reach my brother whilst he is near. Or something."

Mrs. Griswold nodded. "Deborah was absolutely right. Had your brother appeared at the séance?"

"He seemed to. Briefly."

"Then yes, we will want to have the séance soon. I'll speak with Lysander and let you know." Mrs. Griswold glanced toward the doorway. "In fact, I'll do that now. Please excuse me."

As the medium left, another man entered. He looked familiar.

Tilda leaned toward Hadrian. "Isn't that man one of the footmen who served dinner at Mrs. Frost's?"

Hadrian surveyed the man's oval face. He had deep-set eyes and a cleft chin. "Yes, I thought I'd seen him before."

"Let us confirm." Tilda moved toward the young man before he could progress to join anyone. She smiled warmly. "Good afternoon, I'm Miss Wren. Weren't you at Mrs. Frost's the other evening serving dinner?"

The man's dark blue eyes rounded. "I was, er, yes."

"I'm Ravenhurst," Hadrian said. "And you are?"

"Michael Crocker," the young man replied, clasping his hands nervously. "I know who you are, sir." He squeezed his eyes closed briefly. "Rather, my lord."

Hadrian wondered why the footman was here outside of his capacity as a domestic servant. "Are you a member of the society?" He kept his voice smooth and genial to put Crocker at ease.

"I am."

Hadrian wondered how a footman could afford to be a member of the society. Perhaps they had different levels of patronage. Still, a society that welcomed a duchess and a footman was an oddity.

"What is your interest in spiritualism?" Tilda asked Crocker.

"I, er, my parents died when I was young, and when I learned I could speak with them, I wanted to try."

"Is that how you came to join the society?" Hadrian asked. "Pardon me for asking, but I am curious how you can afford that on your salary."

"Because I am employed by the society, I am allowed to be a member. I am training to be a medium myself." Crocker blushed faintly and didn't quite meet their eyes.

"How wonderful," Tilda said warmly. "Do you live here with the other mediums who are training?"

"No," Crocker answered quickly, then paused. "The mediums who live here are more accomplished, but I am hopeful that I will progress soon. I conducted my first séance last week, and it was very well received."

"Have you learned how to move objects or levitate?" Hadrian managed to keep a straight face. "I imagine that is difficult."

"I can levitate, yes." Crocker sounded proud, but there was another flash of color in his cheeks. "I did not attempt it at the last séance, however. It was enough to contact the spirit realm. Perhaps next time."

"Were you able to speak with your parents?" Tilda asked.

"I did, not long after I came to the society a few months ago. In the séance I conducted, I practiced by contacting John Tabor, one of the mediums' spirit guides." He blushed again. "But you know that from Mrs. Frost's séance."

"Who attends a practice séance? I should think that would be most interesting," Tilda said.

"Members of the society," Crocker replied.

"Are there many people like you?" Tilda asked. "Those who are currently working as retainers who hope to become mediums?"

"Not too many," he replied vaguely. Was he being evasive, or did he not know?

"You must pardon me." Crocker inclined his head toward them before moving to join the man and woman at the hearth.

Tilda turned toward Hadrian. "I find this process of training mediums fascinating."

"It reeks of corruption, if you ask me." Hadrian scoffed. "I should think mediums would have a gift that cannot be trained."

"They might if their ability is the same as yours. Actually, even with your gift, it seems you can learn new things, such as smelling a memory." She glanced toward Crocker. "Do you suppose the footman is able to experience another's memories?"

"If so, how does Mallory find these people? And does that mean Crocker's story about wanting to speak with his dead parents is a lie?"

Tilda's attention flicked to the doorway. "Here comes Mallory. We can ask him."

Hadrian turned his head to see the leader of the society. Mallory's blond hair was bright against the unrelenting black of his costume. Even the man's shirt was black. Why was he dressed fully in mourning whilst no one else was?

Mallory walked toward them. There were dark circles under his eyes, as if he hadn't been sleeping well. "Ravenhurst, Miss Wren."

Quickly removing his glove, Hadrian seized the chance to at last shake the man's hand. He reached out to the medium. "Mallory, my condolences."

They briefly clasped hands—very briefly, for the medium released Hadrian immediately in order to take Tilda's hand. Hadrian hadn't seen any kind of vision or felt any sentiment. Mallory's skin was clammy, and Hadrian had experienced a flash of cold, which he attributed to not particularly caring for the man.

Mallory released Tilda's hand. "I understand you've come to inquire about a new medium for your mother's séance? Mrs. Griswold told me—and she has offered her services. She is excellent." He fixed on Hadrian. "Dare I hope you've decided to become a patron?"

"How much would it cost me?"

Mallory waved his hand. "We needn't discuss that now, particularly with all that is going on this week. Generally, members make a donation they feel is appropriate for their level of involvement."

That sounded rather vague to Hadrian. "I can't imagine some of the members are able to give much. Particularly the retainers who work at the séances and are also members."

The medium's dark eyes glittered. "The donations do vary a great deal. We never turn anyone away." He looked to Tilda and back to Hadrian. "I understand you'll be attending Victor's séance tonight."

"We will," Tilda said with a nod.

"Are you acquainted with Her Grace, the Duchess of Chester?" Mallory asked Hadrian. "She will be present."

"Somewhat," Hadrian replied.

"I was hoping you might know her," Mallory said. "I thought it may be comforting for her to have an acquaintance there since the purpose of the séance is to speak with Cyril. Her Grace is most distraught over his death."

"Do you expect Mr. Ward will provide the name of his killer?" Tilda asked.

Hadrian closely watched Mallory to see his reaction. Did the man believe his own nonsense, that he and his mediums in the society could speak with spirits?

"I am not sure Her Grace will ask that, and we must allow her to guide the conversation."

"Are you not afraid that there will be another murder?" Tilda asked.

Mallory's jaw tightened. "I would be a fool to not be concerned about that, but with constables here and at Victor's house, I am relieved. We cannot allow ourselves to hide in fear.

Furthermore, Her Grace is eager to speak with Cyril. She loved him like her own son, and we must continue for her sake."

Tilda's brow furrowed as she regarded the medium. "Have you any idea who the killer may be? It seems as though someone is unhappy with the spiritualism society—perhaps a disgruntled former member?"

The medium's cheeks flashed pink. "Honestly, I can't think of a single person I've ever met who could commit crimes such as these."

"And yet someone recently interrupted a séance here and made threats," Tilda noted. "What about your former partner—Grenville? Are you certain no one of your acquaintance could be seeking some kind of vengeance?"

Mallory's nostrils flared the barest amount. "You've learned a great deal, Miss Wren. I will leave it up to your investigative skills to find that person. And I will be most grateful."

Tilda inclined her head. "Do you know if Mr. Montrose will be in attendance tonight? We wondered if he might be a suitable replacement for Mrs. Frost since he'd already sat in a séance with Lady Ravenhurst."

"He is not a medium," Mallory said crisply.

Tilda's brows arched briefly. "He's not? I thought he might be, given how close he and Mrs. Frost seemed."

Hadrian admired how Tilda had brought Montrose into the conversation by suggesting him as a replacement for Mrs. Frost. She was most adept at seeking information in subtle ways.

"I maintain that Mrs. Griswold will suit wonderfully," Mallory said. "But if you prefer a male medium, I recommend Nigel Edwards. Have you met him yet? He is one of our newer mediums."

"We have not," Tilda said.

"He is just over there." Mallory gestured to the man who was standing near the hearth with the other woman Hadrian had seen at Ward's inquest. Crocker was no longer with them. "Would you like an introduction?"

Tilda gave the medium an appreciative smile. "That would be lovely, thank you."

Hadrian didn't think she would pass up the opportunity to meet and speak with more mediums. He followed Tilda and Mallory as they moved toward the hearth.

Edwards and the other woman turned to greet them.

"Nigel, Isidora, this is Lord Ravenhurst and Miss Wren. Lord Ravenhurst's mother attended Deborah's last séance earlier this week and is seeking a new medium. And Miss Wren is a private investigator who is inquiring into the murders of our dear friends." He looked down for a moment, his expression grim. Then he addressed Hadrian and Tilda. "Allow me to present two of our rising mediums, Nigel Edwards and Miss Isidora Dryden."

"Pleased to make your acquaintance," Tilda said.

Edwards inclined his head. "It is a privilege, my lord, Miss Wren." He was of an age with Hadrian, with light brown curls and a squarish face with a short, blunt-edged nose and an affable smile which he flashed at Tilda.

Hadrian didn't think the medium was flirting, but the man certainly displayed charm. "Edwards." He turned his attention to the other medium, a woman who appeared slightly younger than Tilda. She had dark hair and arresting gray eyes that were locked on Hadrian in a frank perusal. "Miss Dryden."

"My lord." The medium sank into a brief curtsey. "I have not met an earl before."

"You'll find him pleasantly devoid of pretense," Tilda said with a wink. Hadrian believed she was doing her best to win these mediums over. The better someone felt, the more likely they were to share information.

"That is good to know," Miss Dryden murmured, her cheeks flushing faintly pink. "Thank you, Miss Wren."

"Are you close to catching this horrible killer?" Edwards

asked. "I don't mind telling you it's cast a horrible pall over the society. We are doing our best to continue onward, but it is difficult as we wonder if the killer will strike again."

"We are safe with the constables watching over us," Mallory said earnestly. "But any medium who wishes to retreat from practice until the murderer is captured is welcome to do so."

Hadrian wondered if anyone had done that.

Edwards and Dryden both shook their heads. "We know our services are needed now more than ever," Miss Dryden said. "Interest in the society has only increased with the news of the Levitation Killer."

Mallory wrinkled his nose. "How I loathe that moniker."

Tilda looked to Edwards. "To answer your question, Mr. Edwards, I am still conducting my investigation into the murders. We—I and the police—are trying to determine possible motives. It does seem there may be people who were unhappy with the society for some reason. I understand someone interrupted one of Mr. Ward's séances recently?"

Mallory's lips twisted with disgust. "Eldred is of no consequence. He is bitter and angry, but he would not resort to murder. He is also rather small and thin. How could he do what was done to Cyril and Deborah?"

"I find it's best to never underestimate people, including their ability or their resources," Tilda said. "Why is he bitter and angry?"

"I'm not entirely sure." Mallory blinked. "He attended, I think, two séances conducted by Cyril and was apparently disappointed in the result."

"Was Cyril not able to contact the spirit realm for Eldred?" Hadrian asked.

"I'm sure he did," Mallory insisted. "Cyril was our most experienced medium, apart from myself, of course. It may be that Eldred didn't care for whatever he heard."

A maid entered carrying a large tray with tea and sandwiches.

As she went to place them on a table, Mallory invited Tilda and Hadrian to stay.

"We should probably be going," Tilda said. "I have one last question I'd like to ask, if you don't mind. How do you go about recruiting mediums for the society?"

Mallory frowned. "I wouldn't say I 'recruit' them at all. People who are interested in spiritualism come to the society, and some of them have a sensitivity and talent to become a spiritualist. The society provides a place of fellowship and support that allows them to reach their full potential."

"Could I become a spiritualist?" Tilda asked.

Hadrian had to press his lips together to keep from smiling.

"I confess I have been wondering if you might possess the necessary talent," Mallory said. "May I take your hand?"

Hadrian's attention snapped to Mallory's hands. Was he hoping to see Tilda's memories?

Wait. Did Hadrian believe that Mallory—or any of the other mediums—actually possessed the same power he did? He had to admit he could not dismiss the notion, even if it made him uncomfortable. And why should it? He ought to be glad to find someone, or several others, who shared his gift. Except to confer with them, he'd have to expose himself, and he wasn't even able to do so with his own mother.

"My bare hand?" Tilda asked. At Mallory's nod, she removed her glove and presented her right hand.

Mallory clasped it gently. If he closed his eyes, Hadrian would assume he did not have the ability to see her memories. Hadrian had to keep his eyes open or the vision would disappear.

The medium did not close his eyes.

After a moment, he released her. "Hmmm. I don't feel any special energy in you, Miss Wren. My apologies. That doesn't mean you aren't able to develop a sensitivity. If you'd like to explore doing so, I can recommend several books here in our library that could guide you. I would also suggest you join the

society, where you would be surrounded by like-minded people."
He gave her an encouraging smile.

"Thank you," Tilda replied as she pulled on her glove. "I shall
consider that." She looked at Hadrian. "We should be going."

"Yes."

"I'll show you out," Mallory offered.

"That isn't necessary," Hadrian said. He wanted a chance to
look at the séance table in the parlor and wouldn't be able to if
Mallory accompanied them. As it was, they'd have to find a way
around the butler. "Please enjoy your tea."

They exchanged departing pleasantries with the other
mediums before taking their leave. Outside the library, Hadrian
told Tilda of his intent to investigate the table in the parlor.

"I'll distract the butler," Tilda said with an eager glint in her
eyes.

"Brilliant." Hadrian hung back as Tilda went into the entrance
hall.

She began speaking with Tuttle and positioned herself in such
a way that the butler's back was to Hadrian so that he could steal
into the parlor.

Moving quickly, Hadrian dashed to the table where he
dropped to his knees and crawled beneath it. Though it was dim,
he could see the shape of the pedestal matched those of Mrs.
Frost's and Mr. Hawkins's tables. He made his way to the
pedestal and felt for the carving of the name Clifton. His fingers
found the indentation, and he confirmed it had been made by the
same cabinet maker.

Hadrian whipped off his glove and touched the pedestal. In
his mind, he saw a small hand, perhaps feminine, press on one of
the feet. One side of the pedestal swung outward like a door. The
interior of the pedestal was hollow.

Whoever's memory he was seeing then crawled inside where
it was completely dark. He could not see anything, but he knew
there were levers to pull and a small mallet to knock on the

underside of the table. Someone ensconced inside the pedestal manipulated the table and made the raps attributed to the spirits.

Triumphant satisfaction raced through him, and his heart pounded as he withdrew his hand. He pulled on his glove and crawled from under the table as fast as he could, hoping Tilda had been able to continue distracting the butler.

He walked stealthily into the entrance hall, working to keep himself out of the butler's line of sight. Then he approached them from the direction of the library.

"Ready?" he asked Tilda.

"Oh, yes." She gave the butler a wide smile. "Tuttle was just telling me that Mr. Mallory informed him after we arrived that he is soon to be promoted. He will move into the headquarters and begin conducting regular séances here."

"Congratulations, Tuttle," Hadrian said.

"Thank you, my lord. I am quite chuffed."

After saying goodbye, Hadrian escorted Tilda outside and into the coach, where he told her what he'd seen with the table. She listened intently, her eyes taking on a sheen of excitement as he revealed the details of the hollow pedestal.

"I don't think we need to visit Clifton now," she said. "I think we can unequivocally say that the society engages in trickery in their séances, including the part where the table indicates that spirits are present. And the raps that are supposedly communication from the dead."

She frowned. "However, we still cannot explain how these mediums know the things that they do. I think in some cases, it's possible they are merely guessing at truths, as you suggested."

"I would think the mediums would become quite good at that."

"It is a form of investigation, really," Tilda said. "I confess I was affronted when Mallory said I didn't possess the right sensitivity to be a medium. I think I am rather good at reading people," she added with a sniff.

Hadrian couldn't help smiling. "You are indeed. Perhaps Mallory only said that because he is hoping you will join the society and add to their coffers. He has a great many people to support with so many mediums and retainers in his employ."

"He does indeed." Tilda's eyes narrowed. "You believe the entire society is a fraud. A money-making scheme to enrich Mallory?"

"It seems highly possible." Hadrian lifted his shoulder. "I sense you want to continue the investigation into how the mediums learn specific things about people—whether it's through the power I have or something else, such as simple investigation into the people who attend séances."

"I would like to know. Wouldn't you? Particularly if it's the former?"

Hadrian exhaled. "I must admit that I would like to find someone who experiences what I do. It would be helpful. And it would make me feel less … peculiar."

"You are not peculiar." Her eyes glinted with ferocity. "You are *singular*. And that is a wonderful thing."

Though she was referring to his gift, Hadrian imagined she could think that about him entirely. But he would never ask. They'd reestablished their friendship, and that would have to be enough.

CHAPTER 11

*T*ilda decided to wear black to Hawkins's séance since the purpose was to speak to a recently departed gentleman. As they rode in Hadrian's coach to Clerkenwell, Hadrian had applauded her choice and regretted he hadn't thought to do the same.

"I apologize for not suggesting it," Tilda said. "It was a last-minute decision. In fact, it was my grandmother's idea when I told her that the Duchess of Chester would be at the séance. She found it shocking that Her Grace would emerge from mourning to attend."

"How did your grandmother know the duchess was in mourning?"

"She read it in the newspaper. There are countless stories pertaining to the Levitation Killer, and the duchess has been identified as a patron of the spiritualism society."

Hadrian frowned. "These murders and everything associated with them are the talk of London."

They arrived at Hawkins's house, where a constable stood outside. He stopped Tilda and Hadrian before they could approach the front door.

"Are you here for the séance?" the constable asked.

Tilda didn't recognize the young man. "We are. I am Miss Wren, and this is Lord Ravenhurst. May I ask your name? My father was with the Metropolitan Police."

The constable's expression lit up. "Thomas Wren?"

Nodding, Tilda asked, "You've heard of him?"

"I have indeed. My father worked with him. I'm Phillip Gibbs."

Tilda thought the name Gibbs sounded vaguely familiar but didn't recall the man specifically. "Is your father still with the police?"

"He's a sergeant in F Division. I'm in G, which is why I'm stationed here."

"Aren't there supposed to be two of you?" Hadrian asked.

Gibbs nodded. "The other constable is at the door at the back of the house. We'll make sure no one is allowed inside who isn't supposed to be." He gave them a firm look that showed his intent to keep everyone safe.

"I feel secure knowing you are here," Tilda said warmly.

They continued to the door and were greeted by a familiar face—Michael Crocker.

"Good evening, my lord, Miss Wren." Crocker welcomed them inside.

"Evening, Crocker. How pleasant to see you here." Hadrian escorted Tilda into the entrance hall.

"Have you been promoted to butler in this household?" Tilda asked.

"I have." Crocker gave them a proud smile. "This way." He led them to the parlor where they'd met with Hawkins the other day.

Several other people were already there, but no one Tilda recognized. Their host approached them. "Welcome, my lord, Miss Wren. I'm grateful you could come this evening."

He offered his hand first to Tilda and then to Hadrian who'd already removed his gloves. Tilda's breath snagged as she wondered if Hadrian was seeing a vision. Upon releasing Hawkins, Hadrian looked at her and shook his head subtly. She took that to mean he hadn't seen anything. Perhaps because the touch had been brief.

Tilda noticed a woman standing on the other side of the table. She wore black, including a heavy veil that obscured her features. "Is that Her Grace?" she asked quietly.

Hawkins glanced toward the woman. "No, that is Miss Sullivan. Her Grace is not yet here. Indeed, I don't expect her for a short while. She prefers to be the last to arrive. Please excuse me whilst I greet the next guest."

Hadrian guided Tilda farther into the parlor, but not too far from the door. "I want to be close when the duchess arrives."

"Is that so we can pounce?" Tilda asked wryly as she also removed her gloves and tucked them into her reticule.

A smile flitted across his mouth. "I want to introduce you, and yes, I thought that would give you an opportunity—however brief—to perhaps ask one question."

"I appreciate your forward thinking." Tilda looked toward the doorway, where Hawkins was greeting an older gentleman with thick, round spectacles.

"Miss Sullivan is coming this way," Hadrian murmured.

Tilda pivoted as the veiled lady approached them. She was slightly hunched, but still tall for a woman.

"Good evening," the woman rasped, her scratchy voice revealing advanced age or perhaps the ravages of respiratory damage. "I am Miss Cordelia Sullivan. I belong to the London Spiritualism Society and often participate in séances." She offered her hand to Tilda.

"I am Miss Matilda Wren." Tilda took the woman's hand, which was encased in a knit glove. Except Tilda felt the warmth of Miss Sullivan's bare palm against hers. Dropping her gaze to their clasped hands, Tilda removed her hand and looked at the woman's exposed palm.

Miss Sullivan chuckled, a deep, rich sound. "I prefer to keep my hands covered, but touching with bare skin is necessary for the energy of the séance. I knit my own gloves for these occasions." She clasped her hands together in front of her waist.

Tilda wished she could see the woman's face. She possessed a charming demeanor. "Ingenious. I'm afraid I've no talent for such endeavors."

"I'm sure you have plenty of other talents," Miss Sullivan assured her. "What brings you to the séance this evening?"

"We attended one the other night with Mrs. Frost," Hadrian replied.

Miss Sullivan tipped her head toward Hadrian. "My apologies. I did not introduce myself to you. An oversight, for I'm afraid I already know who you are, Lord Ravenhurst. Mr. Hawkins told me you would be here tonight, and I deduced you must be the esteemed earl."

"What brought you to that conclusion?" Tilda asked.

"Just look at him, my dear. If this man isn't an earl, I will eat my veil." She emitted another low, husky laugh.

"It is difficult to argue with that," Tilda said, flashing a smile toward Hadrian, who did not seem amused.

"I do apologize, my lord," Miss Sullivan went on. "It was rather gauche of me to ignore you. At my age, I find I prefer the company of like-minded people, which are primarily those of the gentler sex. To be perfectly honest, Mr. Hawkins told me your companion is a private investigator, and I am *most* intrigued by that. Are you truly investigating the murders of Mrs. Frost and Mr. Ward?"

"I am," Tilda replied.

"She has solved several murders, in fact," Hadrian told the older woman.

Miss Sullivan gasped. "Goodness. That is astonishing. Are you close to finding the killer?"

"That is difficult to say." Tilda edged closer to the woman.

"Since you've attended many séances and are familiar with the society, can you think of anyone who would want to kill the mediums?"

"Absolutely not. They are lovely people. I am aghast that someone would kill them."

"And worried too, I imagine," Tilda said. "It doesn't concern you to attend the séance tonight?"

Miss Sullivan gave her head a shake, which sent the veil moving about her shoulders. "Not at all, especially since there are constables present. I am glad the society has continued to conduct séances. Perhaps I am being selfish, but I would hate to see them stop, even temporarily."

Tilda noted the arrival of another woman. Of average height and with a somewhat thick middle, she also wore black and a veil, though hers was sheer enough to allow her facial features to be seen, while Miss Sullivan's was not.

"Her Grace has arrived," Miss Sullivan said.

Hawkins announced the duchess's arrival. Everyone in the room bowed or curtsied, including Tilda. She worried that Hadrian had missed his chance to intercept her immediately, but he moved toward her with alacrity.

Tilda looked to Miss Sullivan, murmuring, "Please excuse me," before following Hadrian.

Hadrian approached the duchess with a mild smile. "Good evening, Duchess."

Though Tilda hadn't had much occasion to recall formal address, she knew that Hadrian could call her "Duchess" as her peer. Tilda, however, and everyone else here, would call her "Your Grace."

"Ravenhurst," the duchess replied. Her voice sounded a bit tremulous. "It's been some time."

Hadrian inclined his head. "Indeed it has. I am deeply sorry for your loss. I understand Mr. Ward was a special person to you."

The duchess cleared her throat. "Like a son." She sounded stronger now.

"Allow me to present my friend, Miss Matilda Wren." Hadrian took a small step to the right to allow for Tilda to present the duchess with another curtsey.

"I am honored to make your acquaintance, Your Grace."

The duchess did not reply. She turned her head slightly to address Hadrian once more, and Tilda wondered if she was invisible. "What brings you to this séance?" the duchess asked. "Are you a patron of the spiritualism society?"

"I am not. I attended a séance the other evening—conducted by Mrs. Frost—and wanted to come tonight."

"Be warned," the duchess said thickly. "They are addictive. Were you close with Mrs. Frost? Perhaps we should try to contact her as well."

"I was not," Hadrian said. "Her death is a great loss."

Hawkins nodded in agreement, his features solemn. "We are deeply saddened by the deaths of Deborah and Cyril. But tonight we will hear from Cyril and know that he is well and safe in the spirit realm."

The duchess turned her head toward Hawkins. "That is my fervent hope. May we please begin?"

"Certainly," Hawkins said quickly. He addressed the room. "Please take your seats." He turned to the duchess. "You are at number ten, of course."

Tilda wondered if "of course" meant that was her usual seat. "Where would you like Lord Ravenhurst and I to sit?" Tilda asked.

Hawkins gave his head a shake. "I neglected to tell you, my apologies. Miss Wren, you will be at number six, and my lord, you will be at number five." He moved to escort the duchess to her chair.

Tilda saw that Miss Sullivan was making her way back around the table. She stopped at number eleven. "I see that Miss

Sullivan will be next to Her Grace," she whispered to Hadrian. "That does not follow the typical man-woman arrangement."

"The same as the vision I saw with Hawkins seated beside Montrose," Hadrian noted. "It seems Hawkins does not adhere to that rule, despite him saying it was typical."

"There must be a reason," Tilda murmured.

"I'm sure it's something to do with *energy*." Hadrian did not roll his eyes, but if that action had a sound, he'd made it with his sardonic stress on the word *energy*.

When everyone had taken their places, Hawkins sat at number twelve and smiled serenely. He took a long, deep breath before speaking. "Good evening, friends and neighbors. Tonight, we honor the memory of our dear friend, Cyril Ward. Hopefully, we will speak with him, or perhaps someone who is with him."

As Hawkins spoke, Crocker went about the room extinguishing all light except the large branch of candles at the center of the table. The young man then moved to stand in the corner, his hands clasped behind his back.

"Let us join hands," Hawkins said before closing his eyes.

Heat flushed through Tilda as she took Hadrian's hand. His touch never failed to heighten her awareness of him. And of the attraction she felt toward him. Still. Apparently, it didn't matter that she didn't want to feel that way. Her mind and body were not in alignment.

The man on Tilda's opposite side held her hand loosely. Tilda wondered how he knew Hawkins and whether he was a member of the society.

Silence reigned for several moments. Tilda watched their host as well as the duchess. Miss Sullivan sat between them, and Tilda wondered why she and the duchess had been placed next to one another. It seemed that Miss Sullivan was leaning slightly toward Hawkins.

"I would ask that you all clear your mind of excess thoughts and direct your energy toward the spirit realm. Think of Cyril

Ward. Say his name over and over, either silently or aloud if you are moved to do so."

Tilda sent Hadrian a sideways glance. His lips were pressed tightly together, as if he were determined not to speak. Or as if he was annoyed. Tilda gathered it was likely both.

Cool air moved over the table, causing the candles to flicker. Tilda looked about to see the source of the breeze, but the candlelight from the center of the table did not provide enough illumination for her to see into the corners of the room.

"My guide is with us," Hawkins announced, though he did not open his eyes. "He says he has seen Cyril and that Cyril is well!"

Murmurs sounded around the table. The duchess bent her head.

Hawkins's brow creased. "He also says that Cyril is there, that he wishes to speak."

The table moved then, a gentle rolling. Hawkins flinched, his body jerking forward and then back against the chair. His chin lifted, but his eyes remained closed. When he next spoke, his voice had altered. His accent shifted, making him sound as if he hailed from north of London, in the middle of the country.

"My dear Agatha, I am so pleased you are here," Hawkins said. Though perhaps he was speaking as Ward.

Tilda felt the unknown man beside her tense. She glanced over at him. He had long sideburns and a crooked nose.

"Oh, Cyril!" the duchess exclaimed. "I am bereft!"

"Do not be," Hawkins—or Cyril—said. "It was my time, and I am quite safe here in the spirit realm, not that I ever doubted I would be." Hawkins did not open his eyes, nor did he turn his head toward the duchess.

"It is too cruel for me to lose you after losing my son," the duchess nearly wailed. "How am I to carry on? I wish I could be in the spirit realm with you and my beloved boy."

"Have strength, Agatha," Hawkins replied in Cyril's voice.

"The society is here to support you. Lysander and Victor will guide you. You mustn't be distressed."

"I fear I cannot help it, my dearest Cyril." The duchess sniffed, then took a long, wavering breath. "What am I to do?"

She sounded so forlorn that Tilda could not help but feel sorry for her. Whether this was real or not, she wasn't sure if it was helpful or cruel. Because in the end, the duchess could not be with her son or with Cyril, not unless she died. Which, of course, would mean there was a spirit realm where everyone gathered after death. Tilda truly hadn't spent much time thinking of such matters. But now that she did, she understood the woman's desire to be reunited with someone she'd lost. Tilda would give anything to see her father again.

"You are to continue on," Hawkins as Cyril advised. "You will wake every morning as you normally do, taking your special tea. And you will walk each day around your garden, just as we used to do. You have not walked since I left, have you?" He sounded almost as if he were admonishing her, but his tone was gentle.

The duchess's head dipped once more. "No, I have not. How well you know me."

"You must promise to stop crying as you gaze at my portrait. No good can come from so much grief, especially since you needn't grieve me. Not when we can still be together like this."

"Can we?" the duchess asked hopefully. "I miss you terribly. But if we can continue our chats with Mr. Hawkins as our intermediary, I may just be able to manage."

"Of course we will continue our talks," Cyril said. "For as long as I am able. Until you join me here in the spirit realm."

"How I long for that day!"

"Do not wish for that, Agatha," Cyril cautioned. "You've much life to live yet."

The duchess stilled. "How much?"

"I cannot say."

"But you must know," the duchess persisted. When he did not respond, she sighed. "I wish you would tell me."

"It is time for me to go for now, Agatha. Until next time." Hawkins twitched again, his body shuddering several times before his eyes fluttered open.

"Is he gone?" the duchess asked.

"Yes," Hawkins replied gently. "But I'm sure he will return another night."

The duchess began to weep softly. Surprisingly—at least to Tilda—she did not release the hands of those next to her.

"There is another spirit who wishes to pass a message to one of our guests," Hawkins said. "Let us see to whom they wish to speak."

The medium spoke the name of the person seated at number one. There was a single rap in response, which meant no. He continued around the table until he reached Hadrian. The response was also no.

Tilda was aware of the fact that the table had a hollow pedestal within by which someone was delivering these responses. If that much was fake, was Hawkins's channeling of Ward also false?

Hawkins called out Tilda's name. The answer was three raps.

Yes.

Tilda stiffened. Though she wanted to see her father again, she knew in her heart it wasn't possible. She did not want to receive a message from the spirit realm, even if it was real. Whilst that may be comforting to some people, it was not to her. Especially in this instance, when she had not asked to communicate with any spirits. It felt … intrusive.

"No, thank you," she said clearly.

She was aware of everyone's eyes on her, including Hadrian's. He no doubt gazed at her with understanding, but the rest of them were likely watching her with bated breath. She did not care to be the source of their entertainment, for that was surely what a séance amounted to.

Hawkins's eyes clamped shut and he jerked. "Tilda, darling. Do you have my hat?"

Tilda's blood went cold. How would Hawkins know about her father's hat? It was one of the few belongings of her father's that she'd kept after his death. But he'd never called her "Tilda, darling." He'd called her Tilly when she was young and then Til as she'd grown older.

This couldn't be real. But then how did Hawkins know about the hat? Was it another guess that had proven correct? Or was it a memory Hawkins had seen when he'd taken her hand as he'd greeted her earlier? It *could* be a memory, for Hadrian was never able to hear what was said. It would make sense for Hawkins to call her by the wrong name.

Tilda was torn between wanting to end this immediately and trying to determine what was happening. She felt Hadrian squeeze her hand and looked over at him. His expression was one of deep concern and care.

In the end, self-preservation won out, and Tilda released the hands of the men on either side of her. She did not want to be the center of this spectacle, whether it was real or not.

Hawkins's eyes opened. "The circle has been broken." He looked to Tilda. "You did not wish to speak with your father?"

"No. My apologies for ending the séance so abruptly, but I was not prepared for that. I did not realize spirits would come and speak to anyone in the circle."

"Oh yes, that happens sometimes. I'm sorry for your discomfort," Hawkins said kindly. "I understand that it can be overwhelming. We can try again next time when you are prepared."

The hell they would. Tilda had no intention of becoming entertainment for anyone. She was even more invested in discovering the truth behind the society's séance performances.

Everyone else had released their hands. Crocker moved about the parlor relighting candles.

Tilda pushed her chair back from the table, and Hadrian rushed to stand and hold it for her.

"You're upset," he said quietly.

"I was taken off guard. I'm fine." She turned toward him and kept her voice low. "I would like to know how Hawkins knew about my father's hat."

Hadrian arched a brow but didn't say anything because Hawkins was approaching them.

Their host gave Tilda an apologetic look. "I am sorry to have surprised you like that. I'm afraid the spirits can be very forceful sometimes."

Was he saying Tilda's father was an aggressive spirit? Tilda would no more believe that than she thought any of them could levitate.

"Forgive me for ruining the séance."

"You did nothing of the kind." Hawkins gave her an encouraging smile. "I hope you'll stay for dinner. Crocker is pouring wine. That may settle your nerves." He departed, and Tilda resisted the urge to glower after him.

"I do not have *nerves*," she grumbled.

"Would you care for wine anyway?" Hadrian asked.

"I suppose." She watched as Hadrian made his way to the corner where Crocker was filling wine glasses on a small sideboard.

"Are you all right, Miss Wren?" The unmistakable husky voice of Miss Sullivan drew Tilda to pivot.

"I am, thank you."

"You went quite pale." Miss Sullivan sounded concerned.

"I was surprised by what happened."

Miss Sullivan grasped Tilda's hand. "You must listen to the spirits when they wish to speak. You never know what unfinished business they need to conclude."

Tilda's blood chilled once more. She hated the way her father had died—so suddenly and violently. He'd deserved much better, and so had she. Not being able to tell him that she loved him, that she would miss him, that he was the best person she'd ever known was salt in a wound that never seemed to fully heal. To think that her father was somewhere with the same open wound was agony. Still, none of that was fodder to entertain these people.

"I would think that mediums could better control what happens in a séance," Tilda said. "There is … grief involved, and some people may not wish to share that publicly."

"I do understand," Miss Sullivan said kindly. "I think the mediums believe that if someone is attending a séance, they are open to conversing with the spirit realm. That is, after all, the point."

Tilda couldn't help feeling as though she were being scolded, however politely. "That was not made clear to me."

Miss Sullivan gave Tilda's hand a gentle squeeze, their bare palms pressing together, then released her.

Hadrian returned with two glasses and handed one to Tilda. He looked to Miss Sullivan, who abruptly took the other one from him. She did so almost clumsily, her hand covering his briefly before she managed to clasp the glass.

"Pardon me," she said with a throaty chuckle. "Thank you, my lord."

"My pleasure," Hadrian said, though Tilda was almost certain the wine had been for him. "Will you be staying for dinner?"

Tilda hoped so. She wanted to see the woman's face.

"I'm afraid not." Miss Sullivan held her veil out and lifted the wine glass beneath it to take a sip. "It was lovely to meet you both. I hope we'll encounter one another again." She turned and walked away.

Hadrian looked at his hand, his lips bent in a slight frown.

"What's wrong?" Tilda asked.

"When Miss Sullivan touched my hand, I felt an odd sensation. It was akin to an electric current, but also cold at the same time." Hadrian gave his head a shake. "What did she say to you?"

Tilda related their brief conversation. "I found her counsel annoying, which was disappointing since I was rather charmed by her before the séance. I wonder about her relationship to Hawkins, besides being a member of the society, and why she and the duchess were seated next to one another."

"Perhaps they share a special energy." Hadrian waggled his brows.

Tilda stifled a smile. "Did you see anything during the séance?"

"From the woman on my other side, you mean? I did not." His gaze moved toward the doorway. "The duchess is leaving."

"We should bid her goodnight."

"Too late," Hadrian said. "She's already left the parlor."

"Would you mind if we take our leave?" Tilda asked. "I don't think I can tolerate dinner after what happened."

"I don't mind at all."

Tilda returned her glass to the table where Crocker stood. "I didn't drink any, if that matters." She set the wine down.

"I hope you aren't too unsettled, Miss Wren," the butler said earnestly. "The spirits mean you no harm. I think you should try to speak with your father."

"I'll have to think on it," she said noncommittally. "Have a good evening, Crocker."

She and Hadrian went to make their excuses to Hawkins and left a few minutes later.

Once they were in Hadrian's coach on their way to Marylebone, Tilda stroked her cheek. The feel of her gloved fingertips prompted her to recall Miss Sullivan's odd gloves.

"I find it strange that we could see nothing of Miss Sullivan save her palms. Not that we were able to see them so much as feel them when she touched us both." Tilda narrowed her eyes. "I'd thought that perhaps Hawkins had seen my memories when he took my hand after we arrived, but it could also have been Miss Sullivan. She touched me before the séance and could have relayed what she saw to Hawkins. It's also possible she could have whispered to him during the séance. With her thick veil, there was no way to see if she spoke."

Hadrian stared at her. "Have you convinced yourself that these people are able to see memories as I am?"

"It seems the most plausible explanation at this point." She blew out a frustrated breath. "Unless they truly are just making rather accurate guesses."

"I still think that is possible," Hadrian said evenly. "Ward's supposed spirit seemed to know things about the duchess, but I think it's highly likely Hawkins could have known enough to offer believable estimations." He paused before crossing his arms. "However the medium is able to convincingly speak with the spirit realm—whether by guessing about things or using a power such as mine—have we concluded that it's all a fraud?"

"Not yet." Tilda saw his eyes darken and held up a hand. "We've still more investigation to do. I wish to speak to Eldred and find out what happened to make him angry at the society. Not just because he may be a suspect as the Levitation Killer. Perhaps he has evidence of fraud."

"Shall we call on him tomorrow?"

Tilda nodded. "We don't have his address, but I think we must visit Teague at Scotland Yard and persuade him to share it. I'd also like to travel to Swindon and question Mallory's former partner. I'm most curious as to why he was denigrating Mallory before leaving London and returning home."

"Let's take the train to Swindon on Sunday then." Hadrian fixed her with an expectant stare. "I think you want to be able to confirm that someone has the same power as I do."

"If that is how they are allegedly speaking to the dead, then yes."

"What if we cannot do that?" he asked. "What if we are only able to catch them pretending to levitate or controlling the table? What about their other tricks, such as the cold air that blows at the start of the séance? Or moving objects, which we've yet to see?"

"This is why we must continue investigating. I am relieved there was no murder today."

"As am I." Hadrian uncrossed his arms and leaned back against the squab. "Perhaps the murderer is finished."

Tilda looked out the window into the night. "That may be, but we will still find them and bring them to justice."

CHAPTER 12

The following afternoon, Hadrian arrived at Tilda's grandmother's to fetch Tilda for their visit to Scotland Yard.

Vaughn answered the door as quickly as his trudging gait allowed. He smiled upon seeing Hadrian. "Good afternoon, my lord." He welcomed Hadrian inside.

The small, marble-floored entrance hall had become quite familiar to Hadrian now. He felt an instant sense of comfort and welcome.

"If you'd care to wait in the parlor, Miss Wren will be down shortly. She ran back upstairs to fetch a different hat."

"Thank you, Vaughn." Hadrian moved into the parlor, which was empty. Often, Tilda's grandmother could be found seated in a chair near the windows, where she would work on her embroidery. There was a round table where he'd taken tea with them.

He'd never spent time investigating the space, however. Likely because he hadn't had occasion to be here alone. He moved toward the hearth and noticed a photograph of a man in a police uniform. That had to be Tilda's father.

Though he wasn't smiling, Hadrian had the sense that the man had done so often. He realized that wasn't something he could tell from a photograph. Rather, it was something he presumed based on what he knew of the man—and his daughter and mother, who lived here in this house. Wren looked a bit like his daughter, particularly in the chin, where he had a cleft very similar to Tilda's.

"Good afternoon, Lord Ravenhurst. It's always nice to see you."

Hadrian pivoted upon hearing Mrs. Wren's voice. Tilda's grandmother wore an outdated gown of dove-gray trimmed with burgundy and a lace cap atop her white hair.

"The pleasure is mine, Mrs. Wren." Hadrian bowed.

Mrs. Wren went to sit in her chair by the window. "What is today's errand?"

"We will be calling on Detective Inspector Teague at Scotland Yard." And perhaps on Eldred if they could ascertain his address.

Hadrian wanted to know about the photograph on the mantel. "Am I correct in assuming that photograph is of your son?"

Mrs. Wren looked toward the mantel, her features softening. "Yes, that is my Thomas. I am grateful we have that. He looks so smart in his uniform. His father was quite proud of him."

The mention of Tilda's grandfather pulled at Hadrian's heart. He'd died more than thirty years ago, so Tilda had never known him. But she felt as though she did through the memories of him shared by her father and grandmother. During their first investigation together, they'd learned that her grandfather hadn't simply died from falling from a horse as everyone had believed. He'd been murdered. His killer was now dead, but that wasn't a comfort. Tilda hadn't told her grandmother the truth, having decided there was no reason to. Hadrian could find no quarrel with that.

"Tilda misses him so. As do I." Mrs. Wren looked toward Hadrian. "Do you also miss your father?"

"Not in the same way," he said. Not at all really, but he didn't want to say that. Hadrian was spared further discussion by Tilda's arrival.

She looked lovely in her burgundy gown with a matching hat. She pulled her gloves on, and her reticule hung from her wrist. "I'm ready."

Hadrian gave her grandmother another bow. "It's been lovely visiting with you."

Mrs. Wren smiled up at him. "You have brightened my day, my lord."

"You must really call me Hadrian, I think."

"Indeed?" Tilda's grandmother laughed softly. "I'm not sure that's appropriate, but I suppose I must if you say so."

"I do." He grinned at her before escorting Tilda from the house, bidding Vaughn goodbye on the way.

Leach greeted Tilda and handed her into the coach. She took her usual seat, and Hadrian sat opposite her. He still mourned the closeness of sitting with her on a shared seat, but he was glad to be conducting this ever-widening investigation with her.

Teague was, thankfully, present at Scotland Yard, and they went directly to his office. He stood from behind his desk as Tilda and Hadrian entered.

"Afternoon Ravenhurst, Miss Wren. Please sit." He gestured toward the seating area and joined them there.

"I wanted to know if you were able to question Eldred," Tilda said, moving straight to the purpose of their visit.

Teague's brows climbed. "You learned his name?"

"I am a private investigator," she replied drily.

The detective inspector smiled. "And a good one at that. Yes, I spoke with Octavius Eldred yesterday. He is an odd fellow. He attended a séance with Ward a few months ago. Eldred claims he was recently blackmailed about something that no one alive would know. He deduced that Ward, who spoke to the dead, was behind it." Teague shook his head.

"You don't believe it's possible that Ward obtained information from the spirit realm to blackmail Eldred?" Hadrian asked sardonically.

Teague sniggered. "Would you?"

"Absolutely not."

Tilda frowned briefly. "Yet, Eldred says no one who is alive would know this information?"

"That is what he insists," Teague said. "And he was *most* insistent. I have to think someone else *did* know. But why would they wait until now to blackmail Eldred?" He shook his head. "Unfortunately, I didn't find him helpful. The only thing we have to go on is the location of where he was to pay the extortion—a grocer in Bedfordbury. I sent a constable to question them, but they said they didn't know anything about blackmail, nor had anyone ever left money there."

"They could be lying," Hadrian suggested.

"Perhaps, but I've no way to know," Teague said ruefully. "I'm hopeful we can find another blackmail victim."

"What was the blackmail about?" she asked.

Teague exhaled. "That was the most frustrating part of our conversation. Eldred refused to say. He claimed disclosing the information would incriminate him."

"That is tantamount to admitting he is a criminal," Hadrian said. "Do you think he also may have killed Ward and Mrs. Frost?"

"I doubt it. Whilst he may have had motive to kill Ward if he was indeed being blackmailed by the medium, I can't come up with a motive for him to kill Mrs. Frost." Teague lifted a shoulder and frowned. "As it happens, Eldred had an alibi—he has been in Bath the past week and only arrived home last evening. His manservant confirmed this. I would add that Eldred doesn't seem large or strong enough to have positioned the bodies without help."

"Well, that is a disappointing dead end," Tilda said. "Though learning that the spiritualism society may engage in extortion is interesting. Perhaps there are other victims, including one who was angry enough to kill."

"I have considered that and will be looking for more evidence. I trust you'll be doing the same," he said with a half smile.

"Of course," Tilda replied. "Did the pearl earring we found at Mrs. Frost's offer any help?"

Teague shook his head. "I believe you already know that it did not belong to Mrs. Frost. We asked everyone we interviewed with the society about it, and no one could recall seeing it. I also took it to a jeweler for assessment. It doesn't bear any jeweler markings and was cheaply made. Since Mrs. Frost held séances in the drawing room upstairs, that earring could have belonged to anyone who visited. I'm not sure it's an actual clue to the murder."

"Would you mind if we question Mr. Eldred?" Tilda asked. "I should like to understand his perceptions of Ward and how he worked as a medium. It would aid my investigation."

"I've no opposition to that. If you happen to learn the purpose of the blackmail, I hope you'll tell me."

"Certainly," Tilda replied.

After obtaining Eldred's direction, Tilda and Hadrian left Scotland Yard. Eldred was located near Bloomsbury Square, and they decided to go there straightaway.

Hadrian crossed his arms over his chest as he surveyed Tilda from the opposite seat in the coach. "Your real purpose in interviewing Eldred is to determine whether the society used his memory to blackmail him."

"Yes. And if they did, I have to think there are others. One of them may be the murderer."

"How do we go about finding them?"

She gave him a sly smile. "We investigate."

~

*T*ilda thought about how they might flush out other blackmail victims. Eldred had done them a favor by barging into Ward's séance and declaring his anger. However, no one else had done anything like that. Perhaps there weren't any other victims. But Tilda doubted that.

She and Hadrian departed the coach and went to Eldred's door. A housekeeper showed them into a cozy sitting room where Eldred was already seated.

Hadrian made their introductions whilst Eldred regarded them dubiously. "You've come to speak with me about the London Spiritualism Society? I've nothing good to say about it."

"That is quite all right," Tilda replied with a smile. "We are seeking the truth about their activities. I am a private investigator."

"You may as well sit then." Eldred waved them down. He looked to be in his sixties, and Teague's assessment that the man was not large or strong enough to move bodies over stair railings seemed accurate. Eldred was slight of frame, and though he was seated, appeared short of stature. His head was mostly bald, save a semi-circle of grayish-white around the sides and back, but he had a neat, gray goatee.

Tilda and Hadrian perched together on a small settee. They weren't quite touching, but they were close enough for Tilda to be utterly aware of his proximity. She could smell his soap or cologne—whatever it was—and reminded herself not to notice such things. They were too … stirring.

"How did you come to speak to me?" Eldred asked.

"I confess we heard of you at the spiritualism society," Tilda said somewhat apologetically. "Someone mentioned you were disgruntled."

He fixed his gaze on Hadrian. "Are you a patron? They only want your money. Your set is captivated by spiritualism, but they are a racket."

"I am not a patron." Hadrian twisted his lips into a brief smirk. "I gravely doubt their ability to move objects or levitate, let alone speak with the dead."

Eldred slapped his palm on the arm of his chair. "You're wrong about that last one. They absolutely can speak with the dead."

"How are you so certain?" Tilda asked.

"Because I was blackmailed by someone who knew something that no one could know," he declared with outrage. Settling back in his chair, he continued in a more measured tone. "I received a letter the week before last about something that happened twenty years ago. The only other person who knew of it died nearly ten years ago. There is absolutely no way anyone could have known what to write in that letter unless they spoke with a dead man. That means Ward had to have been the blackmailer."

"You think Ward communicated with this dead person who knew your secret?" Hadrian asked.

"It's the only thing that makes sense," Eldred insisted. "My former colleague is dead, and he would not have told anyone what we did. The consequences would have been far too great. Even if he decided to unburden himself on his deathbed, why wouldn't anything have come of it until now—nearly a decade after his demise?" Eldred shook his head firmly. "The only explanation is that Ward is behind the blackmail."

"Is it not at all possible that your colleague confided in someone?" If no one possessed the same power as Hadrian, or one similar, there would have to be another explanation. Perhaps they needed to determine if the society made inquiries about the people for whom they conducted seances. Tilda could envision someone like herself working for the society in order to collect information about people that could be used in séances.

"I would be shocked if he did," Eldred replied firmly. "And again, why wouldn't the truth have surfaced before now?"

"Can you tell us about the séance you attended?" Tilda asked.

"There were two. My sister heard about the society and wanted to contact our mother. She'd died a few months earlier and my sister … well, she missed her terribly. I agreed to attend a séance with her, even though I suspected it was merely a performance."

"That was kind of you," Hadrian said.

"At Ward's request, my sister brought a cameo that had belonged to my mother. He said that having an item associated with the person we were trying to contact helped the spirit find us. However, our mother did not appear at that first séance. I was certain it was a swindle, except they did not charge a fee." He pursed his lips. "Of course, they did for the second time, which they insisted would be successful. I didn't want to return, but my sister was so upset that I could not refuse her.

"Ward asked me to also bring something. He hoped two items would allow our mother to hear my sister's call. My sister brought several things, whilst I brought a silver dish that I'd given to our mother many years ago. Ward contacted our mother, and she spoke through him. It was most disconcerting. However, I was convinced she was speaking. She said she'd cherished that dish more than anything. It was how she knew I'd become a success." His face flushed, and Tilda presumed he was feeling a rush of emotion for his departed mother.

"That is very sweet," Tilda said softly. "Pardon my question, but did Ward touch you or your sister before or during the séance?"

Eldred shrugged. "I shook the man's hand when we arrived."

"Did you or your sister sit next to him?" Hadrian asked.

"No, there was a man between Ward and my sister."

Tilda wondered if that was Montrose. She and Hadrian

exchanged a quick glance before she asked, "Do you recall his name or what he looked like?"

Eldred's brow creased as he thought for a moment. "I don't remember his name, but he was Scottish. He had red hair and a red mustache to go with his nearly unintelligible accent."

That didn't sound like Montrose at all.

"Why didn't you attend a third séance?" Tilda imagined Ward would have invited them, especially if Eldred's sister was so eager to speak with their mother.

"My sister wanted to, but I refused to pay to continue, and she does not have the funds. She understood. Then, after several weeks went by, I received a letter extorting me to pay two hundred pounds to a grocer in Bedfordbury or a damaging event from my past would be exposed."

"Exposed to whom?" Hadrian asked. "The police?"

"The letter was not explicit. I didn't care because I could not imagine what proof the blackmailer would have. What he referred to happened twenty years ago, and there were no witnesses to it except myself and my deceased colleague."

"So you assume that Ward somehow received information from this dead person and used it to blackmail you. That seems rather skeptical, doesn't it?" Hadrian mused.

"I tell you that is precisely what happened! That silver dish … it was part of that … event from the past. I have to think Ward used it to contact my deceased colleague." Eldred scowled. "I should not have brought it. You see, Ward had to be the blackmailer."

"That is why you confronted him," Tilda said. "Why did you choose to do it during a séance?"

"I didn't actually. That was a coincidence."

Hadrian frowned at the man. "Why did you threaten Ward?"

"Because the man was despicable. I told him so. I said if he didn't leave me alone, I would make sure everyone knew he was a fraud and that his levitation was an exceedingly poor parlor trick."

"Did you see him levitate?" Tilda asked.

Eldred nodded. "At the first séance. It looked horribly fake to me."

"You believe he can speak to the dead, but not that he could levitate?" Hadrian sounded dubious.

"I can *see* the levitation with my own eyes." Eldred jabbed his finger toward his face. "The man did not appear to be floating so much as standing on his toes or something. But I cannot explain how he knew about my past." He spoke vehemently and now took deep breaths to calm himself.

"You did not pay the blackmail to the grocer?" Tilda asked.

"No. I wasn't going to give them the satisfaction. Who would they tell and how would they prove anything? I waited to see if I would receive a second letter, but I did not. Then Ward was murdered, and I assumed he was behind it. I have to think he was blackmailing others, and someone wasn't going to let him get away with it."

"You mean someone killed him," Hadrian said.

"It certainly wasn't me," Eldred declared sharply. "I will tell you what I already told the police. I was in Bath when Ward was killed. And when that other medium was murdered too."

Tilda found Eldred credible despite his agitation. "Why didn't you report the extortion to the police?"

"That is a difficult crime to prosecute and is often ignored." Eldred cleared his throat. "And I preferred to let the matter die, as it were."

"You want your past to stay a secret," Hadrian said. "I confess I'm surprised you wanted to attend a séance to speak with the spirit realm if you had matters with a deceased person that you wished to keep secret. That seems risky."

"I didn't think the medium would contact anyone in the spirit realm other than my mother." Angry furrows creased his brow.

"It wasn't at all fair that he would communicate with someone else."

Tilda wholeheartedly agreed, of course. Hadrian sent her a look that told her he knew what she was thinking. She gave him a subtle nod toward the doorway to indicate she was ready to leave.

"Thank you, Mr. Eldred, you've been most helpful," Hadrian said.

Tilda rose as Hadrian did the same. Eldred also stood, and Hadrian withdrew his glove to shake the man's hand, just as he'd told Tilda he would.

They left and Tilda hastened to the coach, waiting until they were inside to speak about what had just occurred.

Hadrian didn't wait for her question. "You're hoping I might have seen what happened twenty years ago that prompted the blackmail." He smiled. "You are in luck because I believe that is what I saw. The vision included a man wearing a very outmoded costume—it could have been twenty years ago—who was likely Eldred's colleague. I was experiencing Eldred's memory, and I saw him take a silver dish and slip it into his coat. The other man tucked something else into his coat, but I didn't quite catch what it was. It seemed clear to me that they were stealing things."

"That would be worthy of blackmail, I should think." Tilda pulled the small notebook from her reticule and spent several minutes scratching out notes. "This was a very helpful errand, thank you."

They arrived at Tilda's grandmother's house, and Hadrian departed the coach with Tilda to walk her to the door. "Should we visit the grocer in Bedfordbury?" he asked.

"I'm not sure since Teague didn't have any luck doing so. However, it would be helpful if we could somehow connect the grocer with the spiritualism society. It may be worth a visit. But that will have to wait, as tomorrow we travel to Swindon. Did you already purchase the tickets?"

"I did."

Vaughn opened the door and greeted them. "Welcome home, Miss Wren. A letter was delivered for you a short while ago." He gestured toward the small table in the entrance hall.

She glanced at the letter and saw the bold address: *Miss Wren*. Something about the flourish of the W pricked her curiosity. She plucked up the missive and quickly opened it.

Her flesh went cold, and the hair on her neck rose. Handing the note to Hadrian, she said, "I think the Levitation Killer wants to kill me next."

CHAPTER 13

*H*adrian practically snatched the letter from her. He quickly scanned the scrawled message.

Dear Miss Wren,
You must stop asking questions and nosing about in matters that do not concern you. If you do not, you may find yourself hanging from a staircase.

The offensive note was not signed.

A fury unlike Hadrian had ever known rose inside him. If the author of the message had been present, Hadrian would have torn him apart. How dare they threaten Tilda!

Holding the paper, he managed to pull one of his gloves off. He touched the note, practically crumpling it in his eagerness to see or feel *anything*. But there was nothing. What good was his bloody curse if it didn't work when he needed it most?

"You look quite angry," Tilda said, pulling him from his haze of rage.

"I am more than furious."

Tilda wordlessly inclined her head toward the paper in his grip.

Hadrian realized what she was asking—whether he'd seen anything. He gave his head a slight shake before swinging around to face Vaughn. "Who delivered this?"

The butler's features were creased, his eyes dark with worry. "A boy of about nine or ten. He thrust it at me and ran off."

Wiping his hand over his mouth, lest he start swearing aloud, Hadrian looked back to Tilda. "We must find who sent this."

Tilda met his gaze. "You are very upset."

"Aren't you?"

"I think it is unlikely someone will be able to poison me with prussic acid and hang me from the staircase. Unlike the other two victims, I have a full household. Now more than ever," she added with a smile that struck Hadrian as inappropriate. How could she make jests at a time like this?

And yet, she had a point. It did seem unlikely that the Levitation Killer would get to her here. "Then perhaps you should stay here at home until the killer is caught."

She gave him an exasperated look. "You just said we have to find who sent this. I can't do that from home."

Hell, he wasn't being entirely rational. How could he be when one of the people he cared most about had been threatened? He took a deep breath.

He did care deeply for her. Which was why he would ensure nothing happened to her. He pinned her with a heavy stare. "Will you promise to only leave here with me?"

"That is excessive. I do have errands, and I take walks. I also escort my grandmother to various places."

"Then allow me to give you a footman to be here and escort you when necessary." Hadrian already knew who he would assign the task. Brian was the burliest member of his household.

She hesitated a moment as she studied him. "You're going to insist, aren't you?"

"Yes." Still, he held his breath, waiting to see if she would argue.

"All right," she said on an exhale. "We should take this letter to Teague."

Hadrian was relieved she capitulated so easily. "We should. Immediately." He started toward the door.

Tilda lifted her hand. "Wait." She turned to Vaughn. "I don't want to alarm my grandmother. Please do not tell her about the note."

Vaughn nodded. "I understand. What will you tell her about the footman? She will notice a new addition to the household."

Pursing her lips, Tilda looked to Hadrian. "I don't want to worry her."

"Tell her I am being overly cautious since we are investigating the murders," Hadrian said. "You don't need to inform her that there has been an explicit threat against you." If Hadrian ever had the chance, he would dearly love to put his fist in the killer's face —at the very least. He struggled to agree with putting some criminals to death, but in this instance, he may feel differently.

What was happening with him? The depth of emotion he felt about this was … shocking.

"That is a reasonable plan, thank you," Tilda said to Hadrian before looking toward Vaughn. The butler inclined his head in response. "Please tell Grandmama we've gone back out."

They took their leave and strode quickly to the coach. Hadrian informed Leach they were returning to Scotland Yard, and after that, they'd be going to his house.

When they were settled in the coach, Tilda arched a brow at Hadrian. "Why are we going to Ravenhurst House?"

"So I can assign a footman to you as soon as possible."

"I see." Her brow pleated. "You are most concerned."

"And you are not as concerned as you should be. Someone has threatened your life." Hadrian's fury was calming slightly, but he was still angrier than he'd been in some time.

"I am taking this seriously," she said. "I agree that we must solve these crimes as quickly as possible." She fell silent a moment.

"What are you thinking?" Hadrian asked.

"That the Levitation Killer is threatening me because I am investigating the murders. Perhaps we are close to discovering their identity." Her gaze snapped to his. "*We*. What if you have already received a threat at Ravenhurst House?"

"I suppose we'll find out after we finish with Teague."

"Now who is the one who does not appear concerned?" she asked with a hint of exasperation.

"I am not going to worry about it until I know it's happened."

"How reasonable of you," Tilda said before frowning. "It is disappointing that you didn't see anything when you touched the letter."

"It's bloody infuriating," Hadrian spat. "What is the point of this curse if it can't help me when I need it?" He again considered that meeting someone who shared the same ability might actually be helpful.

When they arrived at Scotland Yard, Teague was just leaving. He was on his way home, in fact. But as soon as Tilda showed him the letter, he returned to his office, inviting them to join him.

Teague read the letter again as they sat down where they'd been just a short while earlier. "I'll need to keep this as evidence. This is a crime of breaking the peace."

"It pales next to murder," Tilda said.

Hadrian gave her a dark look. "It could end in murder."

"I'll dispatch a constable to watch your house." He met Hadrian's gaze, and Hadrian gave him a slight, appreciative nod.

"That isn't necessary," Tilda replied. "Hadrian is already going to assign me a footman."

Teague cast another look at Hadrian. "Whilst I appreciate Ravenhurst's gesture, a footman is not a constable. We will keep Miss Wren safe—you have my word."

Hadrian didn't doubt the man's intent. Still, he might decide to send Brian anyway.

"We called on Eldred earlier," Tilda said, diverting the topic. "He did not tell us what he did twenty years ago to be blackmailed, but based on things he said, I would guess he and a colleague stole some things from someone."

Hadrian wasn't sure if she would reveal that information to Teague since they had no proof aside from his vision. That was the drawback of the things he saw that helped them. On their own, they weren't evidence. The visions could only direct them to hopefully find the evidence they needed to prove someone's guilt.

"Thank you for sharing that information, though I'm not sure it helps us in any way." Teague exhaled with disappointment.

"No, I don't believe it does," Tilda said apologetically. "Hadrian and I are traveling to Swindon tomorrow to interview Roger Grenville. Perhaps we will learn something useful."

Teague's brows shot up. "Are you? I don't have enough men to send someone," he said bitterly. "Nor can I accompany you. It is Sunday, and if I don't spend a good portion of the day with my family, my wife will likely consign me to sleep here." He gestured to the room at large.

"We will conduct a thorough interview and let you know if we learn anything important," Tilda said.

"That sounds as though you are conducting investigative work for the Metropolitan Police." Hadrian sent Teague an expectant look.

"It does," Teague said with regret. "However, I cannot ask you to do that. I would be grateful if you shared what you learn, but I cannot compensate you for your work. What I *can* do is continue to share information with you in return. In fact, your mention of

Swindon has reminded me that we learned the spiritualism society headquarters is leased by Captain Owen Vale of Swindon. I won't ask you to call on him on behalf of the police." His tone indicated he very much hoped they would.

"Do you have any other information to share?" Tilda asked hopefully.

"I have a list of the society's founding members." Teague stood and went to his desk, where he fetched a piece of parchment. He handed it to Tilda. "You can't keep that, however."

"I'll just copy the names down." She removed her notebook from her reticule and began writing quickly. "Do you know who leased the other properties where the society's mediums lived?" She glanced at Hadrian. "The Duchess of Chester leased Ward's house, correct?"

Teague answered. "Yes. And Lysander Mallory signed the lease for Mrs. Frost's house."

"Interesting that he leased that property but not the head-quarters," Hadrian observed. "What about Hawkins's house?"

"We don't know that yet, but we'll find out on Monday, I hope," Teague said. "I'm not sure any of that is helpful. I have my constables interviewing people who have attended séances given by the society's mediums, but it is taking a great deal of time. So far, there has been nothing notable, such as blackmail, but I will keep you apprised."

Tilda closed her notebook and handed the list back to Teague. "I appreciate that."

"A few people have declined to speak to the constables," Teague said with a frown. "Notably, Her Grace, the Duchess of Chester."

"Would you like me to call on her?" Hadrian offered. "We saw her at the séance last night, and I believe she would receive us."

"That would be helpful, thank you." Teague wiped his hand over his face. "Once again, I am treating you as members of the police, and I cannot do that. You must do as you think best, my lord."

"As a member of the House of Lords, I am invested in the safety of our citizens. I will call on the duchess and ask her about the séances she's attended."

"I do wish we could find more evidence of blackmail," Tilda said. "I can't imagine Eldred is the only victim."

"But why would they even need to blackmail?" Teague asked. "The society takes in money from its patrons and members, and they charge a fee for conducting séances."

"They lease at least one property—in Rathbone Place," Tilda replied. "And perhaps two if they also own Hawkins's house in Clerkenwell. The society also employs many domestic servants as well as the mediums. Perhaps the society needs more money than it takes in and has resorted to blackmail. Or Cyril Ward took it upon himself to extort people, or perhaps only Eldred, but that seems difficult to explain, especially when we know he was receiving an allowance from Her Grace."

"You really are a fine investigator, Miss Wren. I am confident we will determine the identity of the Levitation Killer soon." Teague's lip curled. "How I loathe what the press has done to sensationalize this matter."

"It is a sensational case." Tilda stood. "We will bring it to a satisfactory end."

Teague rose. "Without further loss of life."

"Indeed." Hadrian wouldn't let anything happen to Tilda. They said goodbye to Teague and made plans to see him Monday, though he gave them his home address in case they learned something vital in Swindon.

When they were outside, Tilda asked if Hadrian wanted to call on the duchess now.

"Do you have the time for another errand?"

"I do, but what of her mourning?" Tilda asked. "Do you really think she'll receive us?"

Hadrian lifted a shoulder as they arrived at the coach. "Since she came to the séance last night and we were there, I think it's worth trying." He looked to Leach and gave him their next destination.

"Were there any surprising names on the list of society founders?" Hadrian asked as they started on their way.

"Roger Grenville was on the list, but I don't suppose that's surprising. I am very glad we planned this trip to Swindon."

"I am glad you will be gone from London after receiving the letter," Hadrian said.

"Only for a day, but if it will relieve your tension, I'll be glad of *that*." She gave him a small smile.

Though Hadrian had calmed since first reading the threatening letter she'd received, he was still agitated. Knowing that a constable would be looking over her house gave him comfort, but he wouldn't fully rest until the author of the letter had been caught.

Eyeing her across the coach, he hoped she wasn't troubled by his reaction to the letter. "Is it all right that I am concerned for you? We are friends—close friends, I think."

"We are," she agreed. "I hope we shall always remain friends."

"It sounds as though we are both committed to that." And Hadrian was most grateful. Aside from bringing him into a world of investigation that he found exciting and fulfilling, she'd been a wonderful support at a time in his life when he'd needed an understanding confidante. If not for her, he was nearly certain he would be struggling with his odd ability entirely by himself. That alone put Tilda in a unique position as the person he apparently trusted most in the world.

Tilda pulled him from his reverie. "There were two names missing from the list of founders—Miss Sullivan and Mr. Montrose."

Hadrian shook away his deep thoughts about their relationship and leaned back against the squab. "They must have joined later."

"Yes." Tilda shrugged.

They arrived at the duchess's house and departed the coach. A pair of gentlemen emerged from the house as they approached. Hadrian inclined his head toward Lysander Mallory and Victor Hawkins.

"Good afternoon," Hadrian said.

Mallory's hooded brown eyes surveyed them briefly. "Afternoon, my lord. Miss Wren."

"You were visiting the duchess?" Tilda asked.

"I have every day since Cyril's death," Mallory replied. "She says it is a comfort. After Victor's success with contacting Cyril last night, Her Grace requested we both visit today. She didn't mention that she was expecting you."

"We saw her last night, of course." Hadrian flicked a glance toward Hawkins. "However, we weren't able to speak for very long." That was all he was going to say. He glanced at Tilda, whose eyes gleamed with some unspoken communication, perhaps that she approved of what he said.

"I hope you enjoyed the séance last night," Hawkins said, his gaze settling on Tilda. "I did worry that you were upset about your father wanting to contact you."

"It was most startling," Tilda replied evenly. "Please don't let us keep you."

Hawkins touched the brim of his hat as he and Mallory stepped past them and walked away along the pavement.

Tilda looked after them. "I find it interesting that Mallory has called on the duchess every day since Ward's death."

"I expect she is their wealthiest patron," Hadrian said, escorting her to the door. "It makes sense that he would wish to continue their relationship following Ward's death."

Hadrian knocked, and the butler answered the door. Straightaway, Hadrian handed the man his card. The butler didn't hesitate to invite them inside.

Hadrian gave the man a brief smile. "Please tell the duchess we are here to speak with her about Mr. Ward's death. We are investigating the matter, which we think will be of interest to her."

"Thank you, my lord. Please wait here." The butler hastened into the staircase hall and went upstairs.

Hadrian noted how Tilda surveyed the entrance hall. Her gaze lingered on the paintings and a life-size statue of a woman in Roman garb. These things must seem extravagant to her.

"You should take the lead with our questions," Hadrian said.

Tilda nodded. "If she agrees to see us."

Hadrian would press the matter if she did not. However, that was not necessary as they were shown upstairs to the drawing room a few minutes later.

The duchess was once again dressed in black, though she was not wearing a veil. She sat near the hearth wearing a forlorn expression which carved deep lines into her round, jowled face. A black lace cap perched atop her gray hair.

"Good afternoon, Duchess," Hadrian said as he and Tilda moved toward the seating area.

"Ravenhurst." The duchess looked up at him, then glanced at Tilda. "And Miss Wren. Hanson said you are here to discuss Cyril, that you are investigating his … death." She blinked slowly as if she had difficulty saying that word.

"We are," Tilda replied. "I am a private investigator."

"Are you?" the duchess asked in surprise and with perhaps a mild derision. "How strange." She looked to Hadrian. "And why are you with her?"

"We work together investigating cases," he said. "May we sit?"

The duchess waved them toward a settee. Hadrian looked at Tilda, and they went to sit together.

"How did you come to work with one another in such an odd

manner?" The duchess eyed them dubiously. Again, her tone held a touch of disdain.

Though Hadrian had said that Tilda could lead their interview, he felt he needed to speak on their behalf in this instance. "I hired Miss Wren to investigate a matter. We worked together and have done so on several matters since."

"*You* hired her?" The duchess's surprise moved toward incredulity, which Hadrian found irritating. Though he should not. Most people would find hiring a woman private investigator to be … strange or odd—to use the duchess's words.

"I did, and I did so a second time." He stopped short of saying his mother had hired her too because he did not want to reveal their investigation into whether the mediums were frauds. "Miss Wren is extremely clever. Her grandfather was a magistrate, and her father was a sergeant in the Metropolitan Police." That he'd died before he was able to fulfill his promotion was not important. "Miss Wren is working very hard to find Mr. Ward's and Mrs. Frost's killer. I have every expectation she will."

The duchess now looked at Tilda with curiosity, which was an improvement from her earlier disdain, and from last night when she'd all but ignored Tilda. "That is high praise. I want nothing more than my poor Cyril's murderer to be brought to justice. I shall watch him hang with great glee."

Hadrian wasn't sure that would be possible. A law ending public execution was currently under discussion, and Hadrian was greatly in favor. Indeed, he supported eliminating capital punishment entirely.

"I see how distraught you are about Mr. Ward's passing," Tilda said with deep concern. "I would like to help you find the justice you seek. We encountered Mr. Mallory outside. He visits you every day?"

The duchess's features softened. "Since Cyril died. I have asked him to, and he's been kind enough to oblige me. I asked him to bring Victor today as I would like Victor to become my personal medium as Cyril was."

"Did he agree?" Tilda asked.

"He did. I've invited him to move into the house on Willow Street immediately."

"That is kind of you," Hadrian noted.

"There's no reason for the house to sit empty, and it's much nicer than his house in Clerkenwell." An expression of distaste passed quickly over the duchess's features. "I didn't particularly want to return to that neighborhood. However, I am not certain I will be able to attend séances in Willow Street after what happened to Cyril there. I may lease a different house for him. In the meantime, Victor has kindly offered to hold séances at the headquarters for me."

"Very thoughtful of him," Tilda murmured.

The duchess sniffed. "I agree. I don't know that we'll form as close a bond as I had with Cyril, but if he can continue to be a conduit for me to reach Cyril, we may well."

Tilda gave her a gentle smile. "That must be a great comfort. What is it about Mr. Ward that drew you to him?"

A flush moved up the duchess's neck and face, and she blinked back tears. She pulled a handkerchief from the cuff of her sleeve and dabbed at her eyes. "He reminded me of my son, who I miss very much." She looked to Hadrian. "You remember him, don't you?"

Hadrian gave her a respectful nod, though he hadn't known her son at all. "Of course. He was very well liked in the Lords." That much was true.

"And now the title belongs to some cousin I hardly know." She sniffed again. "I cannot help that I did not have more sons or that my son only had daughters."

"What about Mr. Ward reminded you of your son?" Tilda asked.

The duchess tipped her head. "Many things, but I suppose it is that when my son would inhabit Cyril's body to speak to me, I truly felt as if Bernard were here with me. We had so many wonderful conversations about times gone by." She wiped at her eyes again and took a shaky breath.

Tilda paused a moment before continuing, likely waiting for the duchess to compose herself. "It must have been lovely to relive memories with Mr. Ward."

"Not with Cyril. With Bernard. Cyril was merely the vessel through which my son spoke."

"Now Mr. Hawkins can be that vessel," Tilda said. "Do you know Mr. Montrose and Miss Sullivan well? I confess I was quite taken with Miss Sullivan at the séance last night. She was very charming."

The duchess actually smiled. "I do enjoy Cordelia. And Balthasar, though I know Cordelia better. She was almost always present at Cyril's séances. I presume that is why she was there last night. I expected to see Balthasar as he typically attends Mr. Hawkins's séances, from what I have heard."

Tilda glanced at Hadrian before responding. "It sounds as though the mediums specifically invite Miss Sullivan and Mr. Montrose to their séances. I wonder why."

"Cyril explained that Cordelia provided a special energy that he finds most useful in his séances," the duchess replied. "I presume it's the same with Balthasar and with Duncan Parr, though I've only met him once. He had to take Cordelia's place at one of Cyril's séances when she was ill."

"That is fascinating," Tilda said. "We haven't met Mr. Parr. Is he Scottish, by chance?"

The duchess nodded. "He is, with the most vivid red hair I've ever seen."

Hadrian thought she must be referring to the man Eldred had mentioned seeing at the séances he'd attended.

Tilda went on. "I was curious why you and Miss Sullivan were seated together last night. I thought the order of guests around the table had to be male-female."

"Typically, it is, but in the end, the energy dictates everything. At least, that is what Cyril always said." A faint smile teased the duchess's mouth. "He was always so open about his work. Like you, I found it fascinating." The duchess looked to Tilda and then Hadrian. "Have you become a patron of the society?"

"Not yet, but I am considering it." Hadrian told the lie relatively easily. "What is it that prompted you to do so?"

"I read about the society when it opened. I didn't know anything about spiritualism, but when I learned the mediums could speak with the spirit realm, I called at the society headquarters. That is where I met Cyril." The duchess's gaze softened wistfully. "We struck an immediate accord."

Hadrian took the chance to inquire about the duchess's patronage. "I am concerned about the cost of becoming a patron. I want to ensure I am paying a fair price."

The duchess's eyes were wide as she responded. "I don't think there is too great a price. They provide comfort to so many people, many of whom are not in a position to support their work."

Hadrian wanted more specific information and suspected Tilda did too. "Forgive me for asking, but I read in the newspaper that you provided an allowance to Mr. Ward. Was that in addition to your patronage of the society?"

"How I dislike that my support of Cyril was publicized in such a tawdry manner." The duchess's lips pursed with disdain. "But yes, I shall tell you that my patronage of the society and my special care for Cyril were separate. We developed a close bond, and he became a member of my family." She blinked and refocused on Hadrian. "I can't imagine you would take issue with the patronage, Ravenhurst. You can afford it many times over, I'm sure."

Whilst that wasn't specific as far as an amount, it said enough to Hadrian that he didn't wish to continue pressing.

"The society is lucky to have you, Your Grace," Tilda said.

"Is any of this helpful to your investigation?" the duchess asked. "I can't see how it would be, but I also don't know anything about how Cyril died beyond what Lysander and that inspector explained to me."

Tilda gave the duchess an appreciative smile. "You've been very helpful. I have just one more question. Do you know of anyone who was upset with the society or the mediums?"

"Everyone I have ever spoken to has been thrilled with their experiences with the society," the duchess replied. "I think you are trying to ask if I might know who killed my dear Cyril, and I do not."

It occurred to Hadrian that the duchess's family might take issue with her support of Cyril Ward. "How did your family accept Cyril's place in your affections?"

"My two daughters hardly cared. They are quite busy with their own families." She gave Hadrian a pointed look. "One is a marchioness and the other is a viscountess, if you recall, Ravenhurst."

Tilda looked to Hadrian. "I think we've taken enough of your time."

"Thank you, Duchess," Hadrian said, rising along with Tilda.

"Perhaps I will see you at another séance." The duchess looked to Tilda. "You really ought to speak with your father. He reached out to you. How can you not respond?"

Hadrian felt Tilda tense beside him.

"I'm considering it," Tilda replied thinly.

"Good." The duchess nodded. "You won't regret it. I know it can seem strange at first, but you will be so glad to have him back in your life."

They said goodbye and left the drawing room. Hadrian looked over at Tilda as they descended the stairs, but her features were impassive. He surmised she was troubled by the "appearance" of her father at the séance and people's subsequent encouragement of her speaking with him.

Outside, Tilda suggested she could go straight home since Teague had sent a constable. Hadrian reluctantly agreed and said he would still send a footman over as soon as possible.

"I also want to know if you received a threatening message at your house," Tilda said.

Hadrian met her gaze. "You shall be the first to know."

Leach greeted them at the coach and helped Tilda inside. Hadrian was tempted to join her on the forward-facing seat. Being next to her would perhaps alleviate some of his anxiety about the threatening letter she'd received. But he could keep her safe from the other side of the coach.

Tilda spoke as the coach started forward. "I am curious why Mrs. Frost pressed your mother to return quickly so as not to lose the connection with your brother, whilst the duchess has apparently been conversing with her son for a year or more."

"That seems to be more evidence of their deception," Hadrian said. "Just imagine how lucrative the duchess's patronage has likely been for the society."

Tilda nodded. "That is a fair point. I would like to know more about those three people with the 'special energy' that the mediums find helpful." Her eyes locked with his. "I want to know if that energy is actually the same power you possess to see others' memories. It would make sense to sit someone with that ability next to the medium who is trying to contact the spirit realm. When the duchess spoke of Ward—as her son, Bernard—sharing memories, I immediately thought that you could do that."

Hadrian was horrified at the thought of pretending to be someone's deceased relative. "I would never. I'm confused about who wields this power. I would think it would be the medium, but you think it may be these other people?"

Tilda shrugged. "Perhaps it's both? Or perhaps the 'special

energy' is something else entirely. What if that person and the medium, along with whatever power they might have, work together to speak with the dead?" She exhaled. "I'm merely suggesting ideas. We need to expose someone's ability—if in fact they have what you have, or something similar."

"That may be difficult. I wouldn't reveal that to anyone. The only reason you know is because you deduced there was some-thing going on and forced me to tell you."

"It was vital that you did," she said. "Not just because we needed to build our partnership on honesty. You needed to share it with someone," she added softly.

"You are right about that." He didn't regret telling her and would do so again in a trice. But all this talk of his ability and the duchess's questions about how they came to work together made him wonder about the partnership she'd just mentioned. "Do you think we would be investigating together if not for my ability to see memories?" Hadrian wasn't sure.

She took a moment to respond. "I don't know that I can answer that. Your 'curse' is what caused us to meet. You'd seen a memory, and it drove you to my grandfather's cousin's house where we met. And from then on, our paths have intertwined." She paused, her gaze searching his face. "I think you must accept that your ability is part of you. It wasn't before, but it is now, and you can't separate it from yourself."

Her words slammed into him with a brutal but poignant force. "You are right," he said quietly. "It is still difficult for me to acknowledge, let alone accept. I am most grateful that it brought me to you, however."

Their eyes locked and held.

Hadrian had never felt such a tenderness for someone before. Their relationship transcended their work and even their friend-ship. It was … special. And yet it could not be romantic.

The coach drew to a stop. Tilda looked away first.

Hadrian climbed from the coach and helped Tilda to the

pavement. She released his hand with alacrity, and he tried not to be disappointed. Any reason to touch her was welcome. Like wanting to sit with her in the coach, touching her reassured him that she was safe. He would ensure she stayed that way.

"I am looking forward to our trip tomorrow," she said. "I enjoyed our last journey by train."

They'd gone to Brighton to interview someone when they were investigating their first case. "I will hope we can easily find Roger Grenville. Swindon isn't a village."

"It may take us a bit of time, but we'll find him. Unless he doesn't want to be found," she added somewhat darkly. "Hopefully that will not be the case."

CHAPTER 14

Tilda was glad—and relieved—when Hadrian reported that he had not received a threatening note. She was curious as to why the author had only sent one to her when she and Hadrian clearly worked together. They'd decided the person who'd sent the letter probably didn't want to threaten a peer. He, or she, likely hoped that threatening Tilda would be enough. That conclusion had only served to make Hadrian more upset. He didn't like Tilda being targeted at all, but especially not on behalf of both of them.

His reaction to the threat had been visceral. Tilda could see how deeply it bothered him. She was flattered but also aware that there continued to be an undercurrent between them. Whilst they'd returned to their strong working relationship, and their friendship was intact, the kiss had stirred something that was not easily ignored. Because when she considered that Hadrian might also be in danger, she didn't like it one bit. In fact, it made her furious.

And it made her want to protect him.

The primary result of that horrible letter was that they were both eager to find the killer. She hoped today's trip to Swindon would prove fruitful.

They arrived at the railway station in Swindon at midday. Hadrian managed to hail a hack, for which Tilda was grateful as they were traveling uphill to the older part of Swindon. They'd decided that was the best place to start and made their way to the High Street. The hack took them to an alehouse.

Refreshment sounded most agreeable, plus they could ask where to find Roger Grenville.

"Let us go directly to the bar," Hadrian said.

Tilda nodded in agreement. They were greeted by the barkeep. Hadrian first ordered two ales.

As the barkeep set the beer atop the bar, Hadrian asked, "We are looking for a man called Roger Grenville. We believe he's a spiritualist."

The barkeep shrugged. "Don't know what that is. Don't know Grenville either."

Tilda felt a stab of disappointment, even as she knew it wasn't likely to have been that easy to find him. The presence of the Great Western Railway Works had transformed Swindon into a bustling town.

"Thank you." Hadrian picked up the glasses of ale and carried them to a table.

They sat and sipped their ale. Tilda contemplated where to go next.

"Shall we start knocking on doors?" Hadrian asked with a smile.

"I will hope we won't need to do that. We only have a few hours before we must return to London." Hadrian had purchased their tickets to and from Swindon. Tilda hadn't quibbled about it, but she didn't like him paying her way. It was, however, necessary, as train journeys were not in her budget.

She realized this was now the farthest she'd been from London. Her last trip via train with Hadrian had taken them to

Brighton, and that had been her farthest journey. Now, it was Swindon. She had enjoyed watching the countryside as they'd traveled west. The sprawling fields and spring flowers were beautiful. She could see why some preferred to live outside the city, but Tilda could not imagine living anywhere but London.

A man approached their table. He was older, likely in his late sixties if Tilda had to guess. His dark gaze flicked over them with uncertainty.

"Good afternoon," Tilda said pleasantly.

"I heard what ye asked about Grenville. I know 'im. Lives just down the mews there." The man gestured toward the side of the alehouse. "Walk along the street and take the third left. There's a sign what says 'Spiritualist.'"

"Thank you very much," Tilda said.

The man gave a nod, then set his hat atop his head before leaving the alehouse.

Tilda took another drink of ale, then looked at Hadrian expectantly. "Ready?"

Hadrian chuckled. "You are eager." He took a long pull on his beer.

She arched a brow at him. "Aren't you?"

"Yes, let's go." After one more drink, he set his glass down and stood.

A few minutes later, they walked to the mews the man had indicated. Toward the end, they saw the worn sign that read "Spiritualist" hanging over a door to a narrow terrace.

Hadrian knocked, and Tilda worked to temper her excitement. There was never any guarantee that they would learn something useful, but she had great hope that Mr. Grenville would be able to reveal some of Lysander Mallory's secrets.

The door opened and a tall, reedy gentleman greeted them.

"Mr. Grenville?" Hadrian asked. "I am Lord Ravenhurst and this is Miss Wren. We've come to seek your … spiritual advice."

Tilda was surprised Hadrian had phrased it that way but glad.

If they stated their objective outright, Grenville might slam the door in their faces.

"Come in," Grenville invited, holding the door wide.

They stepped into the small, dim entrance hall. A narrow staircase marched up the right side. Grenville gestured to the left toward a compact parlor where a small, rectangular table sat in the center. There were chairs in the corners, as well as a piano against one wall.

Tilda preceded Hadrian into the room. She eyed the table, wondering how Grenville conducted his séances.

"How may I help you?" Grenville asked. He looked to be in his mid-forties. His light brown hair showed no gray, but his neatly trimmed beard had a few strands of white.

"We're from London," Tilda said.

"I surmised that," Grenville said with a faint smile, his gaze lingering on Hadrian. "I can't imagine what has brought you here to seek spiritual advice when there are plenty of spiritualists in London. Indeed, I can only think you heard my name from someone in London." He didn't ask a question, but Tilda recognized curiosity when she heard it.

"Shall we sit?" Tilda asked, glancing toward the table. There was a chair on each side.

"That is where I conduct spiritual inquiries," Grenville explained.

"I am curious how you hold séances at such a small table," Tilda said as she moved toward one of the chairs.

Grenville moved a second chair next to the one she'd gravitated to, then stepped to the other side of the table. "Please, sit."

They took their seats, Hadrian sitting next to Tilda.

"I do not hold séances," Grenville said. "I meet with individuals or families. I suppose it is like a séance, but it is not an elaborate event." There was a tinge of scorn in his tone.

"Do you not care for séances, Mr. Grenville?" Tilda asked.

"I have had my fill of them."

"We did, in fact, hear of you from someone in London," Tilda said. "Mr. Victor Hawkins told us about you. He said you used to work with the head of the London Spiritualism Society, Lysander Mallory."

Grenville's dark eyes glinted. He wiped a hand over his wide chin and gave his head a gentle shake. "I haven't heard that name in some time. Are you here for spiritual advice or information?" His gaze turned wary.

Tilda didn't see the need to prevaricate since he'd welcomed them inside. "You are astute—I imagine that serves you well as a spiritualist. You undoubtedly possess some level of sensitivity to others as well. We are here seeking information about the London Spiritualism Society."

"I do have some sensitivity," Grenville said with a nod. "What is it you wish to know?"

"Forgive me if I cause any offense, since you are a practicing spiritualist," Tilda began. "We have been investigating the society. You may have read about the murders of two of the mediums."

Grenville's forehead creased as sadness passed over his features. "I did. I knew Deborah Frost quite well, and I am deeply saddened by her death. I had met Ward, but I was not well acquainted with him."

"You knew Mrs. Frost?" Tilda asked. "I wondered if that may be the case, since she was from near here."

"She was married to a friend of mine, but he died a few years ago," Grenville explained. "She came to see me to try to contact him. I was working with Thaddeus by then, and she was dazzled by him. They had a love affair for a time, and he convinced her to come to London with him and train as a medium. He said she had a sensitivity with people, and he was right. She was very kindhearted and possessed an exceptional gift for listening to others. I think that is why Thaddeus found her appealing. She never failed to make him feel like the most important person in the world. He liked that."

"Who is Thaddeus?" Hadrian asked, echoing Tilda's thoughts. She had a strong suspicion but needed to hear Grenville confirm it.

"Apologies," Grenville said with a faint chuckle. "Thaddeus Vale is Lysander Mallory's real name. He changed it when we went to London to start the society. He thought a memorable, somewhat bold name would help our cause." There was disdain buried beneath Grenville's affability. Tilda had the impression he was glad to share whatever he could about Thaddeus Vale. "Lysander is Thaddeus's favorite Shakespearean character."

Tilda's pulse quickened at the connection of the name to the captain who had leased the society headquarters in London. However, she wanted to return to Mrs. Frost for a moment. "Did Vale and Mrs. Frost remain lovers?" She hadn't perceived that sort of grief in Mallory following her death.

"They did not. I exchanged letters with Deborah occasionally, and Thaddeus moved on to another woman, someone he'd also recruited to train as a medium. Thaddeus has never maintained his romantic relationships for long."

Tilda wondered if that woman was still with the society—Mrs. Griswold or Miss Dryden, perhaps. One thing seemed obvious, however: there was a connection between Lysander Mallory and the man who'd leased the society headquarters in Cadogan Place. She exchanged a look with Hadrian before asking, "Is Thaddeus related to Captain Owen Vale?"

"They are father and son. Captain Vale lives a few miles from here." Grenville narrowed his eyes at them. "Are you investigating Thaddeus for murder? I would be shocked if he would compromise his own ambition by killing the very mediums he'd recruited, especially since it seems the society has gained several prominent patrons."

"You seem very informed about the society despite leaving it," Tilda noted.

"I have followed Thaddeus's rise." Grenville sounded slightly bitter. Tilda wondered if the man had a good motive for wanting to ruin his former partner's success. But Grenville would have had to travel to London to commit murder. "Are you investigating Thaddeus?" he asked again.

"We are investigating the murders as well as the society in general. We have learned that the society's mediums commit fraud in their séances. They use hollow tables and parlor tricks to impress the attendees." Tilda looked at Grenville intently, wondering if he may hold the key to what they were missing. "Is that what you and Thaddeus did when you worked together?"

"Not at first, but Thaddeus suggested we add theatrics that impress people so they would talk about our séances and entice others to come." Grenville grimaced. "I'm ashamed to say it worked beautifully. We became rather popular."

"Was there anything real about your séances?" Hadrian asked, his tone slightly accusatory.

"Of course," Grenville replied quickly. "I do have a sensitivity to people. I can feel their energy, and sometimes—often, really—I can use that energy to glimpse things. I confess much of it is nebulous—feelings and sensations, rather than actually hearing something specific from someone in the spirit realm."

"And yet the mediums in the London Spiritualism Society somehow know specific things about people. The best we can surmise is that the society conducts investigations to learn details they can share in a séance. Or they actually speak to the dead, which you say isn't possible."

"It isn't possible for *me*," Grenville clarified.

"Are you saying it is for someone?" Tilda asked.

Grenville gave her a wry smile. "I am not aware of anyone who speaks to the dead. However, there are other means by which someone may gather information that seems impossible."

"That is rather vague." Tilda darted a look at Hadrian. His features were impassive, and she couldn't tell if he suspected what she did—that Grenville was referring to some other super-natural ability. "What means are you referring to?"

Grenville hesitated, then leaned slightly toward them over the table. "Can you believe in something that cannot be proven?" he asked softly.

Tilda's pulse quickened as she wondered if Grenville meant a power such as Hadrian's. Glancing toward Hadrian once more, she saw that his jaw had clenched. "We very well might," she replied to Grenville without irony.

There was a long silence as Grenville studied them both. "How refreshing," he murmured. "Still, you may not believe what I am about to say, and I don't share this lightly. In fact, I've never shared it with anyone before. However, I think it is necessary, given the nature of your investigation and the fact that lives have been lost." He paused, regarding them as if he expected they might interrupt. However, Tilda was rapt and a quick glance toward Hadrian said he was the same.

"Thaddeus is able to experience the memories of others when he touches them," Grenville said, and Tilda's pulse leapt. She wished she could touch Hadrian, to convey both her excitement and support. "I would not have believed it myself if he had not performed the trick on me multiple times. He experienced memories of mine that I hadn't shared with others, and in some cases barely remembered myself."

Tilda cast a sideways look at Hadrian, but his expression was blank—eerily so. "That is astonishing," she said to Grenville. "It must have been unnerving and yet exciting at the same time—the ability to relive something you had almost forgotten."

"I'm shocked you understand and that you actually seem to believe me." Grenville stared at them somewhat incredulously. "Truthfully, I found it unnerving. After a time, however, Thaddeus was no longer able to experience my memories, which relieved me. It seemed that as we became close, he lost the ability, at least with me." Perhaps that explained why Hadrian hadn't seen Tilda's memories. They were, as recognized by both of them, close friends.

She could almost feel the tension coursing through Hadrian, but there would be time to discuss his reaction and what this could mean later. "May I ask how you came to meet one another?" she asked Grenville.

"I was working as a spiritualist, and Thaddeus came to see me —in this very room. He said he was an aspiring spiritualist and performed his trick for me." Grenville paused, his expression wry. "Forgive me, I should not call it a trick, for his ability is quite real. It is the manner in which he purveyed it that counted as trickery, in my opinion. But I am getting ahead of the story.

"After I saw what he was capable of, I invited him to join me in my business," Grenville continued. "With his skill, we could help people in ways that could be deeply meaningful."

"How was that?" Hadrian asked, his voice flat.

Grenville looked toward him. "You are skeptical."

"You mentioned trickery, and I do not like the idea of people being defrauded," Hadrian said coldly.

"Nor do I," Grenville whispered. "Though I am ashamed to admit we did just that. But I no longer truck with activities designed to shock and entertain. You will not find me moving objects or shaking the table." He spoke vehemently, and Tilda believed him.

"And yet you still call yourself a spiritualist. What is it you do?" Hadrian asked.

"As I explained, I am sensitive to people and their energy. I help them, usually with their grief over losing someone. Whilst I don't actually speak to their deceased loved one, I can feel the energy around the person, or persons, I'm with and generally ascertain a connection between them and the person in the spirit realm. I ease their mind as to how their loved one has passed on."

"But you don't really know," Hadrian said. "It sounds as though you offer them vague assurances."

"Life is not always as clear as black versus white, my lord." Grenville cocked his head as he studied Hadrian. "I sense you are afraid of what could happen when one lets down their guard to experience the sensations of spiritualism. Perhaps I am wrong about that, but I don't think I am. And *that* is what makes me a spiritualist."

"You read people like one might read a book," Tilda said, hoping Hadrian wasn't too uncomfortable. She rather thought Grenville was right about Hadrian being afraid, but she was fairly certain it came from having gained this strange ability and not knowing how or why.

"Somewhat, Miss Wren," Grenville said with a smile. "I imagine you'd like me to continue my story regarding Thaddeus." At her nod, he continued. "We started working together nearly five years ago. As I briefly mentioned earlier, we became quite a sensation. People would come from all over to consult with us, and we would travel to Bath on occasion, where people would gather by the dozens to attend our séances. Thaddeus suggested we could do quite well in London, and I confess I was wooed by his ideas, which included starting a society for spiritualism. As I mentioned, I was glad to be able to offer meaningful help to people. We would connect them with deceased loved ones via the memories that Thaddeus could sense when he held their hands."

"Why position it like that?" Hadrian asked. "Why make it about communicating with the dead instead of helping people to unlock distant memories?"

Grenville's expression was open and honest. "Because spiritualism is about communicating with the spirit realm and the belief that one lives on after death. That is what comforts people, especially those facing the end of their mortal life."

"You took advantage of a popular endeavor in order to profit," Hadrian said sharply.

Grenville did not respond.

"What was your plan when you arrived in London?" Tilda

asked, eager for Grenville to continue with his tale and hopeful that Hadrian hadn't just put him off.

Thankfully, Grenville went on. "Thaddeus envisioned a society where people would pay a membership fee that included attendance to séances and a place to congregate with like-minded others. We needed a house for our headquarters. We saved our funds, but once we arrived in London, we realized we could not hope to afford a house in a highly desirable area. Thaddeus appealed to his father, who leased a house in Belgravia for us in which to found the London Spiritualism Society."

Now they knew why Captain Owen Vale's name was on the lease for the property.

"But once the society was founded, you left London," Hadrian noted. "Why?"

Grenville frowned, and he looked down at the table between them. "I realized Thaddeus would go to any length to grow the society as quickly as possible. He recruited mediums, which we hadn't discussed, and taught them the silly parlor tricks. He wanted the séances to become more spectacle than spiritualism. I did not agree." He looked up at them, his mouth set into a firm line. "He also set his sights on London's upper crust." Grenville looked at Hadrian. "People like you, my lord. He hoped they would become patrons, and if they did not, he said he would use other means to increase the society's coffers—that was his primary goal."

"The society's coffers or his own?" Tilda asked.

"It was all the same to him," Grenville said bitterly. "He was the society, and everyone else were his minions. I did not care to be subordinate to him."

Tilda watched Grenville's bitterness turn to anger as the man lifted his chin, his gaze almost defiant. "Do you regret that, given his success?" she asked. "The society has a most prominent patroness—the Duchess of Chester."

"I read that in one of the articles about the Levitation Killer."

Grenville's features smoothed. "I am not surprised since that is what Thaddeus set out to do. He is nothing if not exceedingly charming. Indeed, he could persuade a pauper to empty his pockets."

"But it wasn't Thaddeus Vale, or Lysander Mallory as we know him, who was the duchess's personal medium," Hadrian said. "That was Cyril Ward."

"Cyril was also very charming. He and Thaddeus were cut from the same cloth. I've no doubt they worked in tandem to win over Her Grace. When I read of Cyril's death, I imagined Thaddeus was quite stricken."

"He visits the duchess every day," Hadrian said. "But that could easily be because he wants her financial support to continue, as much as any grief he shares with her over Ward's death."

"You are no doubt right." Grenville thought for a moment. "I wonder if he holds anything over her to maintain her support."

Tilda immediately thought of Octavius Eldred and his allegation of blackmail. She also recalled what Grenville had said a few moments ago—that Mallory had said he would resort to any means to enrich the society and himself. "What do you mean?"

"The incident that caused me to leave was Thaddeus blackmailing one of the members. I was appalled. When I demanded he stop, he refused. I persisted, so he offered me a sum of money to leave London and say nothing." Grenville looked down at the table again. "I'm ashamed to say I accepted."

"What sort of blackmail scheme did he employ?" Hadrian asked.

"If it means anything, I don't think he set out to blackmail anyone," Grenville said. "Thaddeus had seen a memory in which the client was being unfaithful to her husband. She was wealthy, and he sent her a letter demanding payment to keep the information secret." Grenville's brows drew together. "I should have stopped him."

"Yes, you should have," Hadrian said with a faint sneer.

Tilda could imagine his outrage at Mallory using the same power Hadrian possessed for malfeasance, whilst Hadrian used his to solve crimes.

Tilda felt confident that Mallory's ability to experience others' memories explained how Eldred had been blackmailed as well as how the mediums "communicated with the spirit realm." But was he the only one? "Mr. Grenville, do any of the other mediums possess the same ability to experience others' memories? I wonder if that is why Mallory recruited them."

Grenville shook his head. "I am not aware of that, however, Thaddeus stopped confiding in me after we started the society. He began to work more closely with Cyril and Deborah, and a third medium named Victor." Grenville's expression grew contemplative. "I do recall him telling me once that he could sense whether someone else shared his gift. However, I don't know how that was accomplished. He may have told me, but I don't remember." He looked at Tilda. "I suppose it's possible that he recruited Cyril and Victor because they had the ability. But I think I would have known if Deborah possessed it. I'd known her a long time."

"Is it something that can be taught?" Hadrian asked, sounding as though he genuinely wanted to know, which, of course, he did. He would want whatever information he could gather.

Grenville arched a brow. "If it is, why didn't he teach me?" Again, he sounded bitter. "I don't have an answer for you. You should speak with Captain Vale. I would think he would know about his son's oddity."

Tilda noted the word Grenville used—oddity—and looked at Hadrian. His lips had flattened into a perturbed line.

"We will speak with the captain," Tilda said. Indeed, she was more eager than ever to speak with him. She hoped they could determine if the other mediums had the same power, but, for now, it was enough to know that Mallory did.

She considered whether Grenville could be a suspect in the murders, but since he lived here, it seemed unlikely. Still, he had a motive—Mallory had ousted him from the society they'd planned together. "You haven't returned to London since you left?"

Grenville shook his head. "I came back to Swindon just over a year ago, and my agreement with Thaddeus is that I would stay away." He met Tilda's gaze. "If I wanted to find the Levitation Killer, I would start with the people he blackmailed. I can't imagine he stopped after the first woman."

"He did not," Tilda confirmed. "Who was that woman?"

"The wife of a fairly prominent MP," Grenville replied. "Mrs. Horace Tarrant. I believe she paid the money, but I don't know for certain."

"Have you any idea how we might discover who else Mallory extorted over the past year?"

"Perhaps he kept a diary?" Grenville suggested. "I would tell you to ask Cyril about the blackmail because he was aware." His eyes lit. "But you can still ask Victor. I think he also knew about it."

"Excellent, we'll do that," Tilda said. "Was Deborah Frost also aware of the blackmail?"

"No, because I threatened Mallory that I would tell her if he didn't stop. I knew she wouldn't like it."

"But you didn't tell her," Hadrian surmised. "Instead, you took Mallory's bribe and left London."

Grenville's eyes flashed with regret and perhaps pain. "Deborah was happy to have an occupation. She enjoyed being a medium, and she was good at it. I didn't want to ruin that for her."

Tilda recalled what Ellen Henry had told them. "Mrs. Frost's maid said that Mrs. Frost had come to London after her husband died and that she wasn't entirely happy, that she was considering leaving the society. Perhaps you were mistaken about her level of content."

Grenville's lips parted. He seemed surprised. "I had no idea. I did offer to bring her back to Swindon with me, but she declined. I truly thought she was happy."

"Did you ever meet Balthasar Montrose, Cordelia Sullivan, or Duncan Parr?" Tilda asked.

Grenville frowned. "Those names are not familiar."

Tilda considered they may also have adopted new identities as Vale had. "Miss Sullivan is older and wears a veil. Montrose is Welsh and has a beard. He also wears spectacles. Parr is a Scotsman with bright red hair."

"I don't know of them," Grenville replied. "Are they mediums?"

"Members of the society who frequently attend séances. They apparently possess a special energy." Tilda cocked her head. "Do you have any idea what that could mean?"

"Only that they may be sensitive—like Mrs. Frost. Or like me." His eyes rounded. "Perhaps they possess the same ability as Thaddeus."

That was precisely what Tilda was thinking. But how could they find out for certain? And why wouldn't they just be mediums?

"Do you know how Mallory—Vale—went about recruiting mediums?" Tilda asked.

"I would have said he looks for people who possess a sensitivity to others and with whom he's forged a personal bond, such as me and Deborah. However, that seemed to change when we arrived in London. Cyril was flashy and alluring, and Victor Hawkins just *looked* like a medium."

"Because of his eyes," Tilda said with a nod.

"Exactly," Grenville agreed. "He and Cyril were most captivating, just like Thaddeus."

"That is true of most charlatans," Hadrian said. "Would you provide Captain Vale's direction to us?"

"Certainly. He lives just off the Bath Road toward Wootton Bassett. The house is large. You won't miss the gatehouse."

"Thank you, Mr. Grenville," Tilda said. "You've been very helpful."

Removing his glove, Hadrian offered his hand to the man. Tilda didn't think it was necessary to see Grenville's memories, but she wouldn't try to stop him.

Grenville clasped Hadrian's hand. A moment passed, and Tilda observed the slight flare of Hadrian's nostrils. They said goodbye and took their leave.

"Hopefully, we can hail a hack on the High Street," Hadrian said as they walked away from Grenville's house.

"What did you see?" Tilda asked.

"Mallory. Rather, Vale." Hadrian was walking very quickly.

"Will you slow down?"

Hadrian paused. "My apologies." He rubbed his temple, then offered her his arm. "I'm feeling slightly overwhelmed to learn there is, in fact, someone else like me."

"Is it relieving?" Tilda said softly.

Hadrian's eyes darkened. "It's maddening. Mallory is despicable."

They continued walking toward the High Street. Tilda felt the tension in his arm. "I know it bothers you that he uses his power to cheat people."

"Doesn't it frustrate you as well?"

"It does. But what are we to do about it? We may believe what Grenville told us, but who else will?"

Hadrian stopped again. "Now you understand how I feel at every turn."

"Of course I understand," she said reassuringly, meeting his gaze. "I truly do."

They started walking once more. At length, Hadrian said, "I'd thought we would question Captain Vale about why he leased the house in Belgravia, but now that we know he is Lysander Mallory's father and that Mallory possesses the same ability I do, the purpose for that interview has changed entirely."

"It's possible the captain isn't aware of his son's gift, just as your mother isn't aware of yours."

Hadrian nodded, his brow creased. "For that reason, I'm not sure if I want to ask the captain about it."

"Hopefully, the opportunity to discuss the matter will arise," Tilda said with a confidence she didn't entirely feel.

Hadrian smiled at her, and Tilda was glad to see him relax a bit. "If anyone can adeptly turn a conversation to their advantage, it is you."

CHAPTER 15

*T*hey were not able to find a hack. Returning to the alehouse they'd visited, Hadrian paid someone to take them to Captain Vale's house and to wait there for them whilst they conducted their interview. Unfortunately, it was a small gig which required the three of them to press in tightly together whilst a fine drizzle fell.

Finally, they were seated together. And not just on the same bench, but pressed tightly enough that they were touching. It was just their arms and the barest hint of their thighs. Rather, it was their clothing that touched, but it was intimate enough for Hadrian to wonder if Tilda was discomfited.

He was not.

On the contrary, he enjoyed being this close to her. She eased the tumult of thoughts spinning in his mind since learning that Mallory indeed shared the same ability to experience others' memories as Hadrian. He felt much better, as if Tilda's presence beside him was a balm.

The driver sat on Hadrian's other side, and he smelled of ale and earth. Thankfully, Tilda's floral scent was a welcome diversion. Because of the driver's presence, they didn't discuss what they'd just learned, nor what they planned to ask Captain Vale.

His residence was a large manor house that Hadrian estimated to have been constructed perhaps eighty years earlier. He wondered how the man had come to be in possession of such an estate, since he'd been a military officer. Perhaps he was a second —or even third—son and had inherited it.

"I'm curious why Thaddeus Vale has taken up a career as a spiritualist when he could stand to inherit this," Tilda mused after they departed the gig, somewhat echoing Hadrian's line of thought.

"I was thinking something similar. I wondered how Captain Vale had come to inherit this impressive pile whilst also serving in the military and decided he was likely a second or third son. Perhaps Thaddeus is not his firstborn and will not inherit."

"We shall soon find out," Tilda said as they reached the door.

Hadrian knocked soundly. It was a few moments before the door opened. A woman in a gray gown with a cap perched upon her sable hair perused them.

"Good afternoon, I am Lord Ravenhurst." Hadrian handed his card to the woman, who was presumably the housekeeper. "And this is my colleague, Miss Wren. We are here to see Captain Vale. Since we have come from London and are due to return later this afternoon, we hope he is able to receive us."

The housekeeper's dark brows gathered as she looked at his card. "I see. Please come inside. Wait here." She indicated they move to a place near the center of the rectangular entrance hall, then she departed through an archway to the right that led into a large staircase hall. She moved past the stairs and turned to the left.

Tilda was looking after the woman and stepped closer to the archway. "That is an interesting room."

Hadrian looked into the staircase hall and noted a variety of swords and other blades adorning the walls. "An inspiring collection."

"Inspiring how?" she asked archly. "Unless you're planning on opening a school for swordsmanship?"

"I suppose that is one use for them," Hadrian said with a chuckle.

"Why didn't a butler answer the door?" Tilda asked. "I would expect a house like this to have a butler." She sent Hadrian a sardonic glance. "I still can't believe *we* have a butler."

"There may be a butler here, but perhaps he couldn't come to the door for some reason. He may be busy belowstairs. Or it could be that Captain Vale does not employ a butler. Some households run on a smaller complement of retainers. I presume the woman who answered the door is the housekeeper."

Tilda pivoted to face him. "Is it strange that I asked about the butler?"

Hadrian wasn't sure how to respond. He did not find it odd, but he could also not ignore the fact that she had asked and that she'd expected him to know the answer. Because of course, he would know how a house like this would run. "I don't think so. And you are lucky to have a wonderful butler."

"That we don't really need," she said with fleeting smile that lingered in her eyes.

The woman who Hadrian presumed was the housekeeper walked back into the staircase hall and continued toward them. She stopped just on the other side of the archway. "Captain Vale will receive you."

She led them back the way she'd come, taking them into a cavernous library. A gentleman who bore more than a passing resemblance to Lysander Mallory strode toward them. His hair was not quite as blond as his son's, but the hooded eyes were the exact same.

"Welcome, my lord, Miss Wren." The captain gave them a

sharp bow that one might expect from someone who'd served in the military.

"Thank you for seeing us," Hadrian said. "This is a magnificent library." He looked about the massive room, thinking it was one of the largest libraries he'd ever seen, including the rather substantial one at Ravenswood, Hadrian's estate in Hampshire.

"My father is to blame. He decided the ballroom would make a much better library, and since he never held a ball, I believe he was right." Captain Vale smiled. "I confess I've added to it since my retirement. I spend a great deal of time here."

"You've a passion for reading?" Tilda asked.

"Shakespeare in particular. I fancy myself an amateur scholar, if there is such a thing," he added with a smile.

Shakespeare. That could explain why Thaddeus Vale had a favorite Shakespearean character. Hadrian exchanged a look with Tilda.

"Did your son inherit your love of Shakespeare?" Tilda asked.

Captain Vale blinked at her. "Which son?"

"Thaddeus," Tilda replied. "My apologies, I did not realize you had more than one."

"Why have you come?" Captain Vale's brow furrowed. "Do you know Thaddeus? Please tell me he's all right." The man blanched. "I knew I should have gone to London after I read about that first murder."

"We do know Thaddeus." Tilda spoke gently. "As far we know, he is fine. Indeed, we just saw him yesterday."

Captain Vale exhaled and wiped his hand over his brow. "Thank goodness. Are you members of his club?"

Hadrian noted the man's use of the word "club" rather than society.

Tilda clasped her hands before her. "No, we are investigating the murders of two of the mediums in the London Spiritualism Society, which your son founded."

"*You're* investigating?" Captain Vale looked at Tilda as he asked the question.

"Yes, I am a private investigator, and Lord Ravenhurst assists me."

Captain Vale assessed Hadrian briefly. "I hope you do an admirable job."

Tilda smiled, and Hadrian knew Captain Vale had gained an ally if he ever needed one. "He is quite helpful," she said. "Do you mind if we speak with you about your son? We know him as Lysander Mallory."

Captain Vale pressed his lips together in a somewhat disapproving expression. "The name he took for his 'character.'"

"You don't care for it?" Tilda asked.

"It's a fine name, especially the nod to *A Midsummer Night's Dream*, but I don't know why he felt he needed it. Thaddeus is a good, strong name. It belonged to my father, in fact." Captain Vale waved his hand. "I'm glad to speak with you if it will help catch this murderer. I am worried about Thaddeus. I may come to London after all, I think."

Hadrian wondered how much Tilda would say. Part of him didn't want to reveal Thaddeus's fraudulent behavior to his father. The man would likely be hugely disappointed. He already seemed somewhat disinclined toward his son's endeavors. And yet he'd leased the house for the society headquarters.

"Let us sit," Captain Vale said, gesturing toward a small round table. "Mrs. Higgins is bringing tea."

"Your son is most charming," Tilda said as they sat down. She removed her gloves and set them in her lap. "His society is very popular. You must be proud of his accomplishments."

The captain's eyes shadowed as he glanced away. His shoulder twitched, and Hadrian had confirmation that the man did not support his son's work. Perhaps Captain Vale already knew of his son's deceptive behavior.

"I am proud of his hard work," Captain Vale said. "Though I

confess I would have preferred to see him pursue an artistic career. He would make a fine novelist or playwright."

If one thought of Thaddeus Vale as the head of a troupe of actors, one could say he had an artistic career. Hadrian removed his own gloves and wondered what he might sense from touching the table or anything else in the house, including Captain Vale.

"He's written several things." Captain Vale stood, moved to a bookshelf, and plucked up a bound volume. Returning to them, he set it on the table between Hadrian and Tilda. "I had his stories bound into a book."

Mrs. Higgins entered with the tea tray and deposited it on the table. She poured the tea but left it to them to add cream and sugar, per Captain Vale's instructions.

Hadrian reached for the cream at the same time as the captain and their hands collided. "My apologies."

Captain Vale came slightly out of his chair and gripped Hadrian's hand, his palm wrapping over the back. His eyes focused on nothing, and Hadrian drew in a sharp breath. An odd sensation spiked through him—a coldness followed by a flash of heat.

Just as quickly as he'd snatched Hadrian, Captain Vale released him. The man settled back in his chair and straightened his coat. Then his gaze met Hadrian's. "Why are you really here, my lord?" The captain's eyes glittered with wariness and an intense curiosity. Had he felt whatever Hadrian had?

Hadrian's heart raced. When the captain grasped him, Hadrian had felt the same frisson of energy as when he'd touched Lysander Mallory.

"You are like me," the captain whispered, answering Hadrian's question . "You are able to experience others' memories. Don't deny it because I could sense it when I touched you."

Hadrian heard Tilda's sharp intake of breath but did not look at her. "I It suddenly occurred to him that he'd experienced a similar sensation when he'd briefly shaken Mallory's hand. "I also felt something…odd when I touched your son." The feeling hadn't been quite the same, for Hadrian recalled only a coldness. That contact had been fleeting, though. Perhaps they hadn't touched long enough for Hadrian to feel the full effect.

"It is not uncommon for a father and son to share the ability. It runs in families, or so my grandfather told me. I have never met another person—outside of my family—with it. Until now."

Families … Hadrian wondered who in his family possessed this power. Surely it wasn't his father, but perhaps that was why he'd been cold? Hadrian could see how it could make a person retreat into themselves, afraid of what they would see whenever they touched something or someone.

It definitely wasn't his mother. He didn't think she'd be able to mask that.

"When did your ability start?" the captain asked. "It is different for everyone."

"I hit my head a few months ago," he said quietly. "I began to see visions that I could not explain. I was certain I was going mad."

Tilda touched Hadrian's arm, and he turned his head to glance at her. Her eyes were full of such compassion. No one had ever looked at him like that.

"You are not mad," the captain assured him. "At least, the things you see are not due to any mental deficiency. However, the ability *can* drive a person to madness." His expression darkened. "I worried that my poor son would end up in an asylum. He had great difficulty at first, for his power is very sensitive. He could hardly touch anything or anyone without being assaulted by visions. He wore gloves almost incessantly for years."

That sounded horrible. Hadrian was very glad he had not experienced that. "Pardon me, Captain, I am shocked to meet someone who shares this curse." To think he could have answers at last … His chest tightened. "I have been at turns bewildered and frustrated. I don't know why this happened or how to manage it."

The captain's brow furrowed. "Was no one in your family gifted?"

Gifted was not the word Hadrian would have used. *Afflicted* seemed more accurate. "Not to my knowledge." Was Hadrian to ask his grandmother or his father's younger brother? Or perhaps some distant cousin?

Captain Vale shrugged. "It doesn't pass directly. I have three sons, and only Thaddeus has the gift. My father did not have it either, but his father did. Someone in your family has this ability, but it may have skipped a generation or two."

Hadrian wanted to travel to the dower house at Ravenhurst and ask his grandmother what she knew, if anything. But how could he do that without revealing his own secret? If she was not aware of the affliction, he would expose himself for no reason.

"Are women not able to possess this ability?" Tilda asked.

"I don't know. As I said, I've only ever known about the people in my own family," Captain Vale replied. "My grandfather said there were others—and that was according to his uncle who had it, but it's not something you go about sharing."

"No, it is not," Hadrian said firmly. "Though your son shared it with Grenville. He told us about it earlier."

The captain did not look pleased to hear that. "I'm surprised to hear Thaddeus would do that."

"He had to because he's using the ability to see the memories of people who attend his séances, and Grenville was his partner. They used your son's ability to their advantage—to fleece people whilst pretending to speak with the dead." Hadrian didn't hide his scorn. "He continues to use it with the London Spiritualism Society."

"I did not realize that was what he was doing." Captain Vale's head tipped down.

"How could you not?" Hadrian asked.

The captain kept his head bowed and did not respond.

"Lord Ravenhurst uses his power to help me solve murders," Tilda said.

Hadrian heard a note of pride in her voice and looked at her. She met his gaze with warmth and understanding.

Lifting his head, the captain smiled briefly. "That is splendid." He sent a wary look at Hadrian. "I am surprised you told her what you could do. I only told my wife after we were married."

"Miss Wren is incredibly shrewd. She realized something was going on and demanded I stop hiding whatever it was." Hadrian sent her a small smile of gratitude. "I don't regret telling her. Indeed, she has been a wonderful support as I've learned to navigate this mysterious ability."

"Be glad for that. It is a difficult thing to bear on one's own. Perhaps that is why Thaddeus told Grenville," the captain mused, seeming to forget—or ignore—that his son had a more wicked intent.

Hadrian wanted to know more about this power, such as why he hadn't seen Mallory's or the captain's memories. "Did you see something when you touched me?"

"No, nor would I ever. Because we both possess the ability, we are immune to one another. The only thing we can feel from each other is that we share the same ability." Captain Vale cocked his head. "Did you not feel the tremor of energy that passed between us?"

"I did." Just as Hadrian had felt it when he touched Mallory. Which meant Mallory knew his secret too. Hadrian did *not* like that.

Captain Vale cocked his head. "I can't decide if you are pleased to meet someone else who shares your ability or if you're distressed."

"A little of both." Hadrian wasn't sure why he was being so honest. Probably because, for better or worse, he had a connection with this gentleman. "I'm rather astounded. And perhaps worried. I don't like others knowing about this."

"I feel the same," the captain replied. "I would not have shared it with you if I had not recognized that we are alike. I will keep your secret."

"And I will keep yours." Hadrian took a sip of the now tepid tea in the hope it would soothe his tension. Setting the cup down, he fixed on Captain Vale once more. "Do you have headaches when you see a vision?"

"I used to, but they lessened over time. At some point, you should be able to control when you see or feel something."

Hadrian's pulse sped. "How?" He would very much like that to happen immediately.

Captain Vale gave him a brief, apologetic smile. "My grandfather told me it's different for everyone. He said I obtained the ability to manage the gift much sooner than he did. And he continued to have headaches throughout his life, but since he could control whether he experienced a memory, he very rarely indulged the ability. You have them?"

The thought of having the headaches forever was upsetting, but Hadrian would cling to the notion that he would someday be able to control the power he possessed. "Yes, and the more visions I have in a short amount of time, the worse and more enduring the pain."

"I'm sorry to hear it. I suggest lavender. It seems to have the best effect for the headaches we suffer. My grandfather's pillow always contained lavender, and his clothing was laundered with it."

"Is there any danger to continuing to use the ability once you can manage it?" Tilda asked with concern. "Sometimes, his headaches are quite terrible."

Hadrian loved how protective she sounded, but then she often inquired after his head after he experienced others' memories.

"I am not aware of any danger, but as I said, Lord Ravenhurst can hopefully learn to manage the ability so that he can choose to use it—and suffer the accompanying headache—or not."

"Do you have any suggestions for how I might learn to wield this power instead of it simply happening?" Hadrian asked.

Captain Vale grimaced. "Does it happen every time you touch something?"

"No. It doesn't happen at my home at all—not with anything there or any of the members of my household."

Captain Vale nodded. "I am relieved for you. What Thaddeus went through was horrid. His ability was triggered when he fell from his horse at fifteen. He was plagued by constant visions for several years. They made him somewhat volatile, until he was finally able to control the ability."

"What allowed him to do that?" Hadrian hoped he didn't sound too desperate.

"I don't think it was anything in particular. It's something that just happened gradually over time. I believe it helps to meditate on ways to control your thoughts. When you touch something, think about what you want—or don't want—to see or feel."

"Or smell," Hadrian said.

Captain Vale's brows shot up. "You smell the memories?"

"You don't?"

"No." Captain Vale shook his head. "My grandfather did warn me that no two of us are exactly alike. I was not aware of him smelling them, but he did hear them."

Hadrian glanced at Tilda. To be able to hear what people were saying would be most helpful in their investigations.

"Does your son?" Tilda asked. "Hear them, I mean."

"He does, but that came to him later." The captain looked to Hadrian. "That may yet come to you."

Hadrian took a biscuit from the tray, his mind churning with everything he'd just learned.

Tilda sipped her tea, then addressed their host. "Can you tell us why you leased the house for your son for the London Spiritualism Society? You don't seem to favor your son's pursuit of spiritualism."

Captain Vale had also taken the break in conversation to sip his tea and now returned his cup to its saucer. "I didn't know it was for this spiritualism nonsense. He told me he wanted to establish a literary salon. I confess I have felt badly for all the difficulty he suffered as a young man, and I have only wanted him to find happiness."

Hadrian was already inclined to like the man, but now it was certain. Captain Vale clearly loved his son, which was not something Hadrian could say about his own father. "I hope your son realizes how fortunate he is to have you."

The captain smiled. "I am not always certain, but I like to believe he does. I may not approve of what he is doing, but he is still my son."

Hadrian wondered what the man would think if he knew his son was blackmailing people. He couldn't bring himself to tell him about it.

"How I wished he'd actually established a literary salon. He is a gifted writer and found such solace in it." The captain glanced at the book that still sat on the table.

Tilda touched the book. "May I look?"

"Please," the captain encouraged as he picked up his teacup once more.

Hadrian took another biscuit as Tilda opened the book. She turned a page and skimmed the handwriting.

"What sort of stories did he write?" Hadrian asked before taking a bite of biscuit.

"Romantic tales, mostly," the captain responded. "There are some poems as well."

The barest intake of breath reached Hadrian's ears. He looked over at Tilda to see her turning another page. Then she moved the book so that it was easier for him to read. "He's an excellent writer," she said in a tone that seemed—to Hadrian—to trill with excitement.

Hadrian popped the rest of the biscuit into his mouth as his gaze fell on the handwriting. He nearly choked.

The lettering matched that of the threatening message Tilda had received. Hadrian would stake his life on it.

He dared to look at Tilda. She briefly met his gaze, but then focused her attention on Captain Vale. "I can see why you hoped Thaddeus would become a writer. Mayhap he will yet."

The hell he would. Hadrian was going to see him arrested just as soon as they returned to London. They would go directly to Scotland Yard.

"We must be on our way," Hadrian said abruptly in his eagerness to get to Mallory. "We've a train to catch."

"Do you need transport to the station?" Captain Vale offered.

"We have a gig waiting outside, such as it is," Hadrian replied. "But thank you for your kindness and your hospitality. This is not what I expected."

"It has been a pleasure to make your acquaintance, my lord. I do hope you'll consult me if you have further questions. Or if you'd just like to talk about our ... uniqueness." The man smiled warmly, and Hadrian fleetingly wished he'd had a father like Captain Vale.

Tilda rose, and Hadrian joined her. The captain followed suit, then escorted them from the library.

"Did I help you at all?" Captain Vale asked as they made their way through the blade-adorned entrance hall.

"More than we ever expected," Tilda replied with a smile. "Thank you again."

They took their leave and rode in silence to the train station. The train wasn't due for a little while yet, so they went to the refreshment hall to wait.

Hadrian guided Tilda to a table in the corner, out of earshot from anyone who may want to eavesdrop. Not that they would, but he didn't want anyone to overhear their discussion. His pulse was still thrumming from what they'd seen in the captain's library—proof that Lysander Mallory, or Thaddeus Vale, had threatened Tilda. *And* that the threat more than implied he was the Levitation Killer.

"Have we found the killer?" he asked after they sat down.

"It seems we may have," Tilda replied, her expression tight with excitement. "The note I received was definitely Mallory's handwriting. We must go straight to Scotland Yard."

"Agreed." Hadrian couldn't wait to see Mallory in irons.

"Are we calling him Mallory or Vale?" Tilda sked.

"I'd say Mallory since that is how we met him. Vale is now the captain in my mind."

"You liked him," Tilda said with a gentle smile. "He was very helpful to you. I'm glad we didn't tell him about the note his son sent me."

"He will find out soon enough," Hadrian said darkly. "I'm sorry for that, for I did like him. That is why I didn't mention the blackmail either."

Tilda's brow creased with compassion as she regarded him. "How do you feel after everything he told you?"

"I am still trying to understand it all. Ask me again tomorrow." Indeed, Hadrian's thoughts were spinning with what he'd learned regarding his bizarre ability and about unmasking the Levitation Killer.

Tilda nodded. "I can understand that." She paused before saying, "I am trying to determine why Mallory would kill two of the most prominent mediums in his society—an organization he worked hard to build."

"Worked hard deceiving people, including his own father." Hadrian sneered. "But I understand what you are saying. It certainly doesn't make sense, especially with Ward, who'd garnered the support of a wealthy duchess."

"Exactly. I am struggling to come up with a motive for him to kill Ward. With Mrs. Frost, perhaps he was upset that she was thinking of leaving. Now that we know they were once romantically involved, we must consider their relationship was complicated."

"Is that what romance does?" Hadrian asked. "It complicates things?"

"It certainly complicated your life after Louis Chambers was killed," Tilda said. "If not for your past romantic attachment to his wife, you would not have been involved."

Hadrian couldn't argue with her logic. He also began to see her perspective on romantic relationships. If she saw them as difficult, why would she want to pursue one?

"Perhaps it was difficult for them to be romantically involved and work together once the society was founded," Tilda suggested. She did not look at him as she said this, and Hadrian was curious about her thoughts on the matter since they worked together. Was it possible she didn't think they could pursue a romance and investigate together?

"I suppose that's possible," Hadrian said slowly. "Grenville remarked that Mallory did not maintain romantic relationships for a long period of time, so perhaps it was simply that. I think it's possible people can work together and be romantically connected without complication."

Now Tilda met his gaze. "And what evidence do you have of that?"

"None whatsoever. I don't know any men and women who work together—except us." He paused, noting her nostrils flaring the barest amount. Hadrian's pulse ticked a bit faster. "I suppose I am aware of husbands and wives who own a business together— Mr. and Mrs. Pollard from our last case come to mind."

Tilda arched a brow. "I would say their business relationship was a failure, given that Mrs. Pollard was a murderer and Mr. Pollard had no idea."

"I suppose that is true, but I think they worked together just fine. Except for the murdering and hiding that," he added drily.

"I am still not convinced, but we digress. The issue is whether Mallory could have killed his former lover."

He went back to the purpose of this conversation. "I find it hard to comprehend, unless she'd done something that upset him, and he reacted in a passionate manner."

"Such as betray him?" Tilda asked, flicking him a glance. "That was the motive for you potentially killing Chambers. Your fiancée betrayed you with him."

Hadrian grimaced. "I do not need to be reminded, thank you. Of the betrayal or that I was a suspect in his murder."

"My apologies," Tilda murmured. "You are completely entitled to be upset about both of those things."

Hadrian knew she wholly supported him and was grateful for the relationship they had. "Setting aside the romance between them, it's possible Mallory was upset about Mrs. Frost leaving for non-romantic reasons. Perhaps he was concerned she would reveal society secrets."

Tilda's brow creased. "Then why not pay for her to go away in silence as he did with Grenville last year?" She fell silent a moment before adding, "I suppose it's possible his emotions controlled his actions. His father indicated he could be volatile."

Hadrian's blood chilled. He'd been so worried he was going mad when he started seeing and feeling things. Tilda had assured him time and time again that he was not. Now she was suggesting the opposite about Mallory. Whilst Hadrian didn't care for the man, he did not want to think that someone like him suffered from anything akin to madness. That would mean that Hadrian was perhaps vulnerable too.

"I still can't countenance him as the Levitation Killer," Hadrian said. "It seems antithetic for him to endanger the very society he founded. Murdering its prominent mediums would turn people away from it."

Tilda looked at him slyly. "Or perhaps draw attention to it.

The Levitation Killer is the talk of London. They're even aware of the murders here in Swindon."

"You are again suggesting that Mallory is perhaps mentally unstable." Hadrian took a breath to slow his racing pulse. "He'd have to be in order to commit such heinous acts."

"I'm only thinking through ideas," Tilda said, seemingly oblivious to the turmoil he was suffering. "We ought to consider that Mallory might be … less than reasonable."

"Struggling to deal with this bloody curse does not make him mad," Hadrian snapped.

Tilda's eyes rounded briefly, and Hadrian realized he'd spoken sharply.

"My apologies," he said gruffly. He was not himself after all he'd learned today. Worse, he wasn't quite sure when he would be. Perhaps the man he thought he was had disappeared in January, when he'd been stabbed and had hit his head on the pavement. This new Hadrian wasn't comfortable.

"Don't apologize." Tilda touched his arm. "I must apologize. You are not like Mallory, apart from the similar gift you each have. I should have realized how deeply our interview with Captain Vale affected you—as it should have. But we can talk about that another time, as you said."

Hadrian exhaled after holding his breath whilst she spoke. He was very glad for Tilda's presence. She calmed him, and she understood him. He worked to focus on their investigation and all they'd learned today. "Our trip to Swindon has given us much to consider."

Tilda's brows rose as she nodded. "Quite. We know much more about Mallory, including that he is really Thaddeus Vale, that he has the power to experience others' memories, which he uses to blackmail others in order to enrich himself and the society."

"And, most important of all, that he is likely a murderer and threatened you."

"Teague will be shocked when we tell him that." Tilda frowned. "Though we can't tell him about Mallory's power. I suppose we could. We wouldn't have to reveal that you possess it too." She was watching him carefully.

Hadrian shook his head. "He wouldn't believe us, and anyway, there's no way to prove it under the law."

"That is true," she said on a sigh. "We will still call on him to disclose the rest. I'm glad he gave us his home address."

"Whilst I hate to disturb him, it must be done."

"Oh, he will want to be disturbed." Tilda's eyes simmered with purpose. "All of London will be relieved when he arrests the Levitation Killer."

CHAPTER 16

*L*each was waiting for them at the train station when they arrived in London and quickly conveyed them to Teague's house. However, Teague was not at home. Mrs. Teague told them he'd been called to Scotland Yard, but she did not know why.

When they arrived at Scotland Yard, the reason became immediately clear: another medium—Victor Hawkins—had been killed.

Consequently, Teague was actually not at Scotland Yard. He was, as a constable explained to them, "At the scene of the latest death by levitation." The description made Tilda frown.

Now, she and Hadrian were on their way to Ward's house, where Hawkins had just taken up residence the day before.

As the coach moved toward Willow Street, Tilda's mind churned and her belly tossed. She was upset to learn that Hawkins had been murdered.

"The society is running low on mediums," Hadrian said quietly, his focus on the window as they neared Willow Street. "I am sorry we didn't learn that Mallory was the author of that letter to you sooner."

"I am struggling to understand why he would kill the mediums he'd recruited for the society he started." Perhaps it really was that he'd lost his senses.

Hadrian fixed his gaze on her. "The letter he wrote to you implied that he killed them. Do we need to determine his motive, or can we leave that to Teague?"

"I am an investigator," Tilda replied. "I keep asking questions until I don't have any."

The coach stopped. Leach opened the door a moment later, and they climbed down. A police wagon was parked in front of the house, and a constable stood at the front door.

Ezra Clement walked toward them on the pavement. "Here again, my lord, Miss Wren?" the reporter asked.

"As are you," Hadrian noted with thinly veiled impatience.

"Even you must agree that all of London wants to hear about this story. I am not the only reporter here." He glanced down the pavement at a small group of gentlemen who were looking in their direction.

"You are the only one, however, who intercepted us," Tilda said.

Clement shrugged. "I recognized the earl's coach. I rather hoped our previous encounters might mean that you would agree to speak with me."

Tilda blinked at him. "About what?"

"Why you are here, to start." Clement's brows pitched together. "Are you investigating these murders, Miss Wren?"

"I'm afraid I can't say."

Clement blew out a breath. "Pity. You never know when I might have information that could help you. Ah, well, I don't wish to impede your progress." He moved aside and gestured for them to pass.

Tilda almost hesitated. What information could Clement have that would be helpful?

"Ignore him," Hadrian said as they continued on their way. "I'm sure he was only baiting you."

Hadrian was probably right. Tilda shook the encounter with Clement from her mind as they reached the door. Unsurprisingly, the constable stopped them from proceeding into the house.

"We've critical information for Detective Inspector Teague," Tilda said. "It involves this murder."

The constable hesitated until Hadrian said, "Superintendent Newsome will not want to hear that our information was delayed in reaching the detective inspector."

"Lord Ravenhurst is right," Tilda put in, hoping the mention of Hadrian's title would also help ease their passage.

The constable's expression pinched. "The detective inspector is not here. He is at the London Spiritualism Society."

"Thank you," Tilda said whilst Hadrian was already spinning on his heel. She hurried to keep up with him. She was beginning to fear they would never find Teague.

They passed by Clement again, and the reporter asked where they were going. Hadrian didn't slow and neither did Tilda. When they reached the coach, Hadrian directed Leach to take them to the society headquarters in Cadogan Place.

"I must say this is convenient," Hadrian said as he tapped his fingers against his thigh.

Tilda hadn't ever seen him so agitated. "Because Mallory will be there?"

Hadrian's eyes glittered with an edge of malice. "I sincerely hope so."

"You must let Teague handle things," Tilda said. "I know you're angry that Mallory threatened me, but you can't intercede."

"Of course I won't." Hadrian's hand stilled. "But I am eager to see him apprehended. Then I will be able to relax."

When they arrived at the society headquarters, they encountered another constable at the front door. However, this one did not try to stop them. He worked for Teague and recognized them. In fact, he directed them to the parlor where they would find the detective inspector.

Teague stood in the parlor speaking with another constable. He looked toward the doorway as Tilda and Hadrian entered. "Ravenhurst, Miss Wren."

"We don't mean to intrude, but we have vital information," Tilda said as they approached him. "We know who wrote that threatening letter to me."

Teague's nostrils flared. "Who was it?"

"Lysander Mallory," Hadrian replied in a clipped tone.

"How do you know?" Teague asked, his brow furrowing.

"We saw an example of his handwriting," Tilda explained. "We both recognized it immediately. His W is most distinctive."

Teague glanced toward Tilda's reticule. "You have this example of his handwriting with you?"

"We do not," Tilda said. "However, I'm sure you can obtain a sample from his study."

The detective inspector turned his head to the constable. "Go and find out where Mallory might keep writings—a diary or anything in his hand."

The constable nodded and left the parlor.

Tilda addressed Teague once more. "What can you tell us about this latest murder? We're very sorry to hear that Hawkins has been killed."

"He was found in the same manner as the others, though Graythorpe will need to confirm the presence of prussic acid when he completes the autopsy. One of the servants—who doesn't live there—arrived this morning and found him hanging from the staircase."

"The rope was painted again?" Tilda asked.

Teague nodded. "Hawkins appeared to be levitating. The constables interviewed the neighbors, and they are understandably upset that this happened again. As with the prior murders, no one saw anyone unusual entering the house. Indeed, no one saw anyone enter at all today, not even the manservant."

Tilda hated to think of poor Jacob Henry finding Hawkins after he and his sister had found Mrs. Frost not even a week ago. "Was it Jacob Henry?"

"No, a young man named Michael Crocker."

Hadrian looked to Tilda at the precise moment she shot her gaze toward him.

"You know him?" Teague asked.

"We do," Hadrian replied. "We met him Friday when we visited the spiritualism society headquarters, and he was the butler at Hawkins's séance that evening."

"I suppose it makes sense that he would work for Hawkins in his new residence," Tilda said. "Was there no housekeeper or cook? Hawkins employed a Mrs. Wilson as housekeeper at his house in Clerkenwell, but she is not affiliated with the society."

Teague appeared intrigued. "How do you know this?"

"We called on Hawkins last week after Mrs. Frost was killed." Tilda glanced at Hadrian. "Her Grace is going to be very upset." She returned her focus to Teague. "She had chosen Hawkins as her new medium after Cyril Ward died."

A deep frown creased Teague's features as he nodded. "I spoke with Her Grace this afternoon. She was most distressed. It was disconcerting to witness. She was nearly hysterical that all the mediums are dying. Her first thought was that she couldn't lose Mallory too. She sent someone to fetch him to make sure he was all right." Teague put a hand on his hip. "You say Mallory sent you that threatening letter. Why? Did he think you were investigating the murders and wanted you to stop?"

"You'll have to ask him." Hadrian fixed a dark stare on Teague. "Where is he?"

"Ravenhurst, you appear angry," Teague said with concern. "In fact, you look furious. Can I trust you not to attack Mallory, even verbally?"

"Of course I'm angry. The bastard threatened Tilda," Hadrian replied in a low tone that wasn't quite a growl but was very close. "I will maintain my composure."

Teague regarded him a moment, then nodded. "He's in the library." The detective inspector turned and led them from the parlor.

Tilda looked over at Hadrian as they made their way to the library. She believed he would remain composed, but she also saw the fury simmering beneath the surface.

The constable who'd gone to fetch a sample of Mallory's handwriting met them near the entrance to the library. He handed a diary to Teague, who then offered it to Tilda. "Is this his handwriting?"

Tilda opened the book and Mallory's hand jumped from the parchment as did the name Joslin. "Yes. When you compare it to the letter at Scotland Yard, you will see they are a perfect match." She showed it to Hadrian, who nodded. He lifted his gaze toward the library with a steely determination.

Teague took the diary back, which was unfortunate since Tilda wanted to determine why Joslin's name was in it, and snapped it closed. "Thank you."

They walked into the library, where Mallory was seated along with Mrs. Griswold and a handful of other members of the society they'd seen on Friday. Their attention shifted toward the door as Teague entered. Then their gazes moved to Tilda and Hadrian.

Teague fixed a frown on Mallory. "Mr. Mallory, it's come to our attention that you sent a letter to Miss Wren threatening her to stop investigating or she would hang from a staircase. What have you to say about that?"

Mallory's face flushed as he rose. "I did no such thing."

"Don't lie," Hadrian barked. "We've matched your handwriting to the note Miss Wren received."

Teague held up the book. "This diary was in your office. Miss Wren and Lord Ravenhurst recognize the handwriting within as matching that of the note Miss Wren received two days ago. I am confident that when I view it next to the letter I have at Scotland Yard, I will see that both were written by the same hand. Given the nature of your threat, it seems you are likely responsible for the deaths of the three mediums."

"I am not!" Mallory shouted. Others in the room also called out. A few of them stood and gestured wildly as they spoke.

"Silence!" Teague glowered at everyone as they closed their mouths. Mallory looked as though he might continue, but Teague took a step toward him. "Do not, Mr. Mallory. Unless you are going to explain yourself."

Mallory took a deep breath, but his face remained red, and his eyes were dark and almost feral. "I did write that note, but not for the reasons you think."

The society members began talking again, defending Mallory, but also shooting him looks of concern. Miss Dryden and Mrs. Griswold moved to stand on either side of Mallory, but he did not seem to notice. His attention was fixed on Teague—and Tilda and Hadrian.

"Explain," Teague said crisply.

"I didn't want Miss Wren nosing about the society anymore," Mallory said.

"Why not?" Teague demanded.

"We have … secrets that should not be disclosed."

"Such as how you use tables with hollow pedestals?" Hadrian asked harshly. "Or tricks to pretend you are levitating? Or that your name is really Thaddeus Vale?"

Mallory's gaze snapped to Hadrian, then narrowed almost malevolently. "Many of our members and the people we serve have secrets they don't wish to have publicized, my lord. I should think you of all people would understand that."

Tilda's breath caught. That wasn't exactly a threat, but it seemed clear to her that Mallory was communicating that he was aware of Hadrian's deepest secret. He knew of Hadrian's ability and could expose him. She looked at Hadrian and saw the tight set of his jaw, as well as the erratic pulse in his neck. Edging closer, she brushed her gloved hand against his.

"What is that supposed to mean?" Teague snapped.

"I believe he's referring to the fact that Hadrian's mother recently attended a séance for the purpose of speaking to her dead son," Tilda replied quickly. She'd wanted to add that Mallory was also using the secrets he just mentioned to extort people, but she didn't dare. She wasn't sure if Mallory would actually expose Hadrian's secret, but she wasn't going to take the risk.

Hadrian and Mallory held each other's gazes whilst Tilda held her breath. After a long moment, Mallory nodded.

"You mention secrets, Mr. Mallory," Teague said. "Does that include the ones you used to blackmail people who attended your séances?"

This was met with more gasps from others in the library. Mallory's color faded as his eyes darkened with worry.

"I'm arresting you for breaking the peace. And I may add extortion, as well as murder, to the charge since you certainly implied that you killed the mediums."

"I wanted to frighten Miss Wren!" Mallory cried, his eyes becoming wild once more. "I wouldn't kill my own mediums, my *friends*. Why would I do that?"

Tilda decided it was time to wade into the fray to support Teague. "It's possible you were jealous of your mediums and the attention they received, particularly from important people such as the Duchess of Chester. You were quick to align yourself with her after Cyril Ward's death."

"Of course I was. Her Grace is our largest benefactor." Mallory shook his head, his lips pursing. "More importantly, she was devastated by Cyril's death—as we all are. I sought to provide comfort."

"Or you were swooping in to take advantage of her in a time of grief, and when Hawkins won her support, you killed him too," Hadrian said.

A few of the members gasped.

Mrs. Griswold clasped Mallory's hand. "He would never do that."

"He didn't kill Victor or Cyril." Miss Dryden clutched Mallory's arm. "Or Deborah."

Tilda noted the two women's staunch defense of Mallory and wondered if either of them was the woman Grenville had mentioned. Was Mallory involved with one of them? Or, looking at how they clung to him, perhaps both? "Mrs. Frost expressed a desire to leave the society." Tilda met Mallory's gaze. "She was also your former lover. Perhaps you grew angry with her or were concerned she would expose the secrets of your society. I don't think it's a stretch of the imagination to believe you would kill her." She said the last in an effort to push Mallory so she could see his reaction. Was he still as volatile as he once was?

Mallory did not disappoint. He pulled away from the women flanking him and took a step toward Tilda. "Watch yourself, Miss Wren. You don't know me or what I am capable of."

Hadrian put himself in front of Tilda, and for the barest moment, she worried he was going to launch himself at the medium. "*You* watch yourself, Mallory."

"Don't threaten me, Ravenhurst," Mallory growled. "If I am exposed, so are you."

There could be no mistaking what he meant. And Hadrian knew it. He grabbed Mallory by the lapel of his coat. Mallory swung his arm and hit Hadrian in the cheek.

Tilda rushed forward and clasped Hadrian's arm—the one that was holding Mallory. "Hadrian, step away!"

Teague and the constable were there in an instant and separated the two men. "Put him in irons," Teague directed, his head moving toward Mallory to indicate he meant him and not Hadrian.

Mallory fought as the constable turned on him, and it took him and Teague to wrestle him into the manacles that clasped around his wrists. Mallory's face was bright red, and he was breathing loudly and erratically, his chest heaving.

Tilda kept a hold on Hadrian, not because she thought she could stop him if he wanted to go after Mallory again, but because she hoped to soothe him. "He isn't going to say anything," Tilda whispered. "Not unless we do first, and there's no reason to. He's done plenty wrong without exposing his ability and how he uses it to defraud people."

Hadrian turned to face her. "I don't know how I feel about keeping quiet on that matter in order to protect myself." His expression darkened and then flattened, as if a veil had passed over him to mask his emotions.

Two more constables had entered the library and now joined the third, who was holding onto Mallory.

"Put him in the wagon," Teague said. "I'll be out shortly, and we'll take him to Scotland Yard."

"I need my gloves," Mallory demanded. Did he still rely on them to keep the visions at bay?

Miss Dryden stepped forward. "I'll fetch them."

Mallory's expression calmed slightly as he regarded her. "Thank you, Isidora."

She hastened from the library.

"Go on then," Teague said. "Miss Dryden can meet you in the entrance hall. If she takes too long, do not wait."

The constables took Mallory away.

Mrs. Griswold advanced on Teague, her eyes flashing. "You can't arrest Lysander. He didn't do anything wrong."

"I would argue he's done plenty wrong," Teague said. He looked around at the rest of the members, all of whom were now standing. "If any of you would come forward to share what you know about Mr. Mallory, particularly with regard to his black-mailing schemes and his relationships with the other mediums, especially those who were killed, the Metropolitan Police would greatly appreciate it. Even if we've questioned you before, we will be doing so again. A pair of constables will return shortly." He gave them all a meaningful stare before turning to Tilda and Hadrian.

The detective inspector addressed them in a low tone. "I would ask that you not stay here." He looked at Hadrian in particular. "I suggest you go home and have a brandy."

"Inspector, we can't lose Lysander too," Mrs. Griswold cried. "The society needs him!"

Miss Dryden returned to the library. "Lysander is innocent!"

The members began shouting and talking loudly over one another. Teague stalked from the library.

"Come, Hadrian." Tilda took his arm and pulled him toward the door. Thankfully, he moved along with her.

They left the house and watched the police wagon depart. Two of the constables returned to the house, passing Tilda and Hadrian.

Tilda turned to look at Hadrian's face. She lifted her hand to his reddened cheek. "Does it hurt?"

"A little," he said.

Tilda brushed her fingertips over his flesh. "A brandy would probably not come amiss."

He held her gaze. "I apologize for losing my composure. It was not well done of me."

"I understand why you did, and I do not think any less of you." On the contrary, she was moved in a way she could not describe that he would fight so fiercely to protect her. He'd done so before, even putting himself into harm's way and suffering the consequences. How could she ever have doubted that they would no longer be friends after that silly kiss? Surely this demonstrated how strong their bond was. It would not be diminished by a lapse in judgement.

It was a long, electric moment before Tilda blinked. She pulled her hand back. "Let's get you home."

"You first," he said with a faint smile.

They returned to Hadrian's coach. After climbing inside, Tilda sat on the forward-facing seat and scooted over to make room for Hadrian. "Sit with me, please."

Hadrian hesitated only slightly before settling next to her. She realized they'd sat together in the gig in Swindon, their bodies grazing one another. But having him beside her here where he'd kissed her not too terribly long ago sent a flash of awareness through her.

That was normal, she decided. They'd put the kiss behind them, but it was still in the recent past. Of course she would still think of it. In time, the memory would fade.

A small voice in the back of her mind said it would not.

She ignored that voice.

As the coach began moving, she turned her head toward him. "I don't think you need to worry about Mallory exposing your secret. He doesn't want anyone to know about him either."

"I hate that he knows," Hadrian said acidly. "It's like an axe hanging over my neck that can drop at any time."

"Will anyone believe him though?" Tilda was trying hard to be rational.

"I'd rather not find out."

"Then we'll make sure he knows that you've no intention of exposing him. Provided he makes the same promise."

Hadrian folded his arms across his chest. "I'm not sure we can trust him. The man is likely a murderer."

Likely, but not certainly. Whilst the motives Tilda had offered were reasonable, they needed more proof. "I am still bothered by the fact that he would kill the very mediums he trained in the society he worked so hard to build."

Hadrian's eyes lit, but not with the same fire he'd displayed earlier. "You saw how he reacted. I don't think we can discount his volatility or that he may even possess a violent nature." Hadrian uncrossed his arms and smoothed his hand over his cheek.

Tilda recalled what she'd seen in the ledger from Mallory's office. "Did you notice the name Joslin in the diary when I showed it to you?"

"I did not." Hadrian turned slightly toward her, his expression shifting to one of interest. "Wasn't he someone who went to one of Mrs. Frost's séances?"

"Yes. Mrs. Langdon mentioned him," Tilda replied. "I think we should call on him tomorrow and try to determine why his name was listed in Mallory's diary."

"You are nothing if not thorough," Hadrian remarked.

"Nothing is more important than the truth," she said firmly. "Even if we don't like it."

CHAPTER 17

*A*fter a poor night of sleep that not even two snifters of brandy could ease, Hadrian was eager to see Tilda. The *Daily News* had contained a rather sensational story by none other than Ezra Clement about the latest victim of the Levitation Killer.

Hadrian wondered how quickly Clement must have written the article, for it included Mallory's arrest, which had occurred late in the day. It also held many other fascinating details that Hadrian was anxious to discuss with Tilda.

Tilda was ready to depart when he arrived. Garbed in her gray gown, she looked smart and beautiful. Hadrian kept himself from complimenting her.

When she settled on the forward-facing seat, Hadrian noted that she sat closer to the side of the coach as she had the day before. He took that as a silent invitation for him to sit beside her again. So he did.

She'd meant to calm him yesterday with her proximity, and he had no quarrel with that. On the contrary, he'd liked her concern very much. And she *had* eased his agitation.

"How is your cheek today?" Tilda asked once they were on their way toward Montpelier Square to call on Douglas Joslin.

"It does not pain me," Hadrian replied. "Mallory's strike caused only fleeting irritation."

"I'm glad to hear it." She angled herself toward him on the seat. "Did you by chance read the *Daily News* this morning?"

Hadrian faced her as well. "I was going to ask you the same. Clement's article was most illuminating."

Tilda pursed her lips. "As an investigator, I am disappointed to learn things from him, but I suppose I must not complain. It is good to have the information however possible. He's interviewed several people connected to the society—or tried to anyway."

Hadrian nodded. The article had included a few quotes from someone called Harmony Smith, a young medium, who said she was leaving the society because of the murders. There were also statements from people who refused to be named—mostly that they fully supported the society and trusted that the Levitation Killer would be caught soon. There were still others whom Clement indicated had declined to comment. Overall, he concluded that the society was somewhat shrouded in secrecy and that it appeared shaken by all it had endured recently.

"What do you think about Harmony Smith leaving the society?" Hadrian asked.

"I'm not surprised that a medium would choose to distance themselves from the society after three other mediums have been murdered. Honestly, I'm surprised more have not done the same."

"Clement certainly painted a portrait of a society that is falling part."

"Especially with the arrest of its leader. Clement made no small point of that." Tilda cocked her head. "I was also interested to read about the pearl earring I found at Mrs. Frost's house when her body was discovered. I have to think he spoke with the Henry siblings."

"We could ask Clement," Hadrian suggested, though the idea of approaching the man for information was unappealing.

Tilda gave him an arch look. "I am not sure he will want to share information after the way we brushed him off yesterday. Although, if we offered him something in return, he may be more amenable. I shall think on it."

They arrived in Montpelier Square and departed the coach. Hadrian rapped upon Joslin's door and handed his card to the butler.

The butler's brows briefly shot up before he invited them inside. He showed them to a sitting room just off the entrance hall, then departed to fetch Mr. Joslin.

"It may be best if you begin the conversation," Tilda said. "Since you and he are acquainted."

Hadrian nodded. He didn't know Joslin well, but they'd conversed from time to time at Brooks's.

Joslin entered the sitting room a few moments later. He'd grown a beard and mustache since Hadrian had seen him last. They were white, which made the man seem older than his sixty or so years, probably because the hair on his head was a mix of brown and gray.

"Ravenhurst, what a surprise." He reached out to shake Hadrian's hand.

Removing his glove, Hadrian clasped the man's hand and immediately saw a vision, though it didn't last long. Hadrian saw the interior of Brooks's—and himself. That was the first time he'd seen himself in someone's memory. It was disconcerting.

Hadrian gestured to Tilda. "This is my colleague, Miss Matilda Wren."

"I'm pleased to meet you, Mr. Joslin," Tilda said warmly.

Joslin inclined his head. "Please, sit. I can't imagine why you've called today."

Tilda and Hadrian sat together on a settee, whilst their host took a chair across from them.

"I hope you won't find the reason of our visit intrusive," Hadrian said. "Miss Wren is a private investigator, and I assist her."

"*You* assist *her*?" Joslin blinked.

"Yes," Hadrian replied patiently. "She is investigating the London Spiritualism Society. Mrs. Langdon informed us that you attended a séance—or perhaps séances—conducted by Mrs. Frost."

Joslin's bushy gray brows drew together over his small, dark eyes. "I've nothing to say on the matter of that society or Mrs. Frost, God rest her poor soul."

"Indeed?" Tilda asked, her tone hinting at surprise. "Mrs. Langdon indicated that you'd been very pleased with your séance experience."

"I was until recently," Joslin ground out. He looked away from them, his jaw tense. "I don't wish to discuss it."

Hadrian leaned slightly toward the man. "Would it help you to know that we don't believe the society is capable of what it claims? They perform cheap tricks and don't actually communicate with the dead."

Joslin shot his attention back to Hadrian. "What do you mean?"

"Exactly what I said."

"How do you know they don't speak to the dead?" Joslin sounded skeptical. "They … knew things that they could not have without communicating with the spirit realm."

"They?" Hadrian asked. "Not Mrs. Frost?"

"I don't know who exactly," Joslin replied. He coughed and looked away again.

"What things did they learn from the spirit realm?" Tilda asked.

Joslin sent her an apologetic glance, his cheeks turning pink. "I'd rather not say in front of you, Miss Wren."

Tilda nodded. "I do understand, Mr. Joslin. I am not sure if you are aware that Mr. Mallory, the head of the spiritualism society, was arrested yesterday. Among other crimes, he has been accused of blackmail. Your name was listed in his diary, and we wondered why."

Their host sucked in a breath. "You think he …" He exhaled. "Yes, I was blackmailed."

Hadrian exchanged a look with Tilda, and though her expression was benign, he could see the light of triumph and curiosity in her eyes. He gave her a subtle nod before addressing Joslin. "Perhaps you wouldn't mind telling me what happened."

Tilda rose. "I'll wait in the entrance hall." She smiled at Joslin. "We appreciate your assistance with our investigation, Mr. Joslin."

She left, and Hadrian gave Joslin a frank stare. "If you prefer that I not share what you tell me today, I will not. However, if you have information that could help with the prosecution of Mallory, that would be most helpful."

"I don't know if I can help you." Joslin's brow creased as he wiped his palms along his thighs. "I never met Mallory. I went to two séances led by Mrs. Frost. I attended to converse with my brother. He'd died unexpectedly." Joslin met his gaze with a frown. "Though she was unable to reach him at the first séance, she found success at the second. He seemed to speak to me through her. But you're saying that was fakery?"

"We believe so. The mediums seem to have certain skills they use to make guesses about people that are accurate enough to appear as though they have some knowledge." Hadrian had no choice but to lie. He couldn't very well tell Joslin about Mallory seeing others' memories.

Joslin blinked. "They aren't really speaking to the spirit realm?"

"No. The society is a money-making scheme run by its leader, Lysander Mallory. I am sorry you were duped by them."

Joslin's eyes rounded as he stared at Hadrian. "I paid a good sum for that second séance, and then they blackmailed me as well."

Hadrian wasn't surprised, given the man's reaction when Tilda had mentioned blackmail. "Do you have proof? Scotland Yard would very much like to see it and hear your testimony."

"Er, I no longer have the letter I received." Joslin flushed. "I paid the money and burned the letter. I'd hoped that would be the end of it."

"Perhaps you could explain what happened?" Hadrian asked. "That would be helpful."

"You say they lied about speaking to the spirit realm, but there is no other way they could have obtained the information they used to extort me. The only other person who could have known died." The man looked away.

Damn, that would be hard to explain without revealing how the medium had really obtained the information—from Mallory. Though Hadrian could not tell Joslin the truth, he wanted to confirm that Mallory had used his power to mine this man's memories. "Did you ever meet Mr. Mallory?"

Joslin's brows drew together. "I'm not sure. Remind me what he looks like?"

"Blond hair, intense dark eyes. He's quite affable. I'm sure you would have liked him." Hadrian kept himself from sneering.

Giving his head a shake, Joslin said, "I can't be certain."

Disappointed to not have the confirmation he sought, Hadrian returned to Joslin's tale. "There is absolutely no one else who could know the information they used to blackmail you?"

Joslin made fleeting eye contact with Hadrian as he clenched his jaw. "Several years ago, I had a mistress and she … was increasing. I was afraid my wife would learn that I had been unfaithful." He glanced toward the upper floor of the house. "She's not home just now."

Hadrian froze when the man said he was afraid. That did not bode well. "What happened?"

Joslin paled. "I paid for a surgeon to remove the babe. Abigail —my mistress—did not survive."

Hadrian felt a flash of revulsion for the man but did not allow it to show. "What did the letter say?"

"It had details about what happened. They knew her name." Joslin squeezed his eyes shut. "And that of the surgeon, as well as how he told me of Abigail's death." Joslin wiped his brow. "I'd never thought to live through that again."

Mallory must have experienced Joslin's memory.

"The note demanded money?" Hadrian prompted.

"Yes. Two hundred pounds, which I delivered to a grocer they indicated."

"You paid the money?" Hadrian would never. "Why not just ignore them? What could they have done?"

"They threatened to tell my wife, and I've no doubt she would have believed them. She learned I had a mistress once and was most upset." Joslin's face flushed. "Abigail was not the first." He closed his eyes briefly before meeting Hadrian's gaze once more. "However, I have been faithful since that tragedy. God has seen fit to give me a chance to redeem myself."

But not poor Abigail. Hadrian kept his thoughts—and judgment—to himself. He was particularly inclined to dislike men who betrayed their wives, as his father had done continually to Hadrian's mother.

"You mentioned a grocer." Hadrian assumed it was the same grocer Eldred had mentioned. "Where was it located?"

"Bedfordbury." Joslin shuddered. "Terrible place."

"And what did you do with the money when you went there?" Hadrian asked.

"The letter said to leave the money with a Mr. Timms, and that is what I did."

"Mr. Timms didn't question why you were giving him two hundred pounds?"

"He didn't seem to, but I didn't say what it was for." Joslin's face was bright red. "I handed him a purse with the funds and said I was there to deliver it as instructed by a letter. Timms nodded and took the purse from me. That was the end of the transaction."

"What does Timms look like?" Hadrian wondered if Timms was another alias used by Thaddeus Vale, though Joslin had already said he wasn't sure if he'd met Mallory.

"He's a small man—very short—with dark hair." Joslin made an unpleasant face. "He was most unfriendly." He straightened, his brows drawing together with consternation. "I think you are wrong about the mediums not speaking with the spirit realm. They must. There is no other way they would know about Abigail."

"Have you considered that the surgeon may have shared the story?" Hadrian asked.

Joslin's features arrested. He was silent a moment. "I had not. That was years ago. How would they even find him?"

Hadrian lifted a shoulder. "I do not know how they manage their tricks, but I promise you they are not speaking to the dead." He exhaled, eager to leave Joslin's presence. "Thank you for telling me what happened. I can see that was difficult to share."

"Will it help the police?"

"I think so," Hadrian said. "However, you will likely need to provide testimony to Scotland Yard."

Joslin shifted in his chair uncomfortably. "I don't know if I can do that."

"I think you will want to help the police, else you may look suspicious," Hadrian said with a faint shrug. "Three of the society's mediums have been murdered, and your blackmail gives you a motive to have killed them."

"I did not kill anyone!" Joslin's face burned bright red. "How dare you insinuate that!"

"I am merely informing you of the facts, Mr. Joslin. I am sure the Metropolitan Police will wish to interview you." Hadrian stood. "Presumably, you have alibis you can provide for the times of the murders."

"Of course I do," Joslin spluttered.

"Good day. You can expect a visit from a detective inspector." Hadrian left to join Tilda in the entrance hall and escorted her outside.

"I heard him shouting," Tilda said.

"He was outraged when I suggested the blackmail gave him a motive to kill the mediums."

Tilda's brows shot up. "You did that?"

"He didn't want to share his story with Scotland Yard. I said that would add suspicion to him when he already had a motive."

"Well done." She sounded impressed. "Did he have alibis for the murders?"

"He said he did but did not elaborate. I assume he will provide them to the police."

"We must go to Scotland Yard to inform Teague," Tilda said.

"Agreed," Hadrian replied. "I'll explain about the blackmail in the coach."

Instead of sitting beside Tilda, he sat on the opposite seat so that he could face her. "It's easier to converse like this," he explained, though he probably didn't need to.

"Sometimes, yes," she said with a smile. "How horrid was Joslin's tale?"

"It didn't make him likeable." Hadrian repeated what he'd learned and watched the horror rise in Tilda's expression.

Tilda briefly covered her mouth with her hand. "Poor Abigail. Did you see any of that when you shook Joslin's hand after we arrived?"

"Thankfully, no. I saw him at Brooks's. Rather, I saw myself at Brooks's because I was experiencing his memory. It's the first time I've seen myself in a vision, and I don't mind telling you that I didn't care for it."

"That would be very strange. What happened?"

"Nothing. It was more of a flash of a vision and was gone as quick as it came." Hadrian exhaled. "I was most relieved. A vision like that does not bring a headache."

"I'm certainly glad to hear that," Tilda said. "We should visit this grocer where the blackmail victims have been directed to pay the extortion. It would be most helpful to establish a connection between the grocer and the society."

"Agreed. Joslin mentioned the man he paid is called Timms. He described him as very short with dark hair."

"That doesn't sound like anyone we've met at the society."

"It does not," Hadrian said. "Bedfordbury is a terrible slum. You should bring your father's pistol."

"I will do that. Perhaps you should also arm yourself." Tilda looked out the window, her expression contemplative. "I'm glad you asked about Joslin's alibis. I don't think we can assume this case is closed with Mallory being arrested. The evidence against him isn't strong. Joslin has a greater reason to want to kill the mediums than Mallory does, as did Eldred, who was also blackmailed. We should probably speak with Mrs. Horace Tarrant about her blackmail experience, though I doubt a woman would be strong enough to commit these crimes. At least not without help."

"I agree. There have to be other victims."

Tilda nodded. "I hope that Teague has questioned Mallory on this issue. Whilst he won't want to admit to blackmail, he may do so in order to help find the killer and prove his own innocence."

"I would certainly do that," Hadrian said.

"*Blast*," Tilda said crossly, her eyes flashing. "I saw Joslin's name in Mallory's diary. Now that we know Joslin was blackmailed, perhaps other victims are listed within it. I hope Teague will let me review it."

"An excellent idea. But why does that vex you?"

She crossed her arms over her chest and pursed her lips. "I should have thought of it sooner."

"You did think of it," Hadrian said. "And it's not as if there aren't a surplus of threads for us to be following at the moment. This investigation is quite complex."

"You're right," Tilda said as she unfolded her arms and allowed her shoulders to relax. "One of those threads is Harmony Smith. I want to find out why she left the society." Her brow knitted. "This isn't a thread, but what about your mother? She will know about Hawkins's death by now."

Glancing out the window, Hadrian saw they were nearing Scotland Yard. "I forgot to tell you that I sent her a note when I arrived home yesterday evening. I apologized for not calling in person and suggested she pause any further séance attendance."

"Did she respond?" Tilda asked.

"Not before I left to fetch you. I may call at her house after we visit Scotland Yard." The coach stopped at their destination.

"Do you think she'll agree to pause her efforts to communicate with Gabriel?"

Hadrian met her gaze. "I hope so because you and I both know for certain that it's never going to happen. Furthermore, I won't allow her to be sucked into becoming a patroness, or worse —becoming their next blackmail victim."

"But will that happen now that Mallory is arrested?" Tilda mused. "I do wonder what will happen to the society without him at the helm."

"I hope it dissolves," Hadrian said. "With complete haste."

CHAPTER 18

Tilda and Hadrian entered the building and were quickly shown to Teague's office. The detective inspector stood upon seeing them. "You look as though you've news to share."

"We just interviewed Douglas Joslin," Tilda said. "Rather, Hadrian did most of the interviewing because Mr. Joslin did not wish to share certain information with me."

Teague arched a brow, his eyes gleaming with great interest. "What was that?"

"He was blackmailed recently, just like Eldred," Hadrian said. "He suspects the spiritualism society, as Eldred did." He went on to relate what Joslin had told him. Tilda did not enjoy listening to the tale a second time.

"If Mallory is responsible for the blackmail, I am very curious how he collects this information," Teague said. "The extortion for Eldred and for Joslin was about events that happened not at all recently."

Tilda slid a look toward Hadrian. They could not tell Teague the truth—that Mallory had seen these people's memories. "I'll be anxious to hear what Mallory says when you ask him that."

Indeed, Tilda wanted to know if Mallory would expose his ability, though she had to think he would not. How, then, would he explain how he obtained the information he'd used to blackmail people?

Teague nodded vaguely. "This blackmail gives Joslin a motive for murder."

"It does indeed," Hadrian agreed. "I told him he would need to provide his alibis to you. He was thoroughly indignant when I suggested he might be a killer."

"I will call on him shortly."

"We learned of another blackmail victim from Grenville the other day," Tilda said. "I apologize that we didn't share that information yesterday. There was much going on."

"There was. Who is this victim?" Teague asked.

Tilda explained what Grenville had told them about Mrs. Horace Tarrant. "I'm inclined to think she is not the murderer, given the strength that is needed to levitate the bodies."

"Still, we will interview her."

"Discreetly, if you can," Tilda urged him. "The blackmail was because she'd been having an affair. I'm sure she won't want anyone to know why you are speaking with her."

"Understood," Teague said with a nod. "I am sensitive to such matters."

"Thank you." Tilda glanced toward his desk. "I'd like to review Mallory's diary. I saw Joslin's name inside when we looked at it yesterday. Now that we know he was blackmailed, perhaps there are other victims listed in the diary."

"That is good to know." Teague gave her an apologetic look. "However, I'm sure you understand that I need to review it first, since it is already evidence against Mallory."

Tilda had been afraid he might say that. "Of course. It sounds as if you've much to do in pursuit of Mallory's blackmail."

"We do, and I deeply appreciate your help. I have to think Mallory will be helpful, particularly if it will help his cause. He maintains his innocence and claims he loves nothing more in this life than the London Spiritualism Society. He says he would never do anything to harm it or its mediums, whom he cherished as family."

"Do you believe him?" Hadrian asked.

Teague shrugged. "He's very convincing. He confessed that the society employs various tricks to entertain people during séances, which gave him a modicum of credibility. He argued that people expect a thrilling spectacle." Teague's brows rose briefly. "I wanted to tell you that we've sent a telegram to his father, Captain Vale. In all the commotion yesterday at the spiritualism headquarters, I didn't have a chance to ask you if Thaddeus Vale was related to Captain Vale, who leased the property. I have since learned he is the man's son."

"We met with Captain Vale when we traveled to Swindon the day before yesterday," Tilda explained. "I expect he'll come to London. Captain Vale was concerned for his son because of the murders."

"He didn't think his son might have committed them?" Teague asked.

Hadrian shook his head. "No. We didn't ask him, but I am confident he would have said no."

Tilda crossed her arms over her chest. "I have to say that I'm not convinced Mallory is the killer."

"There is a disappointing lack of direct evidence," Teague said with more than a hint of frustration. "The fact that he sent you a threatening letter does not prove he is the Levitation Killer." Teague cursed under his breath. "Pardon me. I do not care to use that ridiculous term the press has given this heinous murderer."

"I understand, though it is difficult with so many news stories about it and so much discussion," Tilda said. Mrs. Acorn had said many people were talking about it at the market that morning.

"If the killer intended to create a spectacle, they have succeeded," Teague said grimly. "But why? What would be the point?"

"The obvious answer would be to scare mediums and perhaps prevent them from continuing their work," Tilda replied. "However, they haven't done so."

"On the contrary, they've continued as if nothing is amiss." Teague shook his head in disbelief. "The constable who was stationed at the society headquarters this morning reported that they are overrun with people wanting to attend séances and to see where the murders occurred."

Hadrian wrinkled his nose. "How ghoulish."

They fell silent a moment, everyone seeming to contemplate the case. Teague exhaled. "I'd best get back to it. I'll let you know what I learn from the diary. We will find this killer."

Tilda and Hadrian took their leave a few minutes later.

"I keep thinking about the article Clement wrote," Tilda said. "I'd like to speak with him. I wonder if he could be persuaded to tell us who else he spoke to besides Harmony Smith."

"Would you like to visit Fleet Street next?" Hadrian asked.

"I would," Tilda said. "Thank you."

However, outside the police station, they encountered two of the mediums from the spiritualism society—Isidora Dryden and the male medium whom Mallory had suggested as a replacement for Lady Ravenhurst after Mrs. Frost had been murdered. Tilda recalled his name was Nigel Edwards.

Miss Dryden's gray eyes filled with recognition as soon as she saw them. "My lord, Miss Wren. We've come to see Lysander. Did you see him?"

"Of course they didn't," Edwards, who appeared to be around Tilda's age, said with a faint sneer. "They are the reason he was arrested. I'm sure they were here trying to ensure he hangs." He fixed Hadrian with an angry stare. "Why do you dislike him so much? He's done nothing but help people, including your mother!"

Tilda hadn't taken Hadrian's arm when they'd left the station, but she did so now. Immediately, she felt his tension in the stiffness of his arm.

"You mustn't shout like that, Nigel," Miss Dryden said. She sniffed and blinked, as if she were trying not to dissolve into tears. Her cheeks and small, pert nose were flushed. "My apologies, Lord Ravenhurst. We are very upset about Lysander. He is not a killer. We're sick that he's been imprisoned. I imagine he's cold and hungry. And probably in need of a bath." Her features pinched, making her appear quite stricken.

Edwards put his arm around Miss Dryden and gave her a squeeze. "All will turn out well, Isidora. It has to." He looked to Hadrian and ducked his chin. "Please accept my apologies, my lord. This is a very trying time, and I'm afraid my emotions—indeed, all our emotions—are high."

Miss Dryden nodded as she pressed a gloved fingertip to the corner of one eye.

Tilda didn't doubt their upset, even if they did work to defraud people. She wondered how involved the mediums were with the implementation of the society's trickery. Surely they were well-versed in the cheats that were used during the séances, but what of the blackmailing?

"We shall see for ourselves how Lysander is doing," Edwards went on.

Miss Dryden looked to Tilda. "We are here to visit him. It's so difficult without him," she said somewhat dramatically. "We are doing our best to carry on."

Edwards turned toward Miss Dryden and took her hand. "Listen to me, my dear, Lysander will guide us. Even now, Mercy is settling into Rathbone Place and will hold a magnificent séance tonight. The society is truly thriving."

Thriving? With three dead mediums? Tilda stared at them.

A smile lifted Miss Dryden's lips, and she briefly closed her eyes as she exhaled. "You are right, Nigel." She released his hands and looked to Tilda and Hadrian. "It's astonishing how many people have come to support the society today. They want to become patrons or members, and they want to attend séances. That is why Mercy is hosting one this evening." She looked at Hadrian expectantly. "Will you be coming, my lord?"

Tilda's breath stalled in her lungs. She worried what Miss Dryden's question could mean.

Hadrian had stiffened. "No, I have not been invited. Should I have been?"

Miss Dryden blushed faintly. "I thought you might have been since the séance is for Lady Ravenhurst. Perhaps you have not yet received the invitation." She looked away from Hadrian as her voice trailed off.

Glancing sideways at Hadrian, Tilda could see that he'd clenched his jaw. She smiled at the mediums. "We must be off. Please excuse us."

Tilda pulled Hadrian toward the coach, which was a short walk away. He fell into step beside her, moving woodenly as he stared straight ahead.

When they reached the coach, he blinked and fixed his attention on Leach. "We'll be taking Miss Wren home. Then to my mother's."

Leach nodded as he held the door and helped Tilda inside. She sat on the forward-facing seat and was not surprised when Hadrian sat opposite her instead of next to her. His agitation was palpable.

"You're upset that your mother is attending another séance."

"And didn't include us." His eyes glittered with anger. "I am her son, and you are her investigator."

"Perhaps Miss Dryden was correct, and the invitation is waiting for you at home."

"It doesn't signify as I will be going straight to my mother's. I'm sorry, but I would rather have this conversation with her without you present."

"I understand. If you do decide to attend tonight, I'm happy to go with you. If you want me to," she added. Perhaps he wouldn't want her there either.

Tilda felt a stab of disappointment and wasn't sure if it was due to being excluded from her own investigation or because it hurt to think Hadrian didn't want to involve her in the more personal aspects of his life.

Tilda pressed her lips together and looked out the window. She had no right to think she should be involved in Hadrian's life. They were friends, but he didn't owe her anything, nor should she expect it. Especially after she'd made it clear to him that she wasn't interested in a more intimate association.

More and more, she began to wonder if she *was* interested.

Why was she bothering to think about that? There was no point. Love and marriage were not things she aspired to achieve. She could not be an independent woman and a private investigator if she married. Especially if she married an earl.

Not that he would ever ask. The distance between their stations was far too great.

She realized that by firmly establishing their connection as professional colleagues and friends, she would not be privy to certain things, including his family, even if Tilda was working for his mother. She couldn't help thinking that the kiss had changed things irrevocably, if only because it had demanded they set boundaries. And now that they were in place, Tilda perhaps felt regret.

Hadrian didn't respond to her offer. Indeed, he said nothing until the coach stopped at her house.

"Good luck with your mother." Tilda summoned a smile. "I'm sure all will turn out well."

"Thank you for your kindness, Tilda. I appreciate you more than you can realize."

As Tilda left the coach, she told herself not to think too long or too hard on what Hadrian had said. They had a lovely friendship and an excellent working partnership. And that was enough.

~

*P*everell, Hadrian's mother's butler, directed him to his mother's sitting room, which adjoined her bedchamber on the first floor. Hadrian had rarely visited that space, and he couldn't help thinking she'd chosen to receive him there because it would put him off-kilter.

Or it could be that was just where she was, and there was no ulterior motive.

Hadrian shook his head before he walked in to confront his mother. He'd been angry for over a week—as long as he'd known that his mother wanted to contact Gabriel. His anger wasn't just about his mother being cheated by the spiritualism society. He now recognized the anger as what he'd felt after learning of Gabriel's death. And he had anger on top of that anger because he'd thought he'd resolved those feelings, and yet here they were resurfacing. All because his mother had decided to see a medium.

He was angry with her for stirring up his grief.

Exhaling, Hadrian worked to push the rage and sadness away. He'd done it before, and he could do it again.

"Hadrian, why are you loitering outside the doorway?" his mother called from the sitting room.

"Apologies, Mama," he said as he walked inside. He smiled and that felt better.

"I wasn't expecting you today," the dowager countess said from the table where she was drinking tea. "I did receive your note about poor Mr. Hawkins. Would you like tea?"

"No, thank you." Hadrian moved to sit opposite her at the table. "Did you send a response to my note? I've been out most of the day."

"I did not." She sipped her tea.

"Did you, by chance, send me an invitation to tonight's séance?" he asked benignly, though his pulse was moving swiftly.

She set her cup down with a faint grimace. "I did not. I only spoke with Mrs. Griswold this morning."

"You spoke with her?"

"Yes, she called to offer her services for a séance this evening. She knew I'd been to one last week with Mrs. Frost and that I'd wanted to attend another." His mother shrugged as if planning to attend a séance where the previous medium she'd seen had been murdered was a regular occurrence. "Honestly, I was eager to say yes. Mrs. Griswold was very charming. I have an excellent feeling about her."

Hadrian took a deep breath lest he say something rash. "Mama, Tilda explained to you how the mediums use trickery during their séances."

"Yes, but I don't care about that. I only care that they can speak to the dead, and I believe they can."

Instead of asking why she'd bothered to hire Tilda, he smoothed his palm along his thigh as he chose his words. "We've found no proof they can do that. We have, however, found proof that they have blackmailed people."

His mother's eyes rounded. "That's ... horrible. How did you find out?"

"In the course of our investigation," he replied. "I do not want you to fall victim to Mallory's extortion."

"Mallory, you say? Well, I am seeing Mrs. Griswold. Furthermore, how they could possibly blackmail me?" She blinked at him. "There is nothing I would pay to keep secret."

Hadrian wanted to reply that his father had kept secrets. But he'd no idea how much his mother knew. They'd never discussed his father's transgressions, and he didn't want to start doing so now. Furthermore, he'd have to explain how Mallory had learned those secrets. This was becoming a massive problem—he could not fully expose how Mallory committed his crimes without sharing the man's supernatural ability. And if he did, he had to think Mallory would point his finger right back at Hadrian.

"These are unscrupulous people, Mama," Hadrian said. "I am trying to protect you from them."

"I have already paid for tonight's séance." Her tone held a note of hauteur. "I have seen and heard enough to believe that these mediums channel spirits. You can't explain how they know things that they should not."

He fleetingly considered telling his mother about Mallory's ability without revealing he had it too. But he was afraid of her reaction. What if she laughed or was horrified? In the end, he said, "Trust me when I say they employ trickery to make it seem as though they can speak to the dead."

"Can you prove that?"

"Not yet." Hadrian suspected that Tilda would encourage him to be honest with his mother about his power. Perhaps he should …

"Well, until you can, I am going to continue to try to communicate with Gabriel." She gave Hadrian a stern look. "I need to do this tonight. I may not have another chance. You don't understand why this is important to me." She looked away from him.

"I suppose I don't. It won't bring him back."

"I know that," she said crossly. Taking a deep breath, she closed her eyes briefly. When she opened them, she focused on Hadrian once more and seemed to have released some of her frustration. "I miss him. I want him to know how much I love him. I need to know that he is all right."

Gabriel was dead, not across the world in India as he had been. Did his mother not understand the difference? Or was it easier for her to believe that in death, Gabriel wasn't so far away. Perhaps not even as far as India. "I don't think it's wise for you to go tonight," he said softly.

She clasped her hands in her lap and pursed her lips at him. "This is why I didn't invite you. I know you don't support this endeavor."

"It isn't that." At least it wasn't entirely. "I don't think you should attend a séance where the last medium to hold one there was murdered."

His mother's eyes rounded, and her jaw dropped. "I had not considered that." She lifted one hand to her chest. "Oh, dear. Should I not go? What if you come with me?"

"It doesn't bother you to go where someone was killed?"

"You don't have to keep saying that," she said with a look of distress.

"Mama, if it bothers you to hear this, think how you will feel when you walk into the house this evening."

She fell silent, her gaze dropping to the table as her features creased with contemplation. Hadrian hoped he hadn't upset her. That had not been his intent.

At last, she lifted her gaze to his. Her eyes were surprisingly clear. "I must go. Before I no longer have the chance to speak with Gabriel. You must come with me. Please, Hadrian."

Hadrian could not ignore the desperation in her plea, nor the sense that she was trying to grasp something that was lost. If she believed she'd spoken with Gabriel, perhaps she could finally put this behind her. Against his better judgment, he nodded. "All right."

"You should invite Miss Wren so that the numbers are even. Or Tilda, I suppose." She arched her brows at him.

Oh, hell. Why was she using Tilda's given name?

His mother took another sip of tea. As she set the cup back in its saucer, she asked, "What is between the two of you? I have the sense you've grown close, and now you're calling her by her given name. And not even the full, formal one. Isn't she Matilda?"

Hadrian swallowed. He realized he *had* called her Tilda a few moments ago. "Yes. We are friends, and yes, we call each other by our given names. It's … easier."

"I'm glad to hear you are only friends."

Only friends. Hadrian wasn't glad about that at all. He thought of Tilda's concern the day before and how she'd put him at ease. He realized he still longed for something more, for the chance, at least, to determine if they might be romantically suited. Could he ever persuade her to try?

His mother added, "Whilst I admire Miss Wren, she is not someone you should become *too* familiar with. Certainly, you couldn't ever court her. I trust you will take a bride someday." She sighed. "She must be capable of becoming the Countess of Ravenhurst. Miss Wren would not be up to the challenge. I wasn't sure Beryl would be either when you were betrothed, but she at least had a viscount or something somewhere in her family."

The dowager countess sipped her tea as if she hadn't just insulted Tilda. Hadrian couldn't think of anyone who was *more* capable of becoming the Countess of Ravenhurst. Tilda was brilliant, beautiful, and a master of many skills that would benefit his household, including running a household of her own.

But Tilda wasn't going to be the Countess of Ravenhurst. She had no desire to wed. Hence, Hadrian wouldn't consider the possibility.

"Mama, I'm sure you don't mean to denigrate Miss Wren." He made a point of using a more formal address.

"Not at all. She's a lovely young woman. She just isn't someone you should marry, not that you were even considering that. I can't imagine she'd be interested in marrying you either. She would undoubtedly prefer someone from her own class. I could see her marrying an inspector, actually."

Hadrian now had the idea of Tilda marrying a detective inspector lodged in his mind. He did not care for it.

His mother waved her hand. "I apologize. I know you dislike when I bring up marriage. I would just very much like to see you settled as your sisters are."

Married and with multiple children. "I know." He stood. "I must be off. I'll fetch you later for the séance. Same time as last week?"

"Yes, please. Thank you for coming."

Hadrian paused in walking to the door and turned to look back at his mother. "What will you do if the medium fails to make contact with Gabriel again?" Though Hadrian suspected Mrs. Griswold would pretend to make contact as the mediums typically did during the second séance.

The dowager countess blinked. "I'm not thinking of that. I'm convinced she will speak with Gabriel."

Hadrian didn't reply before taking his leave. He would hope that his mother would hear from "Gabriel" and then move on from this farce without him having to explain what was really happening. But perhaps he ought to consider telling her the truth —and weathering her reaction, whatever it may be.

Leach held the door of the coach as Hadrian approached. "Was that a disappointing meeting, my lord?"

Hadrian realized he was frowning and smoothed his features. "Somewhat. We'll be attending another séance tonight in Rathbone Place."

"I take it that does not please you," Leach said.

"Not particularly." Although it meant he would see Tilda again, and that was never a bad thing. Despite that thought, he had a persistent sense of irritation.

As he climbed into the coach, he identified the source: his mother's denigration of Tilda. More specifically, that she'd pointed out their class difference and declared that they couldn't wed. That didn't sit well with him at all.

Perhaps because he worried that she was right.

~

Tilda had been excited to receive Hadrian's note inviting her to Mrs. Griswold's séance with his mother that evening. She was eager to participate in another séance and had spent the remainder of the afternoon making notes about their investigation. In doing so, she'd come up with a theory about the séances that she hoped to prove.

She followed behind Hadrian and the dowager countess as they approached the door to the house in Rathbone Place. A familiar face answered—Michael Crocker, who they'd met at the society headquarters and who had served as butler at the last séance they'd attended with Mr. Hawkins.

Tilda suddenly worried for the safety of Mrs. Griswold. Both mediums who'd conducted séances she and Hadrian had attended last week were dead.

"Good evening, Crocker," Tilda said pleasantly as he closed the door behind her.

"Good evening, Miss Wren. I didn't know you and his lord-ship would be here."

Tilda shot a look at Hadrian. Had he not notified their hostess?

"My apologies," Lady Ravenhurst said. "I thought it would be all right if I brought them, since they attended last time."

"I'm confident Mrs. Griswold can accommodate you. I'll just inform her that you're here." He led them up the stairs to the drawing room, where he made his way to Mrs. Griswold.

"Should we wait here?" Tilda asked as they moved through the doorway.

"Perhaps so," Hadrian replied with a nod.

Their hostess wore a stunning dark blue gown with gold accents. As Crocker spoke to her, she cast a look in their direction. Mrs. Griswold smiled, and Crocker went to adjust the seats at the table, adding chairs that had been moved to the wall.

The medium approached them, her gaze falling first on the dowager countess. "Welcome, Lady Ravenhurst. I'm pleased you've brought your son and Miss Wren. I should have thought to invite them since they attended last week. I'm afraid there has been much to distract us in the society." Her mouth made a pretty frown before she transferred her attention to Hadrian and Tilda. "My lord, Miss Wren."

"Good evening, Mrs. Griswold," Hadrian said. "I appreciate your graciousness in allowing us to intrude."

"You are most welcome. Lysander says you have a special energy that is most helpful." Her focus drifted toward the door, where someone had just entered. "Please excuse me whilst I greet our final guest. I'll announce your seating arrangement shortly. Now that you are here, I'll need to make some adjustments, but not to worry, it's no trouble."

Tilda wondered at her comment about Hadrian's energy. Had Mallory told her about Hadrian's ability? Hadrian wouldn't like that. Tilda didn't care for it either.

Mrs. Langdon walked toward them with a wide smile. "What a delight to see you here, Ravenhurst, Lady Ravenhurst, Miss Wren. I was so pleased to be invited tonight and am doubly so now."

They exchanged pleasantries for a moment, and then Hadrian's mother and Mrs. Langdon began discussing a card game they'd recently attended.

Tilda took the opportunity to step slightly away from them and motioned with her head for Hadrian to join her. "I've a theory about these séances," she whispered.

Hadrian's brows arched. "Do share."

"I have been thinking about who may or may not share your ability in addition to Mallory. It seems likely that the three people who sit beside the mediums and often speak to them during the séance are able to experience memories through touch. However, I also find it odd that Mallory was able to find three people who not only possess the same ability he does, but who agreed to use that ability to pretend to converse with the spirit realm."

"Yes, that does seem a trifle far-fetched, but I wasn't sure I'd ever meet anyone who is like me, and I have."

Tilda nodded. "That is true, but let me continue. Earlier today, I was making notes about our investigation. I noticed something intriguing about Montrose, Sullivan, and Parr." She met Hadrian's gaze. "They all have first names that are found in Shakespeare."

Hadrian brows arched briefly. "Like Lysander."

"Precisely. It seems all the attendees are here, and I do not see Montrose or Sullivan, and I was under the impression that one of them—or Parr, whom we haven't met—was necessary to glean information for the medium to use during the séance. The fact that none of them are here tonight supports my theory." She paused, anticipating Hadrian's reaction. "They aren't here because they aren't real people."

"Of course they're real people," Hadrian said. "We've met two of them."

"I mean, they aren't Montrose or Sullivan or Parr. They are all Mallory in disguise."

Hadrian's eyes rounded briefly before he grinned. "You are brilliant."

She lifted a shoulder. "I don't know. If it's true, I rather think I should have determined it earlier. It seems obvious, especially with Miss Sullivan's raspy voice and thick veil that completely obliterated her face."

"Not to mention the odd gloves which almost entirely covered her hands. Without them, you'd likely be able to detect she was a man ..." Hadrian's voice trailed off. He snapped his gaze to Tilda's. "Miss Sullivan has the same power I do. I felt that same jolt of energy when she touched me at Hawkins's séance as I did when I met Captain Vale. I'd completely forgotten." He shook his head. "So foolish of me. Is that proof she really is Mallory?"

"That's not foolish at all," Tilda said. "I'm glad you remembered. I don't know that it's proof positive, but it certainly supports my theory."

Mrs. Griswold had stood at the table for a moment, her features in deep concentration. Now, she brightened as she surveyed the room. "Good evening everyone, and welcome. I am grateful to each of you for coming tonight, especially here in this now hallowed place where we lost our dear Mrs. Frost." She paused and her features tightened with resolve. "Alas, we will not be broken by tragedy, and I am confident the murderer will soon be caught."

The medium began to announce the seating for the séance. Tilda and Hadrian would be opposite Mrs. Griswold at seats six and seven respectively, whilst Hadrian's mother was again at number ten.

The medium called a man named Inwood to sit beside her at number eleven. He had thick, dark, curly hair and wore spectacles, which he adjusted after he took his chair.

"Let us keep an eye on Inwood to see if he speaks to Mrs. Griswold at all during the séance," Hadrian whispered.

"You should touch him after to see if he shares your ability."

"I'll do that."

Mrs. Griswold began the séance. She went straight to instructing them to join hands. "I need everyone to put their minds to the spirit realm. Please think of someone departed, preferably someone close to you. Your thoughts will attract them and make our link to the spirt realm more secure."

Tilda hadn't meant to think of her father, but his face rose in her mind. To think he could be close was nearly torture. Then she reminded herself that it wasn't true, that it would never be true. He was gone. All she had were her memories. She slid a look at Hadrian and wondered if she dared have him try to see one.

What good would that do? It would only serve to remind her of what she'd lost.

"Are there spirits with us?" Mrs. Griswold asked. She did not close her eyes at all. Instead, she fixed her gaze on the branch of candles in the middle of the table. They flickered as cool air swept over the room.

Tilda turned her head and tried to see where it may have come from. The room was very dim—Crocker had extinguished all illumination save the candelabrum. She thought the breeze had come from the corner behind her left shoulder and made a note to investigate the area after the séance. It had to be another parlor trick executed by the society.

The table began to move, drawing Tilda's attention from the corner. Hadrian's grip on her hand tightened slightly before he loosened it again. He slid her a look of mild annoyance, and she suspected he wanted to dive under the table and see what was happening with the hollow pedestal. Tilda was curious who would fit inside the pedestal. It had to be a small person, perhaps even a child.

Hadrian leaned forward over the table. He looked as though he was holding his breath. His chest was not moving.

Was he listening for something?

"Speak to us, spirits," Mrs. Griswold called. "Are you here?"

Three raps answered her query.

Hadrian sat back with a brief frown before smoothing his features into a benign expression.

"Captain Becket, are you with us?" Mrs. Griswold asked.

Three more raps.

Again, Hadrian's hand cinched Tilda's. She looked at Lady Ravenhurst, whose lips were parted, her gaze fixed rapturously on the medium.

"Speak to your son, Lady Ravenhurst," Mrs. Griswold urged. Her focus remained on the candles.

Lady Ravenhurst closed her eyes. "Gabriel, my darling boy. I can sense you are here."

Hadrian was stone-faced as he looked toward his mother.

"Mama?" Mrs. Griswold said, her voice deepening.

Lady Ravenhurst gasped. "Gabriel?"

"I am here, Mama. Is Ravenhurst here too?"

Tilda watched Hadrian. His lips flattened, and his eyes narrowed.

"Yes, your brother is here," the dowager countess replied in a higher, more excited tone. "Are you well, my boy?"

"He's *dead*," Hadrian breathed so that only Tilda likely heard him.

"I'm glad to speak with you," Mrs. Griswold said. "I've seen Father here. We are happy to be together." Their father was happy? That didn't sound like the man Hadrian had described to Tilda.

Hadrian exhaled then and nearly released Tilda's hand. She gripped him more tightly. "Don't let go," she said softly but urgently.

Lady Ravenhurst's brow furrowed, and she opened her eyes. She glanced toward Hadrian. Tilda couldn't quite read her expression but thought she may look troubled.

"I am surprised to hear that," Hadrian said loudly, apparently addressing his brother. "You must have resolved the argument you had before you left for India."

What was Mrs. Griswold doing? Did she have wrong information about Gabriel and Hadrian's father? Or was she guessing at their relationship? Since Mallory was absent—assuming he disguised himself as one of the people who usually sat next to the medium—perhaps she had to resort to making estimations and hoping she was close enough to the truth to be believed.

There was a long silence before Mrs. Griswold—rather, Gabriel—responded. "Yes. Father and I recall many wonderful memories together, such as the Christmas you were home from Eton and the snow was as deep as our knees. We built a fort next to the stables and defended it against the groomsmen."

That was a specific memory. Did that mean Inwood was seeing something from holding Lady Ravenhurst's hand? Tilda hadn't seen him speak to Mrs. Griswold. Was it possible that this memory was shared with Mrs. Griswold prior to the séance?

Hadrian's lips parted, then formed a brief smile before his features seemed to harden once more. "Father wasn't there."

"Wasn't he?" Mrs. Griswold, again speaking as Gabriel in a lower tone, asked.

"He was watching," Lady Ravenhurst replied. She looked over at Hadrian. "Perhaps you weren't aware, but he often watched the two of you when you were creating mayhem." She smiled, then sniffed. Tilda wondered if the dowager countess was crying, but she didn't appear to be.

"If he was watching, I have to think it was with disapproval. Has he changed his opinion in the spirit realm?" Hadrian's question held a sardonic edge, and Tilda had to think this was difficult for him. He was revisiting something that was both joyous and fraught because of the relationships between the men in his family.

"Everything changes when you die," Mrs. Griswold said as Gabriel. "Things that mattered to you in the physical realm fade here. There is only love and joy."

"That is wonderful to hear," Lady Ravenhurst said, her attention on Mrs. Griswold. She sniffed again. "Indeed, that is all I have hoped for."

Hadrian frowned toward his mother. "I'm glad to hear you have peace. Please be at rest, Gabriel. It is time for everyone to move on." He released Tilda's hand.

"Goodbye, Mama," Mrs. Griswold said.

"Don't go yet," Lady Ravenhurst cried.

Tilda saw Hadrian flatten his palm against the table. It began to tilt, and if Tilda hadn't known better, she would have said that Hadrian caused it.

"Lord Ravenhurst, please rejoin hands," Mrs. Griswold instructed. Her gaze had shifted to Hadrian, and she appeared perturbed. "Your mother wishes to continue speaking with your brother."

Hadrian's jaw worked, but he ultimately said nothing. He retook Tilda's hand as well as that of the woman on his other side.

Mrs. Griswold looked to Lady Ravenhurst. "I'm afraid Gabriel is gone. However, that does not mean we can't try contacting him again. If we can't reach him tonight, I'm confident he will come again."

"Is there anyone else there?" Mrs. Griswold asked.

The table shifted, and there were several raps, more than three. What did that mean?

Mrs. Griswold looked about the room. "Who's there?"

"Deborah Frost."

Everyone's attention snapped to a woman seated on the other side of the man next to Tilda. She was a few years older than Tilda with dark auburn hair. Her eyes were closed, but they suddenly opened. She stared straight ahead, her gaze unfocused.

"Deborah?" Mrs. Griswold asked.

"Yes."

There were a few gasps, including from Inwood.

Mrs. Griswold smiled briefly, but then she focused on the woman who was supposedly channeling Mrs. Frost. "I'm so glad to hear from you. We miss you."

"I miss you too. I want to be at peace, Mercy. You must bring my killer to justice. It was *not* Lysander."

"Who was it, Deborah?" Mrs. Griswold asked breathlessly.

The woman who was speaking for Deborah slumped back in her chair, her eyes closing. Her arms went limp, and the man between her and Tilda released her.

"Are you all right?" the man asked, leaning toward her. "Mrs. Kelson, are you well?"

Mrs. Kelson's eyes fluttered open. She looked at the man. "What's wrong?"

"You may release each other," Mrs. Griswold said. "The séance is concluded." She looked to Mrs. Kelson. "Mrs. Frost visited us through you. Do you remember anything?"

Shaking her head, Mrs. Kelson lifted her hand to her chest. "What happened?"

"Mrs. Frost spoke through you," the man between her and Tilda replied.

"I don't remember that happening. The last thing I recall is Mrs. Griswold instructing Lord Ravenhurst to rejoin hands." Mrs. Kelson appeared alarmed. She gaped at Mrs. Griswold. "Has that ever happened before?"

"I have only witnessed it once," Mrs. Griswold said. "Typically, spirits communicate through mediums, but on occasion, they choose another messenger. You should suffer no ill effects." She looked to Crocker, who was in the corner. "Crocker, bring wine for Mrs. Kelson, please."

People began to talk amongst themselves. Hadrian leaned close to Tilda. "That was an interesting performance."

Tilda turned her head toward him. "Mrs. Kelson channeling Mrs. Frost?"

"Yes." He darted a glance toward Mrs. Griswold. "This medium is rather dramatic. The entire thing could have been presented on the stage. Indeed, they probably learned their tricks from the theater."

"Speaking of tricks, when the air stirred, I was fairly certain the breeze was coming from that corner." Tilda looked over her shoulder. "I thought I might investigate the area. I realize we don't need more proof that they are frauds, but I am curious. Here come Mrs. Griswold and your mother."

The medium gave Hadrian a slightly scolding look. "My lord, you mustn't break the connection during a séance. If you return again, I must ask that you keep hold of your neighbors' hands."

"My apologies, Mrs. Griswold. I was too swept up in the moment." His smile did not reach his eyes.

"I thought it was wonderful," Lady Ravenhurst exclaimed. "I do think I'll come back next week."

"I'm delighted to hear it," Mrs. Griswold said.

Tilda had a question for the medium. "Mrs. Griswold, I was interested to read in the newspaper about one of the mediums leaving the society. I don't think I met her—Harmony Smith?"

"Oh, yes. She was young and had only been with the society a few months. We shall miss her."

"Why did she leave?" Tilda asked.

Mrs. Griswold's brow furrowed. "Some people are not able to cope with everything happening, which is completely understandable. As I said, Harmony was young and perhaps a bit … naïve." She looked toward Hadrian's mother. "Never fear, the society will rise from these tragedies stronger than ever, especially when Lysander returns to us. You heard what Deborah said —he is not the killer."

"I don't think Detective Inspector Teague will take her testimony from the spirit realm as evidence," Tilda pointed out.

"Perhaps not, but I will inform him just the same," Mrs. Griswold said pertly.

Mrs. Langdon joined them. "That was a wonderful séance, Mrs. Griswold. I confess I am disappointed I can only attend one each month, for I would attend another this week if I could."

"I'm certain we can arrange for that," Mrs. Griswold assured her. "Both Nigel and Isidora will be conducting séances. There is great demand. Excuse me, I must speak with Mrs. Kelson."

"Who would have guessed that multiple murders would have increased the society's popularity?" Hadrian mused.

Lady Ravenhurst glowered at her son. "I know you don't understand why people would want to speak with their departed loved ones, but it is not uncommon. And you saw what happened tonight. I'm not at all surprised that so many people want to experience this wonder."

Tilda watched the pulse in Hadrian's neck tick madly.

He swallowed before responding, seeming to take a pause to settle himself. "You are right that I don't understand, just as I am not convinced they are actually speaking with anyone in the supposed spirit realm. You heard what she said about Gabriel and Father being happy together. And then you looked at me, and I could see you doubted what the medium was saying."

"The medium wasn't saying it. That was Gabriel." Lady Ravenhurst fixed an expectant stare on her son. "Why wouldn't he and your father have resolved things?"

"Because Father didn't know how to do that." Hadrian's voice was hollow. "Perhaps you don't remember."

The dowager countess averted her gaze from his. "I do remember, and I can hope he has improved upon himself in the spirit realm."

Hadrian's forehead creased. However, he said nothing more on the issue. Tilda wanted to know what he was thinking.

His mother did not relent. "How can you doubt that Gabriel was here? How else would Mrs. Griswold have known about the snow fort you made together all those years ago?"

"Perhaps she has a way of seeing our memories," Hadrian commented unironically.

Tilda's breath snagged. What was he doing?

"Don't be silly," Lady Ravenhurst scoffed.

"*That* is silly, but speaking with the dead is not?" Hadrian smiled briefly, then rolled his shoulders back. "Do you wish to stay for dinner?"

"Yes, and if you would rather not, I'm sure Mrs. Langdon will convey me home." The dowager countess glanced toward her friend.

"If you don't mind, I would prefer to leave," Hadrian replied.

"As you wish." His mother swept away toward Mrs. Langdon.

"Is she upset with you?" Tilda asked in a low tone.

"Yes, but no more than I am with her." Hadrian rubbed the

back of his neck. "She had a terrible habit of tolerating my father's behavior when he was alive."

"What behavior was that?"

"Focusing all his attention on me and ignoring his other children." He lowered his hand to his side. "And ignoring my mother in favor of his mistresses."

Tilda considered changing the subject but couldn't seem to stop herself from asking, "What was the argument between him and Gabriel about?"

Hadrian took a deep breath. "Gabriel had endured enough of our father's comments about how he needed to take care in case he was needed as the spare. Father was torn between wanting Gabriel to do his duty as an officer and preferring he not endanger himself. He just liked to control everything and everyone, and he knew he couldn't do that with Gabriel when he went to India. Gabriel rebuked him soundly. I wasn't there, but I wish I had been."

"You don't think it's possible that Gabriel might have forgiven him?" Tilda added, "Before he died, I mean."

"I hope Gabriel found peace with our father, but I don't know for certain." Hadrian realized he would like to know that. But he could not. "Nor do I expect to ever find out. Regardless of what my mother believes."

Tilda glanced toward the dowager countess. She stood with Mrs. Langdon. "I thought you were going to tell her about your ability."

"I confess I did think of it when I saw her this afternoon. But I am glad I did not," Hadrian said. "Because my curse is *silly*, whilst pretending to speak with the dead is not."

She heard an edge of hurt in his tone. "You're afraid to tell her, aren't you?"

His gaze snapped to hers and held it. "Wouldn't you be?"

"I … I don't know. What are you afraid of?"

He looked away, his jaw tight. "That she won't believe me. Or she will laugh. Worst of all, that she will think I've gone mad."

Tilda gently touched his sleeve. "You aren't still worried that will happen?"

"I can't help wondering, especially after what Captain Vale told us."

Tilda dropped her hand to her side. "You aren't mad. And I think your mother might just believe you. She wants to believe that she can talk to her dead son. Why wouldn't she believe that her living son can experience other people's memories?"

He swallowed. "I don't know if I can take the risk. Not yet anyway. But I will continue to think about it."

Tilda smiled at him. "I'm glad. You have a wonderful bond."

"Whilst that is true, I realize I harbor some … ill feelings toward her. She should have done more to protect my sisters and Gabriel from our father's coldness. I don't know what that would have been, but to hear her now, acting as though things were pleasant when they bloody well were not, is disappointing."

"I wonder if her need to hear from Gabriel comes from regret," Tilda suggested quietly.

Surprise flashed in Hadrian's eyes, but before he could respond, Crocker approached them with a tray holding glasses of a red wine.

"Would you care for wine?" the butler asked.

"No, thank you," Hadrian replied. "We will be leaving shortly."

"Did you not enjoy the séance?" the butler asked, his brow creased with worry.

"I don't think séances are for me," Hadrian said blandly.

Crocker looked to Tilda. "What about you, Miss Wren?"

"They are most interesting." Tilda cocked her head. "When will you lead one yourself?"

"Soon," he said excitedly. "Mrs. Griswold says the society needs to promote the mediums who have been training now that …" His voice trailed off. "Well, you know."

"Yes," Tilda replied soberly. "I wish you good luck."

His eyes lit with gratitude. "Thank you."

After he walked away, Tilda inclined her head toward the corner where she thought the breeze may have originated. She and Hadrian sauntered in that direction.

Hadrian tilted his head and looked high up on the wall. "That is a vent." He lifted his hand. "I feel air, but not strong enough to make the candles flicker."

Tilda looked at Hadrian. "I'll wager they use a bellows to blow air."

"That is entirely possible." He moved closer and scrutinized the area. "See how the wallpaper has been recently replaced around the vent—it's a more vibrant hue than what's below."

"Do you think they installed it when Mrs. Frost moved in?" Tilda mused.

"That's a reasonable estimation," Hadrian replied.

"What are you looking at?"

They both turned at the sound of the masculine voice. Inwood, the bespectacled man who'd sat beside Mrs. Griswold, was looking up where they had been a moment ago.

"Just admiring the ironwork on that vent," Hadrian said with a smile. "I'm Ravenhurst." He held his hand out to the man.

"Inwood." He shook Hadrian's hand. "I hope you weren't too troubled by the séance. I know some people find it jarring to hear from their deceased relatives, especially when they were close to you in life."

"This isn't your first séance?" Tilda asked.

Inwood shook his head. "I've lost count of the number I've attended," he added with a smile. "I joined the society late last year."

Hadrian looked at him expectantly. "And how many people in the spirit realm have you spoken with?"

"Er, none. I don't really have anyone I wish to speak with." He shrugged. "I do like attending séances, however. I particularly enjoy watching levitation." He grimaced. "I suppose I shouldn't mention that here. Seems like the society is perhaps taking a break from that sort of presentation."

"Are they?" Tilda glanced at Hadrian. "I can't blame them."

Mrs. Griswold announced that dinner was being served.

"Shall we?" Mr. Inwood said.

"You must excuse us," Hadrian replied. "We won't be staying for dinner."

They bade farewell to the man before ensuring that Lady Ravenhurst would indeed be delivered home by Mrs. Langdon. A short while later, they were ensconced in Hadrian's coach on the way to Marylebone. Once again, Hadrian did not sit beside Tilda. Tonight, after the emotions he'd experienced, Tilda rather hoped he would. She should have explicitly invited him to.

"I felt nothing when I shook Inwood's hand," Hadrian said as he settled back against the squab. "I think your theory about Montrose, Sullivan, and Parr is accurate. Honestly, it makes perfect sense that they are Mallory in disguise. I'm disappointed I didn't see it."

"I didn't either until I wrote their names down and saw the Shakespearean connection. We must commend Mallory's efforts with hair and costumes. He quite transformed himself." Tilda exhaled. "Can we now conclude that Mallory is the only one in the society who possesses the ability to experience memories?"

"That seems likely, though I would like to know how Mrs. Griswold knew about the snow memory with my brother."

"Was it accurate?" Tilda asked.

"Eerily so. Mallory has touched my mother. It's entirely possible he experienced that memory and had already shared it with Mrs. Griswold."

"That was my thought as well—that she knew about it before the séance."

Hadrian's eyes narrowed. "They are quite cunning, aren't they?"

"I think we must assume their capacity for intrigue is limitless."

"As well as their hunger for gullible people to attend their séances and join their society," Hadrian said. "Mrs. Griswold called on my mother this morning to suggest this séance tonight, and I expect her to solicit my mother's patronage. Damn, I should have stayed for dinner after all, so I could stop such nonsense."

Tilda gave him a sympathetic look. "Try not to worry. I would say the future of the London Spiritualism Society is at risk. Even if Mallory isn't the Levitation Killer, he is a blackmailer and sent me a threatening letter. The society is likely to be without its leader. Can it continue?"

"You make an excellent point. I want to be sure Teague has all the evidence he can get regarding the blackmail. Shall we visit the grocer in Bedfordbury tomorrow? I've a meeting in the morning at Westminster, but I can be free by noon."

"Yes, please," Tilda said with a nod. "Don't forget to bring your pistol."

CHAPTER 19

*H*adrian extricated himself from a meeting in the Commons regarding the Thames Embankment in order to fetch Tilda and arrived later than he'd planned. She was waiting for him in the parlor. Her grandmother was not present, which Hadrian found surprising.

"Where is your grandmother?" he asked after greeting Tilda. "I hope she is well."

"She is annoyed with me because I asked her to stay away from the parlor so that you and I may discuss the case." Tilda gave him a dire look. "I'm afraid there's been another murder."

"Hell," Hadrian murmured. "Mrs. Griswold?"

Tilda shook her head. "Teague called a short while ago. Harmony Smith was found in Leicester Square early this morning. It looks as though she died from prussic acid poisoning."

Hadrian removed his hat. He was disappointed he'd missed Teague. "Teague is certain her death is connected to the Levitation Killer, though she wasn't levitating?"

"The prussic acid may indicate she was killed by the same person. I think it's too coincidental that she was a member of the society and died of prussic acid poisoning, even if where she was found had nothing to do with the society." Tilda crossed her arms over her chest. "Teague also said he is planning to release Mallory today. Captain Vale visited Scotland Yard this morning and apparently overheard that there'd been another murder. He argued that since his son was imprisoned, he could not have committed the latest murder. Therefore, he reasoned his son also wasn't guilty of the other crimes."

"So Teague will let Mallory go?" Hadrian scowled.

"He only has clear evidence that he sent me a threatening letter," Tilda said, unfolding her arms. "Teague will see that he is prosecuted for that, but he does not need to be kept in jail. He will also continue to investigate Mallory's blackmail."

"That is most unfortunate," Hadrian said with a deep frown. He turned his thoughts to the new murder. "Why do you think Harmony Smith was killed differently than the others?"

Tilda lifted her shoulder. "I've no idea. There could be a variety of reasons, not the least of which was that she left the society. Perhaps the killer didn't think she deserved to be killed in the same way."

"That's an interesting thought," Hadrian said. "Poor thing. She tried to leave. Do you suppose she was afraid for her life and thought she may be next?"

"That is my fear. I wish we knew more about her." Tilda moved to a table where her hat and gloves were sitting.

Vaughn's voice carried from the entrance hall into the parlor. "I'll be right back."

The butler walked into the parlor, his focus on Tilda. "You've a caller, Miss Wren. Captain Vale is here to see you."

Tilda's eyes widened briefly, and she met Hadrian's gaze. She'd picked up her hat and gloves, but now she set them back down. "Show him in, Vaughn."

Hadrian turned to face the doorway just as Captain Vale appeared. "Lord Ravenhurst, I'm surprised to see you. But pleased." The captain bowed to Tilda. "Miss Wren. Thank you for seeing me. I hope it doesn't trouble you that I've sought you out."

"Not at all," Tilda replied. "Please sit. How *did* you find me?"

Tilda perched on a chair, whilst the captain sat opposite her on the settee. Hadrian moved to stand next to Tilda.

"Detective Inspector Teague told me where you lived after I pleaded with him. I had to tell him the reason for my call in order for him to relent."

"And what is the reason for your call?" Hadrian asked.

The captain glanced at him before returning his focus to Tilda. "I would like to hire you to find the Levitation Killer. My son is not guilty of these murders."

"I have already been investigating, Captain Vale."

"I understand, but I want to pay you to prove Thaddeus isn't the killer." Captain Vale's expression was taut, his eyes dark with concern.

Hadrian was reminded of how he'd hired Tilda for their last case to prove he hadn't killed Louis Chambers. This was not altogether different. Except for the fact that Thaddeus Vale/Lysander Mallory was definitely guilty of other crimes.

Tilda hesitated before responding. "Captain, I can't promise my investigation won't lead to finding your son guilty. No amount of money will alter the truth."

The captain exhaled, but his features were still taut. "Of course. I would never expect you to do anything other than pursue justice. You are a woman of integrity, Miss Wren, which is why I want to hire you. I know you will find that Thaddeus didn't do this. Never mind that he couldn't have killed Miss Smith, who was just found this morning."

"Whilst it's true he couldn't have done that personally, it is possible he could have asked or paid someone to do it for him," Tilda said gently. "I know you want your son to be innocent of these crimes, but you must accept the truth, whatever it is."

The captain bowed his head. "I know," he whispered. "Just as I know that Thaddeus is guilty of defrauding people with his spiritualism trickery. He admitted as much to me yesterday evening when I visited Scotland Yard after arriving in London."

"Did he also confess to blackmail?" Hadrian asked. "Miss Wren and I have found at least three people the society has extorted or attempted to extort by using information he'd learned from their memories."

Captain Vale blanched. "He did not." He bowed his head for a moment. When he looked up, his eyes were dark with resolve. "I still know he didn't kill anyone. He wouldn't. Not ever." He scooted forward on the settee. "Please, Miss Wren. I'll pay whatever fee you require. Detective Inspector Teague said you would do an excellent job."

Hadrian was torn. Tilda was trying to establish herself as a private investigator. Any client, especially one such as Captain Vale, would be a boon for her, not to mention the financial benefit. Still, he didn't like Mallory and wasn't convinced the man wasn't guilty.

But Hadrian ought to consider he was not seeing things without bias.

Tilda glanced at Hadrian, and he detected a slight hesitation. He didn't want her to refuse. He gave her a subtle nod.

She clasped her hands in her lap and addressed Captain Vale. "I will accept your offer."

The captain's shoulders dipped as he let out a breath. "Thank you, Miss Wren."

"Thank you, Captain." Tilda stood. "You must excuse us as we've leads to follow in the investigation."

The captain rose. "Of course. I'm staying at a house in Woodbridge Street in Clerkenwell. It's associated with Thaddeus's club."

"We attended a séance there the other night," Tilda said, her expression flickering with surprise. "It was the home of one of the mediums who was killed."

"Thaddeus told me that, but he said it was the best place he could offer me to stay that would keep me away from the club, as I prefer that." Captain Vale gave Tilda a grateful smile. "Can I expect to hear from you later?"

"Yes, I'll call with a report on my progress. I appreciate your faith in me."

The captain took his leave, and Tilda eyed Hadrian with a bit of wariness. "Are you upset that I accepted his offer?"

"Not at all," Hadrian said firmly. "I am glad you did. I am trying to see past my dislike of the man's son to reasonably determine if he is guilty of these crimes. You are correct that more evidence is needed."

"Precisely." Tilda set her hat atop her red-blonde hair and picked up her gloves. "Rather than start with Bedfordbury, I should like to visit Fleet Street and speak with Mr. Clement about Harmony Smith."

"After you." Hadrian gestured for her to precede him. "I confess I did not expect to have to look to that reporter to assist with our investigation."

"Neither did I," Tilda said. "But we must take any help where we can."

～

They arrived at the offices of the *Daily Mail* in Fleet Street to discover that Clement was not present. He was, however, in a nearby coffee shop.

Tilda easily spotted Mr. Clement seated at a table next to the wall. He wasn't wearing a hat, but he was garbed in his typical outrageously hued plaid pants, and today he sported a bright-blue stock as well.

"Over there," Tilda said, using her head to gesture toward Clement.

"I see him," Hadrian replied. "The trousers give him away."

They walked to his table. Clement's head was bent as he read a newspaper—not the *Daily Mail*—but he looked up as they approached. Surprise flickered briefly in his gaze before he settled an expectant stare on them. "Ravenhurst, Miss Wren. What brings you to this part of London?"

"You do, Mr. Clement," Tilda said. "May we sit?"

Clement gestured to the chairs on the other side of the table. "Please."

Hadrian held Tilda's chair whilst she sat, then lowered himself beside her.

"You published an interesting article yesterday," Tilda began.

"Now you want to exchange information?" Clement asked with a smug expression.

"Perhaps," Tilda said benignly. "Let us see if you know anything of interest."

Clement leaned forward. "You must suspect I do if you've come to find me."

"I would like to know more about Harmony Smith, as well as who else you spoke with from the London Spiritualism Society. Perhaps we could start with the latter."

"And what would you offer me?" Clement asked dubiously.

"We've just come from Scotland Yard. There has been a new development in the case this morning."

"Has there?" Clement's tone was breathless. "Of what nature?"

Tilda gave him a pert look. "I'd like to know who else you spoke with from the society."

Clement exhaled. "They asked that I not identify them publicly, but I suppose I could share their names with you. It was a pair of siblings—Jacob and Ellen Henry."

"Thank you. Anyone else?" Tilda asked.

"No. They were all very close-mouthed. I only managed to persuade Miss Smith and the Henrys to speak with me because they were not at the headquarters."

"Where did you speak with them?"

"I've been lingering around the houses where the murders occurred," Clement replied. "I encountered Miss Smith as she left Willow Street the evening before last, and I spoke to the Henrys on Saturday after they departed Rathbone Place." His brows gathered. "I will say that the Henrys were divided on speaking with me at all. Ellen seemed eager to answer my questions, but her brother didn't want her to. The society frowns on their employees speaking to people about the workings of the society."

"What did they tell you?" Tilda asked, wondering if she too sounded breathless.

Clement sat back in his chair and crossed his arms over his chest. "I'll share that after you reveal whatever you learned at Scotland Yard."

Tilda found that reasonable. "There has been another murder."

Clement's nostrils flared as he unfolded his arms and lightly slapped his palm against the table. "I knew it. Which medium was found dangling now?"

Tilda curled her lip at the crudeness of his question. "First, tell me what the Henrys told you."

Without hesitation, Clement said, "Ellen said they accepted employment at the society in order to train as mediums. They were told they would move up in the household and become full-fledged mediums. As such, they'd earn a robust living—or so they believed. Since the murders, Ellen has decided she wants to leave, but her brother does not share her desire. Jacob ended the interview after that."

"Did they not tell you about the pearl earring that was found?" Hadrian asked.

Clement glanced away and seemed to have grown uncomfortable. "I gleaned that morsel from the police."

Tilda could not imagine Teague saying anything. "Did you bribe someone?"

Eyes flashing with guilt, Clement pursed his lips. "Sometimes it's necessary."

"Who did you bribe?" Tilda asked. "Tell me and I'll tell you which medium was killed—and how. Otherwise, you can wait to find out until the inquest."

"It wasn't someone currently with the police. His name is Padgett."

Tilda kept herself from reacting. Padgett had been the inspector who'd investigated the attack on Hadrian, as well as a similar attack on another gentlemen that had left the man dead. Padgett had been bribed to bury his reports, but he'd escaped punishment by retiring from the police.

Hadrian scoffed. "Of course it was Padgett."

Clement appeared intrigued. "You know him?"

"Regrettably."

Tilda looked over at Hadrian. "Padgett must receive information from someone still working for the police. How disappointing." She pinned Clement with a hard stare. "I would caution you not to trust Padgett."

"He does seem slightly … sordid," Clement said with a faint shrug.

Hadrian settled back in his chair and gave Clement a dismissive look. "Yet that didn't stop you from bribing him for information."

Clement turned his attention to Tilda. "Who was murdered?"

"The very medium you interviewed for your article: Harmony Smith."

Clement paled. "That can't be. She was going home to her sister in Brixton."

Tilda didn't doubt the man's distress. "I'm afraid it's true. Though she was not killed in the same manner. She was found in Leicester Square, likely poisoned." She gave him a pointed look. "You mustn't print that until after the inquest determines her cause of death."

"I can hardly believe it. She did not deserve that end." Clement bowed his head a moment. "This is terrible."

"It is," Tilda said gently. "I am committed to finding the killer before anyone else dies."

The reporter snapped his head up. Color returned to his face. "Mallory has been arrested." He pressed his lips together. "He could not have killed Harmony."

Tilda told him the same thing she'd said to Hadrian. "He could be responsible even if he didn't do the actual deed. I will discover the truth. I've something else to share, but I want you to tell me about Harmony Smith first. Agreed?"

"What do you want to know?"

"When did she become a medium?" Tilda asked.

Clement nodded. "Only a few weeks ago. Like the Henrys, she was hired for domestic service whilst she trained to be a medium. She enjoyed it and said she had a flair for performance, so she was promoted from housekeeping and cooking duties. She was assigned as a maid to Mrs. Griswold and Miss Dryden at the headquarters. After moving to Cadogan Place, she conducted one séance before the first murder. She was to conduct a second the other day, but she said she was too skittish after Mrs. Frost was killed. Then she decided she wanted to return home until the killer was caught." He frowned as he met Tilda's gaze once more. "She was afraid. She said she wanted to be far away from the Levitation Killer. She was also adamant that Mallory is not guilty."

Hadrian studied Clement with a furrowed brow. "Why didn't your story include any of the information about these medium apprenticeships?"

"The newspaper editor preferred I focus on the murders for now," Clement replied. "I hope to publish another article about the society soon."

"You said she moved to Cadogan Place. Why didn't she live at the headquarters whilst she was in domestic service?" Tilda thought of how the other retainers she'd met, notably the Henry siblings, didn't live where they worked either.

"She only said they had to earn their place there. And before you ask, she would not tell me where she resided before moving to Cadogan Place. She said it was a society secret."

"But she was leaving the society," Hadrian said. "Why not tell you?"

"She was leaving temporarily because she was afraid, not because she didn't like the society," Clement explained. "She planned to return once the murderer was caught. Though perhaps he already has been."

Tilda decided Clement had more than earned another piece of information. "Mallory will be released today."

Clement's brows shot up. "Why?"

Tilda explained the lack of evidence. She considered everything Clement had told them about Harmony Smith and was sorry she wouldn't have a chance to talk to the woman herself. She was even sorrier that Harmony hadn't found her way home.

"Thank you for your time and willingness to share information, Mr. Clement," Tilda said.

"I appreciate you doing the same. You *are* investigating this case, Miss Wren, despite your denial. Did someone hire you?"

Tilda couldn't help repeating what she'd told him before when he'd asked if she was investigating. "I can't say at the moment." She gave him an apologetic smile, then rose. Hadrian stood beside her.

Clement also vacated his chair. "If I can ever be of service, I hope you'll let me know. I don't suppose you'll tell me where your investigation is taking you next?"

"We have yet to decide," Tilda fibbed. She didn't want the reporter following them.

"I'd be keen to exchange information again."

Tilda arched a brow at the reporter. "Then you'd best learn

something more to share." She flashed him a smile before turning away from the table.

Hadrian escorted her from the coffee shop, and they returned to his coach. Hadrian told Leach to make sure they weren't followed by a man in loud plaid pants.

Hadrian sat opposite her in the coach and donned a pensive expression. "What do you think of the medium apprentice scheme?"

"I should love to speak with Mallory about why he does that. Perhaps we can call at the headquarters after we visit the grocer. Assuming Mallory has been released."

"I've no quarrel with that. Do you think Harmony Smith knew the identity of the killer?" Hadrian asked.

"I've been wondering that. It's an excellent motive for someone to murder her."

Hadrian tipped his head. "Is that perhaps why the second and third mediums were killed? Ward was killed, and then the others followed because they learned who did it?"

"That is certainly possible, but we still don't know why someone would kill Ward, unless it was one of their blackmail victims."

"And if any of the mediums had known, why wouldn't they have informed Scotland Yard?"

"They may not have had a chance. Or they were too afraid. Or perhaps they weren't certain." Tilda exhaled.

They rode in silence a few moments before Hadrian asked, "What do you plan to ask at the grocer?"

"Well, I can't very well march in and accuse them of collecting extortion for the spiritualism society," she said with a sardonic smile.

"Should we pretend we are paying blackmail?" Hadrian suggested.

"I thought of that, but I have to think they know who they are extorting."

Hadrian sat straight, his eyes flashing with inspiration. "Eldred didn't pay—I could pretend to be him."

Tilda laughed. "I don't think anyone would mistake you for him. We could, however, pretend to be his agents."

Hadrian grinned. "You are very clever indeed."

They arrived in Bedfordbury a few minutes later. The street was in terrible shape, though not as bad as Flower and Dean Street, which Tilda and Hadrian had visited during their last investigation. The coach stopped near the grocer.

"I have my pistol," Tilda said, lifting her reticule.

"And I have mine." Hadrian smoothed his hand over the side of his coat. "I hope we won't need them."

"I can't believe we will, particularly in broad daylight." Tilda stepped out of the coach with Leach's assistance.

Hadrian followed and addressed his coachman. "Keep a close watch. I would make sure the pistol beneath the seat is well within reach."

"Always, my lord," Leach said with a nod.

Tilda turned to Hadrian. "We must appear nervous and worried. Try to lose your earl swagger."

Leach chuckled, and Hadrian smirked.

"I don't swagger, do I?" Hadrian asked. "Leach, stop laughing."

"You walk like an earl, my lord." Leach composed himself.

"Shall I drag my feet?" Hadrian demonstrated a rather lead-footed walk.

"Just dip your head a bit and perhaps stoop a little," Tilda suggested. "Whatever you can do to make yourself look less … impressive."

Hadrian curled his shoulders forward. "Like that?"

"Perfect." Tilda looked down at her gown. "I should have worn something from my old wardrobe. Ah well, here we are."

She took Hadrian's arm, and they walked to the grocer. It was called Timms and Baker, and the upper floors appeared to be dwellings. A couple of windows were open, and thin curtains blew in the breeze.

Hadrian held the door for Tilda as she preceded him inside. The shop was decently stocked, and the floor was cleanly swept.

An open doorway in the center of the right wall seemed to lead into a vestibule of some kind. Tilda peered inside and saw a staircase.

Voices carried from the back of the shop. Tilda and Hadrian exchanged looks before walking in that direction. They couldn't see anyone over the counter.

The sound of a door with a squeaky hinge closing in a room beyond the counter made Tilda think whoever had been there had just gone.

"Is anyone there?" Hadrian's tone was soft and uncertain.

Tilda would congratulate his efforts later.

"Do you need something?" The response came from behind the counter, just before a head popped up over the top. The man must have been bent down, which was why he hadn't been seen. And now that he was upright, he wasn't much taller than the counter.

Tilda assumed this was Mr. Timms, whom Joslin had described as very short. "Good afternoon."

The man scrutinized them both, his blue eyes narrowing briefly. "How may I help you?"

"I'm afraid we're here about a delicate matter," Hadrian said. He looked around nervously, behaving exactly as Tilda had instructed. "Our employer received a letter, and we are delivering something on his behalf. Do you know what I am speaking of?"

"Who is your employer?" the man demanded.

"Mr. Octavius Eldred," Tilda replied as she worried her hands.

"Why'd you bring her?" The man behind the counter asked almost crossly. "This isn't the nicest neighborhood." Again, he studied them in a dubious manner that spiked Tilda's pulse. "I'll be back in a moment."

Tilda turned and moved closer to Hadrian. "I can't imagine you have two hundred pounds to pay him, so I suggest you say we forgot the money."

"I wouldn't give him two hundred pounds even if I had it," he whispered.

Tilda nodded. "Of course."

Footsteps sounded nearby—Tilda thought the sound may have come from the staircase hall she'd glimpsed through the open doorway. Turning her head, she saw a man walk through the doorway. He strode toward the counter.

Tilda clasped Hadrian's elbow. "That's Nicholls. He was Cyril Ward's butler."

Nicholls paused at the counter, but Tilda didn't think he would have heard them. Not that it mattered. Nicholls would likely recognize them. He pivoted and his features registered recognition.

"Lord Ravenhurst?" Nicholls asked. "Miss Wren?"

There went their ruse. "Yes," Tilda replied evenly. "What are you doing here, Nicholls?"

"I, ah, nothing. Please excuse me." He continued behind the counter and disappeared in the same direction the shopkeeper had gone.

"Why is he here?" Hadrian asked.

"I don't know for certain, but we must assume he is informing the other man who we are. Our scheme is no more, I'm afraid." Tilda walked quickly to the doorway Nicholls had come through and moved into the staircase hall. It was very dim, the only light coming from a window on the landing of the staircase.

She turned to Hadrian. "I want to go upstairs."

"Shouldn't we leave?"

"We know blackmail was paid here, and we suspect the society—and likely Mallory—is behind the blackmail. Now we've seen one of the retainers here." She looked up the stairs. "I want to see what is up there."

"Let's be quick about it," Hadrian said.

Tilda went first up the narrow staircase. The landing led to an open sitting room area furnished with a threadbare settee and a collection of mismatched, worn chairs.

Moving through the sitting room, they entered a narrow corridor. On the right, a door stood slightly ajar. Peering inside, Tilda saw a narrow bed and a small dresser. There was no window, and it was rather dreary.

Hadrian stood beside her. "It's a bedchamber."

"I hate to ask, but could you touch something?" She stepped over the threshold and to the side so that he could move past her.

Stripping away his right glove, he walked to the bed and touched the coverlet. He turned his head to look at Tilda, his hand still on the bed. "I see someone in this room. It's Ellen Henry." He blinked. "That's all."

"You wouldn't be experiencing her memory since you saw her. Whose memory do you think you were seeing?"

"I don't know. I wasn't able to see the person's hands or anything else that might help me identify them."

Tilda looked into a battered wardrobe in the corner. "Men's clothing. Perhaps this is her brother's bedroom?"

Hadrian moved toward the wardrobe, but Tilda blocked his path. "I don't want you to touch too many things, and we've still other rooms to investigate." She turned and left the bedchamber.

Hadrian followed her to the next chamber along the corridor. "We're supposed to be quick." He glanced back toward the way they'd come, but no one was there, thankfully.

"We will be," Tilda said as she knocked softly on the next door.

When there was no response, she pushed the door open. Right away, this appeared to be a woman's room. A chemise hung over the back of a chair as if it had been drying.

Tilda stepped inside and Hadrian again went to the bed. He pivoted to face Tilda as he touched the bedclothes. His gaze was unfocused, his features creased intently, as if he were watching something of great interest. She would not interrupt him, but she was eager to know what he was seeing—if anything.

As before, Hadrian blinked before focusing on Tilda. "It was a woman's memory. She held the pearl earring from Rathbone Place in her hand. Or perhaps its mate. There's no way to tell." He frowned. "Whose chamber is this?"

"Perhaps we can find a clue to answer that." The room only contained a bed, a small dressing table with a stool, and a narrow dresser. Tilda went to the table and opened the single drawer.

"What are you doing here?" A shrill voice filled the chamber.

Tilda glimpsed the pearl earring in the drawer and scooped it up before turning toward the door. Hadrian blocked her sight, which meant whoever was there had not seen what Tilda was doing. Tilda gently—and quietly—closed the drawer before moving to Hadrian's side.

A very petite woman—even smaller than the man they'd met downstairs—glared at them. She wore an apron and a cap atop her sable hair. She wasn't just short, but a dwarf like Mr. Timms. Now that they knew this was where the spiritualism society's servants lived, Tilda realized who was likely inside the pedestals of the séance tables, making them move and producing raps to answer the mediums' questions.

"We were looking for someone," Tilda said pleasantly. "Ellen Henry?"

The woman's eyes narrowed. "She's not here. This is a private area. You should not be here."

"We deeply apologize," Hadrian said. "We shall take our leave."

"I should say you will." The woman stepped aside, but her expression did not lighten.

Hadrian waited for Tilda to precede him from the room. She hurried along the corridor and made her way to the stairwell, where she quickly descended. They walked into the shop where

Mr. Timms now stood in front of the counter. He glowered at them as they departed.

Tilda stopped short and faced him. "Mr. Timms? We know you accept blackmail on behalf of the spiritualism society. If you share what you know, I suspect the police will view your assistance most favorably."

The man's eyes narrowed. "You don't know anything. Take yourselves off now."

Disappointed, Tilda turned from Timms and walked outside.

Hadrian came up alongside her as they made their way from the building. "That was bold."

"I thought it was worth a try. I was hoping he might tell us who he'd accepted payments from or what he did with the money. I trust Teague will be able to persuade him to talk." She looked over at Hadrian and held out her palm. "I found this in the drawer. Thank you for blocking me from the woman's view so she couldn't see me take it."

Stopping, Hadrian stared at her hand. "That's the match to the earring you found at Rathbone Place."

"It is indeed." She glanced at his forehead. Though she hadn't seen him touch his temple or any other part of his head, she wondered if it ached following the two visions he'd seen upstairs. "How is your head?"

"Mildly aching. It's not too bad."

"Good, because I want you to hold this earring, but I didn't want to ask if you were in terrible pain. I hate asking even when you have minor discomfort."

He'd put his glove back on and now removed it again. Tilda deposited the earring in his hand.

His gaze became unfocussed once more. He twitched, then his eyes widened briefly. "I see Mallory with a woman—Miss Dryden. I am angry. No, furious. They do not see me." He squinted. His head jerked back. He blinked several times as he dropped the earring back into Tilda's hand.

"I was looking into a bedchamber," Hadrian said. "Mallory and Miss Dryden were in the bed together. There was a mirror over the hearth, and I saw my reflection—a woman with blonde hair. That was Mercy Griswold's memory." Hadrian's eyes darkened. "And she was wearing the pearl earrings you found at Rathbone Place and here today."

Tilda glanced at the earring in her palm. "This belongs to Mrs. Griswold then. And Miss Dryden was the woman Mallory took up with after Deborah Frost?"

"It seems so," Hadrian said with a nod. "But Mrs. Griswold was jealous. Or perhaps still is."

Jealousy was a motive for murder, but neither Mallory nor Miss Dryden had been killed. "If she was jealous, do you suppose she was angry enough with Mallory to kill the mediums he recruited? I think we must pursue that idea." Tilda tucked the earring into her pocket.

"What does it mean that those earrings belong to Mrs. Griswold?" Hadrian asked. "Does that make her a suspect in Mrs. Frost's murder?"

"She could have simply lost the earring at Rathbone Place. What's curious is why its mate was here in Ellen Henry's drawer."

"Agreed," Tilda replied. Then she added wryly, "It's not as if we have much else to go on at this point. We are at a frustrating dead end."

Tilda looked back at the building. "I believe we've found where the spiritualism society's domestic workers live. I wonder why they are here in Bedfordbury instead of living at the headquarters or one of the other properties. And what do you think of Mr. Timms and the woman who asked us to leave?"

His eyes glinted in the afternoon sunlight filtering through the clouds. "I think either of them could fit in the pedestals of the séance tables Clifton made."

"I thought the same thing. They could make the tables move as well as rap in answer to the questions the mediums pose. We must inform Teague of the link between the grocer and this building to the spiritualism society. However, I think we should investigate what you just saw first. How's your head now?"

"Throbbing a bit, if I'm to be honest. I suppose I should stock lavender in the coach." He smiled.

Tilda hated that he suffered when he used his ability to help them solve a case. "I will have Clara make some sachets for both of us to carry."

"Brilliant, thank you. Where are we off to next?" he asked

"I think we ought to speak with Miss Dryden first, so Cadogan Place. Then we should call on Mrs. Griswold at her new residence. Aside from asking her about her feelings toward Mallory, I'd like to know why her earring was in Ellen Henry's drawer."

CHAPTER 20

*T*hey arrived in Cadogan Place at the society headquarters a short while later. The constable outside inclined his head at them as they approached the door.

A butler Hadrian didn't recognize answered the door. He was young, as it seemed most society employees were, with dark blond hair and sky-blue eyes.

"Good afternoon," Tilda said pleasantly. "What happened to Tuttle? Has he moved to another household?"

The new butler nodded, his expression eager. "He has. He's over in Clerkenwell. He's one of the premier mediums now!"

Hadrian slid a look at Tilda and caught the fleeting smile that passed over her lips. "How exciting for him," she said. "Are you new to the spiritualism society?"

"I am," the young man said. "I'm Davis. Come in, please." His cheeks colored faintly as he ushered them into the entrance hall and closed the door.

"Welcome, Davis. I'm Miss Wren, and this is Lord Raven-hurst." Tilda gestured to Hadrian. "We've come to see Miss Dryden."

"She is in the library," Davis said.

Except she was not. Miss Dryden swept into the entrance hall and strode toward them, her expression aloof. "Good afternoon, my lord, Miss Wren. Why have you come today?"

"They are looking for you, Miss Dryden," Davis replied.

"Thank you, Davis," she said pertly. "You may go."

Davis hesitated but then inclined his head toward Tilda and Hadrian before taking himself off.

"Forgive me for not inviting you inside, but after what happened with Lysander the other day, your presence here is upsetting." She'd looked at Hadrian whilst speaking, so he assumed she was referring to his presence and not Tilda's. Perhaps he ought to offer to return to the coach. Except he didn't want to miss this interview.

"We won't take up much of your time, Miss Dryden," Tilda said. "In any case, you should be delighted to hear that Mr. Mallory is to be released from Scotland Yard, if he hasn't been already. Is he not here?"

The medium's eyes had lit with enthusiasm when Tilda mentioned Mallory being released. "He is not here, but I look forward to his imminent return."

Hadrian was certain she would. Rather than ask her about her relationship with Mallory, he waited for Tilda to pose the questions.

Tilda gave her a pleasant smile. "I imagine you are eager to have him back. You are lovers, aren't you?"

Leave it to Tilda to move straight to the heart of the matter. Hadrian bit back a smile.

Miss Dryden's eyes narrowed slightly. "Why would you think that?"

"Because we know you are," Tilda said. "But I should like to know when that started. In fact, when did you come to work for the society?"

"Why does that matter?" The medium sounded suspicious. Or afraid. Or perhaps both.

"We are trying to find the murderer of your colleagues," Tilda explained. "Any information you share could be helpful, particularly if you are eager to prove that Mr. Mallory is innocent."

Miss Dryden's brow furrowed. "But if he's been released, haven't the police decided he isn't guilty?"

"They are still investigating. They have not eliminated Mr. Mallory as a suspect." Tilda smiled again. "I'm sure you want to help him. Now, when did you join the society and in what capacity?"

Hadrian never failed to be impressed by Tilda. She was certain Miss Dryden would want to protect her lover and used that to persuade her to speak. And it worked.

"I was hired as a housekeeper last September," Miss Dryden said.

"And when did you become a medium?" Tilda asked.

"In January." Miss Dryden crossed her arms over her chest.

"Pardon me for the personal inquiry, but when did you and Mr. Mallory become intimate?"

Miss Dryden's cheeks flooded with color. "Is that really important to the investigation?"

"Every detail is, yes." She lowered her voice to add, "I promise whatever you say to us will be kept in strictest confidence."

Exhaling, Miss Dryden's color faded a bit. She looked away before answering. "We grew closer in December."

"Are you still together?" Tilda asked.

"Yes." She blushed again. "Mostly."

Tilda persisted. "What does that mean?"

Miss Dryden glanced toward Hadrian. "Must I say this in front of his lordship?"

"He will be as discreet as I will," Tilda assured her. "Does Mr. Mallory have another lover?"

"I'm not sure." Miss Dryden's shoulders twitched, and she unfolded her arms.

"What does that mean?" Tilda prodded. "I'm sorry to keep

pestering you, but this truly will help the investigation. I know you want to find the killer as much as we do."

"Oh, yes. I truly do." Miss Dryden took a deep breath. "Of late, he's not as … attentive as he has been. I wondered if he'd taken up with Miss Smith. The poor soul."

"I see," Tilda murmured. "Is there anything else about your relationship with Mr. Mallory that would be helpful for us to know?"

After a moment's consideration, Miss Dryden shook her head. Then she met Tilda's gaze with a fiery stare. "Lysander is a good man. He cares about helping people with their grief. He would never hurt anyone."

Tilda gave her a warm smile. "I understand. Thank you, Miss Dryden. You've been most helpful."

"Lysander is truly coming back?"

"You should expect him anytime, I think." Tilda looked to Hadrian, and he could see she was ready to leave. "Thank you, Miss Dryden."

Hadrian moved to open the door for Tilda, and they took their leave.

"That was informative," Hadrian said. "But does it help with finding the killer? I'm afraid I don't see any connection."

Tilda's eyes gleamed with that special light that indicated her mind was hard at work piecing together clues and information. "Mallory has had affairs with both female mediums who are dead —Mrs. Frost and Miss Smith—as well as two more mediums who are still breathing."

"Miss Dryden and Mrs. Griswold?"

"I think we can assume Mrs. Griswold was one of his paramours at some point, given the jealousy you felt when you saw her memory," Tilda said. "And I think we must consider that she —or Miss Dryden—may have had a motive to kill Mrs. Frost and Miss Smith."

"But what about Ward and Hawkins?" Hadrian asked.

"It may be that Hawkins discovered the identity of the murderer and was killed. However, that doesn't explain Ward's death, since he was murdered first."

"What if Ward was an accident?" Hadrian mused. "Poison was the weapon, and I would think you could poison the wrong person by mistake."

"That would be possible." Tilda gave her head a shake. "We are moving ahead of the evidence. We must speak with Mrs. Griswold and see what we learn."

~

*W*hen they arrived at the house in Rathbone Place, Gibbs, the young constable who'd they'd previously seen at Hawkins's house, stood on the pavement and greeted them cheerfully. "Pleasure to see you again, your lordship, Miss Wren."

"I hope there hasn't been any trouble for you," Tilda said.

"None whatsoever." He touched his hat. "But I'm here at the ready if need be."

Tilda smiled at him as Hadrian moved toward the door. "That is a great comfort."

Hastening to join Hadrian, Tilda arrived at the door just as Ellen answered. Tilda was glad, as she was eager to speak with her about the pearl earring.

"Good afternoon, my lord, Miss Wren." Ellen's brow furrowed. "Is Mrs. Griswold expecting you?"

"She is not," Tilda replied. "We have come to speak with you as well as her."

Ellen opened the door wider for them to step into the entrance hall. "You want to speak with me?" She closed the door and faced them somewhat nervously.

Tilda couldn't help thinking that Ellen had seemed agitated every time they'd encountered her. With good reason. She'd found her employer hanging from a staircase and was expected to simply carry on.

"If you don't mind, we'd appreciate if you could answer a few questions," Tilda said. "Like when we spoke last week. After Mrs. Frost." Tilda decided not to mention death.

"I told you everything I knew," Ellen said, again sounding tense.

"I wanted to ask about you." Tilda gave her an encouraging smile. "I know it must be a difficult time after what you've been through. I hope you're doing well."

Relief flickered in Ellen's eyes. "Well enough, thank you, Miss Wren."

"I wondered how long you and your brother have worked for the society," Tilda said.

"Since last summer. August, I think it was," Ellen added with a nod.

"And you're both training to be mediums?"

Ellen blushed. "I'm not anymore. It was more Jacob's dream. He's still training, but I'm content to continue in my current position."

Tilda noted that the female mediums who'd been promoted seemed to have been those who were carrying on affairs with Lysander Mallory. Had Ellen been pressured to do the same and refused? Was that why she didn't seek promotion?

"My understanding is that the society hires people like you and Jacob and trains you as mediums. Is there a certain time when someone becomes a medium? Perhaps they conduct a certain number of séances? Or, and forgive me for asking such a delicate question, are female mediums expected to engage in a particular relationship with Mr. Mallory?"

Ellen's eyes rounded and her face flushed bright pink. "I don't know if that's expected, but several mediums have developed a tendre for him. He is very handsome. And charming." She blushed even more, then darted a glance toward the staircase hall. "I am not supposed to talk about how the society works."

"I do understand," Tilda said sympathetically. "However, we are investigating the murders of the mediums, and any information you can share will be most helpful. We won't reveal what you tell us to anyone," she added in a whisper. "Have you had any kind of … intimate relationship with Mr. Mallory?"

Eyes widening once more, Ellen shook her head. "No. I am not interested in such things."

Tilda didn't like making the maid uncomfortable, but she just needed one more answer. "Did that prevent you from training as a medium?"

"I … I suppose it did. It seemed as though I might need to show a certain level of … affection for Mr. Mallory. However, no one asked me to do that, and I truly am content in my current position."

"I'm so glad to hear that," Tilda said with a smile. "I am curious as to how someone enters the society to train as a medium. Would you mind sharing that? I promise we won't reveal who told us."

"I suppose it won't harm anything to explain how someone becomes a medium," Ellen said with another look at the staircase hall. "We're hired as domestic servants, and we learn how the society works. Then we start to train as mediums. If we are found to have talent as a medium, we're promoted to being lesser mediums who conduct séances at the headquarters. After that, lesser mediums are promoted to premier mediums."

Tilda glanced toward Hadrian. "We understand Tuttle, who was the butler at the headquarters, is the newest premier medium."

"He is indeed. I'm so thrilled for him. I think Jacob was hoping he might be chosen, but Tuttle has been with the society a little longer than we have. Honestly, I thought it would be Crocker. He is the very best of the mediums in training."

"I'm confused about mediums in training and lesser mediums. Those of you in training also do domestic work, but it seems the lesser mediums do not. Is Miss Dryden a lesser medium?"

Ellen nodded. "Yes, and so were Mr. Edwards and Mrs. Griswold—until they were promoted after …" Her voice trailed off.

"After Mr. Ward and Mrs. Frost were murdered," Tilda finished softly. "Was Tuttle not a lesser medium?"

"Not yet, but he was on the verge of promotion. Then, when Mr. Hawkins … you know." She gave them a meaningful look. "When that happened, Mr. Mallory said he had to promote another male to take Mr. Hawkins's place, and he chose Tuttle."

"So, now all the premier medium positions are filled?" Tilda asked.

"Until the society acquires another property." Ellen shrugged. "At least, that's what I think is supposed to happen. Jacob says Mr. Mallory wants a dozen or more premier mediums running séance houses across London. That is why he keeps recruiting mediums."

"Such as Harmony Smith," Tilda said.

Ellen blanched. "Yes. She didn't train for long. Mr. Mallory promoted her to lesser medium very quickly."

Tilda put her hand in her pocket to retrieve the pearl earring. "I have just one other question for you, Ellen. We visited Bedfordbury earlier today, and I think we were in your bedchamber." Tilda opened her palm to reveal the earring. "I found this in your dressing table. It looks like the one I found here last week. I wondered why you had it. I thought you said you didn't recognize it."

What color that had returned to Ellen's face immediately fled. "I … I don't know." She became extremely flustered, worrying her hands and biting her lip.

"It's all right, Ellen," Tilda soothed. "I only want to know why you had it."

"I didn't recognize it when you asked me last week. But then when Mrs. Griswold came here as premier medium, I found it in her things as I was unpacking them. I just … I took it."

"Why?" Hadrian asked.

Ellen looked to him. "I don't know. It seemed like I should tell someone." She returned her attention to Tilda. "I showed it to my brother, and he said I should just hide it away. So I did. Was that wrong?"

"No, but it is helpful for the police to know who the earring belonged to." Tilda tucked the earring back into her pocket. She could see Ellen was worried. "You are not in trouble."

"But what about Mrs. Griswold? I don't wish to cause her trouble either."

"Just because we found her earring here doesn't mean she had anything to do with Mrs. Frost's death," Tilda said. But neither did it mean she *didn't*. And Tilda was now suspicious of many people in the society. Between Mallory and his revolving paramours, and the promotion system that Ellen had just exposed, Tilda wondered if someone might have been moved to murder.

She tamped down a wave of frustration that she hadn't learned this information sooner. They'd been too focused on whether someone shared Hadrian's power and on the blackmail, which had seemed the best motive for murder. And perhaps it still was.

"But she didn't like Mrs. Frost," Ellen whispered.

Tilda's neck prickled just as she saw Mrs. Griswold walk from the staircase hall.

"Ellen, who are you talking to?" Mrs. Griswold approached them. "Ah, Lord Ravenhurst and Miss Wren. How can I help you?"

"We've come to ask you some questions about Mr. Mallory and the society," Tilda replied.

"I'm afraid I don't have time to speak with you," Mrs. Griswold said. "Perhaps another time?" She spread her rouged lips into a wide smile, but it did not reach her eyes. In fact, her gaze crackled with anxiety.

Had she heard what Ellen had said about her not liking Mrs. Frost? Tilda didn't think so, but perhaps Mrs. Griswold had been listening to the conversation from the entrance hall and didn't like what she'd heard.

"It won't take but a few minutes," Tilda said. She had a bad feeling about leaving Ellen just now.

"I don't have a few minutes," Mrs. Griswold snapped. "You must excuse me." She looked to the maid. "Ellen, show them out."

Ellen moved toward the door as Hadrian stripped his glove away. He stepped forward and snatched Mrs. Griswold's bare hand.

Gasping, she turned to face him. "My lord, what are you about?"

But Hadrian was seeing a vision—Tilda was certain of it. He released Mrs. Griswold's hand. "My apologies, but I wanted to stop you from walking away. Miss Wren has questions, and I would like very much for you to answer them. Starting with why you might wish to kill your fellow mediums."

"I did no such thing!"

Tilda realized that Hadrian must have seen something that made him think Mrs. Griswold had killed the others. Did he know it for certain or only suspect? How she wished she could know!

"You were angry with them," Hadrian said. "Was it because you had been Mallory's paramour and couldn't bear to think of him with anyone else? Perhaps Ward knew of your plan and Hawkins knew what you'd done, so you had to kill them too."

Mrs. Griswold laughed. "I don't care whom Lysander takes to his bed. He enjoys women, and that is his prerogative."

"But you were angry with him," Hadrian said.

"Why would you think that? I adore Lysander."

"She was upset that he hadn't promoted her to premier medium," Ellen said softly. "She was jealous of the attention and patronage that the premiers received."

Everyone snapped their attention to the maid. Her shoulders were turned inward, arms straight, as she clasped her hands. She didn't dare look at Mrs. Griswold, who was gaping at her.

Tilda thought she understood at last. "You killed Ward so you could take his place, and when that didn't happen, you killed Mrs. Frost."

Guilt was reflected in Mrs. Griswold aquamarine eyes. And fear.

"However, I don't see how you could have committed these murders on your own," Tilda said. "You would have needed help to hang the bodies. Mr. Edwards certainly appears strong enough, and he has taken the place vacated first by Cyril Ward and then Victor Hawkins. I wonder, will he become the Duchess of Chester's new medium?"

"Nigel had nothing to do with it," Mrs. Griswold cried.

"Then who helped you?" Hadrian asked, and Tilda realized he hadn't seen Mrs. Griswold's accomplice, which was too bad. "You could not have done all this alone."

"That includes killing Harmony Smith," Tilda said. "I believe you poisoned her with prussic acid. But why take her body to Leicester Square and not levitate her like the others?"

"I would guess it's because she wasn't a premier medium," Ellen said, surprising Tilda with her input. The maid's eyes were wide as she added, "Mrs. Griswold has a bottle of prussic acid in her bedchamber."

Mrs. Griswold lunged for Ellen. Tilda opened her reticule to fetch her pistol as Hadrian leapt forward to grasp the medium. He pulled Mrs. Griswold backward as she flailed.

"You prying little wretch!" Mrs. Griswold shrieked.

Tilda pointed her pistol at the medium, not that she would shoot her whilst Hadrian was keeping hold of her, but she hoped the threat would quiet the woman. "Ellen, please go out to the pavement and send Constable Gibbs inside. Then go to Lord Ravenhurst's coach and tell his coachman to fetch Detective Inspector Teague from Scotland Yard. You should go with him."

Ellen dashed from the house, leaving the door ajar in her flight. A moment later, Gibbs rushed in, his face flushed.

"Constable Gibbs, we've a murderer for you to put in irons, if you don't mind." Tilda inclined her head toward Mrs. Griswold, who continued to struggle in Hadrian's grip.

Sucking in a breath, Gibbs pulled the handcuffs from where they hung at his waist and moved toward Mrs. Griswold cautiously. "Stop fighting, Mrs. Griswold, or things will go poorly for you."

Things were going to go poorly for her anyway, Tilda thought as the constable and Hadrian worked together to put the hand-cuffs around the woman's wrists.

"Let us go into the parlor to await Detective Inspector Teague," Tilda suggested, as if they were paying a call and not unmasking a murderer.

Gibbs clasped Mrs. Griswold's upper arm and guided her into the parlor, where he sat her in a chair and stood beside her. He took his truncheon from his belt and held it as he kept his gaze fixed on the medium.

Hadrian stood next to Tilda as they faced Mrs. Griswold. He withdrew his pistol from his coat and trained it on the medium. "You can put your pistol away, if you like, Tilda."

Tilda slipped her father's pistol into her reticule. "You poisoned the other mediums so you could become a premier medium?"

Mrs. Griswold pressed her lips together and glowered at Tilda.

"You don't have to tell us anything, but I daresay it will help your cause, especially if you name your accomplice. Perhaps you won't hang."

Gibbs opened his mouth, likely to correct what Tilda had said, but she wanted the medium to talk. Tilda gestured faintly toward Gibbs and gave her head a slight shake. He closed his mouth and nodded.

Mrs. Griswold paled. "I was upset with Cyril. I wanted him to introduce me to Her Grace—the Duchess of Chester. I hoped she would like me and perhaps recommend me and my séances to her friends." Her lips twisted. "But he refused. He said I had to find my own wealthy client. I was angry, so the next time I was at his house for dinner, I added some prussic acid to his favorite wine. I thought it would make him ill."

"But you killed him," Tilda concluded. "Why hang him from the staircase and make him look as though he was levitating?"

Mrs. Griswold stared at Tilda as if she were daft. "So that it would appear as though someone else had done it. But it wasn't my idea. That was Michael's concoction. Ward was so bloody good at levitating," she said with a sneer. "It was one of the things that had made him so popular."

"Do you mean Michael Crocker?" Hadrian asked, his gaze briefly meeting Tilda's.

"Yes." Mrs. Griswold lifted her chin. "He was glad to help me. We thought the spectacle would attract notice and perhaps increase membership."

"But the two of you didn't stop with killing Ward," Tilda said, surprised that Crocker was her accomplice. "Why did you kill Mrs. Frost?"

"*I* was next in line to be premier medium," she snapped. "Lysander should have given me Cyril's clients, namely Her Grace. But he said Victor should do it, that it needed to be a man because Her Grace preferred that—replacing her dead son and all that." Mrs. Griswold pursed her lips briefly. "Lysander said I would be next to move up in the society, that I would soon be a premier medium."

"So you killed Mrs. Frost to make that happen faster?" Hadrian asked.

"She never liked me anyway," Mrs. Griswold replied, as if that were justification for murdering the woman. "Because Lysander left her bed for mine after I started working for him."

Tilda could see that Mrs. Griswold possessed a dark, malevolent nature. "Why kill Victor Hawkins and Harmony Smith? You had what you wanted—you would be a premier medium."

"Victor was trying to persuade Lysander that Isidora should be promoted over me because her sensitivity was greater." Mrs. Griswold rolled her eyes. "I am the better performer. I would attract more and better patrons. Miss Smith was too uppity for her own good. She thought she could insert herself into Lysander's bed and move quickly up the ranks. That is not how it works. One must toil and earn their way. They must wait their turn."

Except Mrs. Griswold was eliminating those who stood in her way instead of waiting for her own turn. But Tilda didn't point that out. She wondered how Miss Dryden and even Mr. Mallory had escaped Mrs. Griswold's murderous plans. "Who did you plan to kill next?"

The medium blinked and her forehead creased. "No one."

"Not Miss Dryden or even Mr. Mallory?"

Mrs. Griswold looked aghast. "The society is nothing without Lysander. He is the backbone of all we do. We cannot ... function without him."

"Why not?" Hadrian flicked another glance at Tilda, silently communicating that they both knew why.

"He has a special power," Mrs. Griswold said. "We've asked him to teach us, but he says he can't. I sometimes wonder if he's lying."

"Lying about teaching you or lying about his power?" Hadrian asked.

The medium looked up at Hadrian. "Both. How can he know things about people? You'd have to believe that he can truly speak to the dead, which none of us can actually do. I don't know how he knows things, but he does. And we need him for that."

It was almost refreshing to hear someone from the society speak so plainly. "Where can we find Crocker?"

"I don't know for sure, but he's probably at the headquarters."

"Does he live there or in Bedfordbury?" Tilda asked.

Mrs. Griswold's nostrils flared. "You know about Bedfordbury?"

"You'd likely be surprised at what we know," Hadrian said sardonically.

"He lives in Cadogan Place," Mrs. Griswold said.

Tilda would direct Teague to go there next after he arrested Mrs. Griswold. Meanwhile, she wanted to go to Clerkenwell to call on Captain Vale. She'd promised him an update, and she had precisely the one he would want to hear most—that they'd caught the killer and it wasn't his son.

Teague arrived a few minutes later. Hadrian called for him, and the detective inspector strode into the parlor with three constables in tow. He immediately looked toward Gibbs and gave the young constable a nod.

"As I'm sure Ellen Henry informed you, we've found the Levitation Killer," Tilda said. "One half of them anyway. Mrs. Griswold had help from Michael Crocker to hang the bodies."

"Crocker?" Teague asked. "Isn't he one of the society's domestic servants?"

"Yes," Tilda replied. "We believe he may be at the society headquarters if you'd care to go there next."

"I will, thank you." Teague turned his attention to Gibbs. "Well done, Constable. Take Mrs. Griswold out to the wagon. Parker, go with him."

Gibbs and Parker departed with the medium, and Hadrian finally returned his pistol to his coat.

Tilda explained all that Mrs. Griswold had told them to Teague and presented him with the earring she'd found in Ellen's room in Bedfordbury. "This is the mate to the earring I found after Mrs. Frost was killed. It belongs to Mrs. Griswold, and Ellen recognized it after she began working for her. It led us to confront Mrs. Griswold."

"Excellent investigative work, Miss Wren."

"Ellen said there is a bottle of prussic acid in Mrs. Griswold's bedchamber," Tilda added. "The maid was most helpful to the investigation."

"Indeed." Teague instructed the remaining constables to search the medium's bedchamber, and they immediately left the parlor. He looked to Tilda once more. "Ellen is safe at Scotland Yard and currently giving evidence."

"I'm glad you were able to come so quickly," Tilda said.

"As am I," Teague said. "I'm more glad that no one else was hurt." He met Tilda's gaze with a warm gratitude that filled her with pride. "Thank you again for your assistance. Truly."

Tilda could see he genuinely meant it. Whilst she may never be a member of the Metropolitan Police or recognized for her contributions, knowing that she aided justice gave her immense satisfaction. How she wished her father could see it.

After assuring Teague they would visit Scotland Yard to deliver their official statements, they returned to the coach where Leach was waiting, his eyes bright with anticipation. "Did everything turn out well?"

"Indeed it has," Hadrian replied. "One half of the Levitation Killer has been arrested, and the other half—Mrs. Griswold's accomplice—will be shortly apprehended, we hope." At Leach's expression of confusion, he added, "There is another person at large, but we trust the police will find him in Cadogan Place."

"I'm glad to hear it," Leach said. "That poor maid I took to Scotland Yard was in a dither."

Hadrian addressed Leach as the coachman opened the door for Tilda. "We need to go to Scotland Yard, but first we must visit Woodbridge Street in Clerkenwell. You remember the house?"

"I do indeed." Leach held the door for Tilda, and she climbed inside.

Hadrian sat beside her, and she was glad. Though they hadn't been in real danger with Mrs. Griswold, the encounter had been fraught for a few moments. His proximity contributed to her sense of security.

"Captain Vale will be delighted that the case has been solved," Hadrian remarked as the coach started moving. "He was right that his son was not guilty."

"True, but his son is guilty of other crimes and must pay for them."

"I don't think he'll quarrel with that," Hadrian said.

They were quiet a moment, and Tilda reviewed the events of the case in her mind. "I think I might call on Clement after we attend to matters at Scotland Yard. I'd like him to know the case is resolved."

"Are you of a mind to reward him with this information since he was helpful?"

Tilda lifted a shoulder. "I don't think it can hurt. Who knows when he might provide assistance in the future? We also need to speak with your mother."

Hadrian wiped his hand down the side of his face. "Yes, of course. I can do that after we call on Clement."

"You want to accompany me to Fleet Street?" Tilda asked.

"Certainly. We are partners, and I'm eager to help with all aspects of the case, including the conclusion."

"I feel the same," Tilda said. "Which means I must join you in speaking with your mother. But not just because we are partners. Your mother hired me, and I must deliver the final results of our investigation."

Hadrian's expression became beleaguered. "How do we tell her the mediums absolutely do not speak with the dead? She will point to the memory of the snow fort that was shared at Mrs.

Griswold's séance as proof that they do. I can't contradict that without explaining the truth about my ability."

"Actually, you can." Tilda wasn't sure how Hadrian would react to her suggestion, but she was going to make it anyway. "You can explain that *Mallory* has a secret ability. You don't have to tell her that you possess it too. That way, when you decide to confide in her someday, the foundation is already laid." She watched Hadrian's nostrils flare and the muscles in his neck tighten.

"You assume I will tell her," Hadrian said darkly.

"I think you will. Perhaps not now, but you will find a way to overcome your fear that she will somehow disdain you." At least Tilda hoped he would.

"Or that she won't believe me."

"You can find a way to prove it," Tilda said softly. "I've never questioned your ability, not after what I've seen you do. And I'd like to think your mother cares about you even more than I do." Of course she did. She was his mother, whilst Tilda was merely his … friend.

Who cared for him a great deal.

Hadrian looked out the window. "I'll consider it." A moment later, he said, "Would you mind not delivering your investigative conclusions today?"

"I've no problem with that. After the errands ahead of us, I think I will be ready to go home for a respite." She smiled at him, and he seemed to relax.

They arrived in Woodbridge Street and made their way to the door of the brick-fronted terrace that had been occupied by Hawkins until recently. Tilda felt a stab of sorrow for the mediums who'd been lost.

She realized there was no constable present. Tilda looked up and down the pavement. "Do you see a constable?"

Hadrian also surveyed the area. "I do not. Should we be alarmed?"

Tilda's pulse sped. "I don't know. Perhaps the constable is inside for some reason."

They went to the door, and Hadrian knocked. They waited several moments with no response before he rapped again. Still, no one answered.

Now, Tilda couldn't help feeling concerned.

"Don't worry yet," Hadrian said as he looked at her. "Perhaps Captain Vale has gone out."

"But where is the constable?" Tilda wondered. "And Captain Vale was expecting me to call later today." She tilted her head back and looked at the windows on the upper floors.

"Is no one answering?" a feminine voice asked from behind them.

Tilda turned to see Mrs. Wilson, the housekeeper they'd met when they'd called on Hawkins last week. "No," Tilda replied. "You aren't working today?"

Mrs. Wilson frowned. "I am not. One of those spiritualism society butlers came earlier and told me I wasn't needed the rest of the day. I argued with him because I was taking care of a guest —a captain who is visiting London. That snippy young man put me off, so I came back to check on the captain."

Suddenly anxious, Tilda glanced at Hadrian. "Do you know who the butler was?"

"It was that arrogant chap, Crocker. I don't care for him. I saw him talking to the constable too, and then the constable left."

Tilda's pulse began to pound. She turned to Hadrian. "Try the door."

He whipped his glove off and attempted to open the door. Since he removed his glove, Tilda thought he must be trying to see something too.

"It's locked," Hadrian said darkly.

Tilda looked to the housekeeper. "Mrs. Wilson, do you know how we might get inside? We are concerned about the welfare of those who may be within." She didn't want to say too much and frighten the woman.

Mrs. Wilson's expression dimmed with concern. She opened her reticule and removed a key. "Here." She held it out to Tilda.

"Thank you." Tilda quickly unlocked the door.

Hadrian clasped her arm. "Wait. We should send Leach to fetch Teague once more."

"Yes, but we need to get inside." Tilda slipped the key into the pocket of her gown and opened her reticule to remove her father's pistol.

Mrs. Wilson gasped.

Hadrian pivoted. "Pardon us, Mrs. Wilson. You ought to return to your home." Turning his head toward the coach parked on the street, he called, "Leach, we need you to fetch Teague in Cadogan Place. Be quick!"

Leach set the coach into motion as Mrs. Wilson hurried away.

Taking his pistol from his coat, Hadrian gave Tilda a determined look before stepping into the house.

CHAPTER 21

*H*adrian sucked in a breath as he looked beyond the small entrance hall into the staircase hall. He caught sight of a dark red puddle on the floor.

"Tilda, I think there's blood," he said softly. He lifted his pistol, his entire body tightening with an urge to flee but also to confront whatever—or whomever—awaited them.

The sound of something falling and breaking came from the parlor to their left, where they'd met with Hawkins nearly a week ago. Hadrian's breath snagged, and he looked back at Tilda. Her features were set into grim lines as she held her pistol at the ready.

He moved first toward the parlor, letting his pistol lead him. Quickly scanning the room, he determined it was empty. But there was an unmistakable sound of someone making noise. It came from the other side of the settee.

Stepping toward the center of the room so he could see around the piece of furniture, Hadrian saw the source of the noise just as Tilda did. Mallory's father was trussed up with rope and gagged, his eyes wide as he watched Tilda and Hadrian approach. Blood stained his side.

"Captain Vale!" Tilda was careful not to speak too loudly, but neither had she whispered. She set her pistol on the settee and dropped to her knees next to the man. Pulling off her gloves, she tossed them next to the pistol, then pulled the fabric away from his mouth. She reached behind his head and untied the gag.

"You must hurry!" Vale said, tears pooling in his eyes. "He has Thaddeus upstairs. I fear he'll do the same to him as to the other poor man."

"You're hurt," Tilda said, her hand hovering over the bloodied area of the captain's midsection.

"He stuck me when I caught him. I'd just seen him stab the lad."

"Who?" Hadrian asked, fearing he already knew.

"Tuttle was his name," Vale said as tears leaked from his eyes. "You must go save Thaddeus before the madman stabs him next! If he hasn't already." The man practically sobbed the last word.

Whilst the captain spoke, Tilda had loosened the ropes binding the captain's hands and feet. She grasped her pistol and stood. "Stay here."

The captain nodded as he leaned against the settee, his face pale. Hadrian tried to give him an encouraging nod but feared his own apprehension was etched into his features.

Tilda preceded him from the parlor, and Hadrian hastened to grab her arm. "Let me go first, please."

She nodded, her gaze steady but fraught. Hadrian stepped into the staircase hall and looked up to see exactly what he'd feared. Tuttle hung from the railing, but the rope had not been painted to look like the wood.

"This wasn't planned," Tilda whispered. "It's not the same as the others."

Hadrian agreed. "It doesn't seem as if Mrs. Griswold was aware this was happening."

They went to the stairs and ascended cautiously. Tilda followed Hadrian as he paused on the landing to determine where to go. Muffled sounds seemed to be coming from a room to the right.

Hadrian moved as quietly as possible toward the door which stood ajar. He carefully pushed the door open and surveyed the room. It was a sitting room, and Mallory was trussed up like his father had been. However, he wasn't bleeding yet.

Before he stepped into the room, Hadrian looked again carefully. Where was Crocker? Mallory was gagged, his dark eyes wide. He tried to say something, but only muffled sounds emerged from behind the cloth shoved into his mouth.

"Go help him, Hadrian," Tilda said from behind him.

Hadrian did not lower his pistol as he moved into the room. In fact, he would feel better if Tilda helped Mallory whilst Hadrian watched for Crocker.

Pivoting on his heel, Hadrian opened his mouth to tell Tilda to untie Mallory, but no sound came out. He was too late. He watched in horror as Crocker grabbed Tilda from behind and wrested the pistol from her hand.

He fired the weapon at Hadrian.

~

*N*o, no, no.

Tilda would not allow Hadrian to be shot or stabbed or hurt in any way. She was nearly oblivious to the grip of the man who now held her against his solid chest. Nothing mattered more than clawing her way to Hadrian.

Her father's pistol clattered to the floor, now useless. Crocker —she assumed the man holding her was the murderous butler— pressed something against Tilda's neck. "Stop moving."

Stomach churning with fear, Tilda stopped trying to escape his grip. She tried to take a deep breath to calm her racing heart, but she could not inhale as deeply as she wanted with the man holding her so tightly. His left arm curled around her upper middle and lifted her so that her feet barely grazed the floorboards.

"Do not come toward us or she will die," Crocker said, his breath hot against Tilda's neck.

Tilda blinked and realized that whilst Hadrian had dropped to the floor, he was now standing. And he appeared unhurt. Relief flooded her, and she had to suck in a breath to keep from sobbing.

"I'm fine, Tilda," Hadrian said, his tone carved in ice. He still gripped the pistol, but it was not pointed at them. Tilda understood why—if Hadrian fired, he would hit her as Crocker seemed to be using her as a shield.

Hadrian's eyes glittered with malice. "Crocker has terrible aim, thankfully. And he has nowhere to go."

Crocker snorted. The sound was loud in Tilda's ear, given his proximity. "I've an excellent hostage, Ravenhurst. I can go anywhere I like."

"The police will find you," Hadrian said.

"Don't, Hadrian," Tilda snapped. If Crocker heard there was no hope of escape, he may very well shoot her now. "He doesn't care what you have to say. Crocker, you will escape much more quickly if you aren't holding onto me. We won't come after you. Release me and run."

Tilda didn't want to let the man go, but it was their best option in the current situation. The police would catch him.

Crocker moved backward, carrying Tilda with him. "I don't think I can let you live," he whispered so that Hadrian couldn't hear him. "You should not have come here. There is no reason for you to die."

"You just said there was." Tilda hoped to keep him talking to perhaps distract him. "But you *can* release me."

"You'll tell them all what I've done. I still have time to escape.

I'll leave London. Mayhap, I'll leave England altogether. Mercy said she wanted to visit New England. The spiritualism movement is strong there."

Hadrian emerged from the room as Crocker backed them up to the railing overlooking the hall below. Tilda glanced to the left and saw poor Tuttle hanging farther along the railing.

Crocker pressed the knife into her flesh. She didn't think he broke the skin, but the blade was close to doing so.

"Cut her and I will tear you apart," Hadrian snarled, his pistol half raised.

Mallory came from the room and stood next to Hadrian, who must have untied him.

"You've ruined everything!" Crocker shouted, making Tilda flinch. "*All* of you. Mercy and I had it all sorted, then Mallory went and gave my position as medium here to Tuttle. Why would you do that? It was my turn!"

"Because you're a terrible medium," Mallory said without pretense, as if he were not aware that Tilda was currently in danger.

"Don't antagonize him." Hadrian didn't take his eyes from Tilda.

She met his gaze and tried to convey that she would be all right. She wasn't sure how yet, but if he could move a little closer to the railing, perhaps she could push Crocker off balance so that he fell. The key was not to go over with him. It was not lost on her that their last case involved someone falling over a railing.

"I am an excellent medium!" Crocker cried. "If you paid more attention to those beyond your chosen few, or the women you are wooing, you might have noticed. It is you who are terrible."

"And yet without me, the society will falter," Mallory said with supreme arrogance. Was he trying to aggravate Crocker? "None of you can do what I do. I see into people's minds and beyond to connect with those they have lost. Such as your mother, Michael.

She cries in the spirit realm, aching for the son who has turned out no better than his father—the very man who ended her life."

Crocker's entire body heaved in reaction, his grip loosening ever so slightly on Tilda's midsection. It was enough for her to lift her leg and kick back into his thigh. But he did not release her.

Suddenly, they went sideways. A body hurtled into them, and now Crocker released her. Tilda fell to the floor. She flipped around and saw that it was Captain Vale who was grappling against the railing with Crocker. The man had somehow made his way upstairs.

Both Hadrian and Mallory rushed forward. Crocker tipped over the railing. He gripped the captain, and for a horrifying moment, it looked as though both of them would topple to the hall below.

But Mallory grabbed his father and pulled as Hadrian clasped Crocker's arm and wrenched it away from the captain. Crocker flailed, and Tilda's heart stopped as she feared he might take Hadrian over with him.

He did not. Crocker arced over the railing and fell.

Tilda pushed herself up and rushed to Hadrian's side. They looked over the railing at Crocker splayed on the floor below, a red pool forming beneath his head. His eyes stared up at the ceiling, sightless.

"Papa," Mallory cried, sounding broken as he clutched at his father, who was slumping toward the floor.

"We must fetch a doctor," Tilda said. "I'll go ask a neighbor."

As Tilda turned toward the stairs, Hadrian grasped her arm gently. She met his stare and felt the worry she saw there in the hollows of her own body. It was at once jarring and comforting.

"You're all right?" His gaze flicked toward her neck.

She touched her flesh where the knife had grazed her. "Yes. I am incredibly relieved you weren't shot. We needed *one* investigation where you were not wounded."

A smile lifted his lips, and Tilda's breath caught. "So we did." He released her arm, and Tilda was sorry to no longer feel his touch.

Before she could allow that sentiment to take root, she turned and fled down the stairs.

CHAPTER 22

"*C*an you wed her?"

Mallory's question jerked Hadrian from his reverie as he'd watched Tilda descend the stairs, her gray skirts moving about her ankles.

"What?" Hadrian asked, blinking.

The medium sat on the floor with his father's head and shoulders cradled in his lap. He'd removed his stock and held it to the wound on the captain's side. The captain's eyes were closed.

"You and Miss Wren appear to care deeply for one another," Mallory observed. "You hail from completely different classes. Are you able to wed her?"

Able. As if there were something that would forbid Hadrian from doing so. "I can do as I bloody well please."

Mallory laughed softly, his lip curling as he finished. "Of course you can. You're an earl. I shall congratulate you now then."

"We are not betrothed, nor do we have plans to be." Hadrian wondered if the medium had seen the memory of him and Tilda kissing. He could have seen that when he'd touched Tilda's hand last week. "What have you seen?" His tone was skeptical, bordering on accusing, but he didn't care.

"Nothing between you. It doesn't take someone with our ability to see the connection between you and Miss Wren." Mallory smirked. "Though now I'm going to ponder what has happened."

"Leave him be," the captain croaked without opening his eyes.

Mallory's brow creased. "Yes, Papa. Try not to exert yourself. The doctor will be here soon."

"Talking is hardly exerting myself."

"Perhaps not," Hadrian said. "But managing to climb the stairs in your wounded state was most taxing. You must rest. Thank you for coming when you did." Hadrian didn't want to think of what might have happened if Captain Vale had not launched himself at Crocker at that precise moment.

The captain opened his eyes and looked up at Hadrian. "Thank you for rescuing my son. I know he's done wrong, but I told you he's not a killer."

"No, Papa," Mallory said softly. "Nor will I continue as I have."

"Truly?" the captain asked.

Mallory nodded. "There has been enough harm."

Captain Vale looked at his son with love. "I'm glad to hear you say that. Our ability was never meant to be used as you employed it."

"About that," Hadrian said hesitantly. He didn't particularly want to discuss it with Mallory, but he wanted to make sure his secret would be safe. "You haven't told anyone that we are … alike, have you?"

"No," Mallory replied quickly. "I would never. And I would ask that you do the same. No one at the society knows precisely what I am able to do."

"But some of them knew that you disguised yourself as Montrose, Parr, and Mrs. Sullivan," Hadrian noted. "Did they not know you were doing so in order to experience the memories of the person next to you in order to assist the medium?"

"They did not know what I was doing, only that I was able to give them information that would be helpful to them during the séance."

Hadrian thought of Tilda's suggestion that he tell his mother about Mallory's ability. "I need to explain to my mother how Mrs. Griswold knew about a memory of hers from when I was young. I don't want my mother trying to see another medium, so I need her to understand that none of what you were selling was real."

"That is why you and Miss Wren were sticking your nose into the society?" Mallory asked. "To investigate what we were doing?"

Hadrian inclined his head. "My mother hired Tilda to determine Mrs. Frost's authenticity."

"I see." Mallory's expression turned pensive.

"Tell Lady Ravenhurst you provided the memory to give her what she sought," Captain Vale suggested. "Then apologize for deceiving her."

It wasn't a terrible idea, but his mother likely wouldn't believe him, given his lack of encouragement for her endeavors to speak with Gabriel. "I would do that except she saw quite clearly that I did not support her efforts to speak with my brother, nor did I think it was even possible."

"You can explain that you saw how much it meant to her, so you arranged for the medium to 'speak' with your brother." Captain Vale gave him a gentle smile. "And you are telling her the truth now because you feel guilty about everything. All you want is for her to be happy."

"That is the truth," Hadrian said simply. "Thank you."

Tilda came dashing up the stairs. Her cheeks were lightly pink from her exertions. "A neighbor has gone to fetch a doctor and says he should be here soon. I'm surprised you didn't move the captain to a bedroom."

"Hell," Hadrian swore. He looked down at Mallory. "Let's pick him up."

Hadrian took the captain's legs as Mallory rose and carried his father's shoulders.

"That way." Mallory inclined his head behind Hadrian.

"You lead," Hadrian said. Mallory moved to walk backward as they carried the captain into a bedchamber. They set him on the bed and Hadrian stepped back.

Tilda followed and stood at the foot of the bed. Suddenly, Mrs. Wilson appeared in the doorway carrying a tray with a bowl of water and some strips of cloth.

"Thank you for offering to help, Mrs. Wilson," Tilda said warmly. "I encountered her a few houses away. She'd gone to fetch a constable. He's downstairs assessing the situation. I told him Detective Inspector Teague would be here shortly."

"I appreciate you telling me to take the back stairs, Miss Wren," the housekeeper said with a gentle twitch of her shoulders.

Mrs. Wilson set the tray on a table and wet one of the cloths. Then she moved to the bed and dabbed at the captain's brow.

Teague's voice carried into the bedchamber. "Miss Wren? Ravenhurst?"

Tilda left the room, and Hadrian accompanied her. They encountered Teague near the staircase railing.

"Bloody hell, I am sorry to see this has happened again." Teague's frown was deep as he set his hands on his hips.

"But this is the last of the Levitation Killer," Tilda said. "You have Mrs. Griswold, and Crocker has met his end."

"Indeed," Teague said. "I dispatched the constable who was stationed at the society headquarters to fetch Graythorpe. He'll want to look at everything as part of his investigation ahead of the inquest. In the meantime, tell me what happened."

"We're not sure what happened to the constable who was supposed to be here, but it seems as though Crocker sent him away," Tilda said. They hadn't asked Crocker what he'd said to the man to make him leave.

Teague nodded. "I'll find out what happened—and make sure that constable doesn't make that kind of mistake again," he added with a deep frown.

Hadrian and Tilda told the tale in turns. They each managed to sound somewhat unaffected as they recounted the most terrifying aspects of the events that had transpired. That was purposeful on Hadrian's part, for he was now worried that his deeper feelings for Tilda were obvious to everyone. Was she also trying not to sound moved by what had happened?

Whilst they were speaking, the doctor arrived, and Tilda directed him into the bedchamber to tend to Captain Vale.

When Tilda and Hadrian finished, Teague asked where Mallory was.

"I'm here." The medium came from the bedchamber and joined them. His gaze was wary as he regarded Teague.

"How is the captain?" Tilda asked.

"The doctor says he is lucky the knife did not damage any of his organs. He's stitching him up now and has prescribed him to rest for a fortnight before returning home."

"He's welcome to recuperate at my house," Hadrian offered.

Surprise flashed across Mallory's features. "Thank you, my lord, but that won't be necessary. I'll take him to Cadogan Place. I need to close down the society. Unless I am in jail." He sent an expectant look toward Teague.

"You likely will be for some period of time," Teague replied. "Blackmail was not your only crime."

Mallory dipped his head. "No, it was not."

"What will happen with the society?" Tilda asked. "I imagine the Duchess of Chester will be despondent without it."

"*I* will be despondent without it." Mallory looked at Hadrian. "I only wanted to help people, and I was good at that, even if I didn't always go about it in the right way. I believe I was meant to do good. It doesn't make sense otherwise."

Hadrian understood what Mallory was talking about. He saw

the ability they both possessed as a gift that he could use, much as Hadrian employed his to assist Tilda with solving crimes. In some way, Hadrian could understand how Mallory had lost his way a bit, especially if he'd come from a place of desperation when he'd been so completely overwhelmed by his ability at first. Hadrian had to imagine Mallory had thought it was a curse, just as he had when he'd first become afflicted. The only way to make peace with—or sense of—feeling cursed was to try to find some positive way to accept it. Hadrian realized that he'd done that, mostly, and would continue to adapt in the best way that he could. He would hope for Mallory's sake that he would do the same.

"I will hope you may find a way to actually do good when you are released from prison," Teague said. "Now, excuse me whilst I deal with this." He gestured toward the staircase.

Hadrian, Tilda, and Mallory moved away toward the captain's bedchamber, but they stopped short of going inside.

Tilda looked to Mallory. "What about all the people you employ in the society? Such as the Henry siblings?"

"I would offer to write them a recommendation, but I doubt that would help them." Mallory grimaced.

"I will help them find work," Hadrian said. He flashed a smile at Tilda. "It's what we do following a case. In fact, Tilda's household keeps increasing. Surely you could use a groom and perhaps an upstairs maid?"

"No!" Tilda shook her head, but a smile teased her lips briefly before she quashed it. "Absolutely not. I can barely afford the people I've taken on recently, nor do I have need of them. But yes, we can endeavor to help them." She looked back to Mallory. "Why did they all live in Bedfordbury instead of at the other properties?"

"It's a bit complicated," Mallory said, raking his hand through his blond hair. "I came to London with a friend."

"Roger Grenville," Hadrian interjected.

Mallory's eyes glinted with surprised. "You know him?"

"We traveled to Swindon a few days ago and met him," Tilda said.

"Ah." Mallory glanced toward the bedchamber. "My father told me you called at his house, but I didn't realize you met Grenville as well. He will likely be glad to see that I have fallen."

"He did not support your plans for the society," Hadrian said tersely.

"No, he did not. We came to London and took lodging in Bedfordbury. That was where we met Mr. and Mrs. Timms, and I came up with the idea for the hollow pedestals that they could fit inside and move the tables during séances."

Hadrian met Tilda's gaze. "We were right."

"You sorted that out?" Mallory asked. "Of course you did. I then found someone to build the tables."

"Clifton," Tilda supplied.

"Damn, you are thorough," he said with obvious admiration. "I went to my father for money to pay for that first table and to obtain an impressive headquarters in order to attract the clientele that would allow us to be successful."

"You couldn't very well prey on the Duchess of Chester and others like her from your lodgings in Bedfordbury." Hadrian didn't hide his derision.

"No, we could not," he said ruefully. "I am sorry for what I've done, Ravenhurst. Not that I expect you to forgive me."

"It is not my place to do so," Hadrian said. "You must accept what you've done and find a path forward. My sentiment matters not at all."

"Would you mind confirming a few things for me?" Tilda asked. "I think I've worked out how you managed all the aspects of the séances, but I'm not certain about the cool breeze that typically accompanies the arrival of the spirits. Am I right in thinking someone uses a bellows to blow air through a vent?"

"Exactly." Mallory nodded with approval. "You are most

clever, Miss Wren. It's a shame I didn't meet you sooner and employ you for your investigative skills. They could have been most helpful."

"She would never have accepted such a position," Hadrian said flatly.

Tilda sent Hadrian a faint smile before responding to Mallory. "I confess we did wonder whether you may employ an investigator to learn about your clients and patrons, but once we discovered your ability to see memories, it was apparent you would not need to do that." Tilda paused as she cocked her head. "What of smells? Mrs. Langdon said she could detect her father's scent when he supposedly visited her séance."

"Another trick," Mallory replied sheepishly. "Someone found out what her father's scent had been, and we blew that into the room with the bellows as well."

Tilda nodded vaguely. "My last question involves the spirts who were conjured. You—as Montrose—said that John Tabor was your grandfather. Is that true?"

Mallory shook his head. "No. John Tabor was pure fabrication."

"And Mrs. Kelson who attended the séance last night did not actually channel Mrs. Frost," Tilda noted. "Was she an actor?"

"Yes, we do employ them from time to time as the need arises."

"Everything you did in the name of society was pure theatre," Hadrian said with disdain. "Your father thinks you would be a good playwright. Perhaps you should use your time in prison to direct your theatrical senses toward a better purpose."

"I may do that," Mallory said softly.

The doctor called for Mallory, and they all returned to the bedchamber. Captain Vale looked much improved. Mrs. Wilson had gone downstairs to make tea.

Upon learning that the captain would move to Cadogan Place

to rest, the doctor said he would call on him there the following day. Then he took his leave.

"Will you be there with me, Thaddeus?" the captain asked.

Mallory shook his head. "I'm to be arrested again. But I will ensure there is someone there to care for you."

"Employ the Henry siblings to do so," Tilda said. At Mallory's nod, she looked at the captain. "They are downstairs now. I'll send them up to meet you."

"Thank you," the captain replied with a smile. "Please deliver an invoice for your services to me at your earliest convenience."

Tilda's forehead pleated. "I'm not sure that is necessary, Captain. Most of my investigative work occurred before you hired me."

He met her gaze intently. "You prevented my son from being killed. That is worth a great deal to me. I insist on paying for your services. You decide what is fair, and I'll decide if I agree." There was a glint of humor in his expression, and Hadrian had to stifle a smile. He really did like the captain.

"I'll do that," Tilda said. "Thank you."

Hadrian looked to the captain. "And I must thank you for your … guidance."

"I hope you'll let me know if I can ever be of further help. Ours is a very small club, and we must take care of one another." Captain Vale shifted his gaze to his son. "I trust you will treat our ability with more respect in the future."

"Yes, Papa."

Hadrian escorted Tilda from the bedchamber. Graythorpe had arrived and was investigating the bodies.

The coroner did not even look in their direction as they departed the house and made their way to Hadrian's coach. Leach stood at the door and opened it as they arrived. "All is well?"

"Well enough," Tilda said. "Thank you again for your assistance, Leach. You have become a vital part of our investigative team. I shall ensure you receive extra payment for your service."

A faint bit of color flushed in Leach's cheeks. "That isn't necessary, Miss Wren."

"I think it is," Hadrian said firmly. He clapped Leach on the shoulder. "You were instrumental today."

"Thank you, my lord."

Tilda climbed into the coach, and Hadrian followed her after directing Leach to take them to Scotland Yard. He decided to sit on the opposite seat, probably because his conversation with Mallory about whatever might—or might not—be between him and Tilda was still fresh in his mind.

"My apologies," Tilda said. "I should not have directed Leach."

"Why not?" Hadrian asked. "As you aptly stated, he is part of the investigative team, and you are the leader."

She blushed faintly. "I suppose it's just unusual for me to direct a coachman. I have never employed one or lived in a household that did." She leaned her head back against the squab. "I'm exhausted, I think."

"We've had a very busy day, what with investigating and avoiding being murdered."

Tilda smirked at him. "You make light of that?"

"What else can we do?" He pinned her with a serious stare. "I could tell you that I was terrified you would die, but I doubt either of us wants to belabor that."

"I do not," she said, shifting her attention to the window. "I was also frightened you would be shot. Again. I am most relieved you were not."

"What happened to your father's pistol?" Hadrian asked.

She patted her reticule. "I picked it up when I returned from asking the neighbor to fetch the doctor." Her brows drew together. "I do not like that it was used against us."

"That is not your fault," Hadrian said. "Crocker surprised you. There was no harm done."

"There would have been if he had more accurate aim."

Hadrian heard the agitation in her tone and longed to reach out and steady her with his touch. If he could. "I am fine, Tilda."

She gave him a somewhat tremulous smile. "This time." Again, she moved her focus away from him. They fell silent for a few minutes before she said, "Can we call on your mother tomorrow, so that I may deliver the results of my investigation?"

"What will those results be?"

"I suppose they are moot since the society is dissolving. However, she may wish to seek out a different medium." Tilda studied him a moment. "What will you say if she wants to do that?"

Hadrian blew out a breath. "I don't know. I find her need to ensure Gabriel is at peace and to believe that he and my father have made peace frustrating. Last night you suggested that her need to hear from Gabriel comes from regret. I've been considering that, and I think you may be right. Looking back, I suspect she wasn't as blind to my father's behavior as I thought. I wonder if it wasn't just too difficult for her to face my father's transgressions. Perhaps it was easier for her to pretend all was well in spite of my father."

"That makes sense to me," Tilda replied thoughtfully. "Sometimes people aren't able to confront difficulty. I think my mother is like that to a certain extent. She never wanted to discuss my father's death or help me with my grief." She paused before adding, "I think there are things I choose to avoid on occasion, particularly regarding my father and how much I miss him." She shifted uncomfortably. "It is probably odd that I wouldn't embrace the chance to speak with him in the spirit realm. Most daughters would want that, I would think."

Hadrian couldn't help thinking of the things he wasn't addressing. Sharing his ability with his mother came to mind, as did the situation between him and Tilda. Whilst they had settled back into their friendship, the kiss would always linger—at least in his mind—and he didn't allow himself to fully explore why that was. "Fear keeps us in check," he said softly. "And perhaps from pursuing the truth or even happiness."

Tilda nodded. "This is an unsettling conversation." She laughed softly—and nervously—but quickly sobered. "We could all do with confronting difficult things, I suppose. In our own time, however. Perhaps your mother won't ever feel comfortable doing so and that is a nettle in her mind. Communicating with Gabriel might give her solace."

Hadrian eyed her. "How are you so clever about everything?"

Tilda laughed. "I am not. Indeed, I would argue I am not particularly wise about familial relationships, but even a clock standing still points in the right place twice each day."

Now, Hadrian laughed, and it felt rather wonderful after the stress of the last few hours. When he sobered, he said, "You don't need to pay Leach anything extra. I can do that."

Tilda held up her hand. "Nonsense. It is an expense of *my* investigation. Indeed, I should start compensating you for your contributions."

"Absolutely not," Hadrian said vehemently. "I won't accept a shilling from you, so don't even try."

"I suppose it isn't worth arguing about," she said somewhat unconvincingly, so that he thought this could very well come up again in the future.

"That is correct." He straightened his coat. "Now, tell me what you plan to share with Clement. I'm not certain I agree that we should support his predatory behavior, but I suppose he was helpful."

"He was indeed," Tilda said. "And as I pointed out, he may be again. Information is a valuable resource, and it behooves me to cultivate relationships with those who can provide it."

"You are a cunning investigator, Tilda. I have to think this case will bring more opportunities to you."

The anticipatory glint in her green eyes was unmistakable. "I certainly hope so."

CHAPTER 23

The day after the Levitation Killer was caught, Hadrian and Tilda called on his mother so that Tilda could give her full report on the London Spiritualism Society. Tilda had detailed the ways in which the society had defrauded people with their fakery, as well as how Mallory had blackmailed people through means that were not entirely clear.

That had been an opening for Hadrian to reveal his ability to his mother, but he'd chosen not to do so. It wasn't a conversation he'd wanted to have in front of Tilda. Furthermore, he'd wanted to conduct a small investigation of his own. Namely, he'd wanted to visit his grandmother at the dower house at Ravenswood to learn what he could about his family and whether anyone might have possessed the same ability as he did.

What he'd learned had both confirmed his suspicions and validated his fear. His great-uncle, whom Hadrian had thought had died at a young age, had been committed to an asylum due to hallucinations that drove him mad. His grandmother was not aware that they were not hallucinations, of course, nor did Hadrian explain the truth.

The revelation had sent him into a rather dark frame of mind for a couple of days. But he'd managed to calm himself by acknowledging that he wasn't mad, and he didn't think he would ever be. At least not from this.

That realization had given him the courage to call on his mother and address whether she would continue to try to communicate with Gabriel. When she'd learned of the society dissolving, she'd said she would have to think about whether she could trust another medium.

Hadrian arrived at his mother's, and Peverell directed him to the drawing room where she was taking tea. She looked up from the table as Hadrian strode into the room.

"Hadrian, I was not expecting you," she said. "Would you like tea?"

"Yes, thank you." He sat down opposite her as she poured out and fixed his cup exactly as he liked it.

Hadrian smiled. "You have always been an attentive mother. You knew exactly how we all took our tea, our favorite foods, the things that frightened us and made us laugh with joy."

"Did you know that Caroline still looks under the bed before she goes to sleep at night?" his mother asked. "Though she can laugh about it, at least."

Caroline was Hadrian's oldest sister and four years his senior. He was the middle child with two older sisters, a younger sister, and, of course, Gabriel.

"Things become less dire, or at least easier, as we grow older," Hadrian observed.

"Mostly, yes." His mother sipped her tea. "How was your visit to Ravenswood?"

"Uneventful," he said. "Grandmama is well."

"I'm glad to hear that," she replied, and Hadrian knew she meant it, even though the two women were not close. His grandmother was somewhat cold, particularly when compared with his mother.

"Have you given more thought to whether you plan to consult a new medium?" Hadrian asked as he helped himself to a cake.

"I don't think I will, which I am sure you find most welcome." She gave him a wry look.

"I want you to be happy, and if that means you find a new medium, I will support you. I will even attend another séance with you."

"But you and Miss Wren proved they are a farce." His mother frowned. "Though I still don't understand how they knew about that day in the snow with you and your brother."

This was the moment. Hadrian could tell her what Captain Vale had suggested—that he'd supplied the information to give her the experience she wanted. Or he could tell her the truth.

"Mama, what if there is another way—other than speaking to the dead—to explain how they knew?" Hadrian said slowly.

She fixed on him, her eyes glinting with disbelief. "I'm not sure I understand."

"Perhaps there is something else at work—some way that certain ... *sensitive* people are able to read others' feelings, or even their thoughts and memories."

"That is still a supernatural occurrence," she said. "Which I thought you did not believe in."

"I think I might actually." Hadrian's pulse had sped, and he forced himself to take a deep breath. "Or at least, I'm open to it."

He couldn't tell her about his ability. Not yet. Perhaps when he felt more in control of it. He wanted to, he realized, but he was still just a little afraid. He wondered if he would have told Tilda about it if she hadn't correctly determined there was something going on with him.

And how had she noticed and no one else had not? She'd noted his headaches and caught him touching things. Her curious mind had demanded answers. She'd also cared enough about their burgeoning association to insist upon honesty. He was glad they had that—and so much more.

"That is most surprising to hear," his mother replied. "But I still don't wish to see a new medium." She paused and looked at her teacup for a long moment. "You said that things get easier as we grow older. Often they do, but sometimes they do not. My grief over losing Gabriel has eased, but that isn't to say it has diminished." She lifted her gaze to Hadrian's. "I miss him. But it's more than that. You also said I am an attentive mother, but I should have done more to keep you all—well, your siblings, in particular—out of your father's way. I did my best. I know he wasn't the warmest father—"

"Or husband." Hadrian hadn't meant to interrupt her, but the words had leapt forth of their own accord. "I know you struggled, Mama. Sometimes I wonder if you know how much you struggled."

She looked toward the hearth. "I do. Just as I chose not to dwell on it. You shouldn't dwell on it either. Let us remember the happiest of times. Can we do that?" She met his gaze once more.

"Of course." He didn't want her to feel bad about Gabriel anymore. "We all love you, including Gabriel. And he knew you loved him." He was her youngest child—her baby, as she'd said countless times—and they'd shared a particular bond. "So let us remember the happiest times with him. I am grateful for them."

His mother sniffed. She pulled a handkerchief from her sleeve and dabbed at her eyes briefly. "Look what you've done. Amuse me with a silly story about your valet or the dogs at Ravenswood, please."

Hadrian laughed. "I am happy to, Mama."

~

*I*t had been a week since the conclusion of Tilda's investigation into Lady Ravenhurst's medium. The day after Mrs. Griswold's arrest, an article by Clement had appeared in the *Daily News* detailing her capture and the death of Michael

Crocker. He'd described Tilda's role in solving the case of the Levitation Killers, and as a result, she'd received several inquiries regarding her investigative services. She was rather grateful to the reporter.

The inquiries had come via the office of Mr. Forrest, the barrister she sometimes worked for. She'd also received a handful of rude missives that had denigrated her as a private investigator. None of those obnoxious people had signed their names.

Clement also penned an article dedicated to the dissolution of the London Spiritualism Society. In it, he quoted the society's founder, Lysander Mallory, admitting that their séances were fraudulent and that they did not speak to the dead. Tilda had heard from at least one person—Mrs. Langdon—who did not believe that was true. No one would convince her that the medium hadn't communicated with her father in the spirit realm.

Tilda hadn't seen Hadrian since they'd called on his mother following the conclusion of their investigation, but he was coming this afternoon for tea. She surveyed herself in the mirror, turning her head to see what Clara had done with her hair.

The maid held up another mirror so Tilda could see the artful plaiting and twisting she'd accomplished at the back of Tilda's head. "Can you see?" Clara asked.

"Yes, thank you. It's quite extravagant." Tilda stood and smiled at the maid. "And lovely."

Clara's cheeks flushed pink with pleasure. She set the mirror down on the dressing table. "I'm glad you like it."

Tilda had intended for Clara to be a temporary addition to the household, but she already had one case and might likely accept another. If that kept up, she'd be able to employ Clara permanently.

Though Tilda wasn't entirely certain she needed a maid. Her grandmother, however, adored having Clara, since the maid also styled her hair and took care of her clothing. It had freed their housekeeper up to focus on other areas of the household. In truth, things had never run more smoothly.

Hadrian was due to arrive soon. Tilda went downstairs to join her grandmother for a few minutes before she left to have tea with a neighbor. Grandmama had been disappointed to learn she would miss seeing Hadrian, so she'd asked Tilda to delay his departure until her grandmother returned.

Vaughn greeted Tilda in the entrance hall. "Miss Wren, there is a letter for you. I think it must be another inquiry for your services." He smiled with more than a hint of pride. The entire household was delighted to see Tilda find a modicum of success.

"Thank you, Vaughn." Tilda accepted the missive and opened the parchment, quickly scanning the lines. "It is indeed another inquiry. Someone would like help finding stolen items." Most of the inquiries had been of that nature. And all but one had been from women.

"You'll make short work of that, I expect," Vaughn said.

"Finding stolen items in London is akin to searching for a needle in a haystack," Tilda replied with a chuckle.

She walked into the parlor where Grandmama was just drawing on her gloves.

"Did I hear you've had another inquiry?" Grandmama asked.

"I have. More stolen items."

"Splendid!" Grandmama's eyes gleamed with enthusiasm. "You will be busy, I think. But then, you were quite busy during your last investigation." She exhaled. "I am so relieved that is over and that none of these new cases involve *murder*."

"I am too, Grandmama." Tilda was glad to have work that didn't require someone to have died, though her cases seemed to start that way and then veer into murder.

Her grandmother gave her a pointed stare. "Remember, make sure Hadrian doesn't leave until I return."

Tilda smiled. "I will, Grandmama."

She departed and Tilda reread the inquiry she'd just received.

The woman suspected her former housekeeper had stolen some silver. Tilda would start with tracking down the housekeeper. But first, she would meet with the woman who'd written to her and establish her fee. She planned to collect a deposit before beginning work for anyone.

Lost in thought, she did not hear Hadrian arrive. Vaughn announced his presence at the doorway to the parlor.

Tilda stood to greet him. "Afternoon, Hadrian. Come in."

He'd already removed his hat and given it to Vaughn. However, he still wore his gloves. "Good afternoon, Tilda. I'm pleased to see you. It's always an adjustment to be apart after spending so much time together during an investigation."

"I agree." Tilda had missed him. But she didn't say so.

Hadrian moved to the table where she'd been seated a moment earlier. They sat, and Tilda explained that he would need to linger long enough to see her grandmother.

He chuckled. "I would be delighted."

"How is your mother?" Tilda asked. When they'd visited her the week before and delivered the news about the murders, as well as the imminent closure of the London Spiritualism Society, she'd been glad to hear the killers had been caught but hadn't decided whether she would consult another medium.

"I saw her yesterday, and we had a nice conversation. She has decided not to find a new medium." Hadrian smiled at Mrs. Acorn as she entered with the tea tray. "Good afternoon, Mrs. Acorn. I trust you are well."

"Quite, my lord. It's been a boon to have Clara with us. And if Tilda continues to receive inquiries at the rate she has been, who knows what other changes may abound?"

The housekeeper flashed a gleeful smile before departing.

Tilda poured the tea.

"You've received inquiries?" Hadrian asked, at last removing his gloves.

She nodded as she added cream and sugar to their cups. "They are mostly from women seeking help finding stolen items."

He grinned. "You must be thrilled. I am. For you, I mean."

"I am very pleased." She considered telling him about the obnoxious letters she had also received but ultimately decided it didn't matter. No one had threatened her. They'd just been disparaging.

"If you ever require my assistance—in any way—with your searches for stolen items, I hope you will ask. I am more than eager to help."

"I appreciate that, thank you. Your ability is incredibly useful." Tilda sipped her tea.

Hadrian had also taken a drink of tea and now set his cup back on the saucer. Tilda couldn't help watching his hand. It was odd, but when he'd taken tea here before, which he'd done on a few occasions, she hadn't considered whether he'd experienced a memory when he touched the teacup.

"What is it?" Hadrian asked.

Tilda shook her head. "I was fixated on your hand. Rather, I was wondering if you saw anything when you touched the cup. Or if you have in the past."

"I think I once had a fleeting vision of your grandmother, but there has been nothing strong." His brow furrowed. "I've been paying more attention to what I see—when and for how long, as well as the depth of the vision. It's hard to explain. Some of them —many, in fact—are just a quick impression. Others are fuller and more real, if that makes any sense."

"It does actually." Tilda smiled. "It sounds as though you are coming to understand this ability better and perhaps even manage it?"

"I am trying. It certainly helped to speak with Captain Vale." He moved a biscuit to a small plate and set it in front of him. "As it happens, I've been away from London a few days. I visited my estate in Hampshire. The dower house, specifically."

Tilda knew his grandmother lived there. He'd mentioned her a few times. "Is your grandmother well?"

"Yes. I wanted to see if I could learn anything about my family and whether anyone had the same ability I do."

"*Oh.*" Tilda leaned slightly forward, eager to hear what happened. "How did you manage to speak with her about that?"

"I didn't start by telling her I could experience others' memories," he said drily, a smile teasing his mouth. "I asked about my grandfather and his brothers—he had two of them. One of them died rather young. I never knew why."

Tilda had the sense that was important. "Did you find out?"

"I learned he didn't die. He was sent to an asylum as a young man, and the family decided it was best to just say he'd died." Hadrian shook his head. "It's horrific, really."

"Why did they send him to an asylum?" Tilda's flesh prickled. She feared she knew the answer.

"My grandmother didn't know anything specific, just that he was haunted by seeing things he could not explain. Apparently, he went … mad." Hadrian looked down and then swept up his teacup for another sip. As he set it back down, Tilda noted his hand shook very slightly.

"You are not mad, Hadrian."

"I know. At least, I don't feel mad." He gave her a half smile. "I was going to tell my mother about my ability yesterday, but I am not quite ready. As you correctly pointed out, I am afraid. But I am less so than I was, and I credit you."

Tilda could understand him needing time. He was still adjusting to having this supernatural power. "I don't know what I've done."

"You have been incredibly supportive and considerate," Hadrian said. "I am fortunate to have someone with whom I could share this distressing malady. Someone who has not judged me or been frightened of me. Someone without whose encouragement and support, I would have surely been lost."

Hadrian's gaze held hers, and for a long moment she allowed herself to bask in their shared connection. It was friendship, certainly, but it was perhaps something more. There was admiration and affection. And right now, in this moment—at least for her—an overwhelming desire to embrace.

Tilda put her hand on the table, sliding it toward him. Hadrian did the same, at nearly the same moment. Their fingertips met.

"Pardon me, Miss Wren?" Vaughn interrupted them.

Inhaling sharply, Tilda withdrew her hand as she turned her head toward the doorway. "Yes, Vaughn?"

"An inspector is here to see you."

"Teague?" Tilda sent a bewildered look toward Hadrian. "I am not expecting him."

Hadrian shrugged.

"Not Detective Inspector Teague," Vaughn said. "He said his name was Inspector Maxwell."

Tilda didn't recognize the name. "Show him in." She looked to Hadrian. "You don't mind, do you?"

"Not at all. I could never deny your curiosity." He winked at her, and she laughed softly.

Tilda rose and Hadrian did the same, moving slightly around the table to join her in facing the new arrival.

Inspector Maxwell entered. He was tall, though not as tall as Hadrian. He held his hat, which left his head bare to reveal thick, light-brown curls. He had a neatly trimmed beard and warm hazel eyes that regarded Tilda with respect. He flicked a glance toward Hadrian.

"Welcome, Inspector," Tilda said. "Allow me to introduce Lord Ravenhurst."

The inspector inclined his head toward Hadrian. "Good afternoon, my lord."

"Good afternoon," replied Hadrian.

"How can I be of help?" Tilda asked the inspector.

The inspector rotated the hat in his hands. "I'm with the City of London Police. I've come to speak with you about a case."

Tilda's pulse quickened. Was he here to consult with her? She didn't dare to hope that could be true. Scotland Yard would never do that. But Maxwell was not from the Metropolitan Police. She decided he was likely there to interview her about something. "I'm happy to provide whatever information I can to help you."

"I didn't come to interview you," Maxwell said. Again, he glanced toward Hadrian. He seemed to hesitate.

"I don't mind you speaking in front of Ravenhurst," Tilda said, trying not to sound too eager. But the thought of consulting with a police department was more than she'd ever dreamed. It occurred to her that Maxwell likely knew of her because of Clement's article. Unless Teague had mentioned her, but that assumed this man even knew Teague.

If it was the newspaper article, Maxwell wouldn't know that Hadrian participated in her investigations. Clement did not include that fact. Tilda added, "The earl is exceptionally discreet. He assists me with most of my investigations, in fact."

Maxwell's expression flickered with surprise. "Does he? A woman private investigator is astonishing enough, but I was not prepared for her to have a nobleman as an assistant."

"And yet she does," Hadrian said benignly.

The inspector nodded at Hadrian before regarding Tilda once more. "Miss Wren, I am in need of a female investigator, and I am desperately hoping you will consent to help me. I would like you to be my wife."

Don't miss the next book in the Raven & Wren series, A WHISPER IN THE SHADOWS when Tilda poses as the wife of Inspector Maxwell to investigate London's burial clubs. Hadrian is none too pleased to be cast aside as her partner, however, when there's a murder, Tilda needs his assistance.

But how can Hadrian use his ability to help her investigation with Maxwell supervising?

Would you like to know when my next book is available and to hear about sales and deals? **Sign up for my Reader Club newsletter** which is the only place you can get exclusive bonus books and material.

Join me on social media!

Facebook: https://facebook.com/DarcyBurkeFans
Instagram at darcyburkeauthor
Pinterest at darcyburkewrite

And follow me on Bookbub to receive updates on pre-orders, new releases, and deals!

I hope you'll consider leaving a review at your favorite online vendor or networking site!

I appreciate my readers so much. Thank you for reading!

AUTHOR'S NOTE

I was thrilled to conduct research into the spiritualism movement for this book. One cannot do so without reading about perhaps the most famous mediums in America during this period—the Fox sisters. They began their career communicating with spirits in their home, convincing their parents of their supernatural gift by way of raps that sounded on the walls and furniture. They went on to conduct séances for hundreds of people and became celebrity mediums. Decades later, they confessed to cracking their joints—their toes in particular—to create the rapping sound.

The spiritualism movement had many important and famous supporters. Mary Todd Lincoln held séances in the White House in Washington, DC, and Queen Victoria had many séances at Buckingham Palace in London after the death of her husband, Prince Albert. Arthur Conan Doyle, the creator of Sherlock Holmes, became very interested in spiritualism and spent decades dedicated to the movement. In the early twentieth century, he spoke publicly about spiritualism even though it negatively impacted his reputation.

Many people investigated mediums in order to prove they

were charlatans. None were more famous than Harry Houdini, the magician known for mind-boggling escapes. His initial foray into spiritualism was well intended as he sought to speak with his deceased beloved mother. However, he became convinced it was all fakery. Conan Doyle wanted to prove to Houdini that spiritualism was, in fact, real. The two became friends until Houdini attended a séance during which Conan Doyle's wife, who was an automatic writer (meaning she communicated with spirits through writing), produced several pages of communication that had supposedly come from Houdini's deceased mother. However, the writings were in English, a language Houdini's mother didn't speak. Houdini also found it suspicious that though the séance was held on his mother's birthday, she didn't mention it. The friendship between the two men did not recover.

The London Spiritualism Society is a fabrication for this novel. The levitation trick that Hadrian learns was one way that mediums used to pretend to levitate. The table with the hollow pedestal containing controls operated by small people is my own invention.

ALSO BY DARCY BURKE

Contemporary Romance

Ribbon Ridge

Let Go (a prequel novella)

Get Lucky

Sparks Fly

Fall Hard

Can't Stop

Break Free

Hold Me

Turn On

So Right

This Love

Historical Mystery

Raven & Wren

A Whisper of Death

A Whisper at Midnight

A Whisper and a Curse

A Whisper in the Shadows

A Whisper of Secrecy

A Whisper in Darkness

Historical Romance

Rogue Rules

If the Duke Dares

Because the Baron Broods

When the Viscount Seduces

As the Earl Likes

Until the Rake Surrenders

Since the Marquess Demands

What the Scoundrel Desires

How the Devil Sins

The Phoenix Club

Improper

Impassioned

Intolerable

Indecent

Impossible

Irresistible

Impeccable

Insatiable

Marrywell Brides

Beguiling the Duke

Romancing the Heiress

Matching the Marquess

The Matchmaking Chronicles

Yule Be My Duke

The Rigid Duke

The Bachelor Earl (also prequel to *The Untouchables*)

The Runaway Viscount

The Make-Believe Widow

The Untouchables

The Bachelor Earl (prequel)

The Forbidden Duke

The Duke of Daring

The Duke of Deception

The Duke of Desire

The Duke of Defiance

The Duke of Danger

The Duke of Ice

The Duke of Ruin

The Duke of Lies

The Duke of Seduction

The Duke of Kisses

The Duke of Distraction

The Untouchables: The Spitfire Society

Never Have I Ever with a Duke

A Duke is Never Enough

A Duke Will Never Do

The Untouchables: The Pretenders

A Secret Surrender

A Scandalous Bargain

A Rogue to Ruin

Love is All Around

(A Regency Holiday Trilogy)

The Red Hot Earl

The Gift of the Marquess

Joy to the Duke

Wicked Dukes Club

One Night for Seduction by Erica Ridley

One Night of Surrender by Darcy Burke

One Night of Passion by Erica Ridley

One Night of Scandal by Darcy Burke

One Night to Remember by Erica Ridley

One Night of Temptation by Darcy Burke

Secrets and Scandals

Her Wicked Ways

His Wicked Heart

To Seduce a Scoundrel

To Love a Thief (a novella)

Never Love a Scoundrel

Scoundrel Ever After

Legendary Rogues

Lady of Desire

Romancing the Earl

Lord of Fortune

Captivating the Scoundrel

ABOUT THE AUTHOR

Darcy Burke is the USA Today Bestselling Author of sexy, emotional historical and contemporary romance. Darcy wrote her first book at age 11, a happily ever after about a swan addicted to magic and the female swan who loved him, with exceedingly poor illustrations. Join her Reader Club newsletter for the latest updates from Darcy.

A native Oregonian, Darcy lives on the edge of wine country with her guitar-strumming husband, incredibly talented artist daughter, and imaginative, Japanese-speaking son who will almost certainly out-write her one day (that may be tomorrow). They're a crazy cat family with two Bengal cats, a small, fame-seeking cat named after a fruit, an older rescue Maine Coon with attitude to spare, an adorable former stray who wandered onto their deck and into their hearts, and two bonded boys who used to belong to (separate) neighbors but chose them instead. You can find Darcy in her comfy writing chair balancing her laptop and a cat or three, attempting yoga, folding laundry (which she loves), or wildlife spotting and playing games with her family. She loves traveling to the UK and visiting her beloved cousins in Denmark. Visit Darcy online at www.darcyburke.com and follow her on social media.

facebook.com/DarcyBurkeFans

instagram.com/darcyburkeauthor

bsky.app/profile/darcyburke.bsky.social

goodreads.com/darcyburke

bookbub.com/authors/darcy-burke

amazon.com/author/darcyburke

pinterest.com/darcyburkewrites

tiktok.com/@darcyburkeauthor